Other AvoNova Books by
Michael Scott Rohan

CHASE THE MORNING
THE GATES OF NOON

THE WINTER OF THE WORLD Trilogy

THE ANVIL OF ICE
THE FORGE IN THE FOREST
THE HAMMER OF THE SUN

CLOUD CASTLES

MICHAEL SCOTT ROHAN

AVON BOOKS • NEW YORK

CLOUD CASTLES is an original publication of Avon Books. This work is a novel. Any similarity to actual persons or events is purely coincidental.

AVON BOOKS
A division of
The Hearst Corporation
1350 Avenue of the Americas
New York, New York 10019

Copyright © 1993 by Michael Scott Rohan
Cover illustration by Rowena A. Morrill
Published by arrangement with the author
Library of Congress Catalog Card Number: 94-14459
ISBN: 0-380-77554-9

First AvoNova Printing: August 1995
First Morrow/AvoNova Hardcover Printing: August 1994

AVONOVA TRADEMARK REG. U.S. PAT. OFF. AND IN OTHER COUNTRIES, MARCA REGISTRADA, HECHO EN U.S.A.

Printed in the U.S.A.

RA 10 9 8 7 6 5 4 3 2 1

For Maggie Noach and Ellen Levine
—ten years on!

Knowest thou the mountain, with its bridge of cloud?
The mule plods warily; the white mists crowd.
Coiled in their caves the brood of dragons sleep;
The torrent hurls the rock from steep to steep . . .

Knowest thou the land? So far and fair!
Thou, whom I love, and I will wander there.

GOETHE, TR. FLECKER

Prologue

The Spiral . . .

"Tell you something, Steve," said Jyp (that evening when the Wolves were running, and he took me to see Le Stryge). "The world's a lot wider place than most folk ever realize. They cling to what they know, to the firm center where everything's dull and deadly and predictable. Where the hours slip by at just sixty seconds to the minute from your cradle to your tombstone—that's the Core. Out here, out on the Spiral, out toward the Rim—it's not like that. It's adrift, Steve, in Time and in Space as well. And there are more tides than one that ebb and flow about its shores. One time or another maybe everybody'll find one lapping about their feet—and they look out on infinite horizons! Some bow down, slink away, forget; but others, they take a step forward, they cross those chill wide waters—from Ports like this one, often enough, where comings and goings over a thousand years and more have tied a knot in Time, to all the corners of the wide world. Lord, lord, how wide! And Steve, know what? Every which one of those corners is a place. Places that were, that will be, that never

1

were save that the minds of men gave them life. Lurking like shadows cast behind the real places in that reality of yours, shadows of their past, their legends and their lore, of what they might have been and may yet be, touching and mingling with every place at many points. You can search your whole life long and never find a trace of them, yet once you learn you may pass between them in the drawing of a breath. There, west of the sunset, east of the moonrise, there lies the Sargasso Sea and Fiddler's Green, there's the Elephants' Graveyard, there's El Dorado's kingdom and the empire of Prester John—there's everywhere. Riches, beauties, dangers—every damn thing within the mind and the memory of men, and more too, probably. But are they the shadows, Steve—or is your reality theirs?"

I had no answer for him. I still don't.

Chapter 1

The driver stamped on the brake. The car swerved violently, and the bottle sailed past us, lazily almost, and popped into fragments on the scarred pavement. No flames, just a spattering of stale beer. That made us a lot luckier than many others today.

Lutz was leaning out of the window shouting, but the armored police stationed around the hotel were already surging out toward the little knot of rioters, who scattered, baying like animals and hurling any missiles that came to hand. They were brandishing torn fragments of a banner whose pole had evidently been put to other uses. I made out part of the slogan—something . . . RAUS!

Probably *Kapitalisten*—or *Juden*; they were beginning to equate the two again, openly. As they passed the car they kicked it, thumped the roof, beat and spat on the windows. I glimpsed blunt, coarse faces, jail-cropped heads, round eyes staring, mouths stretched wide with wordless shrieks of hate—so many of them alike, somehow, as if the kinks in their minds created some common cast.

Lutz snorted and sat heavily back, brushing down his

3

thick white hair with both hands. " *'S tut mir leid*, Ste-phen," he rumbled. "These baboons! They do not realize at just whom they are throwing things!"

I didn't suggest their aim might improve if they did. Baron Lutz von Amerningen was a little too sure of his own importance to appreciate that; besides, the success of the launch had left him in one of his high expansive moods. I'd as soon have pricked a baby's balloon. A hotel flunkey opened the door, and Lutz bounced out after me. He wrapped a massive arm around my shrinking shoulders, and breathed sour Dom Perignon into my face; the launch had been lavish. "Now, you're sure you won't come straight on with me? We could catch a set or two of tennis, a sauna, a few drinks . . . "

"Lutz, thanks, but really—I still have things to do—"

"This evening, then? You are not just going to sit and vegetate, a fit young fellow like you? Sure, you are tired now, but that's just the excitement. You need to *unwind*, boy!"

Lutz's English was so good he could have perfected his accent too. I'd decided he just liked the Erich von Stroheim effect.

"Look at me, I'm years older and effery bit as fit! I don't just flop down, I keep going! Partying! That's the way to stay young! So—tonight, out at my place, I am giving one of my liddle *affaires*!" He chuckled, and passed me a stiff white envelope. "You have not been to one before, eh? It will be an education—you know?"

"Lutz, that's . . . incredibly kind of you," I said, slightly dazed. I knew, all right. The fourteenth Baron von Amer-ningen's "little *affaires*" were famous, the stuff of tabloids the world over, not that reporters or *paparazzi* ever got beyond the front gate. Or mere business associates. Well, as of now I probably was one of the idle rich. "I've got a lot of stuff to attend to," I repeated, "and I'm feeling worn out." That at least was the truth, in a way. But I didn't want to offend him outright. "Maybe I could look in a bit later, if that's—"

"Of course, of course!" He waved a massive flipper of a hand, "You know the way? Okay! Don't just sit in your room sucking at a bottle! Or any other solitary vices, hah? Well, *ciao, bambino!*"

I returned his goodbye flourish as his stretched-Merc limousine purred back out onto the rubbish-strewn road. The street was empty now, but a stink lingered in the air, partly the garbage from scattered dustbins, and partly other odors from the city center where they were still strong. Smoke from the burnings, the pepper gas they'd started using instead of tear gas and CS, petrol from the Molotov cocktails—I could taste it on my tongue, and I wanted to spit.

"Bummer, isn't it?" remarked another guest hurrying down to the taxi rank, stuffing bundles of trade-fair literature into his attaché case. "You know they overturned my cab? Tipped it right over! Goddamn fascist bastards! You over for the fair too—hey, aren't you Stephen Fisher? Right, right!" He grabbed my hand and pumped it with slightly awestruck enthusiasm. "Jerzy Markowski, VP, Roscom-Warzawa, electronics sub-assemblies, that kinda thing! Hey, that was some show you gave us! One helluva eye-opener! Know what all this paper is? New business that's suddenly becoming cost-effective, that's what! Haven't seen the figures yet, but we're gonna be buying a *lot* of C-Tran capacity!" His face fell. "And our goddamn competitors, you bet! You won't forget us?"

I was surprised he'd managed to recognize me from my brief spiel at the launch, surrounded as I was by holograms and dancers and the whole razzamatazz. But as I came into the lobby I found out how: my face was plastered right across the newsstand. I hadn't made *Time* or *Newsweek* yet, but the Europeans hadn't wasted any time. There I was staring out from the covers of *Elsevier* and *Spiegel* (alongside Lutz, naturally) and *The Economist* had a cover photo of a crate with a mortarboard and little beady eyes, captioned *Smart Packaging? C-Tran—Shipping for a New Europe*.

I picked up a copy, and the man behind the counter smirked and said loudly, "*Gratulieren*, Herr Fisher!" Heads turned in the foyer; the hotel was lousy with business types for the fair, of course, and suddenly they all wanted to shake my hand, even some big boys from the multinationals. I escaped into the lift with aching fingers and standing invitations to drop by just everywhere from Grenoble to Groton, Conn. I'd felt idiotic at this morning's extravaganza, as if I was pretending to be some kind of celebrity; now it was dawning on me that that was exactly what I was.

But all I wanted to be right now was alone.

That was pretty funny, when you came down to it, me pulling a Garbo. I'd spent years learning not to, and not on any analyst's couch trip either. On heaving decks and dark jungles, among cloud archipelagos in worlds that stretched out beyond our own like endless shadows in the setting sun. On quests so strange and desperate that the very memories they left were fleeting, all too liable to fade. On the Spiral I'd faced tasks and perils that had taught me the real meaning of success—and I had been forced, at last, to face myself.

I flipped open *The Economist*, and my eyes lit on the end of the lead article.

. . . the single most dramatic innovation in the movement of goods since the introduction of containerization in the 1960s. Unquestionably it will make Stephen Fisher, both as chief executive and shareholder, the multimillionaire he deserves to be. But C-Tran, like its enigmatic creator, often seems to have its gaze fixed on wider horizons. Undoubtedly, by rendering the tiresome complications of international shipping as irrelevant as yesterday's frontiers, C-Tran will further draw together an Eastern Europe still torn and tottering from post-Communist trauma, and a West plagued by instability and rising extremism. As such, it may well find its place not only in the dry economic treatises of tomorrow, but also . . .

The door indicator chimed softly for my floor. I rolled up the magazine hastily in case somebody caught me reading it, and snorted. Lord, Lord—as an old friend of mine called Jyp was given to say—all that just because of a little boredom! But now it was over. Now it was done. I shoved the plastic keycard into my door so hard I almost bent it.

I tossed the magazine aside and checked my little computer. The fax dump was choked with messages; so was the answering machine facility—congratulations all. Tapping a few keys dumped them down the line to home office for my PA team to answer. But as I broke contact a window flashed up suddenly in the center of the screen, the format reserved for urgent system warnings. I peered closer at the glaring red pixels.

URGENTIN IMMINENT EVENT SYSTEM WIPEOUT*INTERFACE PORT S WITH PORT G**URGENT**

Interface what with what? I'd never seen this one before. I was pretty sure this machine didn't have any such ports, let alone any means of interfacing them. A joke? A virus, maybe? It had a suggestion of hidden meaning, *double entendre*, even. More probably I'd accidentally triggered some redundant developers' instruction left lying around in the operating software. I touched the *OK* icon, and the frame faded; but with the persistence of liquid crystals the bare letters lingered an instant like fading fires. I shut the lid and went off to shower and change.

By rights I should have forgotten the whole thing. But

an hour later, duly showered, changed into casuals and armed with a great big gin and tonic, I was still brooding about it—if only because I had something worse to brood over when I stopped. The hotel bar terrace was empty— hardly surprising. The management had done its best with marble and shrubs and striped awnings, but they couldn't gloss over the car park annex beyond, and the grotty row of dwarf conifers marking its boundary with the hotel next door, a better view than the multilane road out front, but not much. Still, it was peaceful; and at least the car park opened up a great swathe of unobstructed sky. After days stuck in the exhibition center the sheer sight of it eased my claustrophobia wonderfully. I ordered another g and t, and settled back to admire.

Above the stunted treelets the clouds came surging up in steep walls of blazing white shot with deep gray, un- stained by the smokes of human stupidity. In the crisp air of early autumn, still faintly sunwarmed, they loomed stark and solid against one of those darker azures that draw the eye into infinity. It's common enough to see patterns in the clouds, but this one stood out clear as a painting. To either side they became high craggy rock-faces, higher on the right and linked by a striated slope soaring to a level sum- mit, the base of a flattened V. You could almost believe you were looking up a broad road curving between high cliffs toward the crest of a mighty mountain pass, and rearing above it, like a sentinel, the summit of a white tower. The falling sun tinged tower and path a fiery pink. A dramatic backdrop, fit for a great drama, a film or an opera or some- thing; yet nature and chance alone had created it in minutes, and in minutes more it would be gone.

It reminded me that at least I could slip away for a few days' climbing now, though I'd be lucky to find anywhere that unspoilt. A few days? I could spend the rest of my life climbing. I was a success now—wasn't I?

I'd built up our shipping firm so well that when Barry retired early the step from deputy to managing director was

almost automatic, young as I was. But now my friend and
deputy Dave was running things better than I ever did, and
what was I? A figurehead. Not that he meant to cut me out.
For all his usual disrespectful banter, he still deferred to
me over anything I chose to take an interest in, sometimes
almost embarrassingly. But wherever I looked, I found his
hand firmly on the tiller, steering the whole enterprise with
the cheerful autocracy he'd inherited from his West African
chieftain ancestors—and this while bringing up a big family into the bargain. He was everything I'd tried to be, and
more; my solutions had been good, his were better, and I
began to understand why Barry had quit. But I was barely
past forty, fit and fond of my work—what else did I have
to love, after all? Over the years I'd had ideas about how
our business really ought to operate—crazy ones, mostly,
but I'd begun to fiddle with them, and . . .

And suddenly C-Tran was a reality in seventeen countries, ready to launch in ten more, with a massive expansion
program to spin its web out beyond Europe to envelop the
world. But not in my hands. It had gone beyond me and
my vision now, beyond any one man's control. All I had to
do was give interviews, chair the odd consortium meeting
and rake in the cash with both hands. That was my success,
one mighty bound, from helmsman to figurehead again.
Not all the millions would give me the satisfaction I'd got
from the bagful of battered guineas, *moidores*, *reales* and
soft Spanish ounces I'd held as hard-won profit in my first
trading voyage on those stranger, wider oceans that flowed
between the worlds of the Spiral. That had been two years
ago, when the growing pains of the new system had pressed
in on me. In desperation I'd fled, crossed the threshold and
found old friends, a captain and crew and goods to trade
from one strange port to another. Then just a year later I'd
done the same again, this time as my own captain on a
longer haul. Longer, more perilous and this time with less
profit, but it was a start.

Twice before I'd been driven to seek the Spiral, once by

chance and curiosity, once by need. Now I wasn't driven, but drawn—and the pull was tearing me in two. What did I have to live for, stuck here like a maggot in the Core, when out there was a universe of infinite possibilities? The Core paled before its fierce bold colors. But this world I knew, I could control—as far as men can, and better than most. And the Spiral had a curious way of magnifying both strengths and weaknesses. Better I solve my problems here, or out there they might rise up and overwhelm me.

After all, I knew what the worst one was. Here or there, Core or Spiral, I was alone. The stupidity, the guilt, the cold emptiness of my past life I'd thrown off. I'd resolved to live again, to make real friends, relate, marry even. But I was past forty now, and they lied when they said I didn't look it; I did, from inside. And I was used to living my work, eating and sleeping it, too. Not a good start. And the Spiral itself got in my way. How could I explain a double life like that? Or involve any woman I knew? Claire and Jacquie, they'd both seen it. They'd both backed off from it, and from me. By now, no doubt, they'd forgotten; people did. There were women out on the Spiral, in plenty; but lasting relationships were rare in that shifting mêlée of space and time, where to stop for too long was to lose memory and mire down in dull mortality once again.

I drained my glass angrily, and the dregs were bitter. I stared at those clouds, at that great insubstantial barrier, and longed to escape there, wished as deeply as I'd ever wished that I could just go running up and over that pass and out into the wild blue yonder, to lose my restless self in infinity.

The waiter put down another glass, though I didn't remember ordering. But I didn't touch it. As I turned to read the bar chit a movement caught my eye, a splash of white, as if those scrubby tree-tops had torn loose a fragment of cloud. But as my eyes focused, my mind blurred. It was a horse, and a pretty big one by the look of it. A gray—which is to say pure, dazzling white—just standing there, with neither rider nor groom nor anybody else in sight. Saddled, bridled, but neither tethered nor hobbled, it calmly lowered its head and began to browse on the meagre grass patch under the trees.

I glanced around again; there really was nobody about. The animal must have strayed from somewhere—a trade-fair presentation, most likely. Thank God our agency'd settled for a big-name dance troupe and some really impressive audiovisuals. Over the last couple of weeks I'd seen others rope in everything from strippers to hippos. Anyhow, somebody ought to do something before the poor animal strayed out onto the *Autobahn*, or encountered one of the car-park speed merchants; and I liked horses. Scooping up a handful of sugar lumps from the bowl on the table, I vaulted over the rail and made my way across the tarmac with studied ease, careful not to alarm.

I needn't have bothered. It looked up and saw me, tossed its head a little and just stood there, as if waiting. "You're a tall fellow, aren't you?" I said quietly, and the closer I got, the bigger it looked—not as bulky as a Shire or Percheron, but tall and solid, like a very large hunter. I couldn't name the breed; there was nothing of the Arab or Lippizaner about that long head. The tackle was strange, too: heavy and ornamented, with a high-pommeled saddle, but not cowboy style, more oriental, if anything. I peeled the paper off the long sugar lumps; it sniffed them and took them with a delicate curl of the lip, and let me stroke its slab-muscled neck and shoulder; it felt well fed, well groomed. But then it looked around and snorted, as if to say, *Well—what're you waiting for?*

This was no stray publicity fodder. This had the smell of the Spiral about it—of magic, and of mystery. And the Spiral could be a horribly dangerous place. But right then I didn't give a damn. I tried the girth, and it was rock firm. I caught the pommel, set one foot on the concrete verge, the other to the stirrup and swung myself up and over. My foot slid into the other stirrup almost without trying; they could have been set for me. And the instant they took the weight, the great horse whinnied and wheeled, and plunged toward the screen of trees.

I ducked as the foliage rushed toward me, grabbed frantically at the reins and found them looped around the pommel. But before I could rein in, we burst through the trees, and the soft clump of dry grass beneath the hooves changed. Not to the dull clop of tarmac; earth drummed and stone rattled as the great beast's gait settled to an easy canter. I looked down—and almost lost my stirrups. The ground beneath those effortless hooves was invisible, lost in the flowing gray mist that enveloped us, so we seemed to be hardly moving, just racing on the spot with the mist flowing by us, as if the hoof-beats struck it solid for a moment, only to melt away again as they passed. Except that, as I stood in my stirrups and cast about, I could sense something else: the ground was sloping, we were rising, rising fast. Then, abruptly, brightness burst around us, and the fresh bite of open air. Dazzled, I blinked at the looming shadows above; were those still clouds? But I had to look away and down again—and this time I did lose my stirrups, and had to cling frantically to the pommel.

The ground was solid enough now, a rough path of light gray stone and dusty soil scattered with pebbles of white quartz, but there wasn't nearly enough of it. Not far beyond those flying hooves it fell away sharply, and the pebbles they kicked up went bouncing down a sheer stone crag into giddy emptiness, depths I couldn't guess at. Smooth mist lapped the cliff-face, like a lake of milk. Only it wasn't mist, because it stretched out from the crag to meet that same infinitely distant azure; it was cloud, and we were above it, climbing a mountain flank. The abyss clawed up at me, and my hands went slick with sweat, but I clung tight to the saddle and the climbers' litany, that height doesn't matter, that you can survive a thousand-foot fall and be killed by ten. Gasping, I forced myself to sit up and look up. My eyes adjusted, but I knew already what I was going to see: that selfsame landscape, those same rock walls and between them, rising no more than a couple of hundred feet to the summit of the pass, the road I'd longed to travel, the road I was climbing now. Icy shafts of excitement thrilled through me, only heightened by the swift pang of apprehension. The wind was keen and fresh, and it swept out the tainted city breath from my lungs and poured in life unending. The air was a hundred times more refreshing than the coldest, sharpest gin. I shook off the fear of the abyss, dug my feet back into the ornate metal loops and pressed my knees lightly to the working sides, catching their rhythm and finding my seat, enjoying the animal strength and making it my own. I took the reins, tipped with little cones of silver, and felt the stallion's swift response, as if acknowledging my control at last. It was what I'd wanted, wasn't it? And come what may at the pass, at least I'd see the other side.

The road was rough, but the beautiful beast never so much as broke stride, let alone stumbled. His sure hooves struck sparks from the quartz, his harness rang and jingled, his mane flew in the wind like a banner; I found myself laughing aloud with the manic pleasure of it. At the last slope before the crest the path turned inward, away from the cliff; I dug my heels in and flicked the reins gently, urging the horse on. I needn't have bothered; he went at that slope like the last furlong. We positively flew up and over that crest, and out onto the path that stretched out beyond. But even as we passed, I heard from high above the urgent chiming of a single bell. That tall pale tower was here with the rest, on the crags of the far wall high above us; it was coming from there; and from somewhere below us a deeper bell answered.

But it was what lay beyond that transfixed me. The mountain flank dropped away again, less steeply; but the path didn't fall with it. It ran on level along the crag, out and around the curve of the mountainside, looking down over that shimmering sea. The horse was following it as surely as ever, as if to make some urgent rendezvous; he answered my touch, but hardly seemed to need it. Riding almost automatically, I gazed out across the clouds, looking for some clue to where we were going. Other shapes broke its surface, other peaks rising in a jagged row of dragon-teeth, so we were in the midst of a chain; but closer, much closer and lower, something else speared up. A shadowy spike that barely broke the cloud roof, too thin and delicate to be another peak—and too regular. As we moved out along the cliff path the image split; there were two of them, close together, parallel, the same height—identical. And somehow insubstantial, though the sun cast their shadows clearly on that dazzling white.

Then something moved at the edge of my vision—another shadow. Only this one was below the clouds, sliding through them like a fish, swinging parallel to the path. As well I saw it, or I might have had less warning. With alarming suddenness, like a whale, it breached, and rose, fast. I goggled. It was an airship, a dirigible, but not like any model I'd ever seen in pictures, leaner and sleeker than the *Hindenburg* or a Zeppelin. Its white hull swept back in only nine or ten smooth segments to a finned tail made of square sections like a vast box kite, and the motor units belched smoke in sharp little puffs. And yet it was making impressive speed, effortlessly overhauling us, and the cars beneath looked capacious and streamlined. Primitive? Maybe not. I began to see more of an alternative technology about it, sophisticated design operating on simple princi-ples. Certainly it was a beautiful machine, as sleekly func-tional as a Viking ship. It came swiftly closer, till I could hear the soft gasping chuff distinctly—some kind of a steam engine, surely. I rose in my stirrups to wave—

Something sang past my head. No insect, that was for sure. I ducked, flinching. Above us the hillside exploded in a shower of dust and pebbles. I gaped like an idiot; being shot at was the last thing I'd expected. I tried to wave again, to show I wasn't armed; there was another loud crackle, and this time the path leaped and spattered. I hunkered right down, jammed my heels into the horse's flanks and yearned, uncharacteristically, for spurs. I needn't have bothered. The canter became a gallop, and we positively flew. The next explosion was ragged, and the air sang like a bee-swarm. More than one shot; it took me that long to register it. Volley fire—that meant trained men. Somebody's soldiers were shooting at me, without identification or a challenge or anything. They hadn't even waited; they could have got a lot closer and made sure of me. But they'd fired the moment they came in range—as if they were scared, or something. Of one man who couldn't be carrying anything larger than a pistol? It didn't make any kind of sense.

But they weren't giving up. A shark shadow glided across the path ahead, very close to the hill. I looked up, tried to signal, found myself staring straight up into the sullen glitter of gun barrels from both cars. I yelped and flattened out in the saddle; they vanished in a streak of orange flame, earth and rock tore up around us—behind us! We were going too fast. The airship almost smashed into the hillside; the engine pulse quickened suddenly to a roar, and the air was suddenly full of spray as it shed ballast. The nose pulled up, around, and it swung violently; the motors roared and wavered. I imagined the men in those cars staggering, sprawling, sliding down into a bruised heap in one corner. I grimaced vindictively; I hadn't so much as glimpsed a single face, but I hated their guts. Being shot at does have that effect.

The airship was steadying now, chugging outward in a great circle from the mountainside, ready to come swooping back at me from ahead. I patted the horse's neck, feeling a flush of sick anger. Speed wouldn't save us, then; we needed cover. I couldn't remember any on that upward path—and I wasn't sure I could turn this great beast back. Just trying to rein in at these speeds could spill us both

down the mountainside, or cause so much confusion we'd
be left as sitting ducks. Then, just beyond the corner ahead,
two great standing stones loomed up, towering over the
path like rough seconds from the Stonehenge factory. Our
best—our only—bet. I flicked the reins and hissed, *"Go,
boy! For your bloody life!"*

And go he did. I nearly lost the reins, clung to the lathered neck and gibbered. I could have sworn he'd reacted
an instant before I did, as if he too had seen and understood; maybe he had. We were at the bend now, hooves
scrabbling in the dust, almost in the shadow of the
stones—but darkening the sky ahead was the airship, descending like a glittering cloud charged with deadly
lightning. Still a chance—

Out from between the stones a figure glided, hooded and
cowled like some kind of monk. He didn't spare us a glance,
but lifted his hands in a brusque, dismissive gesture, like a
slap. Quite lightly—yet the sense of contained violence was
so strong that the stallion shrilled and reared, forelegs
striking at the air, and I fought to keep my seat. Not surprising, given what followed. The path convulsed, the very
air bent and shimmered like an image in a distorting mirror, and through the heart of the distortion the dust and
earth and loose rocks lifted and sprayed out in a great curving stream, straight at the oncoming airship. Rocks crashed
off the coaming of the cars, drubbed at the fabric of the
canopy, struck screaming off the airscrews; the machine
lurched and shivered under the impacts, its gasbags in danger. I heard the distant splintering of glass. Again the motors roared, ballast blew, and the machine went swinging
out over the path's edge into emptiness. A single shot,
aimed by brilliance or luck, splashed off the stone near the
newcomer's cowled head, leaving a bright streak of lead. He
didn't seem to notice, but he stood watching the machine
slide away sideways down the sky, its pilots wrestling with
it as I was with the horse.

I managed to quiet him; so apparently did he, for I saw

`

the great machine come about and rise a little, begin moving forward again. I expected it to soar back for an answering volley, but instead it sank down swiftly, till the cloud roof swallowed it. I sat an instant, feeling the horse's ribs expand with great shuddering breaths. His neck trembled, and he shied slightly when I patted him—still nervous and no wonder. I looked down expectantly at my rescuer.

He looked up. It was my turn to shudder then. I had to swallow before I could get the name out.

"*Stryge!* I mean, . . . Le Stryge. What the hell—"

"Am I doing here?" The harsh nasal accent was the same, the continual rasp of anger behind the voice unaltered; but a crooked smile belied it. A wry, thin-lipped thing, sour as green persimmons, but a smile all the same. "Saving your wretched neck, my boy. My usual occupation in your company, is it not?" I blinked. Something about him had changed. There was the same almost sickening impact in the cold gray gaze. The face could have been one of those classical busts, scholar, philosopher, priest or ascetic idealized in white marble. But the life that burned beneath made it a deadly weapon, a blunt instrument, square and stone-hard, the pallid skin deeply lined, the nose a thin flaring blade and the mouth a bloodless, lipless slash above the arrogant jutting jaw. How would you tag that bust—fanatic, madman, psychopath? That's what I'd thought of him at first sight; now I knew a better one.

Necromancer.

A dangerous one; murderous, if all I'd heard was true. And yet, startlingly, he had changed. Instead of the tattered black coat and belt there was that dark robe, figured velvet by the look of it; and the white hair, once matted and straggling, was tied back with an elegant bow of black velvet—and powdered? The old swine looked like some kind of eighteenth-century priest—one of the racier French *abbés*, maybe. But what else had altered? The dirt of the ascetic still ingrained his face, shadowing its already deep lines. Along his high forehead the powder was clotted and gray,

and little yellow drops congealed at the edges of his eyes;
and I could still smell the dank tramp's odor around him.
I wasn't alone: the horse was wrinkling its nostrils. Even
the velvet robe was caked in places with ancient filth. A
leopard *can* change its spots—by becoming a black panther. Better keep this polite.

"You're looking well," I told him, and he bowed slightly.
"I assume I owe all . . . this," indicating the horse, "to you?"

He bowed again. Was he trying to make some kind of
good impression? "I felt the least I could do was provide
you with suitable transport. The fact is, young man, that
just as you once felt in need of my services, so I feel in
need of yours."

"*What*—I mean, pardon? Of—"

Gravel ground in his throat; he was chuckling. "Ah, en-
tertain no fears, I would hardly call upon you for anything . . . touching on my greater concerns. Let us say
rather that I find myself in need of exactly those qualities
I no longer command. I am an old man now, I grow tired
easily. And I did not want your long-standing obligation to
be a burden, a lingering concern. Better, I thought, to—"

"Er, excuse me a moment, my . . . *obligation*?"

He smiled deprecatingly, though his eyes glittered. "Why,
yes. Our first encounter. You would not deny I was of help
to you then? At every stage, material help? Without me,
would you have found the fair Claire? Would you have
stopped the Wolves' ship in its flight—or tracked them
down once more when they escaped you? And my precious
young helpers, who were sacrificed in that cause. Even
among the clouds of the Great Wheel, you surely cannot
have forgotten?"

"Well, no," I said, flustered. I'd had the odd nightmare
about those "young helpers," when I found out what they
were. "Of course not! I thanked you, didn't I? I gave you a
small fortune in gold!"

"Very graciously," said the old man, with that contemptuous crackle still in his voice. "But could it have bought

that help elsewhere? My young creature of commerce, not all debts may be repaid in gold. And what I would have of you entails only a brief and simple effort. Better, I thought, to give you the chance to be quit of it now, thus, and wipe clean the slate. Why, I had not looked for even this slight show of reluctance!" He grimaced. "I would not try to pretend any such thing could wound me. But I must warn you, I can conceive of no easier way to clear your debt."

The horse was restive, shifting his stance and swinging his head impatiently as if he was growing more, not less, uneasy. I didn't blame him one bit. I made a great play of patting and calming him, to give me time to think. Le Stryge! Yes, he had helped me all those years ago—though at the end, if anything, I'd saved him. A long time later I'd thought of turning to him again; but the idea had horrified my friends of the Spiral. Jyp the Pilot most of all, Jyp who had taken me to him in the first place. Hadn't he stressed how dangerous Stryge was—how untrustworthy? How he might make use of any claim I gave him against me—but had I already given him one? What power would it lend him if I had?

The great horse was responding, answering to my voice and touch; it was Stryge who made him nervous, that was obvious and interesting. The old swine might have sent him, but the horse was no creature of his. I sat up straight in the saddle, and stared down at him.

"I pay my debts, Stryge, when they're fair. But I know why you helped me. It wasn't for nothing. It was to clear one of *your* obligations—to Jyp; it's him I owe, if anyone. Anything you want done would tip the scales the other way. A long way, only I might have trouble collecting. You used to call me a fool, Stryge. Well, if you want some rushing-in done—*find another*!"

I reined in with a jerk, dug in my heel. With a loud whinny the great gray, jumpy already, wheeled and reared high. His hooves kicked sparks from the stone above the old man's head, and Stryge, caught beneath, staggered and fell back behind the monolith. As I'd hoped, I flicked the reins as the horse settled, but it needed no telling; he sprang away with a wild glad cry, back along the path, the way we'd come. I sank low, my back crawling at the thought of what might be launched after us any minute. Another stone-storm, some blast or blight or fireball—or some terrible snare to draw me back, a fish struggling on a swallowed hook. More likely something I literally couldn't imagine. I was far more afraid of that than I had been of bullets; I longed to dodge, to swerve, but up here that'd be fatal. No, there was only the speed of those strong legs.

The turn, at last, and we were rounding it, out of direct sight of the stones. We were back where we'd been shot at, but it felt safe by comparison. The horse remembered, that was obvious. He went like the wind, that noble beast, and the dust flew up behind us like a shield. I glanced anxiously over at the cloud roof, but nothing stirred; and ahead of us loomed the crest of the pass. We had to slow here, and I risked a long look back. Far behind, surprisingly far, a small dark figure stood in the midst of the scarred roadway, as if watching us; rising cloud coiled and writhed behind him in a dragonish corona, but he made no move. I shuddered again, and the horse whinnied, as if to reassure me. With surefooted grace he picked his way over the lip of the path and onto the stony slope below, skipping and sliding down that steep stretch, around and out on the broader mountain path. There he picked up the pace again; I glanced back, wondering if I'd see that short silhouette against the sky, ready to drop an avalanche on our heads, but nothing stirred.

The sun was sinking now, the sky darkening. The heights were becoming less distinct in the reddening light, inchoate swathes of shadow spreading across the summit. The cloud pool below grew grayer and dimmer, and as we came down toward it, cantering again, it washed up around us. Sight dimmed in the mirk; I barely made out a shadow-wall ahead. But before I could rein in we were onto it, and tree branches stung my cheeks. Only for an instant; then there was a hard harsh sound beneath those hooves, and we came out into shadow. The acrid air caught at my throat and stung my eyes. The horse shied slightly at the sound of a nearby sports car revving up, and so did I. Shaken, I slid out of the saddle, and the tarmac heaved beneath me at first. I hung onto the pommel for support, and fumbled in my pocket for more sugar.

"I wish I knew your name," I told him. "Ought to be— what? Bucephalus, Aster, Grane, maybe . . . " I made the best fuss of him I could, loosening girth and bit, wishing I could give him the rub-down and proper stabling he deserved. But though he lingered willingly enough, he began to look away, back beyond the trees; and I guessed he was uncomfortable here. Maybe he was being summoned, somehow. I gave him one last lump, and watched him sniff the air, turn and trot back under the branches. I turned too, and strode away back across the car park—or tried to. It was too long since I'd ridden much; my legs and backside were one glowing hoop of agony. I prayed devoutly that the terrace was still empty and nobody watching as I hobbled up the steps, limped to my table and slumped down—carefully, minding my blisters. In the sky now the sun had hardly shifted, yet the difference was vast. The light had changed, reddened slightly, and the clouds were only clouds and nothing more, as immense and insubstantial as the imaginings of men. Only in my mind it lingered, in the pain I'd earned, and the nagging worry. It had happened; there was no arguing with pain. I had ridden up over that path, as I'd wished to, and what had I found? A deep cauldron of cloud, and an even deeper enigma. And to go with it? Danger, deadly danger maybe. Just think, only an hour or two ago I'd been feeling bored—or was it hours?

Unconsciously, answering my thirst, my hand had sunk to that untouched gin glass; and it was still chill in my fingers. I raised it—and stopped, staring. It was the same glass, unquestionably, but in all this warmth the ice cubes hadn't even had time to melt.

Chapter 2

So I'd wanted to be alone, had I?

Not now. I was too badly jarred, and not just in the seat. Already that weird ride was becoming remote and dreamlike, as Spiral memories tend to; yet I couldn't stop turning it over and over in my head. I lingered on in the bar, though it was filling up with trade-fair types doing roaring business—literally—with the local tarts. When the gin had blunted the physical aches a bit, I hobbled off to the crowded grill room to pick at an unmemorable dinner, and sat brooding over my cardboard coffee. I needed advice, that was obvious; but the Spiral was the only place I'd find it.

I might be able to reach it. Seaports, river junctions, the great historical hubs of traveling humanity, it was around places like these, with their tangled web of shadows, that the misty borderland between the Core and the Spiral was broadest and easiest to penetrate. They didn't have to be ancient; I'd had one very strange encounter in the half-lit underpasses at Chicago O'Hare. There could easily be ways and byways here too; but I didn't know my way around, and

23

that was always dangerous. But Stryge might be watching them and, above all else, I didn't want to run into him again. He was a vindictive old bastard, that I knew, and a determined one; if he really did have a use for me he wasn't likely to forget it. He could have stopped me, and just thinking how brought me out in a cold sweat: I'd seen him strike the wind from a great ship's sails once, with an act of sheer cold cruelty. So why had he just let me go like that?

I swore softly. I'd been over that barren ground too often already; I was driving myself nuts. I needed some distraction, better company than the sweaty row in the bar. There was Lutz's party, of course. I'd meant to give it a tactful miss, but maybe some thoroughly worldly glitz and glitter would be therapeutic. Best I caught an hour or two's rest first. I heaved myself up, leaving my coffee, without bitterness, and walked stiffly out to the lifts. I was more or less on automatic pilot; it took me a moment to realize that the soft insistent beeping was coming from my pocket. But when I fished out the little case with the red light flashing, I snapped awake at once. It looked just like a miniature calculator, and so it was; but it was also an incredibly expensive pager, linked to the phone in my briefcase—and the infrared motion sensors built into the front. I made for the stairs, dithered on the first few steps for an instant, then saw sense and bolted for the lifts. Running up twenty-five storeys might be a little faster, but how much use would I be when I got there?

I jabbed the big central button and sprang into the first door that slid back, alternately blessing and cursing Dave. Blessing, because he was the one who'd brought in the top-flight industrial espionage consultants and bought us their most expensive gear; cursing, because it was probably just playing silly buggers, detecting the heating or the maid or something. All the leisurely way up I tapped my foot and fumed, swearing at my taste for high-rise rooms. When I reached my floor I more or less exploded out, sure I'd find

some moustachioed Turkish *Stübenmaderl* turning down
the bed. But from the glass-fronted landing I could look
across the face of the hotel to my windows; and they weren't
lit. Yet the little display showed the alarm was still being
triggered. I stormed down the corridor, but quietly now,
and sidled up to my door, listening. There wasn't anything—or was there? If that was a chambermaid she was
moving damned quietly.

I swallowed, wondering whether to go and phone the
desk, or just retreat behind one of the pot plants and wait
till somebody emerged. Either way I could make a really
total prat of myself, if I turned out to be imagining things.
But I didn't like the idea of leaving somebody free to monkey with my stuff. Gingerly I slid the plastic card into its
slot, and with infinite, agonizing slowness I turned the handle. I knew the door mechanism was ghostly quiet; but
what about the hinges? I leaned on it, gently, fractionally:
no light showed. I tensed, leaned a little further: a line of
utter darkness seemed to flow down the gap. I was about
to open it when two incredibly uncomfortable thoughts occurred to me: firstly, if somebody was in there with the
lights off, they could well be lurking behind the door; and
secondly, this might be something to do with Le Stryge.

I should have thought of that sooner; would have, if the
world of alarms and lifts and coded locks didn't seem so
remote from his. But as I'd found out before, to my cost,
it might not be. Himself, or one of his helpers, his
creatures—either way, about the last thing to bump into
in the dark. I held my breath, and I did hear something,
right enough, a faint creak, a click, a soft hiss . . .

My pulse was pounding in my ears; but if I tried to shut
that door now I might not make it. My fingers sweated and
itched for the weight of the great broadsword that hung
over my mantel at home. If the Spiral really was accessible
here, I might even be able to summon it; but that might
involve some interesting explanations if I was wrong. Better

to wait. I slid the door a fraction wider—and saw the thread of light beneath the bedroom door.

No ordinary light, not the mellow glow of the bedside lamps or the frank brightness of the bathroom fluorescents; it was dim and grayish, too dull to be called opalescent. Yet somehow it looked familiar. Against it, dim as it was, I could peer through the hinge crack. Nothing lurked. And nobody anywhere else in the sitting room either. So whatever this was, it was in the bedroom. What else was in there? Then I heard that clicking again, and the soft hiss of impatient breath, and I realized just what that dull light must be. I was across that room in three strides, before the door swung shut behind me, and flung the bedroom door wide.

Against the dim glow of my computer screen's backlight a dark figure sprang up from the bed. The computer tipped over, I had a brief impression of something lean and leopard-fast, then I was knocked back against the door frame as it sprang past. But not quite fast enough: I might be stiff and sore but I'd learned how to be fast, too. I grabbed an arm. It felt like a sheaf of silk-wrapped steel cables. Its owner, swung around by his own speed, wasted none of it, and went for me. A fist glanced off my cheekbone; another scrabbled at my throat. I tucked my chin down against my chest, which happened to set my head at a convenient angle. Fighting fair wasn't on the agenda right now. I butted hard, and the figure went reeling backward across the bed. I sprang, crashed down as it rolled aside, but still landed on its outflung arm. The hand clutched at my groin and nearly connected, too; then the other fist pounded a dizzying rabbit-punch on the back of my neck. I slid down, gurgling, and the shadowy figure jumped up and ran.

Who was I to argue? I lashed out with one foot; my long legs make good leverage. My sole connected with the intruder's buttocks and shot him right the way he wanted to go, only a little faster. The dark figure caromed off the door jamb and fell in a heap. Still giddy, I rolled off the bed on top of him, swung a punch at his nose and caught something silky instead, which ripped. Then a swiping punch caught me on the chin, another fist thumped into my guts and if I'd been the average businessman I'd have been mugger's meat from there.

I fell back, the intruder sprang up—and I grabbed him from behind and threw him against the bathroom door. That gave me a minute to get to my knees, struggling not to retch. The intruder swung upright. I saw a gloved hand stiffen and ducked. A really classic neck chop parted my hair and thudded harmlessly into the bed—then the other hand scythed into my left arm and nearly numbed it. Desperately I grabbed the arm with my right as it went past, threw the intruder flat on the carpet and jabbed an elbow into his kidneys. He kicked me on the kneecap, hard enough to break it if I hadn't pulled back. All the same, I yelped in agony and punched out; and we became an indescribable flurry of tangled limbs and flailing blows— killers, some of them, if only we'd had the space to deliver them properly. I'd been well schooled in the low arts by a number of friends, and a lot more enemies; but this character was a serious opponent. And a very nasty one. Fingers slithered toward eyes or crotch at every chance they got with an unnerving insistence, or tore at mouth, nose, ears or any other soft tissue. It wasn't a way I could fight, even if I'd had the room. As it was, we were throwing each other around in the space between the bed and the wall, and each time one of us tried to get up the other kicked the heels out from under him, or something of the sort.

It was dinner time on Saturday, the suites around were empty, or somebody would have heard. It can't have lasted long, though it felt like a century, and I began to realize something. I'd been put off by that arm: it felt strong, it *was* pretty strong—but it didn't have my strength. The more I stopped hitting and tried to tangle, to pinion, the more desperate the intruder got, the more evil the clawing. At last, as fingers jabbed into my nose, I let go, startled—

and doubled up with a groan as a knee swung at my groin.
The intruder sprang up, went for the door—and collided
with the bed as I heaved it bodily into his path. Not something he'd expected, because he couldn't have done it himself. He staggered—and I was already on my feet behind
him. I caught him a tremendous clip at the base of the
skull. He fell forward—and I was on him with my full
weight, grinding his face down into the stifling embrace of
the heavy hotel bedspread.

My gamble had paid off; it had been worth faking that
last fold-up just to con him into making a break for it. He
wasn't going anywhere now. I had one knee in the small of
his back, the other on his neck. His arms were tangled in
the bedspread, and his legs flailed uselessly; I could feel him
heave as he fought desperately for breath, giving great snor-
ing noises. If I didn't let him up soon, he'd suffocate. My,
oh, my.

I sat and got my breath back, massaged my bruises, generally let my adrenaline levels subside, and simply luxuri-
ated in being able to breathe freely. I'd had maybe one
harder tussle than that, and it wasn't with a human being.
But just sitting got a little boring. I decided to search the
body. The struggles redoubled, but I ignored them; he wore
some kind of close-fitting shell-suit, radiating a smell of
sweat and—that must be some aftershave. Where were the
pockets? I found one, spilled a ring of metal instruments
and a sheaf of perforated plastic plaques; lock-picking gear,
I guessed, and pretty sophisticated if it could handle these
doors. Anything else? I rummaged inside a trouser pocket—
then my hand closed with sheer shock. The body beneath
me convulsed; not half as much, though, as I would have.

Dislodged, as much by astonishment as anything, I rolled
back across the bed. It all went to prove I was a cleaner
fighter than I thought. If I'd launched a few more below
the belt, I'd surely have found out a lot sooner that I was
wasting my time.

I swung off the bed, retrieving the computer on the way,

and snapped on the main light. I stared at the face that lifted from the cover, scarlet and dripping and trickling blood from one nostril, dangling the ragged remains of a ski-mask.

"Don't even think about it!" I barked, as I saw the murderous flicker in the one open eye. "There's an alarm on the phone—one move and I press it. I don't think you're in any state to cope with me now, anyhow, are you?"

The woman's head sagged, and she gave one great gulping sob. It was a lot more emphatic than any curse. I looked down, feeling ridiculously ashamed of myself. It was then I saw the leads running from my computer to the extra phone socket they put in for fax and modem lines. I looked at the screen, and felt a great light dawn: the main window was running my communications software. I tapped the *Pause* key.

"So just where were you copying my files across to?" I inquired. The woman said nothing. *"Ich fragte, wohin Sie meine Feilen copieren wollte? Je viens de vous demander où exactement vous avez voulu copier mes fichiers? Hein? Mei archivi—dovei? Los ficheros—"*

She muttered something which sounded fairly obscene.

"Okay, we'll stick to English, then. Such as the words *industrial espionage*—they mean anything to you?"

Silence. I contemplated her for a moment, not that she was anything much to look at. Tall, probably; nicely enough built—lithe as a panther, in fact, and not entirely flat about the chest; but the whole effect was spoiled by her face. Right now it looked terrible, with one eye swelling and blackening, a split lip bulging and her nose still trickling slime and blood; but even at the best of times I suspected she wouldn't win any contests. It was a sour, hard face, hard as her fists, from the deep V between the eyebrows down to the discontented furrows either side of the long nose and heavy mouth. The open eye looked deep-set and very dark, slightly slanted, narrowed with lines of tension and temper. Her hair was short and black and slicked to her head with sweat, and that was about all you could say for it. With that look on her she could have been any age, mid-forties maybe; but looking at her neck I took ten years off that, or more. I'd seen faces like that on women athletes, the losers. It wasn't a yielding face, at all; it was a hating face, the kind that goes on hating whether it's right or wrong.

Still, I tried again. "You wouldn't happen to feel like telling me anything? Like who you are and what you're doing here? You might need a few Brownie points right now. No?"

"There are people who know where I am." Her voice was low and flat. "If you do anything to me, they'll be on to you."

I shrugged. She was stonewalling, and she'd go on. I looked at the phone number—010 33. France, which didn't have area codes; but that looked remarkably like a Strasbourg number. I tapped in a command to record it, inserted a pretty comprehensive obscenity and broke contact. Then I jumped, just in time to avoid her lunge across the bed. I whipped the computer out of her reach and tore the leads from the socket. "Naughty!"

For a moment I thought she was going to go shrieking for my throat; but instead she swung her feet wearily to the floor, and sank her face in her hands. I put the computer down carefully, without taking my eyes off her. "You don't learn, do you? I think I'd better just ring down right now for a brace of nice hefty porters and have you turned over to the cops."

She snorted, making a disgusting rattle, and swallowed hard. "You go right ahead! You just bloody try! But you're not going to, are you? Or what'd happen to your precious secrets then?" Her voice grated. I'd heard something like it before somewhere—where? The same harsh monotone, leaden with sarcasm and self-righteousness, the kind that knows it's right and gets no pleasure out of it. "Might find they've a few questions to ask you, when they see the stuff in that machine of yours!"

I blinked. There were commercial secrets in those files, okay, but nothing too crucial. "What stuff?"

She almost spat. "About you! You and your little friends, your so-called colleagues in this European transit scheme. Oh, don't you go thinking people don't know what you're really up to! Those names, they spell the whole thing out to anyone who knows!"

"Spell out what, exactly?"

"Oh, come *on*! Those SOBS? As if they'd all be involved in anything that innocent! When half of them are leftover *nomen-klatura* from the old Communist regimes, high-fliers even—and the rest are the corrupt fatcats they used to deal with? And extremists—such as your bosom buddy the Herr Baron!"

"Lutz von Amerningen? What about him?"

She shrugged theatrically. "Oh, nothing much. Just all those new movements mushrooming lately, not just here in Germany but all over Europe. The way they all go in for training camps and arms caches and street politics—like today. Under all sorts of names, too, but they all spell out neo-Nazi, every one. And he's a big wheel in most of them. But, then, you didn't know that either, did you?"

I leaned against the wall. "You know, as it happens, I didn't."

"Oh, *no*, perish the *thought*!" she leered. "And, of course, you don't believe a word of it, do you?"

I shrugged. "Does it matter? I wouldn't be too surprised—of some of them, anyhow. It's a sad fact of business in the old East, you can't avoid dealing with characters like that. When the crash came they were the only ones around with managerial skills, and naturally they got really well dug in. They're harmless enough, in their way. And Lutz, I could believe it, I suppose. His father had some kind of dodgy war record, didn't he? And I never have much liked the man himself."

"His father?" For some reason that made her grimace. She looked around, and suddenly snatched out at the dress-

ing table. I tensed—she was alarmingly fast—but she was
only picking something up, a long white card. She tossed
it at my feet. Lutz's invitation. "And this?"

"My first," I said evenly. "I wasn't sure whether I'd go or
not."

She mocked me with a twisted smile.

I shrugged again. "Think what you like, I don't give a
damn. I'm not the one who's trying to prove anything here.
All I know about any of these people is that they're widely
respected businessmen, both in their own countries and
throughout Europe, and it's as that that my firm's dealt
with them. Even supposing there's a word of truth in what
you're claiming, that there's anything shady in their back-
grounds, nothing like that's ever crept in. Not in dealing
or fraternizing, business or pleasure—not that we've ever
hung out with them much. And there's never been
anything—and I mean *anything*—about my firm. We've
got an impeccable race record, we've no political involve-
ment, no party links, *nothing*! So where do you get off,
suspecting us? Whoever *you* are, exactly."

She glared at me and said nothing; I hadn't shaken her
in the least. Now I knew who the voice reminded me of:
one of my infant-school teachers, no less, a crabby old sour-
puss with the fixed conviction that children were somehow
conspiring against her and a vindictive delight in catching
them out. After a while, of course, they were. This one
might have the same sort of problem. I pondered, taking
my time. I didn't think she was a cop—she'd called them
they. And she seemed a bit too unstable. I was rapidly coming to the conclusion that I had some kind of manic in-
vestigative reporter on my hands. I could prosecute or sue
on any number of counts—invasion of privacy, assault, data
theft, whatever the German equivalent of breaking and en-
tering was. But this self-righteous biddy in the dock could
throw a lot of mud about, and some of it might stick.

"Well?" she demanded. "In a hell of a hurry to call the
police, aren't you?"

"Right," I said. "I've had about enough of you. Out!"

"Want me to dial them for you?" she inquired sweetly. "No? Funny about that—"

I grabbed her by the scruff of the neck and hauled her to her feet. "We don't need your kind of mucky publicity right now," I told her, going through her remaining pockets and turfing out a trail of sinister little instruments, plus a room key. No ID, no nothing. I could feel the seam where the suit's label had been cut off. "That's the only reason you're getting off this lightly. But listen to me. If you're not checked out of . . . " I read the tab and tossed the key back to her. "1726, first thing in the morning, I will have you chucked out. D'you understand me? I can, you know."

"I believe you!" she hissed.

"Okay, then!" I stabbed a finger at the main door, and she hobbled past me. But she mooched through the living room with such studied insolence, actually stopping to pick up a sheaf of papers, that I caught her by the arm and more or less propelled her into the corridor. She stumbled in the thick carpet, but didn't fall. She drew herself up, cast one flaming glance back at me, snarled something under her breath and set off down the corridor with exaggerated dignity, rather too obviously trying not to limp. I looked after her for a moment, then let the door swing to. But the damper stopped it just short of closing, and I heard an explosive wail, hastily choked. Suddenly I felt a lot less self-righteous myself; and that annoyed me all over again.

I went off to the bathroom to wash, avoiding my gaze in the mirror. I couldn't have helped it, could I? She hadn't pulled any punches with me. If I hadn't defended myself to the limit she'd have beaten me to a pulp and got away, maybe with my computer. At least she hadn't tried playing the woman's card in either of its two main forms, though with the obvious one her looks might be against her. That face—or was it just her set expression? I tried to imagine her without it, and couldn't. Good disguise, if she could only control it. Who was she, anyhow? I began to regret letting her go so easily. I should have found out more; but I couldn't very well have beaten it out of her, could I? I winced as the hot water stung various bruises and scratches. She'd damn near beaten a lot out of me. Where had she learned to fight like that? And how did she keep that fit? By climbing, like me?

Climbing.

Room 1726, which meant floor seventeen. Four down. Where would Room 26 be? At this end of the building, but around the side, one of the cheaper rooms. It figured. I picked up one of those little devices she'd spilled; a bug, if ever I saw one. Near enough for easy pickup. I flushed with anger. Near enough for other things, too. And I had my gear all ready for that little holiday I'd promised myself. I wriggled uneasily. It was a daft idea—but the grim joke began to grow on me. I crushed the evil little gadget between my fingers. Snooping, was it? By God, I'd show the bitch how to do it! I ran to the closet where they'd stowed my cases, and began to rummage.

None of my normal gaudy Lycra gear would do. I tugged on a gray blouson with a hood, dark jeans, snapped my heavy harness over them and began filling the racks with crevice nuts, slings and a nice selection of camming pegs I'd been looking forward to trying out. Another minute and I had my boots on, the ones with the ultrasoft soles, and a length of featherweight line unclamped, fitting screwgate karabiner anchors and a descender. The window had one of those heavy two-way frames, it'd easily take my weight, even swinging. Thinking of that made me look lovingly at my helmet, but its Day-glo gold would flash like a beacon under the outside lighting. Swiftly I opened the window, belayed the line around the main pillar and through my harness fastenings. Then I swung a leg out, looked down to the window-ledge and beyond—and gulped. The car park was a softly glittering mass of roof-tops now, and it was only too easy to imagine myself speeding down toward them, maybe even seeing my reflection in the expensive gloss, coming up to meet me in one annihilating instant of identity, particle and anti-particle . . .

I shook myself. I was used enough to the horrors; any climber who says he doesn't look down is a liar. It can stiffen you for minutes at a time, even when—as I preferred to—you start from the bottom and work up, getting used to it. This abseiling wasn't altogether my line but the need for speed prodded me. I'd climbed down the side of a Bangkok hotel once, hadn't I? Higher than this, too. Admittedly, I hadn't actually *known* I was doing it, but did that really matter? Gingerly I swung out the other leg, winced as I hit a bruise, then felt down for that ledge and leaned away back and out, letting the doubled line pay out, further and further until I was practically walking down the smooth concrete castings of the hotel's façade. A few floors lower and I couldn't have managed this. I'd have fallen foul of the exterior lighting. But up here it was muted, so as not to dim the roof sign; in its shadow all cat-burglars were gray.

Going down was the easy bit; when I reached what looked like the right level I tied off for a moment and looked for somewhere that might take a peg. Nothing; this trendy façade was covered in slots and sockets, but they were all too big for even a hex nut. I sweated a moment, but there was no help for it; it was slink back up, or do the whole damn pitch in one. I risked a look down; nobody shouting or pointing down there—not yet. No time to lose; I began to jump, pushing myself out from the wall, further and further each time. And just as I was reaching the apex I suddenly saw myself coming crashing through a window, ripped ragged to the bone by plate-glass claws . . .

The hell with that! I flung my weight sideways and slipped the brake. With a noise like tearing canvas I flew, out and around, falling, until the line bent suddenly on the massive side-pillar and swung me in. I clamped the descender, the concrete rushed in to meet me and slapped stinging into my hands, my knees, anything that could cling. I bounced, held, slid and scrabbled; a finger caught in a slot, another, a foot—my bruises swore, but I was fast. I took a deep breath, looked up and counted floors. One down—fine. And on this side I was almost invisible from below. I began to climb, taking in the slack, careful not to let the line sag across somebody's window. Above and to the right there, that ought to be 26's window, its transom open a crack—and just as my fingers closed on the ledge beneath, the light came on.

With frantic haste I mantelshelfed myself up, half crouching, hanging on with cramped fingers and creaking back. I had to be careful: almost certainly there'd be others in there, the usual back-up team for this sort of bugging operation. The curtains were open, and pulling the dark hood down over my face I peered over the sill. There she was, moving slowly, just shutting the door; she must have taken the stairs rather than face anyone in the lift—a long, slow, painful hobble. She only just reached an armchair before she folded up and shook with what looked like exhausted sobs. Nobody else spoke; nobody moved. She was alone.

My stupid irrational conscience needled me again, and I sank back. My fingers and calf muscles protested; I searched hastily till I found slots into which I could sink a couple of pegs. Their weird-shaped double-cam heads expanded to grip the grimy concrete, and I krabbed their straps to my harness. I caught a flicker of movement; she was standing now, unzipping her shellsuit. She crossed and recrossed the floor, and I saw the discarded suit fly across the room with some force; she must have kicked it. Then a T-shirt flapped after it, and I saw her bare arm lift as she gingerly probed the red blotches around her ribs; testing for breaks, no doubt. That conscience of mine was really shrilling now; on the other hand, I had a good few aches of my own to account for. Besides, not to mince matters, I was enjoying myself; she had a nice back, as far as I could see, which wasn't quite enough. Then she moved out of view. Slowly, carefully, I hauled myself up behind the folded curtains, and very slowly peered around.

The first thing I saw was a pair of knickers beside the discarded shellsuit. Oh, God. There she was, still with her back to me—a really nice back, right enough—pouring a long drink from the single bottle on the minibar, gulping at it, topping it up, brushing her hand across her eyes impatiently, and gulping again with the glass clutched in both hands. She turned, I shrank back into the shadow of the curtains and saw her limp over to the chair by the telephone. She bent over it—she really did have a nice back—touched it tentatively, as if it frightened her, then swore violently, sat down and began to tap a number.

"Hallo? Centre d'Ordinateur, please—Computer Room? Georges, yes—well, Georges? You did get those files through . . . you did, good . . . good!" A great spring of tension seemed to give out in her; she sagged and gulped at the drink. "Well? Was there enough?" A long silence. "What d'you mean? Georges, you don't know what I went through to get those files out. If you've screwed them up somehow—"

An even longer silence; and then an anguished cry. "I don't believe it! Georges, there has to be *something*! I mean, we agreed, didn't we? We did, we did, you said it yourself! Mr. fucking Clean, in the middle of that ratpack! With all those little disappearances he can't quite explain! You checked his address files, right?" Silence. "You're sure they're all just bimbos? How about the Chinese bitch—all right, all *right*! So he's a cold-blooded bastard, he treats them like muck, what'd you expect? All right." She brooded a moment, evidently simmering. She wasn't the only one.

"All right," she said again, in a voice that meant the exact opposite. "But you should have seen him, the bastard! Today, these riots, Pretty Boy just driving through them with von Amerningen, looking around cool as cucumbers the pair of them! It's like Weimar in the nineteen thirties, they're testing the system for something really big—

maximum disruption. They could even be planning to use this new shipping network of his, maybe, getting everyone to rely on it, then screwing up, shafting the economy at just the right time! How about moving supplies, armaments, even—with no checks till they get to destination? And fast—we're talking *blitzkrieg* here! Listen, Georges, this is too big for just one little departmental team, it's got to go to the Commissioner—I mean, not just what he has already, the whole thing on this man Fisher! Take him out, and maybe the Baron, and we can kick the rest apart." Silence. "Well, no, as it happens I did get some new evidence—chummy's been trained, one hundred per. How would *I* know? With the IRA in Libya, could be. Wherever it was, he's good—too good. Yes. Well, I held him off, he had to let me go, you know there isn't a man in the department who—oh, come *on*, Georges, you're as bad as the rest of them! That's enough! It's *got* to be him! Now we just go in and rip him apart and throw him to rot. . . Georges! Whose side are you on, anyhow? Don't give me that! So this one didn't pay off, so what? Yes. Yes, I got burned. How do I know if he got the number? He may have, I don't think so. Forget that, he probably knew it already—he's the mastermind, isn't he? Oh, come on! If you go telling tales to Bernheimer I am going to get whipped right off this case, you know that? I mean maybe . . . *No, Georges!* No!"

Her hand faltered, and the handset sank; she almost dropped it, then I thought she was going to throw it down. She looked at it, and her face twisted. "Fuck you, then," she said, and put it down softly. She stood up, and I saw, almost more clearly than her nakedness, the reddened and blackening blotches of her bruises. She looked as if she'd been through a mincer. But I thought of my ravished privacy, riffled files, my girlfriends checked up on, the baffled venom in that voice as it twisted and tortured the truth to suit its own suspicions. My conscience shut its mouth, folded its arms, and enjoyed the view.

She considered her drink, put it down and walked with stiff dignity, like a sort of robotic ballerina, toward the bathroom. After a moment I heard the toilet flush, and the shower come on. Not a bad idea; I could use the same myself. I flicked the cams free, gathered my strength and kicked out hard, out, away and into the open air with a rush, then back around the arete to the face of the hotel. This time I didn't need to cling; I hit, bounced, clamped on an ascender and began to haul myself up at speed with creaking arms, passing the rope under my battered buttocks to keep it away from windows. I had relief to fuel me, now that I knew what all this had been about.

A Strasbourg number, and Goran Bernheimer, deputy trade commissioner for the European Community. So Joan of Arc here was an EC trade investigator; nice job for a paranoid. But by the sound of that little lot, she'd be off my back soon enough: Bernheimer was no fool. The relief lasted all the way back to my room—almost.

I was on the window-sill when the cold feeling crept over me. Okay, she was just an overzealous cop with a fixation, the type that tends to end up planting the evidence. Let her try that now! But a cop of sorts she was, and not just some muckraker. That gave more weight to the other things she'd said, a lot more. Okay, she was wrong about me—but the main reason she suspected me seemed to be the company I kept. I'd assumed she was just as wrong about them—but was she? About them she sounded absolutely sure; and as if the absent Georges did too. And surest of all about Lutz.

I slid back in, wincing at my injuries, and headed for that haunt of philosophers, the bathroom. I needed to get clean all over again now. There was a television tilted over the broad bath, but it gave me little comfort as I let my aches soak away into the steaming water. The news was full of riots, both here and in Warsaw, Polish skinheads battling it out with neo-Communist thugs, both equally horrible; the ringleaders in particular looked practically interchange-

able with each other—or with those here, for that matter.
Europe was beginning to wear a common face, and it wasn't
one I liked. Grudgingly I hauled myself out of the water
and phoned down to the valet service for my evening *frac*,
and the garage for my car. I was going to look in at Lutz's
party after all.

I'd rented a top-line BMW sport, and this late the roads
were clearing; I made good time out of town and onto the
byroads. They led me a curling way out to the little village
that was the only material remainder of the once-vast
Amerningen estates, squatting dourly beneath the shadow
of their baroquely decorated gates. The men at the gates
were in tuxedos, too, but there was no mistaking them for
either guests or waiters, impeccably polite as they were;
they were uniformly huge, great square-headed Prussian
grenadier types. You thought they'd clump, but they moved
with easy athletic grace. One of them chatted lightly in
good English while the others gave me and my invitation
the unobtrusive once-over, checking me against some invisible list; then they threw open the gates with enough
ceremony to make anyone overlook the delay. Soft glows
awoke among the shrubbery as I drove by, then dimmed
again behind me to leave the long drive in shadow.

You might have expected a Bavarian baron's family home
to be a Gothic extravaganza of towers and battlements, or
a beamy old rustic *Schloss* full of stags' heads and open
fires. Instead I pulled up under the porte-cochère of a wide,
sleek stately home which must have been the latest fashion
for an eighteenth-century gentleman of leisure, glazed
dome in the roof and all. Evidently Lutz's ancestors were
smoothies, too. If there was an old castle anywhere around,
it was probably an artistic ruin in the gardens. This place
suggested sips of Cointreau more than steins of beer,
though by the din that rolled out as the tall front door
opened, there was some pretty active sipping going on right
now. A tide of flunkeys spilled out, headed by a fifty-fiveish
Juno who must have been quite something in her youth

and, despite the severe business suit, was still well worth a
look. She greeted me like a favorite nephew, introduced
herself, with a conspiratorial smirk, as Inga-Lise, the Herr
Baron's major-domo; and assuring me that the Herr Baron
was expecting the Herr Ratspräsident, meaning me, she
whisked me gracefully off into the depths of the house.

Beyond the hall double doors opened onto a massive ballroom. Once its colonnades might have echoed gentle
waltzes and quadrilles; now it was a swirling blur of decorations and colored lights, strewn with couches and cush-
ions and sprawling, giggling bodies. The air was thick and
smoky, aromatic tobacco tinged with pot and an unholy
mixture of expensive perfume and wealthy sweat. It glowed
and flickered in the path of an occasional laser, overspill
from the disco in the promenade outside, flaring and coruscating on swinging earrings and iridescent gowns, tracing a hot insubstantial finger over bare shoulder blades and
into cleavages. As we picked our way down the side of the
hall, over bodies recumbent or entwined, a side-door
crashed open amid shrieks and shouts. Bare feet pattered
on the marble floor, and we were momentarily enveloped
in a warm crush of half-clad bodies, the girls looking hastily
dressed, most of them, though one or two were in their
knickers, the men in shirts, shorts, socks, rumpled and hot
and glassy-eyed. Someone thrust a hand under my nose and
cracked a little pod; I smelled the sweetish tang of amyl
nitrate and jerked away, among shrieks of laughter. Inga-
Lise smiled at me approvingly. Then they were gone, piling
down some steps that evidently led to an indoor pool, judg-
ing by the splashes and shrieks. One or two thought better
of it, and vanished, giggling, through another door ahead;
with a look of guileless naughtiness Inga-Lise let it swing
back a crack to shed a little light on the goings-on within.
The two of us exchanged glances and chuckled.

"Quite a show. I hope they're not going to overdo those
poppers, or you might be sweeping out the odd corpse in
the morning."

She gave me that half-teasing, approving look again.
"The Herr Ratspräsident doesn't indulge so?"

"Oh, I can be pretty indulgent. But I go for different
highs, real ones. I think they'll keep me younger in the
long run."

She smiled, and handed me a tulip glass of champagne
from a passing servant's tray. "The Herr Ratspräsident looks
younger than I was led to expect, for one who achieves so
much. That is a good thing in a man."

"So does the Herr Baron. You must look after him really
well."

She dimpled, but seriously. "Alas, he is too good at looking after himself."

"I don't doubt it." I grinned. But I wondered whether
that expression was just her unwieldy English, or whether
she really was giving me a gentle warning to watch my
back. Nice of her, but I didn't need it. Right from our early
dealings with the Baron von Amerningen I'd decided that
for all the Pan-European guff he spouted, the interests he
was most devoted to were his own, a man of powerful survival instincts. My good friend Dave had simply commented
that it took one to know one. I hoped he was right.

I was looking out for Lutz right now, but there was no
sign of him among his guests, and Inga-Lise seemed to be
leading me somewhere specific. We moved through the
great house, tripping over minor orgies here and there, and
toward what must be the back stairs. They led us up and
overhead, two floors up, to where even that deafening disco
was just a minor thudding in our feet. There were other
doors ahead, not as large as the ballroom's but heavy and
businesslike. Servants lounging on tilted chairs before them
sprang up as we approached—no, not servants exactly.
More of the types that manned the gates, but where they
had been fairly personable, these were plug-uglies, quite
extraordinarily so, all bulbous noses and cauliflower ears,
and a malevolent gleam in their piggy little eyes. Inga-Lise
handed me over to them with a faintly apologetic smile,

saying, "I go no further," and taking her leave with that impish smile again, a little forced. I heard her footsteps hurrying away down the corridor, and it struck me that it was almost as if she wanted to be back at the stairs before those doors opened.

When they did, though, it was almost an anticlimax. After the glitz and groping among the *beau monde* downstairs this inner sanctum looked absurdly peaceful, a sedate gathering radiating nothing more than the buzz of quiet conversation. At second glance, though, it seemed a little stranger than that, because though the talk was quiet, the talkers weren't. As the doors closed behind me and one of the servants exchanged my champagne glass, I found myself eye to eye with a pair of wild-eyed rock musician types, middle-aged unisex Goths in two-tone hair, black PVC and laces straining with midriff bulge. What was probably the woman rolled black-rimmed eyes at me and demanded, "All aboard for the Brock, eh?" in strident middle-class Cockney. I gave a meaningless smile and drifted aside, only to see somebody tall and camel-like gazing vaguely around and wiping thumb and forefinger over his dangling little moustache. That had to be Lino Mortera, one of our Italian board members and about my least favorite; and there was fat little Pontoise, for whom I had a lot more time, gesticulating furiously to a couple of hefty harridans who would have had a promising career as Russian trawler skippers or Belsen guards. I didn't want to meet either man right now, so I steered hastily for the far side of the room. I rubbed elbows with other business types I vaguely recognized from the fair, hard, intense women with the gloss of TV producers or executives and slightly less glossy ones who might be their academic counterparts. A tall rangy woman who looked like a successful German executive was standing by herself, so I breezed in on her with a borrowed conversational gambit. "Well, it's all aboard for the Brock, isn't it?"

She turned a very strange look on me. *"Verzeih'n—ah. Dem Brocken. Ja, dauert's nicht lang."* She sounded heavy, depressed; yet even as she said the word her eyes narrowed and her tongue traced her lips slightly. She looked as if she was going to shiver. *The Brocken. Yes, it will not be long.*

Brocken! So that was what they were talking about! I knew what it was, all right; I'd been there. A mountain in the Harz range, the highest if I remembered rightly, along what had been the old East German frontier, a long way from here. But I seemed to remember the name from somewhere else as well, somewhere that set the shadows gathering in my mind.

"Listen," I said urgently, "about the Br—"

Abruptly she turned away, pressed her forehead to the wall, and brushed me away when I tried to intervene. I slid away in case she attracted attention, past a couple of German longhairs arguing about performance art, plastic form and *Guernica*. I took refuge among a knot of relatively normal types, mostly overdone jetsetters like burnt-out graduates from the set downstairs, sweating copiously into their collars and discussing the shortcomings of their brokers and their own idiotic ideas of what the markets were doing. I was injecting a little basic economics when two women converged on me, lean, fortyish types with bright nervy eyes, wearing fantastically expensive-looking polyester jumpsuits and puffing at one bloated joint. One leaned over and said, "I know *you*," in breathy accented English. "You are the capitalist, *nicht wahr*? You know, Putzerl? From the article, the man who makes parcels think."

They weighed me up with bright sardonic eyes, and giggled. "What have you come to peddle, Herr Kapitalist?" inquired the other.

"Your ass?" suggested the first, and they shrieked.

"No," I countered coolly. "Yours." The listening men cheered.

"*S'ist's nicht z'verkauf'n!* Is not for sale!" protested the second. "I buy it all up since years ago!"

"Show her yours," whooped the other. "She's always buying, the dirty slut!"

"What's point? I see it later, anyhow! I watch out for you, Herr Peddler! I like you!"

"As long as you are not Jewboy!" the other put in. "Putzerl doesn't like nasty snip-snippety *Juden*, does she, mmh?"

"I see that too!" squealed Putzerl, and they doubled up, coughing great clouds of pot. It smelled like expensive stuff, but it left a bitter taste on my tongue—hellish bitter.

One of the men wrapped a meaty arm around my shoulder. "You watch those two, they breaks your balls for you! Break them," he persisted, "*crr-acck*!" in case I hadn't got the point. "Like my wife does to me. Like my goddamn kids. You wait till later. *He* tames 'em! Tcherno, he tames those two, I've seen them crawl, just crawl. You know what I've seen?" He shook his head, slick with sweat, and I looked down into his eyes, bloodshot and dark, very dark. It was like looking down into pools of pure terror. "You know what I've seen?" he repeated. "*Liebe Gott*, you know . . ."

His arm slumped, and he sagged and turned away, shaking his head. The men around him were talking louder as he lurched through them, heading for a side-door. They were sweating, too, though it wasn't unduly hot here and they didn't seem to be drinking much; there were only a couple of waiters, elderly types, and their trays were seldom touched. There was a lot of pot in the air, though, and I began to feel a bit lightheaded myself. The tensions I'd sensed in that last exchange—or was it just the pot, just that wrongness that can infect a party, leaping from one head to another like lightning and warping the whole ambience? Had that happened here? But there was another kind of agitation, too, an uneasy, unhealthy thing that was almost excitement—the emotion of a group of people about to do something that's illicit and irresistible in equal proportions. I remembered the college climbing club as we prepared to make a highly illegal bungee jump from a local bridge, all bravado and Buck's Fizz while the perspiration trickled down our spines into our shorts. That kind of feeling. The difference was that these people were hardly bothering to conceal it from each other, as if they'd been through it all before, and had little to hide, except perhaps from themselves. I found myself wondering if I'd strayed into some sort of *really* peculiar perversion ring—but there was that accusation of neo-Nazism, and that mention of the Brocken. It was a well-known place, it had been like the Brandenburg Gate, a point of German partition. Could the name have been borrowed for some sort of neo-Nazi *Bund*? Only too likely; or it might mean nothing. Except that I had heard it somewhere else, all right, in a voice I didn't care to remember.

Take me back to the pines on the Brocken, where the dark powers meet . . .

So said a very discontented Le Stryge; and my friend Jyp the Pilot grew pale at the mention.

A low rumble startled me out of my dark memories. Not far away an inner door was being locked back, to let some bulky furniture be carried out of an inner room. I looked through, and saw that the room beyond was much larger than this one and its ceiling was the great glass dome. Men in their shirt-sleeves were bustling around, evidently preparing for something; they were clearing the place, rolling back the carpet, even. Surely this could have been done earlier, before people arrived; so why wasn't it? Unless it was something secret, so secret that it could only be prepared under the cover of the party. The floor beneath looked like marble, sounded like it as they laid out jugs and bowls—no, vessels and ewers, fantastically ornate things of gilt or gold with an undefinable air of age. There was gold in the floor, too, in mosaic patterns inlaid into the marble, one great central shape that looked familiar. Only familiar wasn't friendly, given some of the things I'd seen; where had I ever run into *that*? The Nazis, now, did they have any other symbols beside the swastika? But as I sidled closer, straining to make it out, I almost jumped out of my skin. A hand landed on my shoulder, a great flipper of a thing, and turned me irresistibly around. A pair of slightly bulging blue eyes stared down into mine, and the glitter of rage was sudden and sharp.

"*Stephen? Teufelschwanz, was machst du Verfluchter in diese Stelle?*"

"Well, hold on a minute, Lutz—you invited me, didn't you?"

The eyes wandered an instant, and then his tone was mild; but in men like Lutz mildness doesn't come naturally. "Yes. Yes, of course, I am sorry! To the party, *gewiss natürlich*! Though I had given up hope of your arriving! But to this? I am sorry, Stephen, but this is a meeting of a particular—what is the word? Of a Lodge. A private one, that it was convenient to hold in conjunction with the *assemblage* below. How on earth did you come to be admitted?"

"Fraülein Inga-Lise brought me here to find you, that's how!"

"Ah . . ." His whole countenance changed. "She had no call to do that. The silly girl! She must have assumed, because you were arriving so late, that it was for this alone. Hmph!" He huffed a moment, rubbed his hands, and looked at me slightly askance. "I will have to have a word with her. The fact is, I am a little annoyed. You and she between you have somewhat deflated a surprise I was hoping to prepare for you. Specially for you."

"For me?"

"Why, yes. I was hoping that I could invite you—and please do not laugh!—to enter this very Lodge! Perhaps even this very night! And here you have forestalled me!"

I drew a deep breath. Time to tread very carefully. "Lutz . . . that's a real honor. And extremely kind of you. Only . . . well, perhaps it's for the best. You know how often I've been invited to join the Masons? But I've always had to refuse. It's a company tradition—no fear, no favor." I thought of my old boss Barry, never joining any of his beloved Jewish societies, but somehow I didn't feel like mentioning that to Lutz. "We stop short at the Rotarians, more or less. So . . . "

Lutz snorted good-humoredly, though his eyes still glittered. "You and that company of yours! There you are, you see, I knew I vould need time to tell you about us, as much as I'm allowed to. For this could be very important to you, Stephen. The Masons, that is a petty thing, a local thing. We also are related to Freemasonry, Stephen, but in the much older tradition of the continent. Much older and more powerful, descended from Lodges that numbered among their members Mozart and the Emperor Joseph II. We have long been accustomed to number men of power among us, the more enlightened men of their time. Governments have been made or toppled in our salons, kings overthrown, fortunes made and destroyed. In times of turbulence or war we offer a shelter, an understanding, a constant mutual help that goes beyond mere national boundaries." His voice sank. "And to those with the imagination to grasp it we offer a knowledge of the forces that truly underlie the world. I say no more of that for now, but it is there."

I was walking on eggs. "It sounds fascinating, but principle—"

"You?" he woofed. "You are old enough to know that principle is what you make it. And principle is not everything with you, is it?" He chuckled, and passed me another champagne glass. "Veuve Cliquot, and not for my noisy young friends downstairs to gulp. Though you know, Steve," he chuckled, and I thought he was going to dig me in the ribs, "we could show them a thing or two. We who work hard, we also play hard—I already know that is true of you! Those girls I've seen you with—uh? Well, after hours here . . . "

He raised his eyebrows, making those pop eyes look round and impish. "You take my meaning?"

I glanced around, and he gave a chortle. "Oh, not with this lot, no, not these old *Katze*! They are just along for the ride—*verstehn? So gut.* But I can promise you an experience that will turn you inside out, Herr Ratspräsident—inside out. There are girls, beautiful girls who—words fail me. It must be experienced."

Internally I winced, but I still didn't want to offend him outright. I sought for an answer along the right lines, a gentle turndown that wouldn't give him any excuse for immediate offense. "Lutz, I . . . I'm impressed as hell. But, on the whole, you know how it is? I prefer to roll my own."

He stared at me for an instant, then let loose a thunderous guffaw. *"Jo, g'wiss, und wer soll denn den papier lecken,* hah? And are you careful always with the filter-tips, hah-hah-hah? Well, I can respect that. But you must be careful, Stephen, lest you turn down knowledge. For nobody has enough of that."

"Believe me, I know. Maybe if you feel able to talk to me some more about it. Some other time, maybe. Right now I'm kind of tired, harder to persuade about anything . . . "

"Aber natürlich. But it is getting late, and—" He glanced around. The men in the next room were looking at us uncertainly; so were the guests. "You understand? If you do not join tonight . . . "

"Of course I understand, I don't want to get in anybody's way."

"Fine, fine. Of course you may join the party below, no? Then I will see you out myself." He turned and loosed a blast of instructions to the others—not in German, it sounded more like Polish or south Russian. The men scurried back into the next room, and I saw several of the guests, or Lodge members or whatever they were, moving as if to help, with a growing sense of urgency. I caught one last glimpse of that complex inlaid floor, but at once Lutz put his arm to my shoulders and shepherded me out. We took a shorter way this time, down darkened stairs and past closed doors, avoiding the row below, but just as I thought I would be ushered out of a side-door, Lutz suddenly di-

verted us through the main hall. He stopped there to in-
troduce me to one or two people, not very relevant ones,
it seemed, and then scooped me away. My car was already
waiting, motor running and lights on, and as I clambered
in Lutz stood over me woofing unnecessary instructions for
getting back to town. He seemed determined to take care
of me, and stood waving after me as I pulled away across
the gravel forecourt to the drive. Again the lights rode with
me as I moved through the grounds—some sort of sensor
mechanism, I guessed, so as not to ruin the night with
glare, but it made me feel exposed. Which was ridiculous,
but the hair under my collar crawled. As if I was being
watched . . . as if something was following me among the
shadows. I couldn't shake it off. I touched the brake,
glanced around.

Just beyond the car an overhanging rhododendron twig
leaped and flew up, landing on the bonnet in a shower of
leaves. I braked violently, and something else sang down
and threw up a spatter of gravel at the driver's door. I more
or less stamped on the accelerator; no mistaking what *that*
was. Just as the car lurched forward an intense green point
glittered on the windscreen; then there was another whine
through the open window, past my ear, and a rear window
crazed. I ducked, changed up like a maniac and saw two
more gravel fountains spout around the car. Then I was at
a bend in the drive, and nearing the gate. The gatekeepers
sprang up, and I half expected them to leap into my path
with machine pistols; but instead they flung the gates open
with as much of a flourish as before, so I hardly needed to
slow down. I sailed through with a nonchalant wave, half
expecting a bullet in the back, and saw their faces stiffen
as they registered the crazy cracking on that rear pane. Too
late; I was through, away and down toward the village. But
it wasn't till the cobbles of its main street rumbled under
the tires that I slowed down and stopped, shaking, to wonder just who the hell had been after me with a long-range
laser gunsight.

I couldn't have offended Lutz *that* much; or if I had, there were a hundred easier ways he could have disposed of me, and not on his premises either. And he wouldn't have let me slip through that gate, not Lutz. But whoever it was had missed. Could it just have been a warning? I reached out and touched the shattered window; another centimeter and that would have been my head. Warnings don't come that close. Which meant that our sight-wielder was an assassin all right, just not a very good one—lack of practice, maybe, at least in real-world situations.

I drew breath and started the car up again, heading for the *Autobahn*; these winding little lanes were unnerving now. At every bend I kept expecting to see that green glimmer again, and then—nothing. But on the *Autobahn* I could build up a bit of speed, and be harder to hit, impossible in traffic. The *Einfahrt* sign, which normally made me chuckle, looked like the gate to paradise when I reached it, and the bumpy concrete-block surface, a legacy of the Third Reich, rumbled with safety and security. I'd been shot at more than most people, and if anything I liked it even less now; every miss brought that inevitable hit one statistical notch nearer. I put my foot down and let the car's power take over, snatching me up and sweeping me away. I'd have liked the road a bit less empty, for cover's sake, but at least I could open her up.

It was the roar from beside me that caught my attention, the sound of a fast car being pushed; and it was too close. I glanced around, saw the dark saloon loom up, the window slide down. The sight of the slingshot almost made me laugh, till I realized its purpose. A bullet in a crashed driver's head causes comment, but there are a hundred ways a lump of jagged metal or stone could have got there. Frantically I ducked, wrenched at the wheel to swerve away—and screamed aloud.

The big black truck which had been quietly minding its own business some way ahead had become a roaring, swinging monster right in my path, driving me toward the

outer lane, the concrete lip of the road and the blackness
beyond. I swung the car, braked, and the truck smashed
into the concrete in front of me, rebounded in a spray of
chips, and here was that bloody Merc again! I swung right,
only to see the truck wheels loom above me like whirling
mincers, too close to avoid now. There was a thudding
crash, the broken back window exploded—and the Merc,
cutting in toward me, burst off them like the ball off a
roulette wheel. As I struggled to steer into my long skid I
saw it leap the center and go skidding along the crash barrier, then overturn with a noise like crumpling tin. I pulled
the car around as the truck bore down on me, clamped
down hard and felt some two hundred and fifty horsepower
take hold of the road and heave. Friend or foe, the truck
couldn't even hope to keep up. It fell away behind, and good
riddance; there'd been nothing accidental about any of this.
The wind from the empty light behind whistled savagely; it
would have been my side window, and probably me, if it
hadn't been for that truck. I'd been shaking earlier; now I
was just plain and fancy furious.

It was nearly two when I pulled back into the hotel, causing the sleepy night porter to goggle at the sight of my car,
with its side stove in. I'd stopped to report it, not that it
would do any good, but it would keep the hire company off
my back. The police were politely skeptical, asking if driving
on the right had not by chance confused my lane discipline,
and squaring up to breathalyze me—until they found out
where I'd been. One mention of Lutz and C-Tran, and it
was yes, sir, no, sir, three bags full, sir, which isn't supposed
to happen, but does. That put me in an even filthier temper,
and to avoid another set of explanations I said I'd park the
car myself. I trundled around to a suitably obscure corner
in the shadows at the side of the hotel, and that made me
think of 1726. I looked up at her window, but the light was
off. I resisted the temptation to rush up there and wring
some more explanations out of her, though; the best thing
for me would be getting out of here, fast, and back home,

to find some more reliable advice. And somehow, during all this lunatic pursuit, my subconscious had placed that strange symbol on that beautiful floor, and disturbed me deeply in the process. I wished it had been something like a swastika; that I could almost have comprehended, loathed but related to history, to purely human horrors. But the last place I'd seen a shape like that was among the ghastly tangles of obscene carving on the high stern transom of the Wolfship *Chorazin*. A geometric five-pointed star, set within a double circle of inscription, an emblem of ill intent, a pentacle.

Though this one had been filled with what looked like odd mosaic patterns . . .

I stopped suddenly, turned around. Something had moved behind me, something like a momentary flicker of light, a rustle of movement to go with it. When I spun around again it stopped, then sounded again, louder. Over the bonnets of the parked cars something flowed, barely visible except against their mirror polish, a faint misting that moved in tendrils, amoeba-like. Now I could see it in the air, just, as the lights glimmered on it. There was that sound again—not a rustle exactly, more like a faint hoarse exhalation. It looked like nothing at all, and yet the feeling grew on me that it would be a very bad idea to have that clammy cloud wrap itself about me. I backed away, and saw it seem to rear up, facing me, an invisibility no more than a shimmer against the stunted trees behind and their single low lantern—and then, shockingly, whiter, thicker, as mist flowed back into it from all around. It was gathering itself into a thick misty cloud there; and I turned and ran. Out of the corner of my eye I saw the thing move, too, gliding forward, on my tracks, glittering among the parked cars, flowing over their cold metal like a caress. It was fast, too, but I was faster; I made the front, and practically fell through the glass doors as they soughed back. The porter was contemplating me with fascination.

"Mist," I explained. It happens to mean "manure" in

German, but that was all the explanation I felt like right then. I limped over to the lifts and straight up to my room; but though I was bone-weary I poured myself a drink and went out onto the balcony, unable quite to credit the last couple of hours I'd lived through. The physical attacks, maybe, though who had anything to gain I couldn't imagine. But even they seemed improbable now, faintly ridiculous, as if I'd somehow exaggerated them out of distorted memories. And the mist—okay, I'd had strange things happen before; but surely *that* had to be pure panicky imagination. Hysteria, even, triggered off by stress.

But when I looked down all those floors the car park was still shrouded in that faint haze, setting glittering haloes around all the lights, enveloping the ground floor of the hotel. It stirred as I leaned over, and seemed to stretch a long tendril up toward me, like a wave climbing a sea cliff. But it couldn't make it, and like a wave it fell back into the stuff it came from, spreading faint ripples of ghostly turmoil.

I sank into bed that night, very tired and uneasy, wondering just what I'd got into, what I'd created, and I dreamed. More than once it woke me, sweating, but only one image remained from a vaguely terrifying jumble. A map of Europe, a child's map in the dulled colors of an old school atlas, and spreading across it a web, a gray, complex, dirty web, full of shriveled death. At the heart of it, tense, malevolent, ready to spring, there crouched a small black spider.

Chapter 3

The next morning, oddly enough, I had fewer doubts. That was because I harbored some interesting cuts and bruises, which had taken advantage of the night to stiffen up; and because I had to spend ages arguing with the car-hire company and persuading them to send another car to get me to the airport. The whole thing infuriated me so much I almost forgot 1726, but when I called down, the desk clerk, an old acquaintance, assured me that yes, Fräulein Perceval had checked out at six thirty and taken her car out of the garage and, speaking of which, mine had just arrived. It turned out to be chauffeur-driven; which is one way of making a point. I sat in stony silence all the dull and drizzly way, brooding. Perceval, eh? Distinguished, as cover-names went.

I'd meant to spend a few days more, at least, but with all sorts of people gunning for me, and complications straying in from the Spiral, I had urgent business at home. So much for my climbing, too. I was feeling mean as a rat; they wanted my head, did they? Well, they'd better watch out for theirs. With my cases poised on a wobbling trolley I went through airport security, which had become twice as annoying as customs and passport controls ever were, and trundled my way over to the behind-hangars backwater set aside as a heliport. The sight of my own little machine rolled out and waiting cheered me up a bit; I threw my cases into the minuscule back seat, sent the trolley to hell and went over everything even more thoroughly than usual, just in case somebody had bribed a mechanic to loosen a nut or block an oil line.

Paranoia rules, okay—*and who told you*?

All the same, I felt relieved when I'd covered all the more obvious possibilities; there are too many of them on a helicopter. At last, wiping oil off my fingers, I settled into the pilot's seat and pulled on my helmet. I had just time to run through the pre-flight checks with traffic control before the slot I'd booked came up, and the impatient ground staff waved me out. The starter coughed, turned, and unleashed the worst din in the world. It made me shrink a bit, after last night, but I'd no time to spare. Right hand on the cyclic joystick, left on the collective lever, twist the throttle grip and listen to the quickening hiss of the rotors overhead. As it speeded up I rocked the rudder pedals gingerly, checking the tail rotor's response; I'd only been flying solo for two years, and I didn't want to lose it right in the middle of a major international airport. My left hand gunned the throttle and eased the collective forward, angling the rotor blades to generate lift, and the tarmac sank away in my windshield as the little beast lifted and began to swing. I eased down on the pedals, pitching the tail rotor to kill the swing, tipped the cyclic to tilt the whole rotor assembly, angling the downdraft backwards, and inched the collective along, sending her slowly forward and upward, all the while obeying the controller's patient monotone, keeping a wary eye on the airport around me and darting nervous glances at the crowded control display. Flying a 'copter is a whole-body experience, like sex without the fringe benefits.

I made rather heavy weather of clearing the crowded airspace, but patient the voice remained, so I couldn't have been doing too badly. Finally I was up and away, and I could do what I'd been yearning to, just lean on the stick and let her soar. As high as she would, anyhow: she was a middle-aged Bell I'd bought secondhand, nominally a five-seater provided two of your friends were garden gnomes, and a bit lacking in get-up-and-go. Presumably the company would be able to buy me a better model, maybe one with NOTAR technology—no tail rotor—and faceplate control displays, all the trimmings, but that thought didn't excite me so much now. It was in danger of feeling like dirty money.

As I burst up through the cloud cover, though, my mood could hardly help improving. Out of gray damp gloom and over an expanse of cloud sparkling in the sun's long rays, it reminded me of the most liberating moments of my life, when I set sail upon the Spiral. Few other experiences approached the sheer astonished wonder of seeing the bows lift above mundane seas, heading out toward the cloud archipelagos and the oceans of moonlit mist through which great ships pass to all the seas of the world, in every era there has been and even more that haven't. They had their equivalents, those eerie oceans, in earth and air—regions of land and sky where horizon and heavens blended, where time and space became one shifting, hazy borderland where perspectives shrank and parallel lines met, a mass of vanishing points through which you could slip into realms of shadow and archetypal myth. I'd encountered some on land, within the shadows of great cities and ancient centers of worship, but never in the air. I'd heard they were fewer and less easy to penetrate and pass, and I often wondered how they must look. Now I guessed it might be something like this, this glittering dream landscape where snowcapped mountain-top and thrusting cloudcap merged and mounted in towering, infinite ranges. Maybe that was how Le Stryge had summoned me . . .

Even as the thought struck me, so did the surprise. I stiffened, sending the rotor fishtailing behind me. The still low sun mounted over one such row of cloud crests—and its warm light shot two shapes into dramatic silhouette against the blazing whiteness. Twin towers, tall and narrow, just as I'd seen them from the mountain path.

I didn't have a lot of fuel to spare; you never did in a little machine like this. But I didn't hesitate for a moment. I banked steeply and went whirling in toward them, sweeping between phalanxes of reaching cloudy cliffs, crags of mist and insubstantial steeps; and the towers grew, or so it seemed. Tall airy things, Gothic structures that made stone seem almost as light as the mists over which they rose. I stared, forgetting my course. A harsh gray cliff-face loomed, and instinctively I pulled away, forgetting it was no more solid than a dream—or was it? Jagged edges, stark crevice and weathered chimney; I was climber enough to register those things as they reeled across my windshield, as dangerously solid as any stone that ever scuffed my shins or drew blood beneath scrabbling fingernails. I hauled back on the stick, pitched the rotors and pulled hard around, banking across a vast expanse of sheer savage mountainside. The sweat trickled down inside my helmet. Ill-judged; too fast. Had I made that mistake? Or was this how the landward ways of the Spiral opened, where instead of islands in an azure ocean the pathless clouds would resolve into real mountains with fortress summits, castles of cloud into mighty crests of stone—was it like this? The mists swirled before me as the machine plunged away, and seemed to pull me down.

Lost in gray, without up or down, I struggled to control her, swinging this way and that for long moments, until finally I saw the indicator on the artificial horizon line creep level and the altimeter settle at a reasonable figure. I checked the radar, but there was nothing aloft except mountainsides and me. Then I tried to call Frankfurt control. Nothing. Nothing from Munich either; only noise. I thought for a moment, and then I relaxed the rotor pitch and sank; and we burst out into daylight over a wide valley.

It glowed green beneath me, lush and rich, the floodplain of a river that ran down it like a vein of silver, flanked by chessboard fields and rolling meadows. And as I swung the 'copter away from that all too solid mountainside, I saw where it flowed to, and the reason for those towers. Straddling the river via a tall island at its center, a town dominated the valley, and was dominated in its turn. A huge walled fortress town, like nowhere I'd seen except maybe Carcassonne; and this was larger, and even more beautiful, with winding rows of red-tiled roof-tops and golden stone walls that glowed in the mellow light. But above them, rising from the island, were darker, taller walls; and from their heart rose those cloud-piercing towers. They were the spires of a massive building like a cathedral, an escalating mountain of Gothic walls and arches and buttresses and scale-tiled roof-tops and towers that looked impossibly delicate until I realized just how enormous they must be. The whole thing was like a minor peak in its own right, glowing dark amber against the sunlight that streamed down through the broken cloud. I swung closer, looking for any clue to where this place might be. There were boats in the river, mostly sailing ships and barges; but though there were ribbons of dusty yellow road, I couldn't see a single car or truck on them. I thought of coming down, taking a closer look, but I didn't want to overfly the place, draw attention to myself and maybe start a panic. If I was right, they might not be too used to helicopters here.

Definitely it had a tinge of the Spiral about it, this place, a lingering, haunting timelessness of long shadows and late afternoons, Indian summers of the world. And yet if so, it had something else that was strange to the Spiral—a settled, stable look, a hint of order and purpose I'd rarely if ever encountered on those random shores of time, scattered with the flotsam of history and the jetsam of men's minds. I had to know more. I turned for the angle of the hillside, away from the fields. If I could only find somewhere unobtrusive to land . . .

It rose up to me behind a minor mountain spur, a level shelf of lush upland meadow that positively demanded cows with bells. But the green grass was uncropped, and rippled like water as the downblast of the rotors struck it. I landed with only the faintest bump, and let the motor growl down to nothing, till there was just the whistle of the slowing rotors. Then that too died away, and I was left listening to the rustle of the grass I'd flattened lifting in a more natural wind.

I undid belt and helmet, slid back the cockpit door and swung myself down into the grass. It was almost waist high, intensely green, slightly damp; the stalks I had crushed scented the light breeze. After the choking city the freshness of the air was unbelievable; you wanted to expand your lungs just to keep on taking it in. Across the meadow ran a mountain stream, leaping and splashing over boulders and stone outcrops. Suddenly I felt intolerably thirsty, and ran down to it. I was cynical enough to know that the freshest mountain stream may well have a dead sheep in it around the next bend; but not this one, somehow, not this one. I could almost see its source, up there among the faceted cliffs; now there would be some climbing! But not on my own. I ducked down, dipped a hand in the stream and yelped: it was icy, it must be meltwater from high above, kept cool beneath the rock. But when I sipped at it carefully, so as not to chill my stomach, it tasted amazing, with a faint mineral tang that made a fool of everything in a pressurized bottle. Refreshed, I stood up and looked about. About a hundred yards down the stream passed under an old stone bridge, and beyond that a faint track ran downhill, half obscured by the waving grasses. Making sure the 'copter keys were still clipped firmly to my belt, I strolled down that way, with I didn't know what on my mind. The bridge was old and crumbling, but still solid underfoot, and from its hunched back I had a clear view down the slope and into the heart of the valley.

The city shone there still, behind its massy walls,

through a slight haze, but the taste the wind brought me was of sweet woodsmoke, nothing more. I could see something of its buildings; the massed roof-tops looked like the old quarters of places like Nice or Nuremberg, or smaller towns in Austria and Czechoslovakia, winding rows of houses that tumbled and spilled down the slight slope to the river in cheerful disarray, red roofs and high gables sticking up at all sorts of angles. But here and there were walls wholly alien to that background, the black-veined whiteness of true half-timbering, the squat stucco of a Mediterranean tradition, the warm square-cut stone elegance of Scotland—incoherent, out of place, and yet somehow immensely right, adding up to a total effect that was indescribable but powerful. This was how a town ought to look. High above it, like a crowning achievement, rose the towers of the cathedral, almost level with me; and above them, higher yet, the spires, so high that a man in them could look down upon the hillside where I stood.

The more I saw, the more it intrigued me, one of the most beautiful places I'd ever encountered, on or off the Spiral, one of the most timeless. Yet there was bustle in the streets, clear even from here; and on the approach roads there were carts, farm carts by the look of them, plodding purposefully toward the walls. I crossed the stream, found the path and strode briskly downhill toward the nearest road. After a while, somehow, I was running.

It was all downhill, of course, and by the time I reached the first road I was barely out of breath; all the same, that surprised me. I felt on top form, and the brisk walk then only set me up further. The road was empty, but it came to a crossroads, and there, as I puzzled over a signpost with a weathered inscription in old-fashioned Gothic *fraktur*, I heard a genial hail of, *"Grüss Gott!"* The standard Bavarian greeting, so at least I knew where I was. It came from an approaching train of carts, from the old man driving the leader's sturdy black-and-tan oxen, and the men and women riding on the carts behind, or strolling alongside, echoed it.

I tossed the greeting back, adding that it was fine weather and were they going to town? They understood my German all right, and though they obviously knew I was a foreigner, by the care they took to speak clearly, they seemed to accept me quite naturally. I carefully didn't ask too many questions; they didn't ask me any at all. At other junctions we met other carts, some laden with crates and barrels as ours were, others full of what seemed to be grain sacks, and one with sides of beef. I was startled when one driver hailed us with a profuse babble of Italian, even more so when some young men driving sheep across another crossroads, away from the city, greeted us in broad yokel burrs—in English. The carters evidently understood, but they replied in what sounded like every language under the sun. I even thought I heard Romany.

I was still chewing *that* one over when the road led us around a small copse of trees. Suddenly the town wall lay across the slope in front of us, irregular bastions of honey-colored stone running at odd angles to accommodate the lie of the land, punctuated at intervals by all kinds of eccentric turrets, towers and pinnacles. The effect was pleasing, slightly comical, like one of those Victorian architectural follies; it took a second look to register just how formidable a proposition that wall would be, even for artillery. And the cathedral, or whatever it was in the center, wasn't funny at all; it was overwhelming. The road was leading us down to a tall gate, a high-crowned Gothic arch; it stood wide open, but on either side of the road there were men, armed men. Others looked down from the walls above.

It was a bit hard to take them seriously, too. Their uniforms were just too bright, dark blue or scarlet dolmen jackets festooned with piping, tight white breeches, light blue sashes and high boots; their shako caps crowned longish hair and drooping moustaches. Their only arms were long swords at their sides and tall halberds, spear-tipped poleaxes—altogether the sort of display you only see nowadays in cheesy ceremonials. And they could hardly look more relaxed, lounging against the gate pillars, smoking stubby cigars and joking with the passing carters; but as I drew nearer I could see their eyes, clear and bright, flickering across everyone who passed. And I remembered that uniforms like that lingered because they'd been worn in longer, fiercer wars than any we'd had today. Wars that raged the length and breadth of Europe for decades, centuries, even; wars that had shaped Europe and its culture, for worse and better, the brightness as well as the savagery, Goethe and Hitler, Shakespeare and Vlad the Impaler. These men were like the wall; they were serious, all right.

I wondered what they'd make of me, in my modern casuals and suede jacket. Without making it too obtrusive I hopped up between two carts, talking animatedly to their drivers as we trundled under the shadow of the arch. Wood drummed suddenly under our wheels, and high walls blotted out the light. There was an inner gate, with a drawbridge which could be slid back, leaving any intruder trapped beneath fire from above, and all of it in good repair. I bit my lip, wondering suddenly why I'd become so determined to get this close; there was nothing engaging about these businesslike defenses. And yet even the gates were covered in ornamental ironwork, the drawbridge in elegant carving; and there was a sense of lofty power about the whole fortification, a pride in what it represented. Then the note of our wheels changed again; we were coming through the inner gate, and into the cobbled streets of the city.

I looked around me, amazed and delighted. It was everything I'd seen from the meadow, and more. There were gardens and trees everywhere, broad airy streets and winding alleys that teased the eye, open squares that rested it. It was the kind of look town planners only manage in their drawings, but it didn't look planned at all. My curiosity grew even fiercer; I slipped down from the cart and let the procession flow past me. That wasn't the most sensible thing I could have done. We were through the gates, but still in eyeshot; and when I heard the curt challenge I knew exactly who it was meant for. I hadn't fooled the guards at all. Those lynx eyes had spotted me, wondered, decided to see how I behaved, and at the first suspicious move—

"*Halt! Wer da?*"

I stood, irresolute, looking this way and that, as a pair of guards came trotting toward me, halberds lowered. Behind them a burly man in black with gold epaulettes jumped up, stared, half choked on his cigar and shouted, "*Er! Aus dem Bergenpfad! Der Reiter, der Zauberer's Kerl! Ergreifen Sie mir Dieser!*"

That was enough for me. The rider, the sorcerer's man from the mountain path. An officer, he must have been aboard that airship and, of course, it must have come from here—and I was a lunatic to have ever blundered in. If I could only *explain*—but I didn't fancy doing it in the hands of armed soldiers. That way everything sounds thin; and up there on the path they'd have shot me on sight. Would they even stop to listen here? I skidded around on the cobbles and bolted, right through my new friends and their carts and beyond, down the wide street that must surely lead toward the river and the heart of the town. Where else could I go? The gate would be barred, the alleyways a nightmare they'd know much better than I did. There was no way out, no way but deeper in.

"*Du da! Halt, oder ich schiesse!*"

They were bluffing. They'd better be, or they didn't give a damn about hitting other people in this crowded street, children maybe. Somehow that didn't square with the look of this place, and when no shots followed I wasn't just glad for myself. One or two men moved out as if to stop me, but I was fast enough to dodge them; my trainers seemed to get a better grip on the cobbles than their boots. I ran and ran, but I thought as well; there was method in my madness now. That enormous building, that was where I was heading. If it was some kind of church or cathedral I might find sanctuary there, or at least get a chance to put my story to a priest first after I'd had a few minutes to collect my wits. Right now I couldn't spare any.

I was fit enough, but a fast mile or two weaving over cobbles is no joke, even when it's downhill. With my ears roaring and my temples bulging I risked a look back. There were those bloody sentries, still thumping after me, though we were all going so slowly we might just as well have been walking. If I'd only had a moment I could have tried summoning my sword, the one remotely magical trick I'd ever picked up on the Spiral, and that by accident. But I hadn't, and a sword would mean killing, almost inevitably; that would only get me into deeper trouble. I thought of ducking around a convenient corner and tripping or kicking my pursuers as they followed, only they might be wise to that one and then where would I be? Better if I could find a bench or some dustbins or something to tip in their path, but there were no benches in reach, nothing larger than a window-box, and for all its nineteenth-century look this was the tidiest city I'd ever seen. There was horse-dung on the main street, but not a lot, and the side-streets were immaculate. Maybe that was why all those gardens were so fertile. Nothing to do but keep going, anyway, and I was running out of slope. Where the hell was that cathedral? I forced myself to look up—and stopped dead in my tracks with utter astonishment.

It was there, all right. It was everywhere, or so it seemed; even the distant mountain wall was less overwhelming. If it had been solid it would have been brutal, its shadow a sunless burden on the houses it fell across; but the stonework was so airy that it cast strange dappled patterns across roof and wall, a shifting lattice of light. I was almost level with its base now; a little way below me the street opened out into a wide space above the river, and from there a bridge, broad and level as an *Autobahn*, thrust out to the island it stood on. The sight of it spurred me on, and only just in time. Gaping had lost me my lead, the clumping boots were almost at my back. But I'd had a second to draw breath, and that pulled me ahead again; I had the heels of them, if nobody else stopped me. There didn't seem to be any guards at this end of the bridge; the other—I'd just have to take my chances. Down into the square—a brief glimpse of other buildings, taller and nobler than the houses I'd passed through, buildings fit for palaces and parliaments and seats of learning—and then I was weaving among astonished-looking walkers to reach the bridge. Like the road it had no pavement, but its cobbles felt every bit as solid underfoot. It was only when I snatched another glance back, and saw the high bluff it came from and the cliffs falling away to the river, that I realized I was some two hundred feet in the air.

Ahead of me was the island, the same height, and the foot of the cathedral walls—or was it a cathedral? The closer I got, the odder it looked; yet it had towers, spires, yes, and stained glass. What else could it be? Even the island setting was a bit like a gigantic version of Notre Dame, only there was a touch of the fortress about it which made me uneasy. The riverside cliffs were raw rock; those of the island were sheathed in smooth stone, broken only by the occasional tree-lined shelf and the broad stairways that ran between them. People walked there, or sat, as if they were just parks or pleasure gardens; but they would be marvelous fortifications. I ducked and ran between the passers-by on the bridge, and they stared at me but, like almost everyone else, they made no move to stop me. Could that mean the guards weren't popular? It didn't feel like that, either. The looks I intercepted were surprised, but neither hostile nor sympathetic; I didn't see any judgment in them at all, only interest, even a rather distant kindness among older people.

I was coming to the bridgehead now, and there were no guards, none at all. Only a broad path covered with gray flagstones, rather than cobbles, and the steps to the cathedral. The doors were immense, as tall as the city gates and as ornate, covered with one single complex design, and they stood slightly ajar, so only half the design was visible—a stylized bird, a dove gripping something in its foot; the proverbial olive-branch, maybe. That suited me. I bounded up those high steps as if there was no tomorrow, and heard a very satisfying crash as the leading guard came a cropper behind me. The steps were longer than they looked, but I got to the door, stumbling dazed against the iron-bound wood, and more or less fell in. I ought to have been croaking *"Sanctuary!"* or *"Haro, à l'aide, mon prince!"* or something of the sort; in truth I hadn't the wind. I hobbled down a dressed-stone corridor which must have been the length of a normal cathedral in itself, toward the bluish light of an arch at its far end. I wasn't too clear about the routine in this sort of business, but there ought to be an altar or something here I could fall on. I needed to fall on something, and it had better not be the font.

There were openings, railed off, that might have been side-chapels. There were plaques and decorations on the wall; they looked old, and I wasn't stopping to decipher them. Unless . . . No other feet. No other sound, even. Where were my guards? I looked around again, expecting them to charge through the great dark doors. They didn't. That fall hadn't taken care of them both, had it? Suddenly one of them peered around the door. He jerked his head back instantly, guilty as a schoolboy. It looked very much as if they weren't allowed to come in here. So much the better, there might even be a convenient back door.

But when I came to that arch I halted, and for a moment I forgot all about my pursuers, my exhaustion, thirst, everything. That was the effect of the place beyond. It was like a church, but it wasn't. It was vast. I'd been inside Hagia Sophia, but this was larger, and emptier, a great dark oval of a hall encircled by a narrow colonnade, beneath whose roof I stood. Down below, at floor level, it lay mostly in a blue-tinged gloom relieved only by the faint gleam of glazed wall tiles; but immense windows were set high in the wall,

and through them the light came pouring, great slanting
beams that crowned the drifting dust motes with haloes,
some clear, some stained gorgeous hues. Imagine yourself
a church mouse, a real one, peering out of its hole. That's
about how big I felt.

It wasn't only the sheer size of the place. The Soviets
built big, the Kremlin Hall for example, but that just
showed up the little men in it. This place felt as if it was
built for something bigger than men; and as if that something was still here. It had the awesome, numinous quality
I'd felt in many places, in Core and Spiral both—an Anglo-
Saxon barrow, the palace at Mykonos, the Borobodur, the
Great Pyramid. This, though, this was stronger. A dusty veil
of quiet hung about it, yet it was only the stillness of rest,
not emptiness; and even the rest was watchful. My eyes
were constantly darting from shadow to shadow, drawn by
the illusion of swift movement; but there was never anything.

I couldn't figure out what this place could be for. There
certainly wasn't any altar. There was no sign of seating, no
trappings of any kind, not even the inscriptions you find in
the barest mosques, hardly a sign of human use at all. Yet
as my eyes adjusted to the gloom I did make out other
doors beneath the colonnades in the far walls; that was
promising. And there were patterns of some sort, higher
up the walls; frescoes probably, dim patches of somber colors steeped in shadow. The floor wasn't so barren, either;
it was a mosaic. I thought uneasily of Lutz's room, but this
looked purely decorative, a stylized sunburst or a compass
rose that drew the eye in toward the heart of the hall.
There, just out of one great shaft of light, there was something, after all—low and shapeless, but the only thing out-
standing in the whole vast emptiness. I took a tentative step
forward, and my footfall boomed away into the heights of
the dome, echo, echo, echo . . .

I choked my heart back down my throat, and trod more
softly. There should have been clouds of dust; there weren't.

My office didn't get this clean. The dust was in the atmosphere, tiny particles of time swirling, never allowed to rest. I ought to be heading for one of those far doors; I wasn't. I was curious, and maybe the key to the mystery of this place lay there at its heart.

A grave, I guessed; somebody buried, somebody powerful enough to have this whole vast pile for his mausoleum. Somebody a whole nation had believed in, believed in still, maybe, and were waiting for him to wake. Arthur; Frederick Barbarossa; even Attila, as much a hero in the lands east of the Rhine as he was a villain in the west. The dust was in my throat as I approached that hunched shape; and I thought I was right when I saw it closer. It was a low dais, of black marble or some other polished stone, smooth and featureless. Across it, almost carelessly, a great swathe of material lay draped, something like heavy silk with encrusted embroideries. As far as I could make out in that gloom it was a long cloak or robe or mantle, of some dark color; the embroideries looked like Byzantine figures in dull gold, saints or something of the kind, but it was hard to be sure in the dimness. Beneath the robe there seemed to be something long, and beneath that a stone, maybe some sort of marker. But as I very gingerly lifted the edge of the material I saw it was no conventional gravemarker, whatever it was; it looked very roughly dressed, far cruder and more ancient. It was about the size of a small flagstone, and a foot to eighteen inches thick, and it had no inscription, none at all; just rough irregular markings. The only significant one was a deep bowl or cup shape set some way off from the center, and surrounded by a curious pattern of scratched-in rings, some deep-worn, others mere scrapemarks, but all concentric, all very deliberate. And stranger still, lying across the top of this stone, held there by the long cloak, was a short strong-looking shaft of wood, bound with bands of brighter metal and tipped with a very businesslike head of—what on earth was it? Black glass, I guessed, but volcanic glass, obsidian; not chipped but smoothed and honed to a perfect surface.

Mystery piled on mystery, and I was wasting my time in here. They could have surrounded the whole place by now. I lowered the mantle very gently and padded as quietly as I dared toward the colonnade opposite. But just as I reached it, I heard the boom of that outer door thrown back, and the crash of running feet. There was a harsh shout, wordless but threatening, and two men came charging up to the archway; men dressed in hussar fashion, not unlike the guards, but all in gray, with froggings and pipings and epaulettes of chain mail that sparkled silvery even in that submarine gloom. Their drawn swords gleamed a grimmer hue, huge straight sabres with basket hilts, broadswords almost. I expected them to charge across the floor, but instead they dashed into the colonnade, and began circling the hall toward me. I let them come—far enough and I could bolt across the floor and out—but then the door boomed again, and others came racing in. Even from here I could see the swords, and the uniforms: more gray hussars. I thought of my own sword, suspended above the mantel in my flat, as out of place as ever; in my mind I reached up for it, I worked my fingers as if to close about its grip. For an instant I seemed actually to touch the wirebound sharkskin, cool and comforting in my hand, and weigh the solid steel. Then the darkness of the place pressed in on me, and I felt it slither, slip, fall away with a faint fading clatter.

I swore horribly, tensing my fists. What was it now, five, six against one? One weaponless. I could give myself up, take a chance on their mercy; somehow I didn't fancy that. They'd shot at me on sight, perhaps because they'd linked me up with Stryge. The swords were leveled, steady, unyielding; any one could kill. The unfairness of it rose in my throat like bile. I had to defend myself somehow, if only to make them listen; and damn the cost, I'd do it any way I could. I poised, waited till they were all in the colonnade,

circling me like jackals around a fire; and then I dashed
where they wouldn't go, right across that mosaic mandala.
Sliding the mantle down I snatched the spear from across
the stone and swung it, taut and heavy, in my hand.

The result was unexpected, to put it mildly—and electrifying. It sounded like one great gasp, echoing around the
shadowy vaultings above, but it came from all of them, in
horrified unison. And as one those somber swordsmen sank
back and down, tall shapes of menace shrinking to crouching defensives, backed up against the walls like baited beasts
before a trainer's whip. Heartened, I jabbed the spear at
them. Their swords swung wildly in their hands; one
dropped his, another gave a shout of alarm. They were between me and those other doors now; too bad. I strode
boldly toward the archway, wondering if they'd scream and
run; they didn't. They just watched me, six pairs of eyes
glittering in shadow. I glanced at the nearest one as I
passed, and he returned the glare like a parry. He was
blond, with bushy sidewhiskers and upturned moustache
that barely concealed two long scars seaming his red
cheeks.

Despite those, it wasn't a harsh face; there might have
been laughter lines around those eyes normally. But now
they were stretched tight with helpless, contorted hatred,
and his sword twitched in his hand. For half a cent that
man would have jumped at me and cut me to pieces, whatever the cost to himself. So whatever was holding him back
had to be something a lot greater. Fear? I didn't buy it,
somehow. The man on the other side was dark-skinned,
with plump features that couldn't blunt a hawk nose, a
North Indian type with three white bars painted on his forehead. From somewhere I remembered these were the marks
of a warrior and teacher of warriors. He was purple-cheeked
with outrage; but he was just crouching back, sucking in
his breath, watching.

I passed under the arch and into that long corridor, wondering what was going on outside. Maybe things had died

down now, the good citizenry gone about their daily business; maybe not. I looked back; there were the gray swordsmen piling in through the arch. They stopped as soon as I looked at them, but like hounds held back by a leash; and one had poised his sword to throw. Another stopped him with a gesture. I didn't fancy going back, and I couldn't see any more side-doors, so there was only one way to find out. I leaned on the huge door and opened it a fraction; sunlight streamed in, and I wasn't shot at. So I pushed a little further, and stepped out—only to freeze like the swordsmen when the crowd clustering around the steps growled and surged forward. Just ordinary citizens, not guards. Quickly I raised the spear two-handed, swinging this way and that— and again the effect was electrifying. I could have been casting thunderbolts, in fact, because in instant accord they yelled, turned and ran, tripping, falling, being dragged along, spilling over the sides of the steps into the shrubbery. All the scene needed was a bullet-riddled pram bouncing down those stairs—with me cast as the entire Imperial Guard. I swallowed, took a few steps down and saw the panic go rippling out from the heart of the crowd to the mere gawkers and distant onlookers. In minutes the way was clear. But so much for appealing to the people in the street.

I staggered back across a bridge now completely empty except for the odd deserted hat or fur muff; and evidently the word was going ahead. As I reached the street opposite and began to climb, doors slammed, children wailed, figures vanished hastily up side-streets. I looked back, once, and saw the gray hussar types, close together, pacing swiftly across the bridge, swords leveled again; but when I looked they stopped. I started running.

It was uphill now, and a terrible slog over those lumpy cobbles; but I kept going, driven by my own astonishment and confusion as much as anything else. By the time I reached the top of the main street any child could have stopped me with the average feather duster; but nobody even tried. The most I heard was cries of distress, and shutters slamming. Within sight of the gate the burly officer of the watch shouted again, snatching for his sword, and the guards sprang into my path; then I raised the spear. They wilted, gaping in horror; the officer, cursing violently, backpedaled till he was almost flat against the archway, panting and sweating. If I'd been carrying a live atom bomb they could hardly have responded better. I gestured, and the officer groaned despairingly and threw aside his sword with considerable force. I plunged past him and into the narrow inner gateway; carters and farmworkers took one look, screamed and tried to plaster themselves flat against the walls, hiding their eyes. Women burst into tears. Nobody tried to stop me. Nobody so much as threw anything. So I stumbled out onto the open road outside the wall, free of the city, but feeling dazed—and oddly disgraced.

I stood there a moment, gulping. I could have thrown the bloody spear aside there and then, left it hanging in the hedgerow like some king or other's crown. Or rather, put it down carefully, for it was evidently something incredibly precious or sacred. But then horsemen could come after me, ride me down; and somehow I suspected they would. That guy in the church would have hunted me with hounds. I'd leave it by the helicopter, that would do. Leave it clearly visible somehow—trample the grass, maybe.

By the time I'd made it back to the meadow I hardly had the energy. Fall flat on my face in it, maybe. Stashed behind my seat there was a pack of isotonic fruit drinks, and I longed for those as if they were the fountain of youth; my tongue was sticking to my mouth. It almost froze there, though, when the short figure rose from the 'copter skid he'd been sitting on, and nodded with mild contempt.

"Well! A fool has duly rushed in where angels fear to tread. My good sir, you have most admirably completed the task I set you. You have but to hand over that barbaric instrument, and you may go on your way free of all obligation."

"You son of a bitch, Stryge!" I croaked, my voice nearly as harsh as his. "You're telling me *you* made me do all that?"

Why, of course. It was laid upon you from the moment you exchanged words with me up above there. It did not occur to you, did it, that you were not acting entirely in accordance with reason in never exchanging a word with those of the city? In never explaining yourself, or seeking explanation? Of course, it helped that I provoked them into firing on you in the first place. But did you never once wonder what was the root of the curiosity which led you so directly to the Hall? No doubt you rationalized it to yourself, for that is the nature of such . . . obligations. But nevertheless you discharged my instructions with commendable dispatch. You are a tool that comes apt to the hand, young sir."

I unglued my tongue with difficulty. "Do you want to know what *you* are?" I raised the spear. "I've half a mind to—"

Stryge snapped his bony fingers, a sound like dry tinder catching. "Half? You can scarcely claim even that much."

From around the helicopter two huge figures stepped, one holding a long narrow metal case. They bore down on me with a lumbering, menacing swagger to their stride. For a moment I thought they were Wolves, those appalling demi-humans, till I saw that their skins weren't that dead elephantine gray. They were just plain Caucasian pink, but it didn't stop them looking weird. Over the double meter in height, built like the original brick outhouses, with fat heavy limbs, almost hairless heads and nightmare faces, square and crumpled—and yet somehow horribly familiar. They wore heavy coveralls and boots, like caricatures of laborers; and they stank like animals. The old man sniffed, and rasped a thumb over his bristly chin. "I repeat, young fool, hand that over and you may go about your petty business. Or—No. There is no *or*."

I was stunned, exhausted, doubly humiliated; and I was

impelled by an inner drive that I was only just realizing
wasn't my own. It still felt as if it was as much a part of
me as my thirst or my anger and as hard to shake free of.
I really wanted to hand the damn thing over and be done
with it, however much my rational mind objected. It felt
like the only natural thing to do. The two ogreish characters squinted down at me from piggy eyes deep sunk in
creases of pale flesh; one of them broke wind with deliberately noisy contempt. The other rumbled something, saliva trickling down his jowls, and flipped open the case. The
velvet lining had been clearly shaped to an exact fit; and
somehow that evidence of planning and forethought un-
manned me completely. It was exhaustion that saved me,
and shock. I trembled with indecision, Le Stryge hissed his
impatience—and unthinkingly, almost automatically, I
held out the spear to him. He positively hopped back, spry
as a cricket, and snapped at the ogre who held the case.
The brute stamped forward and pointed with a great horn-
tipped finger. I was to put the spear in the case myself.

Something clicked. Disingenuously I offered it to him.
He growled something incoherent and swung back a huge
paw as if to cuff me. The flatulent one gave a gross, belch-
ing laugh. But he didn't make any move, either. They
wanted it so much, but somehow none of them would
touch it.

I made as if to lay the spear in the case—and then I
swung it up in their faces. The one behind blundered back,
knocking Le Stryge flying, but the ogre with the case, less
agile, instinctively cuffed at it. His hand touched it—

There was no transition. One minute he was there, the
next a mere shadow in a roaring spout of fire that almost
took off my eyebrows, capering in a great gargling bellow
of agony suddenly cut off. I staggered back, clutching the
spear. The fire didn't come from it; it rose like a waterspout
around the ogre. The blackened figure was swaying, folding,
sinking down into itself, a dwindling outline. The fire
popped out in a column of greasy smoke, and a charred

lump fell sizzling into the steaming grass, a little stubby parody of the hulking outline of before. No human body would burn so; this was more like a burned vegetable. The other creature let out a high whining squeal and blundered away across the meadow like a stampeding elephant, shrieking. That left me with Stryge, half sprawling in the grass; and of all the things I hated and feared, the invasion of my mind was the worst. He raised himself on one elbow, long dark sleeve swinging, and I lunged at him. I caught one glimpse of his malevolent face; then the sleeve flapped across it, and the spear struck harmlessly down into the grass. The sleeve went fluttering away of its own accord across the field, an early bat swooping after insects, leaving me staring.

I hefted the spear in my hand, wondering what would happen if I touched the head—but I already had, hadn't I, back in the hall? I gave up. Exhausted as I was, I knew I would be best advised to head straight back to the town with it, start talking as I should have done in the first place. It'd be a lot riskier now; but trying to hold on to something like this would be even worse. I was looking back, wondering whether to go on foot or risk the 'copter, when I saw, rising behind the bulk of that mysterious hall, a glimmer of glistening white against the graying sky. A drone of engines came to me over the fields, and up from beyond the towers of that strange hall rose the pale outline of an airship, like the one that had chased me. Behind it, nosing upward like a breaching whale, came the rounded prow of another.

Thanks to Le Stryge's influence I'd evidently left it a little late to talk. Wearily I fumbled for the keys; luckily they were still on my belt. I stared dully at the spear. I was tempted just to chuck it down into the grass for them to find; but Le Stryge and the other brute were still around somewhere, and the airships would be more concerned with catching me. It might easily fall into the wrong hands before anyone got to it. Impatiently I snatched up the old necromancer's case from where it had fallen, and slapped the spear into the velvet. It fitted perfectly, and the case snapped easily shut. The airships were approaching arrows now; and they were fast, far faster than I'd expected. I tore open the cockpit door, thrust the case back behind my seat and leaped in. I twisted the key in the starter and jammed on my helmet just in time to save my ears. No preliminaries; the moment she reached full revs I shoved the collective forward and twisted the throttle, and she fairly leaped off the hillside. I tipped the cyclic, tapped the rudder pedal and sent her sweeping away up and out across the valley. The airships saw me and climbed after me; I banked across the top of them to turn in a tight arc around the tall towers in my path. They tried to follow, almost collided, and fell away to my rear as I soared up and away toward the clouds. A gray shroud closed around me, the note of the rotors changed slightly, and once again I was flying blind.

Radar showed me the mountainside, and I climbed higher yet. Then, quite abruptly, the world was full of light and noise again, the long rays of a sinking sun and the voice of the Frankfurt flight controllers squawking in my ears, demanding my position and flightpath, and how did I manage to vanish from their screens like that?

Unthinkingly I tabbed on my little navigational computer. Its entry rang up on the control screen.

Landed: Ref unrecord: Heilenthal. Stay: hrs 4.
Port reference: 0001-fac. airship Fuel: none.
only.
Frequency: unlisted. Other Service: none.
Portmaster: Adalbert v. Refuel: within hrs
Waldestein, Ritter. 4.5.
Deputy: Arcite v. Lemnos, Ritter.
Authority: nil.
Clearance: nil.

There was a moment of what I could only call strangled silence from the controllers, and then a great shout of laughter.

Chapter 4

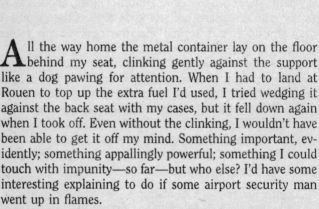

All the way home the metal container lay on the floor
behind my seat, clinking gently against the support
like a dog pawing for attention. When I had to land at
Rouen to top up the extra fuel I'd used, I tried wedging it
against the back seat with my cases, but it fell down again
when I took off. Even without the clinking, I wouldn't have
been able to get it off my mind. Something important, evidently; something appallingly powerful; something I could
touch with impunity—so far—but who else? I'd have some
interesting explaining to do if some airport security man
went up in flames.

As it turned out, there wasn't a problem. This was my
home heliport, the men on duty knew me, and waved me
and my trolley full of climbing gear right on through without checking anything. All the same, I heaved a sigh of
relief as I jammed it into the back of my car; it wouldn't
fit in the boot of this vintage design. I'd been afraid that
black glassy head would get damaged despite all the velvet,
but there wasn't a mark on it. So far, so good—but what
was I supposed to do with it now?

I knew what I ought to do, of course—return it to the city, somehow. But they'd been a touch too trigger-happy for my taste; and besides, that might easily draw Le Stryge down on me. As it was, even on the drive back from the heliport I began to get the feeling I was being marked or followed in some way, though my mirror didn't show any cars tailing me. I wanted to know what it was all about, this sinister object, before I made up my mind. I knew people who might well have more of an idea than I did—not too difficult; I'd find them, and ask. But till then I'd better hide it. It wasn't exactly the sort of thing you hang on your wall, and it wouldn't fit in any of the office safes—besides, I didn't want those kinds of forces attracted to either my home or my business. I'd had enough trouble with that before. Unless . . .

I almost burst out laughing, the idea was so simple; and yet it ought to tie anyone coming after that thing in knots. I'd planned to stop off at my new offices in the C-Tran regional headquarters, anyway. When I got there it was late afternoon, almost everyone had gone home, and when I wandered into the service department, as I often did, it was almost empty. Then, with the spear neatly stowed, all I needed was a few minutes with my desk terminal to set it all up via the central computer. As simply as that, the spear was off my hands. I spent a few minutes more carefully doctoring the records to remove any traces of what I'd done, and touched the on-screen button to log off. But instead of the usual prompt panel an error message flashed up, and I swore. Then I saw what it was.

URGENTIN IMMINENT EVENT SYSTEM WIPEOUT*INTERFACE PORT S WITH PORT G**URGENT**

"Oh, my *God*!" I groaned, with the awful feeling that I, Chairman of the Board, Herr Ratspräsident himself, was about to crash the entire network and throw the business into total chaos. Then I remembered a couple of things, and swore again, violently. Firstly, this software had failsafes on its failsafes, for obvious reasons; I ought to know, I'd insisted on them. Secondly, I was using a smart terminal that didn't *have* anything as plebeian as i/o ports, S, G or Z for that matter; and thirdly, this was totally different software from the stuff in my little portable, a different operating system, even, and yet here was the message in the same format. So it must be a virus, probably originating within the company; somebody playing sillybuggers, right enough. They might have made it funnier; then they'd have something to laugh about in the dole queue, when I caught up with them. But that could wait.

I logged off again without a trace of trouble, and sat back with a sigh, staring at the great skyscape on the wall opposite, copied from the one I'd commissioned with microscopic care for my original office. A vast blue skyscape, an archipelago of moonlit cloud and rising above it a great cloud-arch like a frozen wave, and sailing through it, to the stars beyond, a tall square-rigged merchantman with moonlight silvering its sails. It always used to puzzle my visitors; I told them it was an allegory of the romance of commerce. But for me it could have been painted from the life. I got up wearily; it set all kinds of longings stirring, that painting, but right now I just wanted to go home.

I heard the sirens as I was shutting things down. When I turned off the lights I saw the distant glow through the slats of the blinds. I went over to the window and peered out; it looked bad, a fire slap in the middle of the business district, office country. One more reason to be glad I'd resisted locating us there. I locked up and made my way down along the corridors, deserted now except for a few cleaners and the odd nighthawk still plowing through the day's workload. I waved as I went past, and they waved back, but there was always a touch of hesitancy, of awe maybe; I didn't like that, though I knew it was inevitable. I did want to be open, accessible, able to communicate directly with staff at all levels . . .

I snorted. I was thinking in management jargon. I just wanted to be able to talk to people, that was all, and have them talk to me. It had been that way at the old firm, a friendly place even when it got somewhat tough; I'd always been able to tell Barry to get out of my office when I had work to do, and when I took over I tried to foster the same spirit. Almost everybody had known me on the way up, after all, but here that just wasn't possible. Right from day one I was the Old Man, I had too much power over pay and promotion and prospects. It isolated me at every level. That research chief in the marketing department, Angela something, she wasn't at all bad-looking, she was bright, reasonably unattached or so it seemed; I liked what I'd seen of her, I had a fair idea she liked me. Suppose I dated her, though? Just asking her out was a hundred times more difficult when I was the captain of her ship, the master of her fate, and not just one of the guys from the office. Would she feel she couldn't say no? Would she feel she could take advantage? Suppose we ended up in bed? That took on all kinds of dodgy connotations, and the same questions applied. Okay, they'd never worry a lot of bosses I knew, but I was learning. It was another reason I didn't go for Lutz's kind of temptations, or any of the others you run into on the international circuit. The trouble was that the glow of virtue didn't warm the bed any, and I hate electric blankets.

I stepped out of the lift to the night porter's desk and logged off my security tag, just like the lowliest typist. With the porters, at least, I could exchange the odd casual word.

"Evening, Macallister! Any idea what's going on in town?"

The head porter rubbed his short-cut Navy beard. "Aye, Mr. Fisher—o' course you'd not've heard, you bein' away at the fair and that. It'd be some sort of protest march, from all they say. God knows what kind o' crap they're on aboot, but it wis peaceful enough at first. Seems some rough lots tagged along, hard-line anarchists or whatever they call themselves this year. It's they startit some fights. That's all I hear so far, but it must be gettin' worse, by they sirens—eh?" As if to underline it, another one went by, an ambulance this time.

"Sounds like it. Right. I'll be watching my way home, then. Put a board up, will you? Warn people—and if they need taxis to get them home, get them on the firm's account, all right? Cleaners and everyone. No, don't bring the car around, I'll manage myself. Night!"

I could see the glow in the sky quite clearly as I turned out of the car park. My usual route home led right past there, but it would probably be blocked with emergency vehicles and TV crew and general rubberneckers; I'd better try going around the side, though that meant a much longer and fiddlier drive. So I went zigzagging around the back-streets, and sat drumming my fingers at innumerable traffic lights; and all the time the noise grew louder. At last I was past the center, and turned back toward the old dockland area, now heavily residential, where I lived. But as I turned out onto the broad downhill road that was the main route there, I jammed my foot hard on the brake. The wide street was a rolling mass of smoke, shining a hellish red, and through the air something came flying like a minor meteor to burst on the roadway in front of me. There was a sudden ball of flame, and I locked the brakes, skidded across the junction and fetched up smack against the roundabout in the center. Normally a concrete tub of rather grubby flowering shrubs, now it was a mass of little fires, smoking and spitting.

Another petrol bomb came whizzing out of the redlit mirk and burst nearby; it didn't go off, but the petrol ran down the gutter and touched the rest, and suddenly the street opening I'd come out of was a sheet of fire. There was a roar, a siren wail, and I barely managed to get the car in gear and pull away before a huge fire engine came racing past, right across where I'd been. I saw with a sense of dizzying unbelief that it was on fire itself, trailing flames from one flank. A trail of yelling, jeering forms ran and capered after it, grotesque against the leaping firewall. But it outdistanced them; and then they saw me.

I threw the car about; it was fast, but its turning circle was on the wide side, and I had to swing it around more or less under their noses. Stones bounced off the long bonnet, smashed one headlight—and suddenly there were more of them, running out in my path, cutting me off from escape downhill. I couldn't drive through them, not without building up speed. I kept on turning till I was facing uphill, and accelerated suddenly away as another petrol bomb exploded just behind. I was heading closer to that louring glare, and as I drew closer I saw the fire that shed it: it figured, the Sixties hotel and shopping complex, thoroughly in flames—and, beside it, no fire engines, but the burnt-out skeleton of an ambulance. Debris was falling into the empty road, and the smoke was becoming choking; going back downhill didn't look like a good idea anymore. There was a handy side-road just a little way up, if I could reach it—but as I slowed down, a figure dashed across and sprang up on the running board.

"Get me up top!" he shouted. "To the main street!"

I was about to throw him off when I recognized his dark coveralls as police riot gear, with shoulder stripes. "You'll be lucky!" I yelled back. "How about Ramsay Lane?"

"Don't be daft, man, there's a nest of them down there broken into the pub! We're regrouping up there, we'll get you behind our lines!"

"Regrouping?" I steered us through a chicane of smoldering cars. "You mean they broke you?"

"What's it bloody look like?" he snarled.

"But protesters—"

"These aren't ordinary protesters! They half killed a couple of marchers who tried to reason with 'em! We were in the shopping center, supposed to cut off anyone escaping through there. Escape! They bloody attacked in force. There were thirty of us in there. I don't know if anyone else got out—"

I braked again, so hard he almost fell off. A ragged line of dark shapes was drawn up across the road, facing away from us; plastic riot shields glinted red. Some of them swung around sharply as they heard the car, but the policeman jumped down and hailed them. There was a swift muttered to-and-fro under raised visors, a crackling radio conversation, then he turned back to me. "You'd best head back down the hill. There's trouble up here."

"That's where I came from. Petrol bombs."

He swore again. "Better leave the car, then. Go down by the theater there, cut through the buildings, down the steps—*shit!*" A pop, a flash and the line broke, with men slapping at themselves as patches of flame blossomed on their coveralls, and one man, unforgettably, scrabbling under his visor and screaming. Somebody shouted through a loudhailer, and the whole line seemed to take one deep breath and surge forward, shouting, into the main street. Petrol bombs whizzed through the air; shouts and shrieks carried. My policeman scooped up a fallen shield and a metal bar from a shattered bus shelter, and loped after them. Sweating, I began to turn the car; but the road was narrower here, and I was reversing for the last time when I was suddenly surrounded by yelling, capering figures. As quickly as that I felt the car lift under me, tip sideways; sticks and stones and bare hands battered at my head as I fell sideways.

It was my suitcases that saved me, toppling out with a thump; the crowd on that side jumped back and I was able to roll out before the car crashed onto its side. Somebody aimed a boot at me, I grabbed it and twisted and he fell over, and in the smoky confusion the others started kicking him; I scrambled back in time to see somebody strike a match and flick it away. They must have poured petrol first; the car caught with a roar, and its sudden flare exposed their faces as they jumped back, gloating, manic masks of men and women, square, ugly, heavy. Momentarily forgotten, I grabbed the nearest by the shoulder and punched him right on his flattened nose. He reeled back against the burning car, shrieked horribly and ran off with his clothes alight, trailing sparks; the others ran after him, shouting, leaving me alone with the car. There was nothing I could do to put it out; large parts of a Morgan's frame are ash wood, and the tank was almost full. I'd barely made the nearest side turning when it went off with a tremendous roar, sending me staggering into the dark.

This wasn't an area I knew very well, and to my shocked mind, in the smoke and stark furnace light, with all the streetlamps and window lights out, it could have been the circles of Hell. Demons roamed it, little knots of them all over the place, doing what they liked with nobody to stop them. The power was off, telephones dead; the few times any kind of emergency vehicle appeared they came flocking up out of nowhere and barraged it with stones and petrol bombs. Slinking from doorway to doorway, staying in the shadows cast by the flickering fires, I began to realize what had happened. This part of town was cut off; the rioters controlled it now. That wouldn't last, of course, but while it did they could do an incredible amount of harm. And they seemed determined to, singing, shouting, smashing windows and looting—or so it looked.

But when one lot broke the window of a furniture store, I saw them tear out the tables and chairs and cabinets on display and smash them all over the pavement; they didn't take anything. Nor, more surprisingly, did another lot from the electronics store down the road: TVs, games computers, expensive hi-fi all went spilling across to the gutter. Not one of them so much as put a games cartridge or a Walkman in their pocket, let alone slipped off home with a TV or other expensive prize. They acted drunk, but they weren't; they had crowbars, bolt cutters, garden machetes and heavy knives, and they went through that window, security grille and all, with methodical speed. Suddenly, in the midst of it all, they dropped everything, and went racing off down the street as if they'd been summoned. I moved after them, but more slowly, careful to stay out of sight. I jumped like a startled rabbit when I darted into one doorway, and something squirmed at my feet. I grabbed, hard, and somebody hit me, not too efficiently. We stumbled into the light, and I found myself looking at a young type in crumpled denims, covered with political buttons and the remains of a painted slogan. He was shaking violently, but still trying to punch me; somebody was hitting my legs, feebly. I held him off and looked down. Another figure, sprawled in the doorway—a mess. The young man had the remains of a rich nosebleed and a scraped forehead.

"I won't do anything if you don't!" I said quickly, and he sagged. "Who's this?"

It was a young woman, though I only saw that because her clothes were in rags; her scalp was split, her face a mask of matted hair and blood. I didn't like the sound of her breathing.

"You were on this demonstration?"

"It was nothing to do with us!" he wailed, and then caught a grip on himself. "Okay, one or two wild men joined in the stramash at first, but it was the others, they had knives—and then the cops, and we ran—then we met up with this lot who were breaking up a café and we tried to tell them—and that's what they did to her and they kept on doing it and I couldn't *stop* them . . . "

"Nobody could," I said, knowing it wasn't guilt getting to him, just a helplessness he'd never experienced before. "That's the way the world is, sometimes. At least she's still alive. Maybe we can keep her that way." Her skull felt intact, and her spine, but her leg was oddly crooked—dislocated hip, I guessed. I was about to try reseating it when I felt the grate of bone; her pelvis was probably fractured. I looked around. Rape, robbery, arson—there might be people behind these windows, many of them, but they sure as hell weren't going to be answering their doors.

"I had to run away," he trailed on, "they held me and they were going to—and then when they were gone I came back and . . . and . . . "

I picked up the girl—a hell of a dangerous thing to do, but he'd moved her already and neither of us had any choice. She stirred feebly, moaning. "You did the right thing. The only thing. You couldn't fight this lot on your own. I've run too, at times, with less excuse. Come on."

Across the street and down, scanning the doors till I found one with multiple bellpushes—more likely there'd be someone there. The boy jabbed them at random, but of course there was no answer. I kicked the lock, hard; so did he, and at the third kick something cracked and the door flew in. We piled into the stoneflagged hall, only to stop short. There were people on the stairs, a knot of them, and in the beam of a flashlight a double gun barrel gleamed.

"You stop right there, mister! Or I'll blow your fuckin' head off—"

"Oh, shut up!" I barked. "We've got a girl here, hurt bad. She needs somewhere safe—"

That broke the ice a bit. People grumbled, argued, kvetched as they always do; but soon enough she was stowed away upstairs, with one woman who was a nurse looking after her as best she could. The shotgun wielder and I set about fixing the door.

"There must be people like you all over the neighborhood," I told him. "Just lurking behind their doors while there's robbery, rape and murder all around them."

"Well, what else'd we do?" he demanded, a burly truck-driver type of about my age. "Just wait till the cops get in, eh?"

"That could take hours. They probably don't even know all this is going on yet—they're not psychic, are they? And there's no way to tell them, with no phones, no power."

He considered. "There's Sean down the street. His van's got a CB radio. Don't think he'll be answering his door either."

"How's your kicking foot, then?" demanded the young protester type, clattering down the stairs behind us with a couple of others in his wake. They were carrying sticks, and one had a fearsome-looking fire axe.

"How is she?"

"Okay, I think. For now. But if you hadn't got us in—"

"Aye, well, I get the point," grunted the trucker type. "We'll fix this door solid again, then head down there. Let's hope Sean's not too quick on the trigger, either."

But shouting through the letterbox got us in this time. Sean turned out to be a fearsome creature, a bearded builder shaped like the original brick outhouse; his CB was a horrible thing, full of dangling wires and covered in cement dust and paint, but it worked. He nudged me, when we got a response. "You tell 'em, you've got the posh accent."

We'd reached a cab company on the other side of town, but they had a direct hook-up to the police. The cops had already got the general idea, and thanked us for the more detailed report; they were bussing in reinforcements, and hoped to have the streets under control in another hour or two. That was all they could tell us.

"An hour or two!" echoed the shotgun artist.

"Lot can happen in that time," said Sean grimly.

"Too much already, by the look of it," I said. "If we could only—you don't have any more friends around here we can call up?"

"Or kick down their doors?" Teeth flashed in his beard. "Aye, we might, we might. You're thinking—"

"I'm thinking nothing. We might slow the bastards down a bit, though."

"Permanently!" spat one of the young men, swinging his stick, as we made our way quietly out of the garage.

"Not so fast," I told him, looking warily around the street. "Just chasing them off will be better, breaking up their little gangs. Doesn't get us into trouble same as them. No pitched battles, if we can avoid it, either. That's how they've been tying up the police and they might make hay with us. There's something about this pack—I don't know what it is, but they seem organized, almost. As if they'd been trained . . . "

"That's right!" hissed the protester type. "Infiltrators planted on us, weren't they? To discredit us—"

"Ach, come on!" grunted Billy the shotgun artist. "I suppose they're all from the CIA with wee headset radios? They're just a bunch of squarehead yobbos! You get the same thing down the Costa del Sol onna bad night! Just want their heads bashed in!"

"And yet they do seem to have some sort of control or organization." I told them what I'd seen. "And they are acting more like provocateurs than rioters. But I don't think it's the CIA—or the KGB, for that matter, or the Inner Tranquility Bureau—"

"What the hell?"

"The Chinese secret service, to you. Something a lot more evil than any of them, maybe. I agree about the heads, though. They've got to be stopped."

"All right by me," rumbled Sean. "We'll pick up some more lads, and then you just tip us the word. You're the boss, jimmy."

And so, to my surprise, I was. We picked up people as we went along, not snarling vigilantes but ordinary people, surprised and helpless in a situation most of them had never dreamed of, but ready to act when someone took the initiative. That seemed to be me. I hadn't pushed for it, it just came out that way. Maybe it helped that I was the only one with combat experience, even of a pretty weird kind, and had picked up the knack of command. At any rate, they did what I said without overmuch questioning; and when we came upon the first riot gang, about ten minutes in, we were just about ready. By then there were twenty-four of us, armed with a motley collection of weapons from brickbats to garden forks, plus two shotguns I insisted were kept for real emergency. And one leathery middle-aged woman came out struggling with what could be our most formidable asset, a pair of hysterical Rottweilers on what looked like a very weak chain. The rioters, tearing apart a local clinic with the usual instruments, were about the same number, and I noticed something I hadn't before; they had a leader, too, a square-built thug who rallied them around him with quick gestures of his machete as they came pouring out through gaping windows and canted doors. I knew that was the thing to prevent—a coordinated fight. We had to break them up, scatter them without getting scattered ourselves. I could only hope our lot remembered everything I'd been throwing at them. I swung up a hand, shouted, *"Charge!"*—well, what else was there?—and led the way with a wild rebel yell.

It was only half-way there that I remembered one cardinal precept of command, namely don't forget to look after your own arse. I'd been so busy organizing everyone else that I'd clean forgotten to arm myself, and here I was running barehanded at that machete-wielding thug. Too late to stop now; I could see him grin nastily through his curly beard. There was something familiar about him, but I hadn't time to think what. I clenched my fist because it was the best I could do, sweating like hell, wishing this was the Spiral. The machete flicked back, I thrust out my hand in a desperate counter—

A blur, a rush of air, a glitter. A blow against my palm, stinging, not sharp, not cutting, a dull heavy impact of hard sharkskin and a sudden well-balanced weight. Almost by instinct I followed through. A blade spun away, glinting in the fierce light, severed from its haft. The machete—and its wielder was reeling back, screaming, with his arm slashed from shoulder to elbow by the sword I held. Two of his own, with the same square, crushed faces, grabbed him and hauled him back. I turned on the nearest thug, shattered a six-foot fencepost in his hands, then swung the sabre at a crowbar merchant with a cut that lopped his hand off at the wrist. He bolted, screaming and scattering blood. That sent the others running in all directions. It had some of my own looking a little pale, too. Big Sean kicked the hand, still flexing, into the gutter, and raised a hairy eyebrow. "Where the hell'd you come up with that pig-sticker, then? Have it down your pants? Thought you were walking a wee bit stiff."

"No, that was a woman," I answered absently, staring around me, and hardly noticed his guffaw.

"Bloody interesting life you lead—"

"*Quiet!* Something dangerous is happening—even more dangerous, I mean!" The sword, my sword from above the mantel—things like that don't happen in the Core. Which meant that a threshold had been crossed, somehow—and those strange rioters had appeared. "Anyone know what this area used to be before they built all these houses and everything? And the shopping center back there?"

It was the leathery woman who answered. "Why, nothing much. Just a big crossroads—where the main road came in from the port. It was a separate town then."

I took a deep breath. "That would do it. Listen, we've got to get these streets clear now—but be careful. There may be things about you don't expect—and that's putting it mildly! Don't get led around any corners, don't get decoyed away from the rest of us. It's more important than ever we stick together now. And if I disappear, don't any of you come after me—right? Follow Sean here."

"Why? You planning to leave us?" He grinned. "Daddy, who was that masked man?"

"I'm not planning anything, but somebody else may be. As to who I am—ever read the business pages?"

"Me? You're joking, jimmy. Just page three and the football."

"Good. Keep it that way. Let's move."

Nobody was over-jubilant, I was glad to see. In fact, though we'd had no casualties, they looked more sober and less excited than before. They'd seen how well organized the rioters were and no doubt they'd got around to won-

dering why. Some sort of military organization pretending
to be drunken criminals, with makeshift weapons—pretending pretty hard, with a bit of gangbanging along the
way. What were they really after? And why were they striking where the Spiral was strong, in a place where many
paths had crossed in space and time? Because that was
where they came from?

A couple of smaller groups took one look at us and
bolted, as if the word had got around. We kept on, sweeping
the main streets, picking up one or two recruits as we went,
getting a couple of casualties under cover. That was how
we came upon the second gang, the larger one. We followed
the trail they left out onto a main road, and spotted them
from there. They were busy around the foot of a church;
wisps of smoke were boiling out from beneath its roof, light
flickering behind its leaded panes. Faces turned as we appeared, and this time every single one of them looked alike,
men and women all; the heavy faces, the same faces, piggy,
brutal, blunt.

It was then I made the connection. The German rioters—
these—and those monstrous helpers of Stryge's. Even the
general body shape was the same, in different sizes, in both
sexes. As if they were related. As if the one might be cousin
to the other; or might grow into it. Three ages of man;
three stages of Unman. The more they grew, the less human
they looked. The child is father to—what?

These weren't any kind of rioters. I was looking at another human subspecies, like the Wolves, spawned probably
by God alone knew what blend of abominable conditions
and unearthly forces out along the Spiral. They were moving, quickly now, gathering in ragged ranks—or was that
a spearhead? And if they were anything at all like the
Wolves, they were incredibly dangerous.

I looked at my makeshift troops. Sean and Billy interpreted that look, and unshipped their guns. "That lot'll take
some shifting," muttered somebody.

"Remember," I hissed urgently. "Don't let them trap you

into a full-scale fight—they'll win. Pull back, harass them, keep them busy without sticking your necks out. In, bash, then out again, till they run or the cops come. Now— *move!*"

I hardly needed to tell them. We were already spilling across the road, spurred on by shared anger and fear, breaking into a trot, and then, suddenly, into an all-out run. I saw the heavy figures mass to meet us, then heard a rattle and a sudden frenzied snarl. That woman should have been a general; her timing was just right, the effect shattering. The two huge dogs, freed from their chains, went racing out ahead of me with a furious howl, as if they sensed the inhumanity ahead, jumped the low churchyard wall and flung themselves at the leaders. The others jumped back, and we came pouring over the wall. I leaped over the struggling figures and swung at their followers with great roundhouse slashes that made the air sing. I felled one, maybe injured more, but the main effect was psychological; they hopped like bunnies, ducked and fell over their fellows at the rear. Beside me a shotgun went off, then another, I kept on slashing and plunged headfirst into screaming confusion. A crowbar parried one blow, then bent uselessly; machetes snapped. A squat figure slashed at one of the young men with a garden sickle, then folded at a blow from the fireaxe; wooden poles jabbed out at face or stomach, or tripped up opponents. Around me, weapons lost or forgotten, fighters rolled and traded punches, or clawed at each other's throats. That was what I didn't want. I jabbed at a couple of the strugglers—and then literally jumped as something whistled by, shearing hair from my head and the shoulder padding from my jacket. Somebody else had a proper sword, and for the ursine bulk that was all I could see of him, he was no slouch with it.

We crossed blades, slash and parry. He lunged with appalling force, I gave back, caught his blade outstretched and slapped it aside against a gravestone. I lunged in, connected and heard him grunt. But not enough; he recovered, cut at my legs and sent me stumbling. I slashed out again, expecting to send his sword flying; it was like hitting a brick wall. That, with a wound in him; these characters were strong as Wolves. We had to make them start running, break and scatter. He cut at me again, viciously hard, I ducked down, he bellowed in triumph and launched a fearful downward slash. His sword rang and smashed in two on the gravestone I'd ducked behind; they made them of granite in this part of the world. I sprang up and went for him. With only the stump of a sword he had every excuse for running, but as I'd hoped it broke the others. They pulled away, split and bolted across the churchyard, stumbling over the crosses and gravestones; the locals streamed after them. But my man went limping off around the far side of the church; and if as seemed likely he was a leader, I wanted to get my hands on him. I went after him; but abruptly a flash lit the corner of the building, there was a loud dull bang quite unlike a shotgun's cough, and I saw him stagger back. Another flash and thump, and he was flung sprawling back over a gravestone, and slid down it unmoving, chin on chest.

I was about to duck away, when I found myself looking down the barrel of the original smoking gun. A massive Colt automatic stared at me with an eye blacker than the night, and only the slightest tremor. But I managed to outstare it, and look behind the bunched hands that gripped it, the stiffened arms. "I might have known," I wheezed disgustedly. For some reason my mouth felt appallingly dry. "Aggro before brains, every time, Little Miss 1726!"

"You!" she barked, and her voice dripped venom. "This is all your doing, isn't it? Your idea of fun!" She laughed an angry little laugh, and it cracked at the end. Her face was indistinct in the gloom, but one eye flickered, as if there was a tic in the lid; the pistol hardly wavered. "Christ, you and the Night Children—you must have really thought you were laughing now!"

"The who? Christ. I'm not with *them*—"

She wasn't listening to a word. *"Bloody well laugh at this!"* She squeezed the trigger. At that range she could hardly have missed; but it was her very steadiness that saved me. My teacher Mall had turned a pistol bullet in flight; I couldn't do that, but the barrel made a steady mark, and squinting down it like that she couldn't see me readying my sword. It was close-run, even so, because the clanging impact and the shot were simultaneous, and the bullet and the flame singed my cheek. No second chances here; I hared off at full tilt, hurdled a gravestone with a yelp as her second shot smashed chips off it, and zigzagged away among the trees. My merry men, discipline forgotten, were a long way down the street now, beating the bejasus out of such of their opponents as hadn't run fast enough, and good luck to them; but she was between me and them, and I couldn't attract their attention. Another bullet whined off the wall, altogether too close. Nothing for it; they'd have to manage for themselves now, I wasn't hanging around with little Miss Paranoia 1726 on my heels. I legged it away up a passing side-street, and into the night once more.

I'd no idea where I was, but I kept on running, ducking, weaving, dodging suddenly around corners. I'd encountered some scary people in my time, and more than people; but that woman unnerved me. The gun, of course, had a lot to do with it. So did her sudden appearance. How had she just popped up like that? Had she been following me all that time? But then she'd have known I wasn't with the Children or whatever she called them—or could her hatred of me have warped the facts around enough? It was possible. Every so often I stopped in the shadows, listened for following feet; but there were none. The sounds of riot, though, still echoed around me, coming from ahead now; and at the end of a dark alley alongside a newish-looking concrete supermarket building I saw a familiar flickering red light. I took a firm grip on my sword, and went to see.

Just as I neared the end a dark form dashed into the alley mouth, stopped short as it saw me and sank down to its knees, half gasping, half sobbing. Coming closer, I saw it was a black man, West Indian by the look of him, in an old-fashioned but expensive-looking camel coat, one sleeve badly torn. I was about to go and help him up when a gaggle of other figures dashed up around him, and I heard the sickening thud of boots striking home. *"Hey!"* I yelled, without thinking. *"You stop that!"*

Faces rounded on me, pale faces, oafish faces, but wholly human. That didn't make me like them any the more. One or two of them were oddly uniform, wearing heavy sideburns and oily curls topped with quiffs and cowlicks, and their jackets hung low and long-armed, making them look oddly apelike. The others wore sweaters or leather jackets, tight jeans and pointed shoes. They weighed me up, sniggering softly. "Gonna make us, then?" mouthed one of the curly types.

"Yeah—nigger-lover!" mocked another.

"He's old enough to be your bloody father!" I hissed, wondering where these weird clothes had come from.

"Maybe it's 'is old man!"

"Nah—'is boyfriend! He's a brown-hatter, see?"

They snorted with laughter. "Yer want 'im," said one, "yer come get 'im!" He thrust out his hand, and it spat a short silver tongue. Others flipped their wrists, and blades swung out; a broken bottle glinted green. It was the flick-knives and razors that completed the image—teddyboys from the fifties, before I was born. Somehow I didn't think I'd run into a fashion revival. They'd had race riots then, hadn't they? Serious ones.

"Something's 'olding 'im up!" guffawed the leading ted, and without looking around he backheeled the groaning man on the ground. That did it. I stepped forward and swung my own wrist, bringing the sword up into the light. The teds gaped, I took one swift backhand swing and smashed the leader's knife right out of his hand, probably breaking a few bones on the way. Then I brought the flat of the sword back against the side of his head. It connected with a smack like a shot, he yelled and fell writhing at my feet. I set the point under the chin of the next boy, and backed him up against the wall, yammering with fright.

"Now!" I shouted. "Knives, razors, anything—throw 'em away! Throw, I said, not drop!" I flicked the sword, and a severed kisscurl went flying. Metal clattered in all directions. I grabbed my sick-looking victim, spun him around and booted him hard in the backside. "Right! Now run like bunnies! Run, kiddies, or I'll set your arses on fire!" I herded them out like sheep, landing stinging slaps with the flat of the blade, and chased them along the road a little way, pinking them with the point. It was surprising how fast they could run in those funny shoes, though some of them would be eating their dinner off the mantelpiece for the next few days. Then I went back and found the old man picking himself up, muttering his thanks, and the ring-leader still stunned and groaning. I turned him over with my toe, riffled his stupid-looking jacket and came up with a wallet holding about thirty pounds—quite a sum back then, probably. I tossed it to the old man. "Should help pay for the coat! Want me to see you home?"

"No, thanks. It's not far. You saved my life, man."

"Maybe. It won't always be this bad."

He sighed. "Ah, man, you want to bet?"

"Take it from me. I *know*." I grinned at him again, and set off back down the alley. I'd better try to retrace my steps, if the way hadn't shifted already; the Spiral was like that. I tried not to think about where I might end up next. I cast around for some sort of stable point, some landmark, that might help. There was only one: the column of fiery smoke from the burning hotel. I didn't care to end up there again, but at least it'd be in my own time. At the next turn I was fairly sure which way I'd come, down a narrow street overhung by old buildings; and there was red light down that way, certainly. Maybe Annie Oakley was still there, too, but that chance I'd have to take.

I sidled down, keeping to the shadow of the walls, although that meant treading in some really unpleasant puddles that gurgled as I passed, as if threatening to eat my shoes, and released amazing stenches. There was a roar of voices, the sound of glass smashing, and I tensed, gripping my sword. A flaming billet of wood, tipped with tar or something like that, flew past me and into the open gap of a shattered window—an old leaded window, in a wall of heavy brick. I looked around, through the smoky air. Half the buildings were like that, brick and timber, only a few stone-faced in the familiar city style. I grabbed the torch out and dropped it sizzling into a puddle. A heavy hand slapped me staggering back against the wall. "Let 'er burn!" screamed a big man, looming over me. "That's a godless grafting brewer's house there, that poisons the workers with his filth—burn 'ut for the Charter!"

"For the Charter!" screeched a mass of raucous echoes, and suddenly I realized I was surrounded by a much larger crowd than the mere teds, shadow-shapes of men and women flickering and dancing in a wide arc of torches. "Give us our Charter!"

And they started pitching torches into the gap, all of them, shouting and capering as the flames sprang up. I couldn't believe what I was seeing, the sheer stupidity of it. It started me shouting at them. "You bloody idiots! These old roofs catch easier than dry grass! You'll burn the whole damn street—" and then, as it sank in what they were shouting about and what clothes they wore, battered top hats, long dresses, leather aprons, "The whole damn town, more like! Your homes and everybody's! Is any Charter worth that? Where're your children? This winter where'll they be?"

That had some effect; a lot of the crowd, the women especially, stopped dancing and looked around hesitantly. With a sound like a last gasp the torn curtains caught. I grabbed them, swung on them and hauled. The big man tried to punch me. Hands full, I kicked out and caught him in the crotch, then landed a neat left on his ear with my

sword hilt that dropped him face down in the muck. The
curtains came free and landed beside him, steaming and
smoking, dragging the torches with them. "Now get back!"
I yelled. "Put out the rest—for your own sake! And your
families!"

There was a distant hubbub, a continuous clattering
rumble, and somebody yelled out, "Dragoons! It's the bastard dragoons! Leg it!"

I didn't stop to see if they put the fire out; I was back
into the shadows now, and moving fast. That little detour
had wasted me too much time, and taken me too far out
of my way—the Chartist riots, mid-nineteenth century as
far as I remembered. But I could still see the flames from
the hotel fire, casting long distorted shadows on the high
walls around me, and suddenly I understood what was happening. It really was casting long shadows, that thing, the
shadows of the Spiral, reaching back through timeless
reaches to other fires, other shadows, other riots, other out-
bursts of mindless hate and destruction around this spot.
What I could remember of my local history seemed to in-
clude an awful lot of them; this had been a good town for
mobs. And I was astray among them, till I could find this
latest one again.

Around a corner ahead I saw light, I heard voices; that
might be promising. But as I rounded it I was all but swept
away.

The torrent was human, but it stank like a piggery in the
smoky air. So did the muddy slush underfoot, innocent of
anything as solid as a cobblestone. It almost sucked the
shoes off my feet as I staggered back into the mouth of my
street, but luckily they were tough trainers; I prayed the
laces wouldn't dissolve. The people who milled around me,
hardly noticing me, were mostly barefoot, short squat figures in coarse dark tunics, much the same for either sex
except for length, and crowned with simple headgear; but
there were two in nothing but stained shifts, two women
dragged along on ropes by men in leather and mail, buf-

feted and kicked by anyone who could get close. For some
reason both of them were slathered from head to foot with
what looked like great gouts of pitch or tar. I wondered
why, until I saw what waited ahead, and my blood ran chill
in my stomach—the rickety scaffold, built against a stone
wall for strength; and beside it, in the center of the street,
the huge pile of brush and straw. In this country witches
were rarely if ever burned alive; it was customary to hang
them first, till they were at least partly dead.

I gaped in horror; but there seemed even less chance of
doing anything here. There were hundreds of these people,
their faces gloating and pitiless, and their victims weren't
exactly the romantic stereotypes a man might stick out his
neck for. One old, one young: the crone was a shriveled old
thing that screeched with senile malevolence, as convincing
an old devil as I'd ever seen; the younger was a great
doughy lump of a woman with a coarse red face and crumpled features, howling and roaring at her tormentors. I
couldn't count on any support among the crowd, that was
for sure. Should that make any difference? I'd seen too
much tonight, and been taxed too far. I gathered up my
courage, and as the foul cortège swung close to the mouth
of the alley I plunged out into the human stream.

I stand tall among most ordinary crowds; I towered over
these, and my sword shone bloody in my hand. They gave
back at the sight of me, and I reached the women in a
moment and slashed out—once, twice—severing the ropes
that held them, and hurling them back before me toward
the dark. One startled soldier had the presence of mind to
spring in my way and aim a pike, but one sweep sliced the
head from it and tipped him into the mire. I hope he had
his mouth closed, or he was a doomed man. Stones
smacked painfully against my back, hands clawed at my
clothes, but when the sword swung their way they sprang
away. Often they fell, overbalancing their fellows and free-
ing the passage. The women screeched before me, as afraid
of me as the crowd, and as they reached the alley the

younger clutched the elder's hand and they ran; so did I, but within moments I'd lost them in the dark. What chance they'd have of escape I couldn't imagine, but I didn't dare stop to look, not with that crowd at my heels. I couldn't understand a word they shouted, but I guessed they might think I was these poor creatures' master come to bail them out. In those circumstances, if they caught me they might forgo the hanging first. My long legs were my main advantage, and the column of fire called me mockingly on, as if to remind me of what awaited me in the Core, in my own time. The sounds of pursuit grew fainter, fading into a kind of general hubbub; but I didn't hang around.

Some streets on now, still trying to follow that infernal light, still dogged by that distant confusion of sounds, I realized I was running on a hard surface—cobbles. For a minute I hoped I might have come out into one of the conservation area streets. But these cobbles were awash in a slurry of hay and dung. I was about to turn back smartly when I heard a faint groan, and realized the shapeless heap a few feet from me was a human shape—or had been. I squatted down, panting, appalled. I'd heard of people beaten to a jelly, I'd seen some terrible approximations, but never this. It was just recognizably a man, a tall one maybe; but the features were gone, the splintered bone poking up through the raw flesh. Amazing that he was still alive— and horrible. A sudden steadier light fell on him, and I looked up to see a thin man holding a lantern; he had on a long shabby coat, knee breeches, buckled shoes. Lank yellow hair straggled around his chinless face, but there was something a lot more formidable in his bloodshot eyes. He stared at me, gave back a little as he saw my sword, then gathered himself up as others drifted out of the smoke around him.

"She's escaped, is the whore, but at the least we have made certain of the he-idolator, eh? What, be there life left in him yet? Not so strange that his soul should cling to his filthy corpse, given the torment that awaits't upon the leav-

ing, in the uttermost cauldrons of the pit!" Apparently that
was a joke. At any rate some of the others laughed, a couple
of women among them. They had sticks in their hands
mostly, the odd dungfork and flail. The pale man snapped
his fingers. "Come, we'll speed him thither! Alexander Mar-
shall, hast still thy rope? So then, upon a linklight with it,
and tie a goodly halter."

"You're going to *hang* him?" I demanded, swallowing.
"Why, for the love of God? He'll be dead in a minute, anyway!"

"For the love of God, thou sayest? Call it a pious work
then, that we lift this plotting Papist equivocator as close
to Heaven as's like to come!"

Another joke, apparently. A bundle of laughs, this guy.

"Let me get this straight. You did this to him—and you
still want to *hang* him?"

"Aye, friend. The hand of the multitude, that speaks with
the voice of the Lord against the sin of popery and the
Whore of Babylon that is its Church, was laid heavy upon
him—but aye, mine was foremost, that detected the sinners
in the midst of their sinning. Shall it now be backward?"
He peered at me more closely, and there was an unpleasant
glitter in his eye. He had the look of a man thoroughly
enjoying himself. "And, friend, what might be thy concern
in the matter? I perceive thou'rt of a somewhat strange
mien, art thou not?" He jerked his head at the people behind him. "And has not Master Oates unveiled the deadly
stratagems of foreign princes, that would, by the agency of
their servants sent hither to walk hidden among us, subvert
our land and faith, and vomit upon us the filth of their own
corruption? Shall we suffer those to walk free among us,
or shall we not use them even as we use their willing
pawns, even as we have used this one at our feet?" His soft
voice rose to a sudden galvanizing shriek, and he brandished a heavy-looking stick at me. Gobbets of blood and
hair clung to the silver-banded head. *"Upon him! Tear the*

black heart out of his body, strew his entrails before his eyes! So saith the Lord—"

I grabbed him by his greasy shirtfront and ran him through to the hilts. There was a general scream from his followers as I pushed him off to collapse into the mire by his victim, and turned the sword on them. Their fright gave me just enough time to duck back into the shadows and run like hell.

Turn, turn, twist and dodge, and God help the first of them that caught me. Titus Oates, the Popish Plot—so its paranoid influence had reached this far from London. I didn't remember hearing about that, but maybe too few people had died for this incident to make the histories. Then a less cynical thought struck me; maybe there had been only that one death. Or two, depending on how you looked at it. Maybe the mob had worn itself out in hunting me and, deprived of its rabble-rouser, had gradually cooled off, regained a bit of common sense and gone home ashamed. I hoped so, but I'd never know; I wasn't going back to find out. The sound seemed to be fading away again, but I kept running till I saw light and skidded around a corner—right into another huge crowd of people.

I was so startled I thought they were my pursuers, and almost slashed out at them till I realized how differently they were dressed, how quietly they spoke. They stood in an open space between high buildings, beneath the light of hanging lanterns. This was a richer place and time, later than the last by the look of it, as if I'd finally found the right direction and was headed back toward the shadows of my own time. Here, the long coats were of better stuff, often richly decorated, the hats three-cornered, with badge and cockade. Even the man who struggled in their midst wore a bullion-embroidered coat, evidently a uniform; those who marched him through the crowd were relentless, but they didn't hit him. Those around him neither called nor taunted, but spoke in low voices or not at all. And yet there was a menace in their soft rumbling murmur greater than all the frenzy of the others. Scarcely a moment later I saw it consummated, swift, silent, brutal—a line of washing lifted carefully from a high frame and a cord flung over it, to be placed around the victim's neck. I clutched at a passer-by's arm.

"Why?" I demanded. "What's he done?"

"Do ye not know?" returned the other, civil enough but surprised. "He'd quell a crowd at a hanging by ordering his troop to fire upon it, and fire they did, to many deaths. Well, let him quell this one!"

Even as he spoke a man with a white collar and bands stepped back from the victim, thrusting what was evidently a Bible into his bound hands; as quickly as that the rope was hauled taut. I winced, but I couldn't look away. The man died inches from the ground, strangling slowly on his own weight with no neck-breaking drop. He died hard and long and horribly, and they quietly watched him writhe. I clutched my sword hilt; but who could I fight here? This was a whole city, or near to it, dispensing what it thought was justice.

"Is this right?" I spat.

"Aye, it goes hard," mused the man I'd spoken to. "But it is fitting."

I didn't say anything. By my lights they were a lynch mob, the man they'd hanged was probably only doing his duty as he saw it. But who was I to condemn them? The blood was still drying on my sword. I vaguely remembered the story now, from school histories, but no doubt there'd be a story like it in every city, remembered or forgotten. Any of these things could have happened, anywhere—could still happen, as the night had shown. And from all I'd seen it looked as if forces that fed on them somehow were busy fomenting more. I turned away again, shaken, and let the shadows close at my back once more.

Even from here it beckoned, that column of firelit smoke, across the timeless distances of the Spiral. But I no longer saw it as a beacon. Above ruined roof-tops it rose like darkened battlements among the clouds, a vast shadow-tower that loomed over the land. Beneath its black pall, born of violence and terror, all such evils flourished and grew strong again. I'd tried to help, but had I? Or had I only touched myself with the same dark taint?

I ran, and I ran; and now I no longer turned toward any lesser lights or noises. I kept the terrible column in my eye, and fixed heart and mind upon it, and looked neither to left nor right; for I was afraid now to see any more shadows of what had been. How long I ran I don't know, and there may be no way of defining it. That hubbub was all around me, but I knew better now than to follow; it stemmed from no one place or time, it was all of them, the same from all, the constant tumult of a hundred insanities resounding across the pathways of the Spiral, swelling and feeding on one another, a roaring waterfall of wrath and cruelty and despair. At last, though, I began to make out other, shriller sounds that I thought were just more screams and cries, and perhaps at first they were; but gradually they became clearer. They were sirens, the familiar cutting notes of police and fire and ambulance, slicing through the rumbling disorder. The smoke swirled thicker around me, the road drummed hard and flat under my feet, and I felt the distant heat of flames on my cheek. A harsh blue light hurt my stinging eyes, and I stared wearily around.

The hotel fire still glowed up ahead; but this blaze was nearer. It was the church, with two fire engines playing hoses on its roof, and it looked as if they had it under control. Police cars were halted around it, roof lights on, and beyond them, lit by the swinging blue flashes, stood a motley crowd I recognized, watching the flames. I caught sight of Sean's huge silhouette, dwarfing the policeman next to him, obviously talking amicably. There were the Rottweilers, chained again, licking their chops sleepily. Evidently no trouble there. Best I didn't get involved again; the sword, for example, might take some explaining. I turned and limped away, back toward the hotel blaze and the road that would take me home.

Weariness wrapped itself around me as I walked, a leaden cloak. No point in heading back to the car, it wouldn't be going anywhere ever again. That thought depressed me. When I came out at last on the downhill road, a flock of fire engines were damping down the great blaze, with the firemen in their yellow protective gear stamping around like so many deformed dwarfs. I wasn't going to miss the center or the hotel; still, they'd probably build something even more hideous in its place. Here and there cars were beginning to appear; there might even be a taxi. I remembered the sword, and was already slipping off my jacket to wrap it up when I realized it wasn't in my hand any longer. I looked back in panic, and then remembered this also had happened before. I had a feeling I'd find it safe over the mantelpiece when I got home, as if it had never been away; but there'd be a broken window.

There was. When the lift I hitched dropped me outside, I saw the glass scattered on the pavement. "That your window?" inquired the young driver. "Bad luck, mate—look, not another in the whole damn block touched!" He glanced around. "In fact, it all looks pretty quiet around here—never know there'd been a riot! An' I always thought it must be tough, down by the docks."

"It is, in some parts. Around here it's yuppified enough."

"Yah. Maybe they sent some cops down here, or something, and that stopped the riot gettin' hold. Well, gotta get off, don't want the wife worrying. See yer!"

I looked around, considering. He was right. Most of the town had got off very lightly, even near this end; but here the stillness was almost uncanny. It felt very restful, after the hysterias of the night. I thought suddenly of those great unseen potencies that enforced and guarded the safety of trade in the great Ports of the Spiral, such as this. Could it be their hands that had held this area so safe? They would guess something of where it sprang from; the Wardens it might be.

What would they have made of me this evening? An interfering idiot, probably. They never tried to solve every little problem. They probably knew better than to try. And yet . . . and yet. The girl might still die; the fanatics might find another victim, the witches might still hang. But if I hadn't intervened? I might never know. But this much I felt sure of at last, that I'd been bound to try. Without me things might have been worse—a lot worse. And I wouldn't have been able to sleep the way I was going to, now.

I was too tired to think anymore, and the lift, inevitably, wasn't working. I trudged up and up the floors to my penthouse; and when I reached it I could barely get the key in the door. The burglar alarm would be running on its batteries, so I'd better disable it from the inside; but when the familiar singsong warning whine didn't start, I simply assumed it was one more damn thing broken down, and left it at that. I let the heavy door slip shut and leaned gratefully against it, looking down the length of my enormous living room.

There was the mantel, all right, but the sword wasn't there. It lay on the floor to one side, among a spray of glass fragments, brought in on its return, no doubt. I went forward and stooped to pick it up—then, weary as I was, I stiffened painfully. Maybe I'd sensed something—a sound, a movement. But nothing like that could account for how I knew a gun was pointing at the back of my neck. I just felt it, and that was all. "Nice place!" said the harsh unsteady voice. "Wish I could afford it. But it's just a cold shell; it could use some warmth. And a better burglar alarm too. Stand up. Face to the wall, hands above your head. *Move!*"

Chapter 5

I stood up, very slowly; but I turned around, also very slowly. There was the gun, all right, tipped now with a short silencer, just enough to take the edge off the bang. It jerked up to level with my face, but nothing else happened. I looked the woman up and down. She stood in the classic range posture, legs akimbo, arms outstretched, the gun clasped tight in both hands. It was as steady as ever, and as hard to ignore; but now she looked dangerously disturbed. Or, to put it scientifically, barking mad. Her shaggy black hair stuck up in spikes, her dark shellsuit was crumpled and torn. She was a soot-streaked, battered mess; but then so was I, probably. It was her face: her features were slack, her eyes wild, with that tic still beating away at one corner, and her mouth was working so much she could hardly speak.

I shook my head in awe. "You're really determined, aren't you? Tailing me through all that—how long for?"

She gathered her breath and spoke with an effort. "Since the heliport! You were late! Didn't spot me, did you? No! Too bloody confident after your famous *coup*!"

"Well, I did feel—"

But once started she went plowing on, as if she'd something bursting to get out. "And then the riot, and you heading off down all those back-streets—I lost you then, but it was obvious you knew something, you were going somewhere! I *knew* it was too close to be a coincidence—so I started searching. I knew how to find you. I just looked for the worst trouble, and there you were, right in there with those creatures, whipping it up! Just like in Germany!" Her voice was pitching higher, near cracking. "Oh, you scored a real coup there, congratulations, yes! It made you careless, over-confident, so you thought you'd be safe to come out from under your stone at last, didn't you? Get it off with a bit of rape and pillage!" A trickle of saliva oozed from the corner of her mouth and made its way down her chin. "Get your lousy rocks off! Thought you had us whipped, didn't you? *Didn't you, damn you?*"

She was close to raving. "Look—" I began soothingly. I didn't get any further.

"Thought it was clever, didn't you, getting me suspended like that? Well, you were wrong, weren't you, bloody well wrong, wrong, *wrong*! Because it just gave me more time to go after you! Yes, and more freedom to deal with you the way you should be dealt with—you and *scheissdreck'* like you!" She stopped, gulped in air. Her voice dropped suddenly, almost to a croon. "We don't need you," she said softly.

"Can I just—"

"Whatever you've done, it'll unravel when you're not around anymore. And after you that bastard von Amerningen—"

"Look—"

She sucked in her breath and spoke briskly, as if steeling herself for something. "The hell with the law—stamp on you like cockroaches, it's the only way—"

"*Christ, woman!*" I roared in her face. "Will you *listen*?"

I suppose I was lucky the gun didn't go off just from

reflex. But I'd guessed that mad or not, she was too much in control of it for that. All the same, she jumped violently, and stood blinking and gaping at me like an idiot. "You," I shouted, forgetting all the ideas I'd had about being calm and collected and soothing, "are an obsessive, self-righteous, self-centered, small-minded monomaniac! You jump to conclusions, you do the damnedest things, and you never stop to consider that just once, in any way, Little Miss Crusader might be *wrong*! Wrong wrong bloody well *wrong*! You never stop to listen, you never admit it's possible! That's not conviction, that's mental illness! Who d'you think you are—God?"

She swallowed, and smiled an appallingly sweet smile. "You've given me all the proof I need!" she said brightly. "But sure, do go on. I haven't had many laughs lately." Almost lazily, like a cat, she stretched out the gun again.

I slumped against the wall. The way I felt, being shot might almost be merciful. "I don't know where to start!" I protested. "Look—those back-streets—of course I was going somewhere, I was trying to get home—round the riot! You didn't see what happened afterwards, did you? No! You lost me. Well, you won't find my car in the garage here; it's lying burnt out in the middle of the road up by the shopping center. I got turned around by petrol bombs and then tipped out by rioters. They nearly killed me. Think I staged that?"

She stared at me in scorn. "You could afford a hundred of those little sports cars!"

That made me really furious. "Yes, you stupid bitch, but they wouldn't be *mine*! I liked that car, really liked it. It was the first thing I bought when I got the deputy MD's job. There'll never be another like it—and, Christ, I don't suppose you know there's a ten-year waiting list for those things? They're practically hand built. Think I went that far just to keep up appearances?"

"You might," she said, with even contempt. Smoothly sure of herself, unexpectedly enjoying the battle of words, as if it only made her feel more secure, not less. "Or it might just have been a convenient accident. If the rioters nearly killed you, why'd I find you with those creatures at the church?"

"You didn't find me *with* them! I was *with* a bunch of locals I'd rousted out and organized to stop them! If you don't believe me, look up some of them—a builder called Sean, a trucker called Billy something, I can give you their addresses. They'll tell you what I was doing."

"Just playing it cleverer than I thought, maybe. Stirring up two lots of trouble—vigilantes—"

"Or there was the girl—raped and left for dead. I'd like to know if she was all right. And listen, woman, when you shot that . . . character, he was running, wasn't he? With a broken sword. What d'you think broke it? Who do you think he was running from?"

"You?" Her laugh was as humorless as ever, the brick wall I was banging my head against.

"Me," I said quietly. "With that sword behind you on the carpet."

"If you think I'm going to look back at it, think again. It was there when I came in. I suppose it just flew home ahead of you."

"It did, in a sense. But I could never make you understand about that. Any more than—"

"Yes?" There was a change in her tone, but I couldn't tell what.

"Well . . . there's just one way you may have been right. I found out that Lutz is mixed up in something—but it's not what you think. Not just—if anything, it's worse, but . . .Oh, crap, what's the use? You'd never believe it. It's right outside any frame of reference you'll ever have."

She was silent. I looked up, and saw a very odd look on her face. For a moment it lost some of its ingrained lines, and about ten years with them. I caught a glimpse of what she might have been; it was more striking than I'd have expected. Then suspicion stiffened her features again. "Just Lutz. Not you. Right."

"Yes," I said, meeting the sarcasm head on. "Some of the board members, but principally Lutz. He did want to have a go at drawing me in, that night you called. For various reasons it went off half cocked. Probably would have anyway. I like to think so. I don't think he was too confident either, because he waited to try until it didn't mean so much. He chose that night because C-Tran was all set up, launched, everything. It was only then he was ready to risk alienating me—and having to get rid of me."

"What d'you mean?" she demanded sharply.

"I mean I had an interesting ride home from his place. First somebody takes a pot at me with a high-powered rifle and a laser gunsight while I'm still coming down the drive." Her face had taken on another odd look. "You don't bloody believe me? Well, after *that* somebody tried to knock my block off on the *Autobahn*—a car, a heavy with a slingshot. Nearly did it, too, except a truck got mixed up in it. You should see the car I was driving there, as well. I don't think they're going to hire me one again in a hurry—"

I stopped dead. The woman was looking positively sheepish. "That bloody rifle . . . " I breathed. "That was *you*! I should've guessed Lutz wouldn't want a killing on his own home grounds, or anywhere traceable to him. But you would! It was *you*, you—you self-righteous little—" Words failed me, and I clenched my fists. Instantly the gun jabbed into my face again.

"Me and my team, yes," she said sourly. "Pity I've never used that model before. It was the only one we could get in a hurry, and it had to be at extreme range."

"You're apologizing? And that was your team in the car, too?"

She shook her head. "No. Not us. But it fits the pattern of other—" She pursed her lips suddenly. She'd realized she was implicitly going along with my story; and there was something underneath that still made her determined to disbelieve me. Obsession, maybe, or something more solid—but what?

"So," I said, watching the sweat streak her smudged face, "you may not believe me, but oddly enough I believe you. Lutz took a lot of trouble to make sure I was seen leaving safely. If you'd killed me then, you'd only have been doing his work for him. Maybe you're only doing it now—"

That firing stance is all very well, a nice stable platform; but when you have to hold it too long it becomes a bit stiff. And so do you. I wasn't in prime condition myself right now; but I'd been relaxing. Suddenly, careful not to send any vocal or physical signals, I bent my knees and dropped, fast, to a crouch. I expected the shot to part my hair, but she didn't even get one off before I'd sprung. Not up but forward, catching the outstretched arms as they swung down toward me and forcing them aside, bringing the wrists down hard across my knee, like breaking wood—

The gun made a clattering mess of my floorboards, but mercifully didn't go off. I let the woman go, pushed her back and grabbed it. Then I stepped hastily between her and my sword, but she was still doubled over, hugging her aching wrists. She looked up, biting her lip hard; she seemed to be waiting for something. "Turn around," I ordered, and with a slow weary smile, her shoulders sagging, she turned.

I thrust the pistol in my belt and grabbed her by the scruff of her neck and the seat of her pants. She gave a wild yelp; that wasn't what she'd been expecting at all. I more or less raced her toward the door. *"Open it!"* I ordered. Still sobbing with shock, she fumbled with the lock, but managed it. I ran her out onto the landing, and she gave a wild scream and grabbed the balustrade, evidently expecting to be flung over. I tore her loose and rushed her to the stairs, and she grabbed the rail again, thinking I was going to throw her down this time. She was in a state of complete gibbering panic, and that only made me angrier. I don't know where I got the strength, but I gave her the classic bum's rush all the way down sixteen flights of shadowy stairs, with her flailing and kicking and squealing and getting her leg stuck in the railings. From time to time one of my worthy neighbors looked out. "Mormons!" I explained, and they all nodded sagely. Finally I reached the ground floor hallway, and more or less dropped her on her backside while I got my breath back.

She got hers back first; she hadn't been carrying the weight, after all. She squinted up at me, the way you might look up at a dodgy-looking tree, wondering which way it was going to fall. "You could have shot me more easily up there. Or just quietly wrung my neck. I couldn't have stopped you."

"Oh, for God's sake, woman . . . " was the best I could manage. She started to get up, and I drew the pistol and motioned her down. She stiffened, but when I didn't fire she subsided again.

She kept on looking at me. "You don't add up."

"You can't," I grunted. "You started with two and two and you get twenty-two. Or 1726."

She slapped the smooth marble tiles violently. "What the hell are you on about? I've got to know!"

"Whistle for it," I told her. "There's something going on here, all right, but I'm damn sure it's nothing that ever entered your narrow little horizons. Better to keep your nose out of this. And your one-track mind!"

She bridled. "I could say the same to you! That *Autobahn* incident—do you know what that was? Can you protect yourself against another?"

I groaned. All I could see was bed as a beautiful vista, sixteen floors up. "Yes, yes, yes . . . " I had to do something about what I'd got caught in—to get some advice, some thinking done—but first of all I needed sleep. I reached down, seized her collar again and yanked her to her feet. I skidded her over the smooth floor, too fast to make much fuss, straight at the glass doors. The porter was nowhere to be seen, and that was just as well. I tabbed the lock and they sighed back as we hit the mat; I threw her stumbling out into the night. I looked up and down the road; there was nobody at all in sight, and only the occasional siren broke the silence. The sky was growing pale, the street lights looking dimmer. It'd be dawn soon; I'd have to leave my next move till evening. I needed the sleep, anyway.

I raised the pistol, saw her start, heard the sharp little gasp. I clicked on the safety, then the magazine release, shucked it out and put it gently down on the pavement. My toe spun it twenty yards or so. Then I unscrewed the silencer and dropped it in my pocket.

"Wipe the magazine before you put it back in," I said, and handed her the pistol. "It's a rough night out there. You may need this to get home."

I turned on my heel and stalked back through the door, trying not to look as if I was hurrying, but all too alert in case she made a grab for that magazine. But I caught a glimpse of her in the glass, just standing there unmoving, staring after me. In the pale light, with all that taut malevolence drained from her face, she looked more as she might have—not at all bad, really. But I still legged it for the stairs at speed, trying not to think of the sixteen flights between me, a shower and bed. For the moment that was the most terrifying prospect in the world.

Evening brought others. I saw nothing of the day; I was asleep, dead to the world, for some eleven hours; and I woke with a head like a football, over-inflated, a tongue I could have lathered and shaved. But a bath and a meal restored my interest in the world, and in the news of last night. The rioting had died down with the morning light, but the city was still in deep shock. The police had arrested a few looters and minor troublemakers, but I wasn't at all surprised to hear that the organized gangs had simply faded away. They were still being "actively sought," and lines of inquiry "followed up"; only I knew just how far they'd have to follow,

right outside the bounds of ordinary human experience. I
was headed that way myself.

If I could get hold of a car, that is. Duly slept, showered
and shaved, I spent an interesting hour or so trying to scare
one up; they were heavily in demand right now. The remains of mine had been hauled away somewhere, but my
suitcases were picked up more or less intact, though heavily
scorched and dented on the outside; the explosion had
blown them into a doorway. Eventually, by pulling strings
on the C-Tran account, I got the use of a hideously expensive luxury saloon, not at all my kind of car; but I'd had
interesting experiences around where I was going, the kind
that put you off wandering too far on foot. Now, though, I
was beginning to wonder if I wouldn't be better off that
way. In the early days it hadn't always been easy, finding
my way to the Tavern; but lately the old Morgan seemed
almost to have learned the way itself, rumbling easily
through the streets of the old port, across the cobbles,
down the dark alleys that lead to one place or many, always
guiding me toward the light and the warmth of a place I
felt truly at home.

Now, purring along in this sleek self-satisfied monster
with my sword bumping and rattling uneasily on the back
seat, I began to wonder if it wasn't some sort of jinx. It was
so alien here; the shadows of the old warehouses more or
less slid off its mirrorbright metallic paintwork, the romance of the old street names—Danube Street, Orinokoo
Lane, Chunking Square, Hudson Quay—hardly penetrated
its tinted glass. All it found me were the modern redevel-
oped quarters, more yuppified even than my flat block, full
of little boutiques and restaurants with festoon blinds and
brass circulating fans, discos whose pink neon signs obscured the ageless stone shells they briefly inhabited.
Around and about we went, three times by different routes;
yet always we fetched up back here. I began to feel as if
barriers were being raised across my path, all the more
solid for being unseen.

Exasperated, I tried something I hadn't for years; I braked outside a local pub, one of the seamier, unreconstructed jobs, and asked a pair of ancients coming out if they knew where the Illyrian Tavern might be, or one Jyp the Pilot, if he was in port. They glared at me and muttered something about never hearing the name, then toddled off on their sticks, looking back and grumbling to each other. I sighed, mooched inside, ordered a pint and repeated my question. Often the question warmed the atmosphere immediately; but this time it produced only a sour shrug from the barman, and a sudden looming shadow at the far end of the room. A massive man in black donkey-jacket and jeans, white-haired and balding, with a ruddy sailor's complexion over his yellowing white jersey, rolled up to the bar and leaned on it, that bit too close to me. "What'd be yer business wi' any such fella, eh, jimmy?"

I looked at him. I didn't like being loomed over. "Who wants to know?"

He didn't answer for a moment. "That yer set o' wheels outside, jimmy?"

"It is."

"Better get it out o' here then, or something might happen tae it. Dead rough neighborhood, this is."

"I've got business here. I go when I'm good and ready."

He raised his glass to his lips, and talked around it. "Fella might get himself an awfy sore face wi' an attitude like that."

"Just what I was thinking."

He made a mock-surprised face and looked around the bar, courting a laugh. He didn't get it. There was a taut, repressed atmosphere in the place. An ancient one-bar electric heater was scorching the lino as it obviously had for years, and the faint sickliness caught at the throat. He put down his drink deliberately, and pushed himself upright; so did I. There was more to this than met the eye; and if I wanted to know what it was, he was the obvious person to ask. He might take a little persuading, though.

The barman hurried over. "I'll have no squarin' off in here. Drink up and get out, the pair o' you, or I'll have the cops here in two minutes. C'mon, piss off!"

Neither of us bothered with our drinks. Slowly, keeping an eye on each other, we moved to the door. I opened it; he stood back, and I went out first. But I was still on the step when his heavy hand seized my shoulder, and I was thrown away back against the grime-blackened wall. The huge man swung himself out, and grinned at me, nastily. For the first time I noticed how large his teeth were, great splayed and distorted things, and how yellow. "I could settle ye inside or out," he grunted, "one way or t'other. But this way's better."

He hadn't scared me before, but the sheer strength of that hand altered things a little. And the teeth. Urgently I looked around; the street was empty, the light fading from the sky. From the occluded moon the shadows of the vast Victorian buildings poured down into the narrow way like pools of ink, dark, heavy, impassable. But one of them, above its crumbling ornament, cast a shadow tracery like a gigantic web, and my heart pounded harder at the sight of it. Then the man was looming over me, his white hair falling forward over his face, and his face swelling with it, growing longer, narrower. His lips curled back and blackened, a stench of breath rolled over me and hot slaver fell on my face. The hands that lifted were fingerless, featureless mitts—until black claws burst out between the coarse white fur. Then the moon sailed out into a wide gulf in the clouds. Eyes, narrowed and darkened, glittered above me with hotly vicious rage. The largest living land carnivore, I knew, could have looked a tyrannosaur in the eye; he glared down on me from around eleven feet, an adult male polar bear.

But I had seen the shadowlace, the mastheads of great square-riggers that docked here, scoring the sky. And as the moon crossed it, without any visible change or shift, the gulf in the clouds became, for an instant, that window

opening upon wider seas, the glittering steel blue of the
cloud archipelago. A wild joy overtook me at the sight of
it, the infinite road I'd sailed so often. I laughed in the
creature's face, and thrust out my hands; I expected a crash
of glass, but instead came the faint whirr of an electric
window wind. I was getting better at this. Then, with a swift
spinning rush of air, the sword slapped down into my open
palm. As quickly as that I lashed out, pushing the creature
back across the battered dustbins by the door, and grabbed
him by the greasy fur that had been his sweater. I ran the
blade up under his jaw, where the slightest thrust would
send it up into his brain. "And the inlay's silver, in case
you're wondering. So one twitch too many and you'll never
taste another seal, friend. Now—where's the Tavern?"

There was an abrupt inflowing, and suddenly my fingers
were sunk in a coarse jersey once again. "Is it you that's
got the Spear?" gasped the big man, man once more.

"You're awfully inquisitive for somebody who's about to
have no head," I told him, and shook him by his sweater.
"What if I was? You thinking of claiming a fiver for spotting
me or something?"

"There's prices oot on yer bloody head!" he growled, trying to twist away. "You've got the smell o' it on you! I'm
no' taking you near ony mate o' mine!"

"Prices?" I demanded. "You mean, more than one? And
what mate? You mean Jyp? He's in port?"

His eyes were wide, and he was sweating. "Lissen, if it's
you stole that spear, what the hell use have ye for me? Or
Jyp? What've we ever done tae you?"

"I don't want to harm Jyp, you bloody fool!" I barked.
"I'm his friend! I want his help! And for some reason I can't
get through to the Tavern!"

"Are ye surprised? After yon rioting? The Wardens have
a' but built a bloody wall! You ken fine what could've spilled
over into here wi' the Children loose!"

"I do, Paddington, I do," I murmured, and backed off,
letting him stand up. "I saw some of it. The Wardens, eh?

But we're already over the boundaries, or you couldn't have changed and I couldn't have called my sword. So, you can guide me from here, can't you? Get in the car!"

"If you've got the Spear," he repeated, shaking his head. "There's no barrier could stand against that . . . "

"It's not that simple." I flung open the door. "Get in."

The big man was shaking like a leaf, but he didn't move. Deliberately I tossed the sword onto the back seat. He started as if I'd kicked him, and shook his head wonderingly. And then, mistrustfully, he opened the driver's door and clambered in. "Jist who are you?" he demanded. "You're not like any sorceror I ever met."

"Top marks, Paddington. I'm not. Now—which way?"

The way there had never seemed so long or so winding as it did tonight. Through the old docklands we crawled, afraid of missing a turning, dwarfed by the gloomy bulk of the warehouses around us, stone ghosts of a vanished empire of commerce—vanished, that is, within the Core. In everyday ordinary streets they were more than half of them empty, eyeless shells with windows boarded or broken, grass growing between the crumbling bricks. In places they were demolished, their places taken by rusty corrugated-iron sheds, half-empty industrial developments, timber yards and small grubby engineering shops, or simply vacant lots where the grass and the fireweed blew. But around and behind those streets, in their shadow, older thoroughfares still ran, and tall buildings filled with strange merchandise from every corner of the Spiral, for sale to stranger places still; and above their roof-tops towered the webbed rigging of the tall ships that bore it. We passed a mule train, laden with heavy sacks, led by men with hawk-nosed impassive faces, and it was only then that I began to trust my ursine navigator. The men carried bows, and they glanced around suspiciously at us. We passed a strange silent truck, gleaming in white and gold, that came rolling smoothly down one main road on two black spheres, apparently unattached. The big man and I exchanged glances; even aspects of the far future could be reached along the Spiral, for those who were clever enough to navigate there. But it wasn't that popular, the trade being low and the culture shock immense. And on the pavement outside one warehouse, hooded crouching figures were gesticulating over piles of sacks that twitched. I accelerated past there, and the big man nodded.

"Spooky," he said succinctly.

I might have pointed out, when I was new to this game, that the same could be said of him; but I'd already called him Paddington, and tact is something you learn early. Or never.

"Turn left down here," he said, and where a minute before I'd noticed only a wall there was a narrow lane. And at its end, glowing against the night, mirrored in glistening puddles, were the warm red-curtained windows of the Illyrian Tavern.

"You left your drink," I told him, as I swung the car across the junction, and onto the stoneflagged court at the side of the Tavern. "I'll buy you another."

"I thank you," he said. "But if ye'll but let me out, I'll be on my way. No insult tae you, for I see you're something of a leader of men; but I want nothing of yours, or that clings about you. I smell danger in the being with you. And so may Jyp; but that's for himself to say." He clambered out, tossed his white head and sniffed the air. "You're expected," he grunted, turned and lumbered off into the night.

That didn't altogether surprise me. But even here I hesitated, under the familiar sign that seemed to show a different set of languages every time, all of them gloriously misspelt and unidiomatic. I'd brought danger on my friends often enough, but never so consciously as now. Still, there was no help for it; I had to have their advice. I pushed upon the door, and the familiar waft of spice and beer, strong pickles, woodsmoke and odors less familiar wafted out around me, the low buzz of voices, mostly human but not quite all. It carried with it the memories of kindness and, more, of belonging. I shut out the world behind me, and went down the steps. And at the foot Katjka was waiting.

She draped her arms around my neck, and I wrapped mine around her. It wasn't at all hard to be fond of Katjka, though she could be disconcerting and just occasionally a lot more than that—and though the position made it fairly obvious that, as usual, she hadn't washed quite recently enough. It wasn't in her cultural background, whereas cheap rosewater apparently was, in quantity. She was dressed, also as usual, in one of her peasantish dirndl outfits, if you can imagine the kind of peasant who hangs around under lamp-posts and leans low over bars, somewhere between a milkmaid and Lili Marlene. But tonight there was nothing of her usual sardonic come-on; the wide, innocent gray eyes that were the best of her were troubled, with dark smudges beneath, and the cynical furrows that flanked her mouth were deeper somehow. I bent down and kissed her, and noticed her lips were badly bitten.

"I am glad you are ssafe, Sstefan," she murmured, transforming my name with her sibilant accent. "Sso nearly you were not, asstray in all that. But you did well, sso well!"

"Last night, you mean? You know about that?"

She gave me another highly pneumatic squeeze. "I know, some at any rate, though there is much I do not understand—that bitch who is trying to kill you, for one. But ah, I'm proud of you, proud!" She followed up the squeeze with a wriggle that did terrible things to my self-control, and drew me down into the warm embrace of the tavern's main room. Its customers mostly preferred the privacy of shadow and soft speech, so it was hard to tell how many there were; but today it had a curiously empty, quiet feeling about it. "Come, Master Pylot is here, he must hear from you all about your heroicss!"

"Yes, but how do you know? You weren't . . . keeping an eye on me?"

She laughed, "Would that I could, always! It might while away the long days here—sso long, sso very long! But it would be too much a strain. Besides," she gave me a side-long look, "I sshock easily. This . . . " She shrugged. "This was close at hand, a violence in the Sspiral; that I was bound to esscry by all the means I have. And in doing sso I found many things—and one of them was you."

I stirred uncomfortably. "Making a bloody fool of myself. Trying to stem a flood. Bossing everyone about—"

"Beating ssome sense into their thick skullss!" she spat. "Ssomebody musst lead. I know you, I love you, my Sstefan, but I would not have thought it of you, you who have sstood on a great threshold sso long, never quite sstepping over. Something happens, something grows within you, at lasst. Those times, they called for one who would stand against the flood, who would become a leader of men. And you came forth."

I thought of witches, and scratched my head. "I didn't do much good. It was a God-awful mess—"

"Ssome is better than none!" she snapped, eyes hooding. "Believe me! You used your head, you saw what was afoot, you cut the heart out of it where you could, both in your own time and in the sshadow—and where it was not sso clear, you let it be. Without you that night's work would have been worse—so much, sso much worse! As I feared it would; for already I was uneasy. Ssomething has happened, Sstefan, something you would not know of, but it is ssomething awful, terrible. Something that has not happened in all the days of my being here, and they are very many. We were expecting trouble."

"Which translated," drawled a quiet voice from the shadowy stall near the open fire, "means I was lookin' for the first ship out. Dammit, I'm just in off the Ultima Thule run with a cargo of fire-amber and rhino furs and icicles in parts personal! All I want's a quiet spell and my feet warming, and suddenly here's all Hell breaks loose." Jyp snorted uneasily, and levered his spare frame up to greet me. "Literally, just about. And now look what the wind blew in!"

"It nearly didn't!" I told him, when we'd exchanged the usual backpounding and ritual insults. "Blow me in, I mean. Is it the Wardens, or what? There was hardly a road open!"

Jyp nodded. "Me, I'd've been just as happy to see you back home and out of all this. Still, ol' Sir was a good safe guide, nobody'd bother you with him on board. Glad to see you got on okay."

"The preliminaries were a bit rough, but—*Sir*?"

"Well, just what'd you call a seven-foot guy who—"

"—can turn into a polar bear? Right. But listen, what is all this? What's been happening?"

Jyp sucked his breath between his teeth, obviously very hesitant. He never liked drawing me into the darker affairs of the Spiral, not since he'd accidentally done so on our first meeting and almost got me killed several times over. "Better let that ride awhile. Not the kind of thing you get gabby about, unless you have to. But I can tell you, I'm just hitchin' up my pants ready to sling my hook for quieter climes when Kat here shows me you're right in the thick of it—and I figure that sure as hell you'll be panting up here next morning, so I stick around. Meanwhile everyone else'll have the same hunch, and the devil a berth I'll ever raise, not so much as a fo'c'sle flop on a tin-tray coaster. Things I do for my friends!"

I chuckled. "You know damn well there's hardly a skipper on the Spiral who wouldn't cheerfully trade in his soul, his wife or half his cargo to have you as his sailing-master. But don't think I don't appreciate the thought; I've a lot to tell, more to ask. So why don't we—*Myrko*!"

The landlord, face agleam like an appreciative toad, came barreling out of the darkness, bearing a tray laden with beer steins, *tujica* flasks and bowls of fierce pickled vegetables. "*Daj, daj, panye* Stefan, they tell me you is comink! And I ssay trouble, trouble, *bielzhaje* trouble—hah? Pulls you like lodestone. So I pulls the beer. Skies may fall, spearss be stolen, but beer—that you can trust! Hah!"

"Stolen—*what* was that?"

But he just bustled about the table and wouldn't be drawn; which was unusual. And under the patter he was looking more serious than usual, too. I began to press Katjka, but she pushed me down into Myrko's cushion-draped settles, put my feet up before the fireplace with its crackling logs, and flopped herself down between us.

"It's not sso often I get ssandwiched between two such bravos," she smirked, stretching and writhing like a cat in the fireglow. Then abruptly her mood changed again; her eyes grew hooded and cold. "Sso now—tell of last night!"

"It goes back longer than that," I said. "I was literally just home—I'd been to Germany, for the C-Tran—"

Katjka sat bolt upright, and rounded on me. *"Germany?"*

Jyp put his hand over his eyes. "Oh, Lord," he said quietly; and Jyp had had a religious upbringing. "Say it ain't so . . ."

"You'd better hear it," I said. "From the top . . ."

They listened; and as they listened I felt Katjka's body stiffen against mine, and her breath go faster, shallower, as if she was living every minute of it with me, that mad race across cloud-driven heights, its crazy aftermath, the vision of the city and my terrible homecoming. Jyp stared moodily past his outstretched feet, into the fitful patterns of the fire, and never interrupted; but at the end he leaned forward sharply, shivering, and tossed two big logs into the grate.

"Figures," was all he said at first. Katjka said nothing, only held on hard to my arm, as if striving to weigh it down. But both their faces betrayed their feelings—pale, stricken, appalled.

"What figures, Jyp?" I asked patiently.

"Clouds. Mountains. Both fractal forms, kind of similar progressions. Make the transition easier." He watched the ceaseless shaping and unshaping in the flames as if it meant something to him, and perhaps it did, for he could draw meaning from the flux and flicker of space and time along the Spiral itself, and steer a true course between them. After a while he added, "That town . . . how'd you feel there?"

"You mean, apart from hunted? I . . . I liked it. I think I'd have been drawn to it even without Le Stryge's 'fluence or whatever it was he put on me."

"A *geass*," snorted Katjka. "A brutal thing to wrench at mind and heart."

"Kind of a subtle one, to work so directly and still not tip off the poor guy caught up in it. Stryge's been learning himself some new tricks, it sounds. And you don't even know what the damn place is called? Then I'll tell you. It's Heilenberg."

"Heidelberg?"

Jyp's face twisted. "Heilenberg. And I wish I had a nickel for all the guys who've spent half their lives struggling to find that little town that you just landed and waltzed so calmly into, that's all. It's—what'd be the word?—one of the most powerful places on the Spiral. No, power-filled, that'd maybe come a tad nearer."

"Numinous?" I suggested.

"Yeah. Wish I had your schooling. Numinous it is—and it's one of the most dangerous, too."

"As you say." I sighed. "It figures."

"Yeah. Kind of goes together. See, it's like this. You know the Spiral well enough by now, you know how places have their shadows . . . "

I nodded. Long shadows, like those the fire threw across the stone-flagged hearth; thrown out of the Core into the Spiral, out of time into timelessness. Blending and uniting the changing natures of a place to embody its character. Everywhere men have lived—and more . . .

"Well, like you might expect, whole nations cast those shadows too—only kind of broader, enveloping the others. That's what we ran into back in Jawa. But whole continents, now, groups of nations, they do as well. Only they're less material, sort of misty; but there's almost always some kind of focus, a center, a place that embodies their spirit, their history, all that and more. All that's truest about them, what some folk'd call culture or civilization, but that don't more than half cover it. Heilenberg, now, you could call it the heart of Europe, of European civilization and everything gives it its inner life and strength. That's why you felt right at home."

Even now the rightness of it was startling; but I shook my head. "In Germany? The heart of Europe? I can see some problems with that."

Jyp had sailed in two world wars. He laughed. "We're talking history here, feller, *real* history, from the Old Stone Age onward, or older. Common history—enmities, alliances, tyrannies, they're submerged, they're just ripples in the stream. Even in recent history you could have a bigger beef with France, maybe Holland and Spain too, but that's nothing, that's irrelevant. I mean, look at you—your grandpa fought the Nazis, but you speak German, French, Lord knows how many other tongues, you come and go there as you like. And that's just one generation on—how about a hundred? Another thousand? It's a whole wider view, friend. You'd be at home there; so'd Kat, though she's from a side of Europe that's more of the Spiral than the Core. Even me, though I'm a Midwest boy, 'cause that's where my folks came from. Though we've got a center too; but it's different, its foundations not so deep-dug—not yet. It hasn't got what yours has at its heart. There's a mighty power dwells there in Heilenberg, Steve—a great force, from the outer reaches of the Spiral."

A fearful chill ran in my veins. That great demi-cathedral rose again in my mind, dark and haunted, that sense of presence. "Like that *dupiah* thing, you mean? Like Haiti and the Invisibles? Or the Balinese spirits, or Ape?"

Jyp pondered. "Up to a point, maybe. It's an intelligence, it's only part material—but, Lord, you couldn't measure them against it, any of them."

"Not even Ape?" I grinned. "He was pretty hot stuff. Wish I could set him on Le Stryge."

Jyp, unusually, didn't match the grin. "You better believe it, Steve. This—it's not just stronger, it's . . . vaster. A whole order. And more, it's . . . " He flailed the air with his hand. "It's less rooted in human things, less able to come and go in our world. Less easy to understand. See, Ape, the Barong, even that little creep Don Petro, after a fashion— they were still a whole heap human, in their ways. They'd grown beyond it, but they could still take their old shape, walk and talk and eat and fight and—well, one or two other things, huh? Like the Rangda lady, the way you told it me, huh?"

He grinned; I shriveled; Katjka sniffed, and ran her fingers along the inside of my thigh. "But this," Jyp shook his head, "it don't interact like that, I guess it can't. And what makes it tick is a sight harder to sort out. Mind you, I do hear it was a human mind once, maybe; one that went reaching out further and further along the Spiral, always out toward the Rim." He brooded, while the fire danced. "That could be."

"Like Mall, you mean?"

"A ways. You've seen her in action; you know a little. She's more already than one material body can rightly contain. But this, it's gone a lot further than her, than the Ape, than 'most anything else I ever heard of. Anything got that far, however human it was to start with, it'd be bound to be—changed. Out there space and time, they become more and more one. Things you and I'd call certain, solid, they get less and less fixed, less material; things that're just abstracts here, they take on a real existence, become clearer, more defined, closer to absolutes. *The* Absolute."

"You told me about that, once. And this—thing? It's been there?"

He brooded. "So they say. And come back, to take a hand in the world it left. And the shape it's taken—well, I've never been to that city, I've never seen it. But there's no mistaking that description of yours, that cathedral-hall, for sure. And what it held. Though there was something a mite odd there."

I shivered. "Odd? Christ, no wonder that place was so spooky! I wish I'd smashed that bloody stone—"

"No, Stefan!" murmured Katjka, sounding shocked. "To take a hand, *daj*—but a helping one!" She sighed. "That is how it usually workss out, anyway."

Jyp riffled back his red hair. "Sure. It's a power for good, this, Steve—in the long run, anyhow. Always has been, so I hear. You know it's shifted around, that city? And changed its whole look. Always to places where Europe's identity's been threatened, somehow; always to the borders, always where the dark's creeping in. Nowadays that's somewhere around the fringes of Germany and Eastern Europe, the old Russkie empire; but it's been other places. Last war they said it'd turned up around a corner in south England somewhere. A long while back, the Middle Ages, it must've been, when the Moorish caliphates were boilin' over into Europe from Spain—it stood on the northern slopes of the Pyrenees. It was called Montsalvat back then."

I sat bolt upright. "Now wait a minute . . . " Even I'd heard that name, though I couldn't quite put my finger on the context.

"Yeah," nodded Jyp. "Back in those days the power it sheltered was called the Sangraal, or just Graal. It came to be known as the Holy Grail."

It was just as well I was between mouthfuls of beer. The breath stuck in my throat, and going by Jyp's expression I probably looked like a bullfrog about to burst.

"Bloody *hell*!" I exploded, when I could. "You mean you're telling me that this is—I mean I don't know much about the legend, but I had this storybook—that great lump of stone, you're telling me that was supposed to be the cup Jesus drank from at the Last Supper? That they caught His blood in afterwards? And the Spear was what a Roman soldier—a *blind* Roman soldier? I always thought that one was a laugh—wounded him with? Come on, Jyp! I've run into some pretty weird things on the Spiral, but *this*?"

"Hold hard, hold yer hosses!" drawled Jyp, with wry amusement. "No call to go gettin' all het up with your *ay*-gnostics, you goddamn heathen! The Grail tale's no part of the Scriptures, that's for sure. Me, I was brought up strict, you can take my word on that. It's not part of the Faith. It's a legend about it. See the difference? It's one of those archetype things, like the rest of the Spiral. 'Cause all kinds of folks believed it was a relic of Christ, that's the shape it has for them. But the Graal's older than that legend. Much older. Even in the earliest Christian versions of the tale there wasn't any Christian thing about it. It was a stone, a miracle-stone, like one of those Greek horn things—you know!"

"A horn of plenty? A cornucopia?"

"Right, right! That's how they saw it. It'd been a pagan archetype, see, an ancient thing folks used to worship, like the Golden Fleece. But the Graal, it went back further still. Right back beyond the henges and the standing stones, the dolmens and the menhirs and the great barrow-graves, deep into the depths of the Age of Stone and a cult that spread across savage Europe in the wake of the Great Ice retreating. What the archaeologists call the cup-and-ring stones, from the way they're marked; but the Spear that was the other half of the rite, always tipped with flint or obsidian— that's something the double-domes haven't cottoned onto. The Graal was the center of that cult, their great original. And you—don't ask me why or how, but that's the way you saw it, godless heathen type that you are!"

"Spear and cup?" I protested. "For—those are just symbols, Jyp. Pretty obvious ones!"

Katjka arched her eyebrows. "You have something against them, maybe? That iss not the Sstefan I know and love!"

Jyp chuckled. "Okay, they're symbols. Crude ones,

maybe, by our lights, but potent. Fertility really meant
something then, remember. And like a heap of other symbols, Christianity kind of picked them up along the way as
it spread. You know the strange thing? They stayed the
same; they fitted in real neatly."

"As if," said Katjka soberly, "as if they had been designed
sso. As if it had been intended, all along."

Jyp inclined his head. "Could be. Could easily be. For
one thing's sure, Steve, the Graal's got a daunting power,
and a purpose."

"Jyp, it's just a *thing*, a lump of stone with a spear across
it, and some sort of cloth. It couldn't move, couldn't see or
hear—"

I stopped short as it came back to me all of a rush, the
terrible sense of watchfulness that filled that hall. "Okay!
Maybe it has got senses of some kind—but how does it *do*
anything?"

Jyp shrugged. "The way I hear it is, the stone or the
chalice, the Spear, they're only this thing's kind of sheet
anchors in the material world, channels for its power.
That's why it created that city around it, to give it followers
to work through. The Graal itself never stirs, just draws
them in and rules through their leaders—a king or a
queen, the stories say. Special folk, anyhow, awesome folk,
in harmony with the Graal, sharing its thoughts and its
power. Some followers it keeps around, so there's always a
living community, others—knights or soldiers, I guess
you'd call 'em—it sends back out into the world. The rul-
ers, too, sometimes; not just throughout the Spiral, either,
but deep into the Core, with the power of the Graal behind
them, to help the downtrodden, and pursue the wicked, and
champion good causes in secret."

He took a deep draft of his beer, and chased it down with
a phial of plum brandy. "So that's what Le Stryge sent you
up against. Nice of him, huh? It's a miracle to me you're
still here. Might take an even bigger miracle to keep you
that way. Sonuvabitch's getting ambitious in his old age."

"But why? What on earth could the old bastard hope to gain?"

"Maybe much," put in Katjka somberly. "The Graal is not the only ssuch earthly power. There are otherss, darker ones, and they sstand in deadly opposition to it. Maybe the *Sstregoica* is in bond with one. Maybe he hopes himself to become one. I know ssomething of their long wars with the Graal, and what they would plan sshould it ever fall into their hands. Could they break it, or but imprison it, then that would at least remove the Graal's influence from the world. Should they bend it to their will—what then? *Myne Stefan*, I greet no dawn gladly. But even if the fires must first consume me, that one I pray I never ssee. In their hands that greatness might be turned to terrible ill."

She spat a mouthful of *tujica* into the fire. It sizzled momentarily into eerie blue flame.

"Ssomehow, *Stefan*—and how, it is beyond me to imagine—you have gone and sstolen half this ancient power. Half, perhaps, of its very being."

Chapter 6

I almost laughed. I wanted to—but all too clearly I saw a parade of faces, the horrified soldiers and townsfolk, the uneasy blend of greed and terror under Stryge's acerbic mask, the horror of the consuming fire. The words came out as an idiotic bleat. "But—"

It wasn't doubt, it was protest, against the unfair fate that had dumped me down headfirst into this mess. "But if it's so bloody all-powerful, this thing, what about me? How on earth did I manage to just rush in there and run off with it?"

"It is not omnipotent, this Graal," mused Katjka. "I have heard it said the world wars of the old century dealt it a terrible blow, even to causing the death of its last king. I know that it has become more withdrawn ssince then, perhapss weaker."

Something clicked. "I could believe that," I said. "From all you've told me, that city ought to reflect at least something of modern Europe—but it doesn't. Not a trace. It's stuck firmly in the pre-World War I era. Even so, weaker

133

or not, the Spear blasted that ogre-creature on the spot neatly enough—why not me?"

"Your very innocence, maybe," suggested Katjka. "The Graal would ssense it, and hesitate to hurt a true man."

Jyp's mouth twisted. "Even at the cost of being stolen? I don't buy that one, Kat."

Again I felt that strange little thrill of understanding. "And yet Le Stryge seemed to expect it!" I said. "Expect something, anyhow. Or why'd he go to so much trouble choosing me as his instrument at all?"

"We-ell . . . " Jyp writhed in an unaccustomed torment of tact. "Remember he's not seen you since you were a lot younger. Could be he thought you were kind of—well, steerable. He sure didn't expect you'd just shake off his lousy compulsion the moment you became aware of it."

"No more would I," said Katjka, still thoughtful.

I clutched at my forehead. "Look," I said, as calmly as I could. "I suppose I've got to believe all this, but knowing it isn't going to get me much further. The Spear, well, that should be safe enough for now. Even I don't know where it is at this moment, not exactly. I should be able to get a message through to this city somehow, shouldn't I? So at least they won't shoot me on sight when I try to return it?"

Jyp whistled softly. "Ordinarily that's a main hard place to find. But now, you can bet the knights'll be looking high and low, scouring the Spiral. I can get messages left where they'll surely find them—with Myrko here, for one."

"Okay," I said. "That'll deal with the immediate problem. They can have the bloody thing back any time they want, with pink ribbon around it for all I care. What's worrying me a lot more is, how is my own company tied up in all this, and C-Tran? What's Lutz's stake? He tried to murder me, though I can't prove it. If he'd succeeded, Le Stryge wouldn't have been able to use me—so are they allies, or rivals, or what? Don't tell me there's more than one power hanging around over my head. I'd enough of that out East! If Lutz is planning to misuse C-Tran somehow, I'm the only

one with enough clout to stop him. I've got to find out!
Can you help me there?"

Jyp looked at Katjka; Katjka gave me one of her slow
smiles. Her hand was already over the table, riffling down
the pack of cards she always seemed to carry. Where exactly,
I'd never found out; but as she guided my hand palm down
onto them, they felt warm and soft as skin. They flew in
her long fingers, shuffled and dealt in one sweeping action.
"Thiss time you turn one over, I the next," she said—or
whispered, almost, for very suddenly the atmosphere had
changed, and the crackle of the fire had become harder,
almost menacing, reminding me of those other larger fires.
"The firsst!"

I chose one at random, flipped it. Ten of Spades, like a
thicket of black spearheads; Katjka nodded somberly, and
slid its neighbor over. A court card; I peered at it, appre-
hensively. I'd seen some strange faces on this pack before.
Spades again—the Knave, thickset and bullnecked like
most card figures, clean-shaven, smirking, with its eyes
touched in a bright impenetrable blue that reminded me of
. . .

Katjka nodded as I turned it back hastily. "Your friend
Lutz. He is the Knave—but who the King? Turn another
card!"

More slowly now I reached for one at the end. Hearts, a
seven, and Katjka smiled, and turned over the next. Ace of
Clubs, with nothing strange about it except the way the
flames danced in reflection on its glossy face. Katjka's face
turned stony, and she nodded me to another card. My fingers had trouble grasping it, and kept slipping, but when I
turned it, it was another court card. The King of Hearts;
but there was nothing odd about it at all, although it did
look less stuffed and more alive than the usual card face,
handsome even. Katjka stared, and reached for its neighbor—Queen of Hearts, with a face half-shadowed in the
uncertain light.

"*Agnece Bozji!*" she breathed. "Stefan, this is very

strange, but it is not all bad. You have strong enemies, the *vojevode* Lutz among them—and yes, he plans something, something very great. But the rest of this . . . " She shook her head. "It is good. How good, I . . . cannot say. A chance, not a certainty, therefore it cannot be more definite. About the dark, that is definite. Lutz works with Stryge, of that I am sure, for he is not himself the King. But maybe Stryge is not either; there is a power cloaking him I cannot penetrate. And Lutz has ambitions of his own, he practices rites, gathers dark forces about him—probably how he and Stryge found one another in the firsst place. As you thought, it was something very terrible that Lutz planned for that night."

"What . . . you mean a Black Mass, something·like that?"

Jyp chuckled, which was slightly unexpected. Katjka glared at him. "Light man! He does not take these thingss sseriously enough. Stefan, the Black Mass is largely the invention of fanatical priests and inquisitors, no worse than ssome of their own fiendish tortures save for the blasphemy. But blasphemy, however great, however ugly, conveys no power in itself. It is the ill intent that gives the rite its power, and the evil deed, the sacrifice, the staging of it all in a formal guise; many such rites embody that, in many faiths. Even witch-burning itsself was often so intended, the true demon-worshippers hidden among the persecutors, cloaked in a robe of smiling ssanctity."

I looked at her. "I could believe that, after what I saw last night—or whenever it was."

"And yet witches there are," said Katjka very softly; and for an instant, as she gathered in the cards once again, the fire blazed up with a hungry crackle behind her strong profile. "*Ej daj multito*, there are indeed . . . "

One card fluttered down onto her lap from the bottom of this pack. I scooped it up and handed it to her. Automatically she took it—and then looked at it with sudden intensity, and turned it over.

I wasn't looking at it; I was looking at her, for the most

extraordinary course of feelings chased their way across her face. But all in an instant it set like flint, her lips thinning and whitened, the deep lines from nose to mouth very intense, her eyes gleaming like a fox's. Jyp sat up, too, reached across and turned the card to face us. It was the Ace of Spades—only, as I watched, the dancing shadows seemed to show me the outline of Clubs looming behind it, dark and empty as a half-hidden pit.

"What the hell—" I began.

Katjka smiled, taut-lipped, and slid the card back into her pack. "Don't worry, Stefan. Your charm was over, it can tell you no more. That card was no part of it, not for you. Be thankful!"

"Believe me, I am. So you can't tell me just what it was Lutz was up to? What this rite of his was all about?"

"I would need to know more of it, that rite, its settings, its language, its symbols. I can tell you he was keeping tryst with ssomething, forging or reaffirming some link with forces from Outsside. From near the Rim, I guess; for there is great power in play."

"Another near-absolute, you mean? Like the Graal?"

"Unlike. Even a slight step beyond the Core good and bad become more disstinct. You have felt it yourself, the turmoil it sets within uss, pulled this way and that by our mingled natures. The farther out one ventures, the sstronger each grows, less dilute; the weaker element iss purged, by time and circumsstance, till only the fine hot metal remains, radiant and sstrong. Good, in the Graal; in the one the *vojevode* seeks . . . other. There are many such powerss, some never yet concerned with this corner of the Core. But many turn their gaze this way; which is this I cannot tell you. Not without knowing more of the rite."

"Well, I can hardly ask Lutz for a free demo." I shivered—then snapped my fingers. "That room—the floor! It was inlaid, marble with what looked like precious metals; it must have cost a fortune. All kinds of patterns and characters, that sort of mumbo-jumbo! None of them looked accidental, either. Suppose you'd photos of those, would they tell you anything?"

"They might," she said, quite soberly. "Or they might not. It might not matter, when the getting of them is suicidal. If there is anything of value there, be ssure it will be guarded."

"By Lutz's security agency? I could get past them if I had to, I think."

"By them as well, no doubt," she said sourly. "They are no great peril, they would only kill you. But otherwise— no. It is too great a risk, just for photographs that might not come out, or show the last essential detail. Better that I see with my own eyes."

"No, Katjka!" I protested, appalled. Jyp sat up so sharply he all but overturned his stein. "You've no idea, I couldn't take you into foul places like that—"

"I might know more of them than you guess."

"Hey now!" barked Jyp, sounding as horrified as I felt. "Belay that, for a start! That's not for you, girl, you know that's well as I do! Forgotten just what this could be—what it could lead to? Just what the hell it is you're risking? Look, Steve don't even know the half of it and you've gotten him half-crazy worryin' 'bout you already! You stay right here in this tavern, and that's an order! While we go fetch up Mall."

She nodded calmly. "That we sshould do, yes, for she is powerful in these matters. But even sso, I will come with you none the less."

"Look!" I protested. "Both of you, what's this we? One man—I know this agency, I know their alarms, we've got them all over C-Tran. And I can remember the way well enough. I could just slip into the house and slip out again. Just me. Nobody'd ever know I'd been there."

"Ssome might. Though it might be no body."

Jyp pounded his fist on the table. "Damn! God damn! No!"

"Katjka, look!" I put in desperately. "He means it. I mean

it. This is my fight, if anything ever was! I don't want to risk a friend."

Katjka, calm as a slightly used madonna, took my face between her hands. "What are friends for? And are you sso sure thiss fight is yours alone? But be sure of one thing, Sstefan, without me you will accomplish nothing. To whom elsse will you take the pictures? Who elsse dare you trusst? And suppose I saw something in them that required my presence, what then? You might make it into that place once, never twice. You get only thiss one chance."

I looked to Jyp, but this time he said nothing. "And there is more," she said, her voice remote and cold. "I will have one advantage, where otherss might have none. If what I ssuspect is true, the evil that might threaten you has already touched me. I will have power againsst it that you never could, not even your friend that great mare, sshe with her inner flame." She slid easily out from between us. "I will go to get my coat, and some other things."

"Satisfied?" growled Jyp, as she vanished into the darkness.

I snarled right back. "Come off it, Jyp. You can't stop her any more than I can stop you. She's got us, and you know it."

"Yeah, suppose I do. But—ah, the hell with it. We're going in this whirlybird of yours?" That thought seemed to cheer him up a little. "Okay, we'll stop off for Mall *en route*, I'll guide you in."

"Great. We can leave whenever. But, listen, these Wardens of yours, shouldn't I see they get told about all this?"

"You already have. Katjka's one; and what she learns goes to the rest."

"*What?*"

"Not something she advertises. A privilege and a penance both, tied to this place and this tavern for year after year, to set a balance straight. Using her powers to balance some of the evils she did with them, and in the getting them—and from all I've heard that was quite a heap. That's how it is with a lot of the Wardens—ol' Sir, for one, he's another. But he's free to move around, within limits. Katjka—well, you've taken her from here once, you saw what happened. Time, guilt, grief, loss, a double dose, all descending on her in one go. Oh, she can stand it, sure—for a while. But . . . " He looked around, then leaned over to me quickly as he heard her steps returning through the almost empty bar. "We've got to ride shotgun, look after her every inch of the way, you, me, Mall. She's risking worse than that, a whole lot worse, Steve. If I'd my druthers—"

"But you do not," she said quietly. Trenchcoat and beret made her look more like Lili M. than ever, though mercifully not the Dietrich version. "And the time for argument is done. Come!"

Jyp stood up jerkily. He wasn't the type to waste any more time on hopeless argument; but he drained his beer, and tipped the dregs into the fire. The logs sizzled and steamed. "Okay. Let's go get Mall."

As the tavern door shut softly behind us Katjka unobtrusively took my arm; and as we touched the lowest step she leaned on it. She reached the car without much effort, but she sank down into the deep back seat as if she'd run a mile. On the way out of town to the heliport Jyp reverted to his normal self, bouncing around in the car like an eight-year-old, one minute demanding I go faster, the next insisting I slow down to look at how some place or other had changed since last he'd passed that way. Katjka, though, I could see in my mirror. She let her head loll against the rest, eyes half shut, looking neither to left nor right till the harsh floodlights of the airport fell on her. She jerked her head away and raised a shadowing hand, but not till I'd seen the sudden deepening of lines, the hollow eyes, the seamed, papery skin stretched taut across her cheekbones. Not an old face, exactly; a young face wasted. I was glad when I could pull into the darker side lane that led to the heliport, here a stretch of the old original military airstrip still set among living fields. When I opened the car door for her she slid out as lithe as ever, and her face, as usual, didn't look a day past twenty-nine—assuming you could pick up that much experience so early. She lingered as we walked over to the little terminal, gulping down the wet grass-scented air in breaths that shook her whole body, and as the doors slid shut behind us she echoed their sigh.

What the security check made of us I can't imagine—especially Jyp, dressed in his usual black pea-jacket and sea gear, and twice as hyper at the prospect of a helicopter flight. Just as well we didn't have to bother with passports these days; his and Katjka's would have made interesting reading. But as before they knew me, and let us through easily enough, to the bays where surly late-shift mechanics were still running out and refueling. This late there was no problem about slots, and once a night flight was clear we were free to go. Katjka, after a startled oath at the noise of the engine, gave a tooth-gritting shriek as we lifted off and grabbed the back of my seat, then jammed the headphones I gave her hard over her ears and sat back sulkily. Jyp sat rigid in his seat, his long white teeth flashing in a grin—rather fixed, but definitely a grin. Even here, caged in this noisy trap of modern technology, I caught his excitement, something of the same exhilaration and exaltation of setting sail with him, when a breeze from beyond the sunrise bellied out the sails, and the bows dipped deep and lifted higher, high above the horizons of the Core, over the airs of the earth.

He tapped my arm, and pointed; I looked up, expecting to see the cloud archipelago open before us, as ever. But the gusty wind was rapidly scouring the sky clear to reveal a brilliant moon. Rags of low cloud shot by us like storm-shredded sails, and we scudded among them like a shark among a shoal of silver fish, flashing from moonlight to mist and back again by the minute, a wild disorienting ride. I sent the little machine swinging away westward, following Jyp's excited directions as best I could, and saw on the horizon, mottled by the racing clouds, the steely glitter of the open sea.

Apart from constantly trying to leap up in his seat and lean out of the window, Jyp seemed perfectly at home, though when he realized what the airspeed indicator read he turned slightly pale. Out toward the coast and beyond he directed me, navigating with the same casual confidence as when he steered ships, in an extraordinary series of twisting and turning vectors in and out of the clouds. They made no sense that I could see, but they must have left some cryptic squiggles on the coastal radar traces.

"You're sure you can find her?" I shouted into the intercom, eyeing my fuel gauges nervously.

He pointed. "She's only a week out, that-a-way. Can't miss 'em! From Zakynthos to Hyperborea via the Pillars of Herakles and Folkestone—that's where Mall left me word. Head north a point, maybe. Say, you got radar on this rattletrap?"

I had, but only for other air traffic. I brought her down as close to the water as I dared: over these featureless waves you really had to keep an eye on your artificial horizon, or you might find yourself angling down into them by mistake. The radar sweep showed up a surprising number of images, some of them probably ghosting from the wavecrests; but Jyp took only a second to choose one. "Try that," he said, and it never occurred to me to doubt him. Not, at least, until we actually made visual contact with the trace. At first I felt sure it was the back of a whale, low, dark, gleaming wetly in the moonlight; then, as we banked down toward it, even lower now, it looked disturbingly like some weird centipedal sea monster, crawling its way across the shining surface with a host of slender legs wiggling under its carapace.

"Jyp, what the hell?" I shouted into the intercom. "What is it, one of those jasconey things?" He'd told me horror stories about them, the island beasts on whose broad backs mariners might land and build a fire, only to be dragged down as they submerged. Totally mythical, of course, only this was the Spiral.

"Take her in and have a look!" he yelled back. "Oughta be able to land on that, eh?"

I swallowed, and swung the 'copter around. "You've got to be joking!" But I eased back the stick, and as we sank down toward the thing, very gingerly, I saw that the carapace was flat, completely. It was a deck, wide and level, without rails or gunwales, so it did look a lot like an undersized aircraft carrier. But it was polished planking, that deck, rich dark wood; the whole thing was wood. It knifed across the waves with a faint fluid jerkiness that gave it that look of being alive, not artificial, like a pulse. Not legs, oars, three banks of them, moving with easy strength and flawless co-ordination. The thing was a gigantic trireme.

Jyp was still excitedly motioning me down. None of the oaths I could come up with felt adequate, so I bit my lip and concentrated grimly on bringing us alongside, matching speed and sidling in. As we got close enough to be heard below decks the rowing seemed to falter slightly, and no wonder: oars tangled, and one snapped like a twig.

"We're not going to be that popular!" I sang.

"Wouldn't fret about that!" Jyp called back. "Could be they'll feel a whole lot meaner shortly! You ever going to land or just hang around till the gas runs out?"

I groaned, and slipped the cyclic stick a fraction sideways, eased off the collective and fishtailed us in with the rotor. We hung, swinging slightly, above that deck—was it going to take the weight? As I was looking for some sign of a cross-member, Jyp huffed impatiently and unclicked his seatbelt, then slid back the door and swung himself out onto the skids and down, dropping lightly onto the deck frog-fashion, as if he'd been doing it all his life. He stamped hard, gave me the double thumbs up and backed off hurriedly with his hands over his head as I cut back the throttle and let the 'copter settle. The deck creaked alarmingly, but held. As Jyp straightened up, our welcoming committee appeared in the form of a short bald type in tunic and sandals who came barreling up out of a hatch, waving his hands. One of them had a bow in it.

"Βψγγερ οφφ!" he yelled, or words to that effect, and who could blame him? But he ignored my urgent wave, and the drooping rotors almost rendered him a great deal balder, from the neck up. As he hopped back, another figure came bounding up behind him, a full head taller—and a head much fuller, of long blond curls that streamed back like golden foam in the failing draft. The shoulders it bared were as broad as mine, but the figure was unmistakable in its feline grace; so was the heavy broadsword, and the golden belt it swung from, bouncing at the curve of a thigh. I piled out of my seat, ducking past the still slowing rotors, and ran to meet her.

The short man bounced into my way. This close he was impressively muscled, and he'd nocked an arrow on a bow that looked like a small tree trunk. "Γετ τηισ φαρτινγ ξλο-ξκτωορκ ηαρπχ οφφ μχ φψξκινγ δεξκ!" he commented, in his deep organ of a voice.

"Okay, okay," I said soothingly. Every heave of the deck made me nervous. "Look, there used to be one but it died, all right? I just want a word with your quartermaster here—"

"Γνεσσ τηε ωορδ I ωαντ)ιτη χοψ!" he objected, and made a significant gesture with the bow.

"Leave him, by your courtesy, *kyrios!*" called out a rich familiar voice. "These be old friends and true men, with brave tales to tell. They'd not descend so but at sorest need!"

The burly man looked me up and down with a disconcerting eye, as coldly intelligent as a squid's, and lowered his bow. I bowed politely, because that looked like his kind of thing, and stepped past, to meet another and equally disturbing gaze.

"Well met by loon's light, Master Stephen!" the tall woman said. "You are grown since last we met."

"Well met, Mistress Mall!" I echoed her, and seized the hands she stretched out to me. "Maybe I've just put on weight."

She smiled. "I talked not of the body. In your company that's perilous. You have been touched by something, I see, something that sets you afire."

I shivered. "That was the other guy. Mall—I feel one hell of a lot better just seeing you again—"

She drew back. "Nay, I'll have no bussing, sirrah, for here's no mast for you to go fleeing up after! 'Sides, these lads, if they once saw me permit such liberties then little peace I'd have thenceforth—we're among Greeks, remember?"

"True," observed Jyp. "Might make you safer, though, Steve . . . "

We ignored him. "God help any of them that tried to pinch your backside, angel. But as you said, we've come for a purpose—and I daren't leave the 'copter there long, in case it goes through the deck or slides off it. So here's what's happened . . . "

Mall listened, and her face grew grimmer. She contemplated me with something more than her usual tolerant affection. "Here's dark doings, and a blacker venture yet to amend them. The Graal! The Sangraal! Who dares fix their eye on such a summit? 'Tis too high even for that crabbed old conjuror Le Stryge, my word upon't. There's another behind him, and a greater by far—and such an one with such ambition must needs be dangerous, at whatever they essay! Stephen, my Stephen, it's a strange destiny that'd thus enmesh you." She was looking at me oddly now, very oddly indeed. "As well forbid the sea obey the moon as I to aid you, always—but here also's a peril wider still that must be stopped." She glanced at Jyp, and at Katjka, perched in the 'copter. "That deep one there, she thinks so, or she'd not be here. So be it!" She clapped a hand to her sword. "A minute to gather my dunnage, then I stand to your command!"

"Command? Mall, we need you to lead us!"

Her wide mouth twisted. "Nay, sirrah, I know my place. Your quartermaster at sea I'll be, on land your ancient, a strong right hand, but no commander save at direst need. You are a leader, my master, with all the strengths and foibles of the breed. In your paths I'll tread, willingly. But a moment, I pray you; I must make my peace with the master here. *O kyrios*, a word!"

Evidently the squat man understood English well enough, which made me wish I'd been more polite. As Mall talked to him his face darkened again, and he thumped his solid bowstave on the deck; but she insisted, and he grew more concerned. Finally he thumped the bow again, but gave a curt nod—to me, not her.

"Thanks, *o kyrios*," I told him. "We'll try and get her back to you as soon as we can." *If we can*. That was the unspoken condition, and I saw he knew it too.

He gave me that oddly regal nod again, and growled "Ξηαιρετε!"

"*Chairete, o kyrios!* Let's hope so, anyhow. Got your dunnage, Mall? Okay. Let's ride."

Mall turfed the light bag that held her few necessities behind the seat, then leaned back out and called, "*O Ithaca! I pray you, no more of your strayings against my return!*"

Ithaca, if that was his name or title, smiled sourly and raised his eyes to Heaven, as if she'd made something pretty ripe in bad-taste jokes, but waved a tolerant hand. Mall swung herself lithely up into the undersized back seat. Katjka, overwhelmed on all flanks, accepted the situation with a sour smile; Mall, of course, didn't mind a bit. I slid the door shut and waved the Greek skipper back as I started up. He didn't need telling; but as I gunned the collective and lifted us swinging from the deck, he stood staring after us, rubbing his bristly chin thoughtfully.

"Let's hope he be not inspired!" yelled Mall into her headset, as Jyp showed her how to use it. "Such a *helix-apteryx* device as this would be all the Argive loon requires!

Now, how is't you propose to slip into this sorceror's den of yours?"

"That," said Jyp grimly, "is the original sixty-four-thousand-dollar question."

"For a start," I whispered, lifting my head cautiously over the damp lip of the bank, "there are the guards. Heavies on the gate, and I don't doubt a couple of patrols in the grounds, with dogs—attack dogs."

"Don't light this place much, does he?" muttered Jyp, squinting at the blackness beyond the old fence as if to spy his way through it. The moon flooded the sky with blue, but the treeline beneath was solid black, like a cut-out silhouette. Nothing moved, and the least spark would stand out.

"Avoids light pollution—he's supposed to be red-hot on environmentals." The idea left an unpleasant taste. "But there's lighting there, he's got an automatic on-demand system along the drive, so he could just as easily have every inch of the grounds criss-crossed with floods, tracker spots, you name it. If I know Lutz, he has. You can bet there's some sort of contact wire on the fence, too—even electrified, maybe. Along the top, anyhow—he wouldn't want passing dogs setting it off all the time. And around the house walls there are lights, he had them on for the party."

"Plus a nifty alarm system," Jyp muttered. "And from what Kat says, something a whole lot nastier inside, for a cert. Tough crib. So how're we supposed to crack it?"

I took a deep breath. Katjka and I had done a lot of talking on the way here, and I had something like a plan worked out. Now I had to sound as if I believed it myself. "Well, my first idea was to con my way into the house, being who I am; it's just about the only place Lutz wouldn't want me killed! If he could help it, anyhow. From there I could fake it, get loose on some pretext, snatch a few photos—it wouldn't be too hard. But with Katjka, not to mention the rest of you . . . We'll have to go to my second idea: break in. Three stages: cross the grounds; get in the house; get into the room—"

"Four," interrupted Jyp. "Get our asses out again. Let's us not forget that. Okay, who's got the cloak of invisibility?"

"It might not be any good. The chances are, whatever Lutz has in the grounds, lights or alarms or whatever, they're activated by motion detectors—and the most practical outdoor kind is still infrared. Heat-activated, that is, Mall. Probably with imaging devices, so the security people can get an instant picture."

Mall shook her head. "Ruin for Diana's foresters and all stout fellows that live by the moon! What do we, cloak ourselves about?"

"Not exactly. Clothes won't stop heat radiating—but there are other ways. I'd planned to trace the cables with a metal detector and use a pipe freezer, but Katjka's got a better idea. If you can get us over that fence without touching the top—and quick."

Jyp looked at Mall, she at him. He groaned quietly. "Okay, strongest first. You, then Steve. Just don't tread on my ear this time, okay?"

He stood up, peered about warily, then sprinted lightly forward down the bank to the fence and ducked into the shadow of a great ash, his feet hardly crackling in the leaf-mold. He touched the fence gingerly, then grasped it, splayed his legs and hunched his head down. The moment he was ready Mall rose lithely to her feet, stepped back a pace or two, then with no more of a run-up sprang right from the lip of the bank onto Jyp's shoulders, and in the instant of landing bent her knees and shot straight upwards as if from a springboard. She rolled in mid-air, and caught an overhanging ash-branch as if it were a polished trapeze. The crash as it bent and swung under her weight sounded appallingly loud, but she dangled there quite calmly and let it settle. Somewhere, the other side of the grounds, a dog barked, but no others answered it, and it sank to silence. Mall swung herself easily up over the fence and shinned along onto the heavier branch next door, her weight bending it till it stooped low over Jyp's head. "I'd sooner you climbed, not jumped," came his hoarse whisper. "If it's okay with you."

I clambered from the bankside to his shoulders, my sword slapping at my calf, and straightening unsteadily up I caught the wiry hand reached down to me. It drew me up with little effort, to meet eyes that positively blazed with effort and excitement; and I was reminded that not all Mall's strength was of the body. Below us Katjka was already shinning up Jyp, which he proclaimed he enjoyed a lot more—"though I surely wish," he puffed, steadying her ankles on his shoulders, "that you'd left your fancy heels and brought your broomstick. Got her?"

Katjka joined us on the branch, which was creaking alarmingly. We helped her back to the trunk, then dangled down to where Jyp could just grasp our fingers. For such a lean man he was surprisingly heavy, but Mall took most of the weight. "We should really have left you," I wheezed, "as a pointman to help us back out—but somehow I don't think you'd have liked that, would you? Well, Katjka, it's your play now."

She nodded. "Lower me to the ground. Behind the tree, here." No alarms went off as she touched the mold lightly, then squatted scratching in the earth with a stick, singing an eerie little off-key dance rhythm as if to herself. Sounds pattered on the earth; faint wisps of steam arose; wings rustled suddenly in the branches around us, as if some sleeping small birds had been disturbed. Mall sucked her teeth and watched from above. At last Katjka looked up, and beckoned. "Come!" she whispered. "Come down to me, Stefan!"

It sounded weird, in that damp stillness; but I swung myself down by my hands, and dropped lightly to the earth. Her hand closed on my arm, and the sharp air stung my nostrils. "Sso? Do you feel it?"

The air was slightly acrid but it was also very cool, cold

even. Mall dropped lightly beside us and shivered, rubbing her arms hard before reaching up for Jyp. "A bastard winter's breath you've brought upon us, little spae-witch! I knew not you'd this much of the weather-lore about you!"

"*Nej*, I do not!" She sounded amused, and her whisper made her sibilances creepy as hell. "Thiss iss no crude breath of Boreas, be ssure of that!"

"You're telling me!" exclaimed Jyp, hopping about as much as he dared. "Lord, it's gettin' colder!"

"Cold enough to blind an eye that ssees heat?" inquired Katjka. "If not, it ssoon will be. Come, we must move!"

We were only too willing. Whatever she'd done, it was sucking the heat right out of our bones, and it was no illusion; it clung around us like mist as we moved cautiously out between the trees. But the slight haze seemed to be the result of the cold, not its cause. Only moving kept our blood circulating and our teeth from chattering—though they were ready to. I was unnerved enough anyway, but something right at my elbow was making it a whole lot worse, something I couldn't see. At the last tree we hesitated. The corner of the great house trimmed off the moonlight sharp as a razor, leaving a wide-open space of gray lawn to cross, with only a few bits of bush and topiary to duck behind. But Katjka strode out fearlessly, and the icy cold seemed to stir her skirts like a slow breeze. Mall plunged after her, with Jyp and me in her wake; we ran all the way to the first possible shelter, and ducked down, shivering.

No alarms; no stirring; nothing. We spared a second to draw lung-searing breaths, then, keeping together, we scuttled for the next shelter, a weirdly sculpted privet. As we dropped down behind it I saw, too late, a concealed plastic frontage at the base, and found myself staring straight into what was evidently a PIR heat scanner. A good one, too; but it didn't react. Jyp indicated the casing with a nervous finger. It had the faint rime you find in an overcooled freezer. We were just about to move again when suddenly

Mall, in the lead, thrust out a hand to stop us, and sniffed the air. "Dogs!" she hissed.

Jyp nudged her and pointed. Out ahead something was emerging from the shadow, a brace of sleek Rottweilers, dock-tailed and blunt-jawed, straining at their release harnesses as their handler looked alertly around. Mall slid her hand down to her sword; so did I. Jyp had a two-foot bolo blade, heavy enough to double as sword or cleaver, but it was his double-barreled pistol he reached for. I wrapped a protective arm about Katjka, but to my surprise she shook it off and motioned us forward. "But the dogs'll scent us any moment!" I whispered fiercely. Too fiercely; I saw the blunt heads lift, the teeth flash in the moonlight. The guard couldn't have heard me, but they could. Katjka just gave me an enigmatic smile, and stood up, still hidden. The cold became an icy breeze, swirling around us—

The dogs leaped in the air suddenly, both of them, and fell struggling and snapping at each other, tangling lead and harness. The startled handler barely snatched his hand away in time, and released the harness before the beasts could strangle themselves. Suddenly freed, the two huge dogs leaped up and bolted, haring away around the corner of the house with their handler running furiously behind. "Scared as cottontails!" breathed Jyp. "Or I'm a butternut squash!"

Mall sniffed again. "No more of the brutes near. Yet I'd look to find some roaming without let—"

"No," said Katjka. "They have ssome dogs, yes, for dissplay; but they could not let them run free, not here. Not if the things you fear are practiced here; and that guard, he seemed not as surprised as might be expected. This would have happened before. Even those brutes are clean beasts of their kind, they cannot bear ssuch presences as they would sense here—or with uss."

Mall turned on her. "With *us*? What sayst, little witch?"

Katjka's eyes gleamed the self-same gray as the moonlight, unhealthy and pallid. "I told you I had no weather-lore. But there was another way. Alwayss there is chill, where the dead are walking."

"The . . . " Jyp's whisper failed him. He looked wildly over his shoulder.

"War has rolled over this earth, of the Hundred Years, the Peasantss' Revolt, many more. Many lay unburied on this ssoil, their death hard, their bones scattered. Their shades still look back, and are not hard to recall, for a brief time. We walk . . . in company."

Jyp's face was ashen; Mall's eyes narrowed. I found there was a huge lump in my gullet, and I couldn't choke it down.

"Fear is folly!" said Katjka sharply. "Use them while we may!" Ducking out from behind the bush, she darted the last long stretch to the wall of the house. We almost fell over ourselves keeping up with her, and the biting air swirled alongside us. We piled gasping into the angle of a great old chimneystack, looking up for any sign of movement at the windows. They were huge and heavy, and very probably they had motion detectors set in the frames, like the ones Lutz had had installed in our depots; that didn't worry me. I'd chosen this side of the building carefully. The terrace was here, and high above it an elegant turret; and between them lengths of good solid downpipe and guttering. I latched onto one swiftly, feeling carefully around for spikes, non-drying paint or any other little tricks, but it seemed Lutz hadn't taken this approach seriously; and the metal felt easily strong enough to take my weight. I flashed the others a brief grin, looped a sling around the pipe and began to climb, fast. Four storeys didn't look that high, but I soon began to wish I'd done more freestyle mountaineering, and that I dared use resin chalk. My fingers were more numb than I'd thought, and as I passed a window the panes frosted briefly, as at a passing breath; I had to force myself not to shudder. The dead were still with me, then; but weren't they always? I clamped a grip so hard it hurt, and clambered on.

The pipes were solid and well maintained, and I found

ample hand and toe holds on their joints and fastenings. The hard part was the guttering, between the second and third storeys and again at the top, a great knobbly overhang of water-grooved masonry lined with a lead channel that almost tore free under my scrabbling fingertips, and decanted a tasteful mix of leaves and anonymous muck down my neck. Dead pigeons, probably; by the time I reached the roof I was past caring. Fortunately when this pile was built roof-tops had been places to come and enjoy the view, so there was an ornamental parapet I could pinch-grip, carved into flatulent family mottoes and po-faced pious slogans. I mantelshelfed myself in over the V of HVMILITAS, watching for wires or contacts, and collapsed, wheezing. What felt like a century had actually taken about five minutes, but I still couldn't hang around; I looped my line around the A, which looked the most solid, and let it down. Jyp came shinning up at speed, leaning down to lend Katjka a hand; Mall boosted her from behind, swung her long legs over the parapet and looped in the rope, leaving it tied for a fast descent.

The air up here felt a lot warmer, for reasons I didn't want to think about, but we were still shivering. Jyp produced a bronze flask and handed it around; the contents were clear, odorless, slightly greasy and went off like a bomb in my throat. White Lightning, as fearsome a spot of blockade whiskey as ever dissolved a liver.

"Hope you put the enamel back on the bathtub," I told him as I handed it back.

He snorted. "Where this was 'stilled they don't *have* bathtubs."

It wasn't exactly the Water of Life, but it had a remarkably heartening effect on us all. We turned and confronted what we'd been carefully ignoring, the great glass cupola in the roof. It was curtained and dark, a shadow-pool in which nothing stirred except our mirrored faces. Some of the stained-glass panes were hinged to open. "Ten to one he's got those jiggered," remarked Jyp. "But these ones here don't look too strong-set."

Swiftly we attacked the surrounding lead, and soon we could more or less lift out one of the fixed panes. Jyp held us back. "Hey, how about these here detector things inside?"

Katjka shook her head. "Not if he uses this room as we believe. He could not risk . . . ssomething triggering them, and his guards rushing in. There will be other ssafeguards, depend on it."

I parted the curtains and peered in, with Katjka's breath warm on my cheek. Nothing but silence, heavy and undisturbed, and the faint mustiness of a room seldom opened. Nervously I fished out my flashlight; the darkness seemed to drink the beam, showing me only a narrow circle of pale carpet. "It's under there," I whispered.

Jyp looked to Katjka, who shrugged. "I ssense nothing. That does not mean nothing is there."

Mall was already sliding her legs through the gap. I caught her arm, but she shook it off. "I stand shielded, in some wise!" she whispered, paying out a short length of line. "I first, then let the little witch follow. Only then, you men!" Without further ado she kicked off, caught the line and swung for an instant as it snapped taut, scanning the floor with her light, then dropped the last foot or two to the carpet, landing with feather delicacy. Katjka followed, muttering curses as she snagged a petticoat on a nail. Mall caught her around the waist and lowered her soundlessly, and after she'd sniffed the air a little Jyp and I were allowed to follow. We stood on the deep carpet, shining our flashlights aimlessly around the oval walls, feeling the anticlimax after all the effort of getting in.

Jyp shrugged. "Well, if your friend does mess with things he oughtn't in here, he covers up real well. Looks boring as a bishop's bedroom!"

Mall's grin flashed in the faint light. "Ah, mind, the tales I could tell of prelates . . . "

Katjka spat like a cat, and began to claw at the nearest of the elegant cabinets that lined the walls. It was locked, but somehow the lock popped back under her clutching fingers. Metal gleamed within the mirrored shelves, those ornate vessels I'd seen, silver and gold and silver-gilt. With frenetic energy she rounded on the next one, revealing astrolabes and other marvelous old scientific instruments, richly chased and decorated, worth a fortune if they were genuine.

I balked slightly. "This could be just some of Lutz's antiques, Katjka. He's a well-known collector after all—and seriously rich—" But she opened the next cabinet, and I recoiled. It held only folds of rich heavy cloth, faded and dusty-looking but gleaming with bullion embroidery. But all across them were spatters and stains, and the stink of them rolled out into the still air.

"Trappings!" she said quietly. "I know them, none better. Nothing changes. Now let us look at this ssign you saw. You are sure it was under there?"

"I told you, he had people moving the furniture and everything!"

Jyp scuffed the carpet, then hefted the end of a heavy Empire cabinet. "Take us a while to shift all this junk—"

"Shift, hell!" That bland carpet seemed like every featureless barrier that had been raised in my path. "I don't care anymore if Lutz knows someone's been here. Let the bastard worry himself sick!" I drew my sword and slashed out great sweeping strokes across and across, sending the ruined carpet leaping. The cut gleamed like a welling wound—glossy marble, and here and there a vein of metal.

I kicked back a flap, and we shone our torches. Around the margins of the room the marble was plain gray, the kind you find in expensive office lobbies world-wide. But as Mall kicked away the rest she revealed arcs of richer inlay, obviously the wide circle or ring I'd glimpsed; Jyp and Katjka stepped hastily back, pulling me with them, to be sure we stood outside it. We stared at what lay revealed.

Mall was the first to break the silence, with a soft uncanny laugh. "What pretty plaything is this?"

It was just as I'd glimpsed it, filling the whole center of the room: a ring of darker stone inlaid with fine wire script; but across it, from rim to rim, lay thick straight strips of gold, forming that ill-omened star shape I remembered, its jagged pinnacles joined at the peaks and across the base to form inner and outer pentagons. The design of the shapes, even that cool gray background had a 1930s' look to it—not Bauhaus, but that heavy hard-edged classical line you see dotted all over Munich, with the swastikas chipped off it. But now I could see what lay in the marble beneath, a great streak of textured inlay, almost shapeless; in the uneven flashlight it might have been a bloodstain or an abstract flame.

"E'en as you said, Master Stephen—e'en as we saw on the *Chorazin*'s stern, true enough. A pentacle—but a pentacle's such a device as may serve many a turn, both good and ill, and be made in many fashions. Such as this I never saw before, with that swathe across the heart. Nor can I read this curst inscription! I'd have looked to find arcane signs, Greek figuring, Hebrew or Sanskrit ciphers, emblems elemental or zodiacal—or other alcheme or astrology. Were it not so concealed I'd think little enough o't."

"Seems bare somehow," agreed Jyp softly, thumbing his narrow jaw. "Might be signs tricked up and twisted into all that fine filigree stuff," he added, flicking his flashlight across it. "Good way to conceal 'em, maybe. Or maybe not."

I began to feel stupid. Had I just started at shadows? Had I led everyone on a wild-goose chase? It didn't seem possible—and yet they didn't seem at all excited by what we'd found. "But this pattern underneath, in the pentagon here, what about that? I was hoping—"

Jyp clicked his tongue softly. "New one on me. Might be just a decoration of some kind, no real meaning. Mind you, now . . . " The words seemed to be dragged out of him. "Gone to a mort of trouble just to say nothing, haven't they? And spent a whole heap of spondulicks."

He had a point there. My torch glowed on white English marble, black German, raw-meat pink Carrara that must have cost a fortune, green from God alone knew where and plummy brown with dark red veining, all separated by fine lines of gold. Yet all that costly material had been carefully pieced into nothing but a shapeless splash of color. Seen this close, it was divided into a mass of rough-edged concentric shapes, a comic-book explosion smudged across the heart of the design, as if mocking the stiff regularity of the golden bars above. "Kind of like fire, isn't it? Mall?"

"Aye, though a flame would hardly be limned i' those hues. Nor is it all within the pentagon." She kicked the edges of the carpet wider. "See, it crosses it here—and here, right to the outer margin of the circle."

"Now hold hard there a minute!" said Jyp, softly but with mounting urgency. "Belay! Seeing it whole like that—dammit, I'm beginning to recognize something!"

I began to feel that, too. "Something I've seen before, often, but nowhere like this . . . " An amoeba, maybe. There was something amoeboid about it, with the light spot at the heart like a nucleus and long pseudopods stretching out in every direction. You half expected it to come flowing out toward you—but that was crazy. I swallowed. What was the matter with me?

Mall shrugged. "Then you've the vantage of me; but this is a place such as sets cobwebs i' the head. What says our spae-witch?"

Only then we realized we hadn't heard a word out of Katjka. We turned as one, and saw her standing there, arms outstretched, hands working in convulsive tangling patterns, repeated over and over. *"Idiotss!"* she hissed, grinning with the effort of speaking. "Deluded *fools!* Did I not warn you it would be guarded? Do you not wonder why you are sso uncertain?"

We gaped at each other, slack-jawed. We felt it as soon as she said it, weighing down on us like a stifling mantle, obscuring our thoughts. *Nothing much ... not important ... doesn't matter ... forget it ... forget ...*

Suddenly my heart was stuttering. "You mean ... they know we're here?"

Jyp snatched for his sword. "They're coming? We've gotta—"

Katjka half laughed. "Fear—is the next defense! I told you this was besst left to me! Go, before you trigger things worsse!"

"Not without you!" cried Mall, and drew her sword with a menacing hiss.

I caught her arm. "The sign—our one chance, remember?"

"Jehosaphat, it's a map!" yelled Jyp.

"What?" cried Mall.

"Christ, you're right!" I shouted. "I should've known at once—a topographic map, the kind I use for climbing! And dammit, this one's of a mountain, too!"

"Right!" barked Jyp excitedly. "The colors are the contours, the higher the lighter, right up to the light spot in the center." His torch-beam touched it.

The sound was immediate; it might have been a high wind, or a howling of many voices. So were the shadows, shadows that seemed to fall from the flashlight beam but stayed as it swept back, strong dark shadows across the map, creating strange streaks and pits and hollows, the illusion of detail, of three dimensions. Only it wasn't an illusion. The shape in the pentagon was solid, swelling, rising, a looming mass of shadow spotted with sparks of fiery light, wreathed in swirling streaks like haloes of windborne cloud. And at the same instant the floor seemed to lurch under me, to tilt and slope inward toward that smoky vision. I staggered, lost my balance, fell and slid. I clutched a handful of carpet and caught myself, managed to thrust my sword back into my belt but almost lost my grip. Jyp, hanging on higher up, grabbed me by the wrist and swung me back again. But the slope was steepening, throwing more and more of our weight onto our arms. The thing looked like a model mountain at the bottom of a pit now, pentagon and circle blotted out. I could even see tiny bristlings of dense forest on its flanks, and the bare rock at its summit gleaming under the moon. We were hanging on around the pit mouth, like ants scrabbling to escape an antlion. On the far side dangled Katjka, her petticoats flaring as she kicked out desperately for a foothold; and where the hell was Mall?

I grabbed another fistful of the carpet, so Jyp could let go. I boosted him up by his heel, but he managed only another foot or two before sliding back. I kicked my heels down, and almost lost my grip again when I felt them dig into earth and rock; the slope was a hillside now, a steep valley side sloping down toward the swelling mountain at its heart. I boosted Jyp again, and he gained another foot or two; but he was incredibly strong. How long could Katjka hang on? "Keep trying!" I yelled. "I'm going after her!"

I heard his grunted reply, but it was obvious he couldn't move easily from where he was. I tested my foothold, and let go the carpet. Even as it left my fingers it felt like a grass tussock. I snatched out as my foothold gave, caught the stem of a scrubby bush and inched my way over, kicking another hold. But the slope was getting steeper still, precipitous now, and widening, so that Katjka seemed to be receding. I saw her get a foothold as I had, and called out to her.

"*Get away!*" she screamed. "Idiot boy, you do not know what you rissk! Leave me, get back, save yourself!" Red light from below flickered on her bare legs as she fought the slope. "Go!" she yelled again. "I am not worth it!"

Smoke boiled up around us, pungent, stinging, full of resin and sulphur and worse, and I coughed violently; but I clawed at the earth and stones, feeling my fingernails splinter and tear. I could still reach her—but what then? Fall with her? We'd be on a cliff by then.

Too bad; I was past making sense now. I kicked another hold, reached out to a solid-seeming tussock—and felt it spill loose in my hand. My hold gave, I slipped, twisted, swung by one hand from the wiry little bush-stem, facing outward into the smoky chasm. Then I screamed aloud. Through the smoke, like a falling comet, a great pale flame rushed in toward me, as if to envelop me; and I all but let go. *"Stephen!"* cried the fire; and I saw the human shape of it, the corona of hair that billowed around the head like a halo and streamed out like wisps of smoke behind. It was Mall, centuries old, near-immortal wanderer on the Outward paths of the Spiral, in the aspect that burned within her, yet rose to view only rarely and at times of terrible danger. One day, maybe, it would consume all that was mortal in her, and leave her demi-goddess indeed; for now it was fitful, draining, but terrible to encounter for friend and foe alike. Out of the flame a hand reached, coursing with the same cool fire, and caught mine; tingling agony danced over my wrist. Even in this aspect Mall couldn't fly—not yet, perhaps; but she had caught our rope, and swung over the abyss.

"Jyp—" I choked.

"He's safe! Now save me the witch, for I cannot reach her alone!"

Her voice echoed among vast spaces. Clutching at her, I felt something of the same flame awaken, burning and tingling in my bones. I laughed, lightheaded, and cast loose with a springing kick. Over the abyss we swung, I reached out; Katjka caught my hand.

And screamed, an ear-splitting shriek of real pain; her grip flew off, but I clamped my hand on her wrist again. She struggled convulsively, and I stared down, saw the flames that danced over my arms, not pale, but golden, as if altered somehow. Little electric flickers of them rode down her writhing arm and danced across her twisted features.

"Hang on, you stupid bitch!" I yelled. "D'you want to lose us both?"

Her eyes, screwed shut, flashed open suddenly, and glared into mine. I almost let go. The pupils rolled and boiled like blazing cauldrons, red flame, consuming flame; and beneath her, out of the smoke, something flashed by. She swung, violently, and screamed with fright, as if something had snatched at her. "Haul up!" I shouted. "Up, for God's sake! *Up!*"

I felt Mall's vast strength take hold, lift us easily over the gulf, but even as we came up the speeding thing flew by again, or another like it, and Katjka screamed again. This time I heard tearing cloth, and the coat fell away at her shoulders as if the back was torn. Again that speeding something, half her skirt ripped away and the blood started in shallow welts on her bare thigh as though a claw had swiped her. Higher and higher we rose, but the smoke billowed under us, the mountain peak swelled and grew, and those frightening halo-things, too fast to see, swept by and struck—always at Katjka, never at me. She struggled no longer, except when they touched her, but twisted feebly in my grip.

"Mall!" I howled. "Hurry it up, will you?"

"Easy, Stephen!" came the echoing voice. *"I am e'en now at the roof—you follow!"*

Desperately I kicked up as she hauled me, tried to lift Katjka that fraction higher; but the passing things rose with her, and I seemed to see the arms that swept out to strike—or were they striking? They were human arms or very like them, flung wide. I managed to hook one leg over the lip of the window as Mall hauled me through, and with that purchase I snatched Katjka up high enough to loop her free arm around my neck; but at the same instant she snapped rigid, and I felt another weight, as if someone clung to her legs now. And another, another, till I was trying to support three people, or that was how it felt. *"Mall!"*

I felt one of her hands keep hold, the other release and

reach past me, straining to reach Katjka's arm. But Katjka, staring into my face, gasped, *"Nej! No, Sstefan!* They will pull you all down now, even her! Down to the Great Ssabbat, the unending pool of evil! The Brocken is too sstrong for you, for her, for anyone! Kill its agents! Tell—tell the Graal! But me—*leave me where I belong!"*

Too suddenly for me, the arm around my neck flew away; the extra strain on my hand tore her slender wrist right through my fingers. As quickly as that, her ruined clothes flying free around her, she shot down into the cauldron that had been a room, dwindled and was gone. I swung there, in Mall's grasp, shaking and numbed. Not only by the strain; but by the awful flash of longing I'd seen in those reddened eyes, the instant before she let go.

Chapter 7

It was Mall who hauled me out, Mall aflame no longer, her blond curls plastered to her brow with sweat. Mall who dragged me upright and shook me, though I could see the streaks on her own cheeks. "Lackwit!" she yelled in my face, with the force of a slap. "Must needs look now to our selves!" And she did as much for Jyp. "To heels, man! Afoot, down and away! Or would'st share her fate?"

I saw what she meant. No need for concealment now; the cupola was flickering and flashing like a beacon, and as we flung the rope over we heard shouts and barking. Mall seized the rope, sprang out and went slithering down hand over hand, sea fashion, with only the odd kick off the wall; Jyp and I followed more slowly. When she reached the ground floor windows she sprang loose and dropped onto the lawn, casting about like a wary animal. We abandoned the scientific approach and slipped after her with skin-stripping speed; we jumped from lower down and landed rolling, out from behind the angle of the building.

Suddenly, with no sound at all, the whole gardens were flooded with glaring light. It turned the open lawn stark white and threw the uniformed figures who came charging up into brutal silhouette. Before Jyp or I could move, Mall's anger overrode her weariness. Springing up from her feral crouch, she unleashed a fearful swinging kick that caught the leading guard in the stomach and simply smashed him off his feet and into the man behind. A gun hit the ground and jarred off a burst at nothing, skittering across the terrace on its own vibration. A machine-pistol, safety off, no challenge—these weren't any ordinary security men. The others jumped back. One raised his hand, and the turf spewed fragments where I'd been. But they were too slow, far too slow; they hadn't fought out on the Spiral, and there was no rage in them. I drew and slashed in one savage sweep; the gun spun into a flowerbed, the man whipped around and fell. The last already lay at Mall's feet.

We ran then, shading our eyes, our long shadows racing across beside us like spindly giants. But we weren't halfway to the trees when we heard the thudding of other feet behind us, and the hoarse, harsh panting. The dogs were after us, and our ghostly shield was gone.

Mall was already turning to bay, sword held vertical in both hands. With one stroke she could sever even those blunt necks; but she made no move to. She stood, breathing deeply, as the beasts rushed in on her; and at the last moment she tilted the sword, caught the intolerable glare of the floods and with inhuman accuracy flashed it right into their eyes. They twisted, blinded; and she hit out with the flat only, a swift slapping left and right. They rolled, stunned and yelping. Jyp's pistol barrels spat and smoked in turn; two of the lights went out in a spray of hot cinders, swathing us in shadow again. Mall plunged into the copse ahead of us, bounding through the undergrowth to the fence. I saw her run straight past the tree we'd come down, and take a mighty swing at the swathe of wire along the top. Too late to shout, I winced. There was the whipping twang of razor-wire parting, then a mighty explosive sizzle and a fat spark. Mall knew perfectly well about electricity, but she didn't always remember.

We hauled her out of the bushes, still clutching her scorched sword, shinned up into the gap she'd made, and, sitting astride the fence, struggled to hoist her after us. We had her draped across our knees when we heard the rushing footsteps, and hastily tipped her down. There was a muffled thud in the leaf-drifts below. But as we swung our legs across to jump after, we heard a harsh, *"Halt! Ruhren Sie nicht!"* from outside. They'd used their heads and sent men around the fence. I couldn't see them, but I heard their breathing, harsh and fast. Big men—heavies from the gate, probably. *"Kom 'runter!"* barked the voice. *"Und kein Scheis—"*

More or less at their feet Mall rose up like some sort of local wood demon, plastered with several season's leaves, and enveloped them. As we landed there was a brief thrashing, then we saw her beckoning. Silently I handed her her sword. She snatched it, and ran. Beside me Jyp tripped over something solid, and swore; and that was the first word spoken since we left the roof. We raced up the slope, wheezing and gasping; I was amazed I could still keep up with these two hardened superhumans. I even had the energy to risk a brief look back as we crested the rise. Flashlights were sweeping the woods below, and the grounds still blazed with floods; but the cupola was dark and silent and still.

We ran through the night, not silently, maybe, but light-footed and fast enough to pass unheard. Jyp's night eyes and sense of direction kept us in line and away from obstacles, and the steady rhythm of our feet and the roaring blood in our ears helped to blot out our simmering feelings. Just at the first hedge I heard what might have been a shot far behind, but it didn't come anywhere near us. Across a road, through fields, vaulting a stream to more fields and a small neat farmyard, the kind the EC subsidizes so that German farm-owners can work full-time on the assembly lines. Beyond that, across more fields, by the half-hidden shell of an old church, to the low wall of woodland into whose shadow we'd managed to push the helicopter. I only hoped we'd have the strength to push it out again. We were alert for pursuers, but we saw none. I guessed the guards mightn't feel too eager, given what we'd done to the others. If Lutz had been at home it might have been different.

Somebody had apparently filled the 'copter with lead blocks while we'd been away, and Mall was a shadow of her normal self. Nevertheless we managed to haul it far enough on its skids from under the trees to get a clear take-off. When I slumped down into the pilot's seat, though, I found my hands were shaking too much to press the starter. I knew I didn't have long. It would be dawn soon, and people about; a helicopter in a field would be visible for miles and attract all kinds of attention, not least from the local cops. The sky ahead was growing definitely grayer, behind what looked like gathering clouds. I glanced back at my passengers, sprawled gasping in their seats. They gazed stonily back at me, as gray and drawn as I must have looked. Delay broke down our defenses, and opened the door to memory. "What happened?" I demanded, and was startled at how choked I still sounded. "What *happened?*"

"What d'you think?" said Jyp dully. "Like she said, we weren't wary enough. We tripped the big one."

"Yes, yes, for Chrissake, I know that! I mean, what— Where's she gone? Is she alive or dead?"

Jyp's mouth twisted. "Death she could've coped with. She felt four centuries was too long. She'd have preferred it."

"Why? Mall's lived longer!"

"Aye, free to roam across the seas of the Spiral, to seek out all the hidden corners of the Earth! Free to grow!" Mall, still leaf-crowned, made no move to look up. "She had to live out hers within the compass of a little tavern in a lesser port, seldom straying and that not far, roaming only in the length of her long sight. Yet that she endured, sooner than founder again in the slough she came from. Now she has."

"Well, can we get her out? Get her back? We've got to, dammit!"

Mall's eyelids fluttered closed. "I see scant chance of that. She is gone back to the Brocken."

"The Brocken, the Brocken! It's just a mountain, blast it! Is this something happens there, or what?"

Mall wiped her hair back, and shuddered. "Just a mountain, aye. But mountains cast shadows like aught else, and this one—blacker than most. Places there are—not many—where the powers from the Rim may reach inward, even to the very borderland 'twixt Spiral and Core. Some such you have trodden, many a time. Such is the Borobudur. Such is the City of the Graal, such is the mountain. The pentacle over the map was a gate thither."

Nobody said anything, but the wind swirled outside, and sang a song of cold and emptiness. A few drops spattered across the windshield. Mall's blazing eyes were dimmed. "Even in my day 'twas a name known. From the earliest times it has been a dark hallow, a place of power, and this is no accident; since the forebears of Frank and Saxon first came wandering out of the east, since Germania's *Urwald* held at bay the mightiest marchings of Rome, since the coming of the younger kindred of men drove back the Elder to the mountains in the wake of the Great Ice. Deep within that shadow something settled and made its habitation and its strength, some force that had followed those first of true men on their *Volkwanderung*. Followed, as the wolf follows the herd."

The day was coming, but it was still far from light enough for me. A fine drizzle wept across the windshield. "What kind of force?" I demanded sharply.

Jyp snorted. "Hope you never get close enough to find out. Those who do, don't tell—like Katjka. Or can't. I hope to Hell—because that's what spawned it, for sure."

Hell wasn't something I'd ever believed in. "Something from outside? Something from out near the Rim, like the Graal? Something that was human once?"

The sound Mall made was not a laugh. "Like, yet so very unlike. And as to human—if so, it took sorely against the condition, for it has long wrought havoc upon humankind, joying in pain, spreading malice and disruption where it may. And yet," she added, suddenly thoughtful, "it might well be that it once wore flesh, for it seems obsessed with it, both to revel in and to excoriate, pleasure and pain always to excess . . . "

"Sounds like a classic sadist," I said, and shivered slightly at the thought. "Only writ large."

"Writ, and in letters of blood and fire," said Mall. "The panics over witchcraft that struck so hard through Europe in my time and earlier, they were but shadows. For the most part witches danced only in the addled pates of witch-hunters deranged or evil, greedy for pain to inflict or goods to confiscate. Oh, here and there 'a might find some misremembered shard of old heathendom, maybe, or harmless hedge-wizardry; but they were nothing. And yet there was a core of grim truth, little though the hunters made of it; a terrible timeless focus of ancient evil. A power that sought to ensnare humanity to its service, dangling strange knowledge and arcane arts and pleasures as a lure; and by awful ceremony and the misuse of those arts in malice and revenge, it bound them."

Again, that bitter negative of a laugh. "Does aught happen there? Aye, a happening indeed, a thing of dread, a work without a name, timeless, without beginning or end—the Grand Sabbat of all the witch cults. Once Katjka walked that path, longer and harder than most, until the same strength that had sustained her along it led her to break free and seek atonement. Many times she visited it, suffered much but learned much, and received many powers. Now she has been dragged back there, not for a brief passage but sans let, sans release. Dead she may be, or far more likely tossed back into that fearful cauldron and lost in it, victim and perpetrator both. If so, 'twill never loose her more. There may be some with power to help her, but this

I know, that I do not. It is not in me. She is lost to us."

I couldn't speak, not for a moment. My eyes stung, and if it hadn't been for the iron concentration that flying develops I might have broken up entirely. For me that was rare. There was a time I'd managed to convince myself I didn't need anyone else, that I was better off with casual sex and no entanglements, that I didn't give the old proverbial damn. And then, all of a sudden, the warmth of the Tavern had wrapped itself around me, Jyp and the old couple who ran it, and Katjka. She'd been at once the most accessible—not to say available—and the most remote, a voice out of the shadows, a warm hand on your neck, a brush of the lips and a hooded glance that said everything and revealed nothing at all. Her intimacies were strictly on a cash basis, though she occasionally hinted otherwise, and there was no more forbidding defense than that. All I'd ever learned about her was from others, or from reading between the lines of her rare unguarded remarks. Her powers she seldom revealed except when a good friend needed them—and more than once that had been me. The Tavern without her seemed hardly possible; that stuffy little room under the eaves, with its clutter of odd old-fashioned balms and unguents and its enveloping feather bed . . .

I wrestled savagely with my helmet. If ever you catch the delusion that you don't have a heart, try carving someone out of it and see. "You were right, Jyp," I managed to say, almost steadily. "It's my goddamned fault."

"No," he said firmly. "No, it isn't. Sure, I wasn't happy about her coming along; but I clammed up, didn't I? If it'd been just your own private quarrel, maybe I wouldn't have—but the Graal, now, that's big. That's something that'll affect all Europe and the world, in the end, Core and Spiral both. You're not to blame. We needed our answer."

"And we have it!" I stabbed savagely at the starter, which coughed and missed. "Thanks to her. We know it's this thing on the mountain behind Lutz, and probably Le Stryge as well, and C-Tran's tied up in it somehow, it's all part of a wider plan. And—and—the hell with it!" Anger welled over my grief. "It's too wide for me! I've been blundering about too much! I'm not putting my friends at any more risk!" I stabbed the starter. The engine spluttered and fired, the rotors swished to life, growing stiff and straight, slicing into the chill dawn.

"So what're you going to do?" yelled Jyp, reaching for his helmet.

"What I should've done in the first place. Go right back to the City and get things straight with them, risk or no risk. I won't take the Spear back, I won't so much as touch it. They can damn well send their own guards or Knights or whatever to fetch it. Let them deal with this Brocken thing, and Le Stryge! And after that," I breathed hard, and thought of what I'd like to do to Lutz, "we'll see! Jyp, you said the City was hard to find. But you have the course I took before, and the time. If anyone can find it, you can."

He glanced up at the gray sky, and the equally gray navcom screen. "Well, no law 'gainst trying." He swung himself over into the front seat, and peered around. The clouds were massing into great peaks and columns, vast forbidding fortress walls, the same in any direction; but he gave me a heading at once, and a corridor. I gunned throttle and collective, caught the tail rotor with the pedals as it tried to overswing into the trees, and tilted the main rotor assembly to send us wheeling away upward toward the clouds. Behind us, dwindling in the dawn, burned a patch of bitter floodlit brightness, and my curse went with it. I hadn't finished with it, or its master, yet.

We moved from cloud to cloud, with Jyp's keen eye flicking from my instruments to the shifting patterns of gray beyond. Which gave him the more guidance I couldn't tell, but he seemed to feel there was something ahead; there was a quiet excitement in his voice altogether unlike his normal boisterous enjoyment, and after a while even Mall seemed to catch it. She leaned over our shoulders, shedding damp leaves, and when I glanced up I saw her face losing its lines of weariness and despair, growing keen again at the prospect of seeing this place. That gave me an odd lift, in its turn; these strange friends of mine had seen so much and lived so long I felt like a child beside them. But now, ahead of us here, was somewhere that impressed even them, somewhere I'd found for myself. I looked at the cloud-peaks ahead, and saw them flush and lighten with the first faint light of the hidden dawn. Completely different from the ones I'd first encountered, of course, random as any cloudscape; and yet that didn't seem to matter. There was a familiarity in their pattern, a consistency, as if I was seeing the same landscape from a different angle. "I think we ought to turn a little here," I suggested. "Westward . . ."

Jyp swung around to look at me. "Gettin' to be quite a navigator yourself!" he shouted. "I was just about to suggest that—westward a point it is."

I eased off the tail a little and pitched the rotors to steer us around. My compass settled easily enough, but the satellite navigation display was behaving oddly, and I half expected to hear the Frankfurt controllers demanding what I thought I was playing at; as far as they knew I'd never made that unscheduled landing outside town. I wished I never had—

Mall's shout resounded even over the engines, and her out-thrust arm almost ripped out my intercom cables. But I didn't blame her when I followed her pointing finger, and saw far ahead, in the midst of a wide pool of blue this time, the pair of gigantic spires that topped the Hall of the Graal. I leaned on the pedals, tilted the stick, and swung us away toward the billowing slopes of cloud, away and down. "I'm not going near that place in the air!" I explained. "No knowing what they'd think. I'll land and walk in, like before."

Jyp nodded, and watched in excitement as the clouds thinned suddenly, and the valley he'd named the Heilenthal sprang to life below us. The sky was clearer, and the dawn

sun blazed on the rough white stone of the cliffs and the
greenery at their feet; the rivers shone like steel and bronze,
and down their long stair-falls rainbows glowed. Mall's hand
clutched at my shoulder as she saw the walls of the city
appear around the edge of the mountain, then sagged in
disappointment as I hastily pulled back and down, careful
to stay out of sight. We fell toward rougher ground than
I'd sought out before, but better sheltered. At the margin
of the forest a clearing opened, the hut at its center a roof-
less ruin whose bare gable toppled at the touch of our
downblast; a mighty cloud of fireweed fountained outward
as I brought us in to land, glittering white in the sun. I
eased the 'copter down, stilled the engines and threw the
door wide even as the rotors whistled to a stop.

We sat, and let the sun warm us, and the air of the place
blow around us; and I marveled. I'd felt something before,
some sense of wonder at this place. But how could I have
failed to sense the fullness of it, when even the very air
seemed to carry some special benediction of its own, given
without grudge or question? It took the grief and anger and
desperate worry within us, that crisp dawn air, and without
in any way diminishing it it somehow lightened the impact,
and the weight. I could bear it now, and look to its ending.
The sun warmed the tensions out of us, soothed our bruises
and our weariness, left us content simply to sit and rest. It
was hard to rouse myself up for the long walk ahead; but
I knew I had to.

"You two can wait here," I told them, and overrode their
protests. "Look, it makes sense. First, if something does
happen, then you know where I've gone; second, I'll look
more harmless alone—and be a smaller target; and third,
with you two here I'm a lot happier about leaving the machine. For one thing, I'm less likely to find Le Stryge lurking around when I get back."

Mall smiled. "An we see him, we'll e'en convey him your
love and *benedicite*."

"Do. On the end of a long sharp stick would be fine." I

swung myself down into the deep growth of the old clearing. Fireweed and thistledown erupted around me, hanging in the air like a slow snowfall. "If I don't come back, play it by ear. If these people are all you say they are, you ought to be safe enough. But, for God's sake, be careful, okay?"

" 'S funny," drawled Jyp. "Just what I was gonna say to you. They're good people, sure, but these are hard times, and you ain't exactly endeared yourself to them already." He tossed me one of the forgotten lunch packs we'd laid on. "Long walk. Enjoy yourself, Steve."

Strangely enough, I did. I followed one of the likelier streams down, and the air took hold of me, and lightened my step. It didn't feel long, that walk; I wanted to linger over every moment of it, even though I was ravenous before I'd gone a mile. Partly it was playing tourist, because there were things to see here; strange old standing stones and dolmens, half-hidden ruins that looked distinctly Roman, and once an entire village standing empty. I thought at first they must all be in the fields, till I saw the sagging shutters and decaying thatch, and the empty millrace from which the wheel had fallen. On the far side of it I stopped by the river, and washed down my sandwiches with great drafts of the stream. I slopped it over my head and neck, and managed to forget the amount of sleep I hadn't had lately. It was icy meltwater, clear and fresh, and even more than the air it set heart in me—not by any mysterious virtue I could detect, but by its very ordinariness. Plain water, but the best plain water there could be, without taint or infection, without even the natural staining of some soils, yet with all the full flavor of an ideal mineral content. The more I thought about that, the more miraculous it did seem, after all. If you could bottle this stuff it would knock every other mineral water off the market—but that idea threatened to spoil it. You couldn't bottle this valley, the air, the trees, all that went with it; the water was only one part of something greater. Something that didn't seem to go with deserted villages, though . . .

I sat up. I'd dropped off—only for twenty minutes or so, by my watch, but I felt amazingly refreshed; I'd had less restful nights than that. Through the trees the wall and the towers looked closer than I'd expected. I felt better about facing them, too; the sooner it was over with . . . I climbed to my feet, and went on.

As often happens, they weren't quite so close as they looked. It wasn't far short of three hours' walking before I reached the last rise, and long before that I'd noticed something was different. There was nobody about, no beasts in the fields, or even on their way to them, and this in the middle of the day. The roads, when I reached them, were empty, and I felt conspicuous as an ant on a tablecloth. As I came within clear sight of the walls I ducked back under the trees again. This was worse than I'd bargained for.

I couldn't just walk up to the great gate, as I'd planned to, and talk to the sentries. It was shut tight, and above it was the first sign of life I'd seen—heads pacing back and forth along the walls, a network of sentries. As if they were on a war footing, preparing for a siege, even. That could make them very, very jumpy indeed; I wished I'd brought something to make a white flag. Moving carefully, keeping my eye on those slow-pacing watchers, I ducked through the trees toward the wall. I couldn't get very close, but at least it was in hailing range. I took a deep breath and stepped out into the open, waved my hand and called out. My leg muscles were taut springs ready to hurl me back into shelter, but I raised a hand and waved, as naturally as possible, and called out.

The reaction was instant. The parapet sprouted rifles, and I had to fight my urge to run like a rabbit. From above a hard voice drifted down. *"Wer da? Halten sie zuvor!"*

"Freund!" I yelled back, keeping my hands in clear sight. *"Ich bringe gute Neues! Ich will mit ein Offizier sprechen! Darf ich hereinkommen?"*

There was a hurried conference on the walls. *"Bleib' da!"*

came the answer. *"Man soll' der Kapitan hohlen. Steh', und kein Spass, sonst bist du Rabensfutter!"*

As much as I could expect, though I didn't like that bit about food for ravens. I crossed my arms and stood waiting, until a small wicket in the great gate opened, and out of it stepped two men in black uniforms, crisp and military in an ornate, flamboyant style that hadn't been seen in the Core for a century or longer, redolent of a world that ended in blood, mud and extremism after 1914. Silver buttons fastened the long jackets, encircled by a Sam Browne-style belt in white leather; silver piping encircled the high tight collar and heavy cuffs, and ran in double braids down the seams of their riding breeches. Swords clanked by their sides, ornately sheathed sabres, but they both carried side-arms in their hands. The bigger one, taking the lead as they stalked up to me, had a Mauser machine pistol, a jewel of engineering that looked far too modern for the late nine-teenth-century product it was. His hair was cropped almost to nothing under his black enameled *pikelhaube* helmet, and his moustache was waxed into upturned spikes—a caricature Hun, ridiculous in pictures, but a lot more formidable in front of you and well armed. The younger man was lean and bony, with longer gingery hair and a small-eyed, clean-shaven face, but he moved with an athletic, self-assertive swagger that was threatening in itself. I didn't like the look of either; but if anyone was in the wrong here, I was. Time, decidedly, to be polite.

I raised my hand, and we disposed of a few courtesies. The Hun turned out to be a Hauptmann Dragovic, not a Hun after all, the other a Leutnant von Albersweg, officers of the City Guard of Heilenberg, and they were obviously impatient or edgy. When I told them I had news about a recent disappearance, though, news important enough to be brought to these Knights of theirs, their entire manner changed. The captain gave me one sharp look, and then impressed me by holstering that fearsome gun; the lieutenant only lowered his, but the captain gestured and he followed suit. "Best that you come with us," the captain said in passable English. "You have the right of it, such news should be told at once. Come!"

Encouraged, I let them bustle and chivvy me down to the gate and through, beneath the slow measured tread of the sentries. But I had to stop in the gate a moment and look out to the open square beyond. It was all I recalled, and more, much more. I'd remembered the neat houses, the gardens and the winding alleys, the wealth of trees, the clear air and all the sense of life and freshness that clung around the streets even when they were empty. Now, though, I saw what lay behind their charm. They were a sign of strength, of a near-perfection it took power to maintain. Power that could hold this whole community stable within the constant flux of the Spiral, power that kept it an enduring, unchanging island where other places, or those who dwelt in them, would soon slip back into the Core and be overtaken by history. How had I ever managed to miss the aura of this place? I could almost see the radiant power in the vast buttresses of the wall, in the noble classical colonnades of the larger buildings, in the coronal of white clouds behind the reaching towers. Had I been blind? No, only blinded, by the compulsion laid upon me. This place was a strength, a bulwark; if it looked even a touch over-civilized, that was because it dare not give any opening to what it shut out. These walls, these guards were not for show, or for oppression; this place had enemies real and immediate, and ones with whom no compromise was possible.

"Ah," said the captain quietly, "so I thought. You have been before within the walls of the Heilenberg. If you please, will you come this way? The Knights will be anxious to hear your tidings."

He ushered me swiftly into a small doorway set within the inner corner of the looming double gate itself, and up a long spiral stair of stone, lit only from above and flanked by faceless doors. I thought for a minute we were going to

climb right to the top, but some way short of it he produced
a bunch of keys, opened a door and waved me courteously
inside. The corridor beyond was dark, and I hesitated. Dragovic seemed to catch my unease. "Such Knights as are
still here, and many others, attend a . . . ceremonial," he
said, stiffly apologetic. "We must ask you to wait in the
guardroom while we send word."

I shrugged; I didn't like it, but I couldn't expect them to
let me run around loose. Dragovic led the way to another
door, unlocked, and as it opened on a lighter room he stood
aside to let me pass. But the light came only from a narrow
slot in the wall, and it was an instant before my eyes registered the empty lamp chains hanging from the vaulted
ceiling, the dull banners stacked around the stone walls,
the bareness and faint dustiness of long disuse. No way was
this a guardroom. But even as I rounded on the two officers
I expected to hear the door slam, and find myself alone. I
was wrong. They were still with me; but the lieutenant's
hand was on the hilt of his sabre.

"And now," he said, also in English, "you will at once
tell us where is the Great Spear and how it may be found.
Zur stelle!"

I'd been neatly shanghaied; but not that neatly. "I'm only
too happy to tell," I repeated. "To somebody in authority.
Not you."

"We are all the authority that is required," said the captain, with icy calm. "A spy has been caught returning to
the scene of his crime, as a dog to his vomit. He will, however, make some slight atonement by disclosing the where-
abouts of the property he stole. The Knights need not
concern themselves with such as you, *mein Bursch'*. Now,
for the last time, will you speak?"

Oh, great. Two more over-ambitious cops out to notch
up Brownie points. I'd had my bellyful of the breed lately,
and I dug my heels in. "I told you," I grunted, "I'll talk to
these Knights—nobody else. And that's final."

"As you wish," said Dragovic coldly. "No consideration

of honor arises with such as you. If necessary we will cut the truth from you piecemeal."

I grunted again. "The Knights wouldn't thank you for killing me."

Von Albersweg shrugged. "If you die it will dissolve whatever forces you have used to conceal the Spear, and we will surely set hands upon it then. *Und nun*—"

My sword was in my hand before his left the scabbard. The lieutenant flushed, and swung it up high, into the stilted Heidelberg on-guard. I almost laughed; Heidelberg dueling is fast showy swordplay with the edge only, on a fixed stance and swathed in face and body armor, its main purpose to decorate callow *Junkers* with shallow scars. I'd played rougher games. I stamped forward into a forceful on-guard, setting my body well back beyond his reach, my point leveled at von Albersweg's solar plexus—very steadily, I was glad to see. I braced myself, but the lieutenant hesitated, staring at the blade. *"Zum Teufel!"* he hissed. *"Sehen Sie doch dieser Stahl—"*

Dragovic twitched that vile moustache, and snorted. *"Beruhe dich!"* he barked, and added contemptuously to me, "So you have been stealing other things as well!" Then abruptly he elbowed the lieutenant aside, swept out his own sabre and came on guard, all in the same flowing motion, at least as easy as mine. His point tapped at mine, without any tremor I could see. Not to be outdone, I raised my sword to salute, and after an instant, grudgingly, he followed suit—and then lunged, with fearsome speed, driving me stumbling back against the wall before I could parry properly. His point struck little puffs of nitre from the stone beside my shoulder. Our guards clashed, we met *corps-à-corps* and I threw him aside and launched a fierce riposte over his blade. He disengaged effortlessly, and I found myself parrying a blinding sequence of slashes at shoulder and thigh—and then a sudden lunge at my stomach. I was ready for that, simultaneously side-stepping and cutting fast at his head. He ducked, countered—and drove, appallingly fast. I skipped back, halted him with a stamping *appel* and caught his lunge as it licked at my throat—just.

I sprang forward into his attack, cramping his style, and launched my own best display of compound attacks, never letting the line of engagement move an inch, staggering the rhythm so it never became predictable. One lunge nicked his ear, another came within an ace of clipping that bloody moustache; he fell back and I went after him. He was going purple in the face; but he was holding me, beginning to beat me back. And all the time the lieutenant was dancing around us like a kid eager to join in—a vicious kid, because I could see by the way he was lifting his sword that he wasn't just enthusiastic, he was looking for a clear opening to take a swipe at me himself. He saw one, too, and sprang in, ready to slash out at my back. I'd seen it too, though; I ducked back and stabbed out, spiking him neatly in the thigh. He screamed, skidded and fell, clutching his hip. Dragovic skipped over him with what might have been an amused grunt—and then laid into me again. This was a real swordsman and not just an overgrown school bully, and I was flagging fast. Cut, feint and lunge followed each other in a flickering sequence that held me to the spot, too engaged to risk a move, though the lieutenant was twisting at our feet. Then I skidded in his blood, lost my balance and the initiative together, desperately tried another traverse and completely fumbled it—

"Halt!" The shout jarred the air, high and clear. It galvanized the captain, leaving his vicious riposte quivering in mid-air; I froze, too—then slipped and crashed down on one knee with stinging force, my weight on my sword hand. The captain's moustache bristled, his blade hovered—and the shout came again, with a clatter of boots in the corridor, and the slam of the outer door. *"Halt', sagte ich! Kein Schlag mehr! Versteh'n, Hauptmann?"*

The captain drew a deep breath between his teeth. His sabre sagged, and his heels clicked. He looked to the corridor, his face a study in repressed disappointment and baffled resentment. I risked taking my eyes off him for a moment. But I wouldn't like to think what my face showed then. His last chop, if it had connected, couldn't have hit me much harder; now I'd really had it. Yet all I felt was numb, stunned by that instant of recognition—although what I recognized was hard to say, the transformation was so total.

The soft dove-gray uniform I'd seen before. It looked inconspicuous compared to the gaudy sentries' uniforms or the trim black of the city guard; but even in the shadows of the corridor the flashes of gold insignia stood out—at the breast especially, because this was, quite unmistakably, a woman. Tall, trim, dark-haired, she clicked quickly down the last few steps and into the doorway, taking in the chaotic scene with one crisp glance. It didn't last; she saw me, and her expression went blank. But I'd had my share of shocks already. I managed to speak first. "Well, hi there," I said loopily, staggering to my feet. "Some uniform. It suits you a lot better than your burglar gear, Miss 1726."

Then I had to leap for my life as the captain launched another vicious slash. It would have connected, too, but for one more shock—a sword was suddenly in its path, almost faster than sight, and rock-steady. Mall could have done better, perhaps, but not many others. The captain's sabre rang and bounced; he clutched at his wrist and unleashed a stream of barely comprehensible oaths. "Can you not see?" he bellowed. "This, this is the one—the thief! Caught sneaking back within the walls again, to who knows what purpose this time. He insults you, and you—"

She ignored me completely and rounded on him. One terrible look, and his bluster ran right down. "Control yourself!" she snapped. "You face serious trouble! Just as well I happened to leave the conclave, or you'd have been in far worse! Weren't your orders clear enough? This is a matter for the Rittersaal alone, the City Guard's not free to interfere. You have no business arrogating anything so grave to indulge your personal ambitions! I am taking charge of this prisoner."

His face went from flushed to deadly white. "You are incompetent. You are but newly invested and not fit to decide. I will call out the guard!"

She faced him calmly. "Do, and it will be to detain yourself. I am what I am, and that is not answerable to you."

"You turn your back on a felon armed and dangerous!" he blustered.

"Dangerous?" She glanced at me a moment. There was none of the old anger in her face—not even any special sign of recognition. All she said, quite calmly, was, "Put down your sword."

"Now just hang on!" I objected, though I was impressed as hell. "I came here openly—this time—to ask for a hearing in good faith. I know where the Spear is, I'll help you find it, gladly—if I can only explain!" But then I couldn't hold it back any longer. "You! What the blind bloody hell are *you* doing here?"

She looked at me with steely authority. It was only then I realized just how radically her face had changed. It was like seeing a flattering photograph or an idealized portrait; it was as if those brief glimpses I'd had were really looks beneath a mask. All the lines of temper and resentment were smoothed off her face as if they'd never been, and that in itself stripped away ten years; but there was more. There was a balance in the features that had never been there before, so what had seemed harsh and angular became subtly smoother, less stark. Her hair wasn't that different, cut short and slightly tousled; but it had lost the cropped, aggressive spikiness. Her nose was still quite prominent, but her cheeks had filled out, so it fitted her face better. Those high cheekbones sloped down more delicately now to a jaw that was only well defined, and a mouth fuller but just as firm; the strong chin hadn't changed, but it fitted. The notch between her eyebrows had gone, and the permanent frown, along with the hollowness around her eyes. Now I could see it was their slight natural slant that had made the frown look so fixed. For the first time I noticed they were a striking blue-gray.

The closer I looked, the harder it was to believe that this was the same person and not some twin or clone; yet I never had the least doubt who it was. Even her voice had softened. "Whatever I am elsewhere, or was, here and now I am a Knight of the Sangraal. You will have your hearing, if you offer no further violence. But first you'd better demonstrate your own good faith—or shall I shed enough of your blood to take your sword anyway? Believe me, I can do that."

I didn't say anything to that. I'd bested her before, unarmed. But I was tired, and distrust racked me like physical pain. "Last time I saw you, you were a gibbering wreck trying to kill me out of hand. What says you won't do it now?"

She stiffened slightly, and then, surprisingly, she almost smiled. "Look at me!" was all her answer.

"I am looking! What in God's name's happened to you?"

"Look at me!" she said again, more sharply. I stared. It wasn't so much what was still there, drive and intensity; it was what wasn't. The instability, the paranoia, the sheer hate—it was gone, down to the last traces, so that what was beneath shone through. As if a filthy window were suddenly scoured clean to let in bright day, in one enlightening sweep. And she knew it; and that was almost the most alarming thing of all. As if that day had always been there, and been obscured by the grime of the world, by disillusion and despair. That disturbed me. What did my own window look like? What had the world trodden deep into my face?

Impulsively, formally, I laid the hilts across my arm, and offered her the sword.

She reached out, but she didn't take it; she stared, just as the others had. "You see, *meine Ritterin*?" hissed the captain. "You *see*?" She did; and this time, so did I. The sword I offered her was the image and pattern of her own.

She didn't ask; she just looked.

"You saw this in my flat," I said. "I didn't steal it; I won it in fair fight from someone who'd no better claim to it. The most anyone's been able to tell me is that it looked like Bavarian make."

"It is," she agreed grimly, taking it now and examining it. "But no ordinary make. This broadsword with the basket hilt, of sabre shape, it's of a pattern and strength forged here alone, within the aegis of the Graal. It is the sword of a Graalsritter, a Knight, a very ancient one." She held it up to the light, squinting at the traceries along the blade. "Made around the time of the Emperor Frederick Barbarossa, perhaps. Some have been lost throughout the years; not many. They tend to find their own way home." She shot a sudden edged look at me. "And the Spear? You say you know where it is? Because it was you who took *that* as well?" A shadow of the old anger crossed her features. "Why? And while we're about it, *how* exactly?"

"Why? Because I was suckered by an old bastard called Le Stryge. He helped me once—the time I got that sword. Then he called in the tab, though I didn't know it . . . "

"Hauptmann Dragovic!" she said sharply. She looked down at the gray-faced lieutenant. "You will assist this man to medical attention, then return to your post, pending further orders!" She could still look very sour. Von Albersweg's head sagged. Dragovic clicked his heels, expressionlessly this time, and watched us as she sheathed her own sword, and with mine motioned me out into the corridor and down the stairs. Open air had never felt better as we emerged from the gatehouse, and I was glad when she briskly led me to a bench set around the base of a big old lime tree. I sat, at her order; but she remained standing, putting one foot up on the bench and leaning comfortably elbow on knee, my sword held lightly but ready in her hand. "So," she said grimly. "Consider this your hearing. Make the best of it!"

As briefly as I could, I rattled off the story. I'd expected questions, but not the crisp, continual grilling she gave me at every choice, every turn; obviously she'd been a trained interrogator. But there was something more, a sense of vision; the details she asked for were almost always telling, central, as if she could envisage practically the whole picture from my sketchy account. I'd spent more harassing half-hours, but not many, not least when it came to glossing over that little episode at the window. When she let me finish, she swung my sword up again, considering it. "And this—you took it from someone, you say?"

"Years ago. From a sea-raider, a Wolf, first mate of the privateer *Chorazin*. Where he got it I never knew; he wasn't around to ask anymore."

"A Wolf?" She raised an eyebrow. "That can't have been easy."

"You know them, then?"

"Oh, yes." Her face was hard to read. "I wonder how it ever came into such hands; we may never know. But there's just one thing you haven't told me. You hid the Spear—where? What's happened to it?"

"It's safe—"

"*Safe?*" No trouble reading her expression now. The old half-hysterical fury had turned into something much more controlled and channeled, but her eyes still seemed to crackle with it. "*Safe?* How can you be so sure? How dare you? You haven't a clue what you're playing with here! Half the Rittersaal's out scouring the Core for it—and more than half our enemies, you can be sure of that. If you've somehow managed to keep it safe from them it's pure fool's luck at best!"

"Look," I managed to get in, "I know you don't trust me, but—"

She raised her eyebrows. "Oh, no, I trust you. Implicitly—as far as this matter's concerned."

"That's a change. Maybe even a nice one. Why the sudden conversion?"

"It isn't sudden. I trusted you the moment I knew you were the thief."

I goggled. Maybe she was still crazy, after all. "I—don't exactly follow—"

"You mean you think I'm still crazy? No, Mr. Fisher. A great many things that were wrong with me have been straightened out, in body and mind both. That is the way of the Sangraal. I trusted you because you were able to steal the Spear in the first place. Because you could touch it without harm, as only the Knights can. No ordinary human could approach it, even; and anyone of seriously evil intent—well, you saw. Only a power of great strength could hold it directly."

"Yes!" I swallowed at the memory. "I felt—nothing. So you don't think Le Stryge shielded me somehow?"

"If he could shield anyone, he'd have shielded himself. So, strange as it seems to me, the Graal must have allowed you to steal the Spear. There must be some point, and I can only follow where it leads and await an answer. Personally—well, I studied the Department's dossier on you; my likes and dislikes don't count. But my duty does; and every moment our danger grows more acute." She turned on, eyes glittering. "Do you realize what it means? Without the Spear the Graal has only half its being—it's lost all its power to strike outward. And if they got hold of it, its enemies might even be able to breach its defenses." She looked around at the little square, at column and buttress and tower beyond, and shivered. "The Brocken could do that, or any one of a dozen other dark forces. Even a failed attempt could leave worse scars on the lands."

"In this valley, you mean? What scars?"

"They're there, even there. Didn't you see any of the ruins dotted about, or wonder about them? Once people could safely live the length and breadth of the Heilenthal, and our community extended far beyond the shadow of these walls. But it was the whole continent of Europe I meant; it has enough wounds to bear already. So, Mr. Fisher, where is it?"

"Well, if it's so urgent I'll give you the details and you can send—"

"No! You won't tell, we won't send." She whipped a notepad from her pocket and began scribbling. "Come along! It's urgent!"

She cut off my protest, caught me by the arm and more or less frogmarched me back toward the gate. As we came out into the wide square at its foot, we almost collided with the lieutenant, limping along with one leg of his breeches torn to take a heavy bandage. The woman returned his hasty salute. "You're relieved of duty? Very well, you can have this message sent to the Hall for me, for immediate reply. Then get down there yourself. Maybe the Graal will take pity on you."

"Zu Befehl, Ritterin Laidlaw!" he said sheepishly, tried to click his heels, winced and hobbled off.

"Take a carriage!" she called after him.

"Laidlaw," I said. "So that's your real name. Not bad— from a long line of Border cattle-thieves, eh? Can't stop thinking of you as 1726, though."

She ignored me, and shouted to the sentries inside the gate. In an instant they were all tumbling out, buckling belts and grabbing shakos, forming ranks alongside crisp-voiced NCOs. Clumping after them came Dragovic; he snapped to stony-faced attention at their head.

"Mmh!" she said. "Which other officers are on duty?"

"None, *Ritterin*. There is the conclave, and the others are heading the extra guard on the wall."

"Yes, of course. Well, we can't take them. It looks as if your excessive zeal is going to get a better reward than it deserves. Follow with six guards—picked men for a dangerous mission. Back to the Core."

He clicked his heels and bowed, beaming all over his sallow face. *"Zu Befehl! Zu Befehl, Ritterin!"*

"Now wait a minute—" I began.

She whirled to face me. "We can't wait. We've got to go and *get* the Spear at once. Me, and some guards—just in case I'm wrong about you. That helicopter of yours is a lot faster than our airships. You're not going to tell us, you're going to take us."

"*What?* Don't you want an army or something?"

She tossed her head rather than shook it. "We haven't got one to spare. I've sent for other Knights, but I don't think we'll get them. We daren't strip our defenses, even to get back the Spear. We'd have to recall troops, get them into suitable gear for the Core, and that takes time. And we'd have to use the airships. And it would attract just the wrong sort of attention. No, a small fast strike is the only way."

"Listen, that 'copter can only cram in four people, five at the most—"

"Your friends will be escorted back here in the meantime, as our guests. For yourself, you'll have to submit to the Graal's judgment. If all you say is true, and you prove yourself by getting us back the Spear without trickery or self-serving, you'll have nothing to fear. Now, come on! It's a long flight back."

"Maybe not," I said.

She turned that frown on me. "What do you mean?"

"When we're back at the 'copter—then we'll know."

I reached into the cockpit and switched on the navcom. It wouldn't work here any more than the radio, of course, but the integral pager should have recorded the C-Tran computer's last check-in automatically. I tapped in a number and checked the new page that opened on the screen. What came up gave me a sudden rush of satisfaction—and, to be honest, sheer relief. "Stuttgart!" I said. "Thought it might be. It was sent off just before we came here."

"I'm beginning to understand . . . " said the dark woman, slowly. "But . . . if you just sent it there, wouldn't that be too easy to trace?"

"Here, there, and everywhere," I said, enjoying the suspicious glare she gave me. "You'll catch on. But we'd better be going." I turned to Mall and Jyp. "You're sure you don't mind?"

Jyp's chuckle was drier than ever. "Steve, there's places I'll never have to buy another goddamn drink *ever* when they hear I've been here. You think I'd let a chance like this slip? I know guys who'd sell their souls t' be in my breeches this one minute!"

To my surprise the woman grinned at him. "Tell them no sale's needed—gratuities at the option of our guests, rather. Anyone of goodwill's welcome here, if they can reach it. You do understand you're not hostages? Normally you'd be free to wander, but as things are ... "

Mall smiled back. "Certes. I also, I'm not unmindful of the honor done me, lady. But, Steve, there's peril in this enterprise, it tickles my bones. I should not leave your side."

I shook my head firmly. "I'm not risking either of you again in this, not if I can help it. And this'll be quick—just there and back. You'll see."

The captain and two of the biggest and ugliest guards were attempting to cram themselves into the rear seat; the other four, detailed to escort Jyp and Mall, were rather nervously weighing up their charges. The woman swung her sword out of the way and hoisted herself into the front seat, very gracefully, reminding me—I couldn't help it—of another lissom rear view. But I caught Mall's sardonic eye, and hastily pulled on my helmet and waved everyone back from the rotors. The motors grumbled as we lifted off, but there were no warning signs on the panel; she seemed to be taking the extra weight. "I can find my way out of here well enough!" I said into the helmet link, as the tree-tops and the waving figures fell away. "It's getting back that worries me!"

The woman twitched her lips faintly and swung the mike-stalk down to them. "It shouldn't! In or out, it's the Graal that opens the way. With its will, you can come and go as you please; without it you could search for a million years and never find it." Her face clouded. "Unless you're a great adept, like the Stryge, damn him! He's been prowling around on our borders for years, him and his creatures!" Her fingers knitted impatiently, and she fell silent. The noise-canceling system left her voice and mine hanging in a void, as if we were the only sounds in an empty universe, creating an odd sense of intimacy. Certainly the others couldn't hear us. I glanced at her.

"What's your first name?"

She glared at me. "Why should I tell you?"

"No reason. I need something to call you, though. I can't get around *Ritterin* every time. *Lady*'s the English equivalent, maybe, or *Dame*; but I'd sound like a New York cabbie."

She didn't answer. I concentrated on flying; the weather was getting turbulent, the clouds thick. Half the time I was watching the navcom more than the windscreen. Suddenly she said, "Alison. It's Alison."

"Okay, Alison. I've got the navcom back. We should be there in about twenty minutes."

She twisted around to gesture at the guards, who weren't wearing helmets and were crowded together with their hands jammed over their ears. I hoped Dragovic was getting thoroughly sat on. After a while she spoke again. "Those two . . . friends of yours, the sea-pilot and that swordswoman—Elizabethan, is she?—they're not at all what I expected."

"Thank'ee kindly, Alison. Yes, they're even housetrained; a struggle, but I managed it."

She glared. "Don't be so bloody stupid. You made them sound like thugs. They're not. I liked them. Mall and . . . Jyp; is that his first name?"

"No idea; never found out. I didn't make them sound that way; you assumed. They're good friends, none better."

"They must be. I wonder . . . " She shook her head. "Mr. Fisher, you don't add up."

"That's why I never went into accountancy. You want a mathematician, ask Jyp. Natural talent plus about eighty years of studying, on and off. Incidentally, I shouldn't have to tell you my first name."

"Yes. I know a lot about you. Too much."

"The dossier, you said. You know how much I like that idea, Alison, you keeping files on me and all that?" I gunned the throttle savagely and tipped the cyclic, so the whole craft shook.

"Stop that!" she shouted, nearly deafening both of us. "What else could we do? You didn't suspect von Amerningen, but the Department did. We knew he was mixed up with this neo-Fascist thing—though I didn't know what was behind it then, of course. And suddenly there you were, his bright new *wunderkind* partner, setting up this amazing system and making him even richer than he is already. And you—you looked honest enough in business, Mr. Clean himself—but your private life, God!" She made a disgusted sound. "You came over as such a cold-hearted son of a bitch, you . . . " She shrugged. "I just loathed you. And the way you lived, all those casual pickups, the mysterious absences—it all fitted too well."

I groaned. "Christ, woman, don't your damn files make any allowance for time? All that casual stuff, it was just a phase, I haven't gone in for that for years! It was making me as unhappy as anyone; I just didn't realize it at first, that's all. Sure, I've had affairs since then, but they've meant something—or I wanted them to. As for the disappearances . . . "

"I know." She sighed. "I should have thought but it just didn't click. After all, do you ever pass somebody in the street and wonder if they're another spare-time wanderer out on the Spiral? If they're fighting dragons or trading treasures in their spare time?"

"Yes—yes, I do, as it happens, now and then. Get the odd quiet laugh out of it."

She looked startled. "Oh. But you didn't ever think that about me, did you? Or Baron von Amerningen? Well, then. And with you the patterns seemed to fit too well. I couldn't believe somebody like that could be really innocent, not one of that bastard's top partners. So when we kept on digging deeper and finding nothing, absolutely nothing at all, it just convinced me you were covering up that much better. And I hated you all the more."

"Till you got a bee in your bonnet."

She shook her head. "Not just about you. I wasn't too fond of myself just then. Or the Department. Or the world. But you seemed to sum it all up."

"Thanks a whole heap," I said. "That's pretty damn comprehensive."

"You wouldn't understand. I started out with ideals, you see. That's why I got into the investigation business in the first place. I was fed up saying why isn't somebody doing something about all this—I wanted to do something myself. But the more I tried the less I seemed to manage, it was like swimming through tar, and I found myself more and more fighting my colleagues, fighting the Department, even. They were just chalking up notches, career points, they didn't care about changing the world..." She drummed her fingers on her sword hilt. "I told you you wouldn't understand."

I corrected our heading slightly. "The Graal hasn't changed you that much. You're still jumping to conclusions. Me, I had it all mapped out at college—successful start in business, build up my contacts, my background, move gradually into politics. I managed to screw up my first real relationship chasing that hare. That stuck; I thought I'd done something clever, cutting loose, staying uninvolved. Only somehow the more successful I got, the less I cared. I told you I was going through a phase. Then one night I turned the right corner—"

"And there was the Spiral!" I could hear the shiver in her voice. "God, yes! I was scared stiff. And then I could hardly remember—I thought I'd got drunk or had a breakdown at last. It was a year before I even tried to get back. I couldn't at first and then, it was like losing my virginity again and I hadn't enjoyed *that* much either—"

The swift flush across her cheekbones and the dark sidelong glance dared me to make something of that. I resisted the temptation; I was still too struck by how different she managed to look. That rather Scandinavian slant to the eyes, which had made the frown look nailed on, seemed faintly exotic and serene now, and the mouth more sensual than heavy. The lips didn't look bitten anymore, either. There were still furrows down either side of her mouth, but the twist they gave it became wry and intelligent, quirky or humorous even; I could almost like it. I decided I'd like to see a proper smile, not one of those grim judicial twitches she'd come up with so far. She saw me looking, and turned away to stare out of the window.

"I know what you mean," I said. "I got hurt—and then frightened out of my skin. Then I poked around in the wrong place, and the whole thing just blew up in my face—like a fist punching into my everyday life."

She looked around, startled. "Into the Core?"

I knew that would fetch her. "Right in. And it grabbed somebody else instead of me. I had to help, really fast. That's how I got in hock to Le Stryge—or so he claims—and how I got that sword. And took to sailing the seas of the Spiral. But it was seven years before I dared try it again, seven years of forgetting it'd ever happened. Except in the odd daydream."

"I was lost," she said. "I was skiing. I took the wrong slope, or so I thought. I tried to turn back and I went over a cliff, I thought I was going to die, but it was lower than it looked and there was drifting at the foot. But I sprained my ankles so they were swelling up in my boots and it hurt like hell to walk, let alone ski. I couldn't find a way back up, the night came down and more snow, I just sat there and cried like a little girl. Then I saw a light, far away; and I made myself get up and trek, with my sticks. I came to this place—and it was a monastery, a genuine medieval monastery, at the edge of a tiny little village. They spoke Latin! But they had a hospice, they were good people; they spoke English when they heard me. They gave me mulled wine, bound up my ankles; it was like a dream. They seemed used to getting people from all over the Spiral— they tried to explain to me about it, but I didn't take it in, not then. There was a man in there, he didn't speak any language I knew, he looked—God, he must have been something ancient, he had a flint knife! And a bronze axe. But he was very polite. Nervous, but polite. I went away next day, with my ankles cured somehow—but I wanted to go back, with a gift. I memorized the way. Only when I tried—"

"You couldn't get through?"

"No. Oh, no. I know what you mean, but it was there, eventually. Only now the village around it was burning. There was a fight going on; and I had a pistol." That flush again. "Department issue, duty only—but I'd fiddled that, I always carried it in case of well, men. Always. So I waded in—and boy, were those things surprised!"

"Things?"

"Awful. You don't want to know. Something like Wolves, semi-human, but adapted for mountains. Not Abominable Snowmen or anything, spidery and strong, like gibbons, and shaggy. *Rubezahlern*, they called them. Anyway, those monks, they were the first friends I made on the Spiral. They knew a lot; everyone came to that hospice."

"Like the Tavern, I suppose. A haven in the fringes of the Spiral. Or that bar in Bangkok."

She gave me a very old-fashioned look. "You would know that one! Anyway, I took to wandering about on the Spiral whenever I could, sometimes with people I met there, sometimes on my own. At first it scared me—but it fascinated me, too. And toughened me up, a lot."

I heard my breath rasp across my helmet mike. "That's an understatement! And you never forgot?"

"No. Not really. The first time was pretty incredible, but I had those odd bandages on my ankles, soaked in peculiar herbs; they worked, too. I couldn't forget that. If I stayed away too long the whole thing'd begin to drift out of my head at times, seem more and more like a silly dream; so I always went back when that started to happen. I was scared I'd lose it. But there was more than that. Somehow out there I could achieve things, I wasn't always fighting the weight of events or the people pressures I was here. A complete contrast—and it just made me madder with things here. I got more and more determined and more insecure; I blamed myself. If I could do good out there, why not here?"

"And you began to feel torn?" I didn't know why I volunteered that just then. She looked at me, just as startled.

"Yes! Until one day, I stumbled . . . No, I don't want to tell you about that. It was the Graal, anyway; it called me, and I followed. I was dazed, but I couldn't make the break, I wasn't ready. Out here, it was great, but—I couldn't really believe in its problems when I wasn't in the thick of them. I didn't want to abandon the Core, the Department—they seemed more real, somehow. The tension pulled me this way, that way, till I got really afraid I'd tear apart, crack up completely, have a breakdown. That was where I was about the time we started probing you." She shifted uneasily, but she didn't look away; I would have had to.

"You . . . you looked so bloody successful, so self-satisfied and sleek and sharply dressed and handsome in that sort of way. And you drove the kind of car I couldn't afford even on a good EC wage. And at first you had a ghastly private life; later on, you seemed to have less and less private life at all. I thought all wanderers would be like me, unhappy sideliners; it never occurred to me that you might be another. Or I might be seeing just one side of you, and the best might be . . . somewhere else. So I thought, *Just let me get him, just him—and then I'll be free to go. Really free.*" She clutched the edge of the control panel, and shuddered. "That's why I went after you, even when my boss tried to cool the file because we weren't getting anywhere. And then you caught me and beat the daylights out of me, and blew my cover . . . and I got referred for psychiatrics . . . and suspended pending transfer . . . That's when I thought I'd have to shoot you outright."

She rubbed a hand across her lips. "God, why am I telling you all this? Only, when you could have put me out of the way so easily . . . when I tried to shoot you . . . you would have. If you'd been von Amerningen's man you'd have done it in a second, you wouldn't have dared do anything else. But you didn't. You even gave me my pistol back." She slumped down in her seat. "I nearly used it on myself. I didn't understand, I couldn't grasp a thing, and yet I knew I'd been wrong, wrong, wrong. That was the last straw. I quit, I moved out, I ran. I ran to the Graal, and it took me in, and healed me. It gave me back myself, the self I should have been. The years since then have been just—"

"*Years?*" I barely stopped myself letting go the throttle. "My God, that was just a couple of nights ago to me! I haven't even caught up on my sleep since then . . . though that nap in the valley was amazing."

"It would be," she said, and her face softened suddenly. "I remember the first time I slept there. But you know what the Spiral's like. It's been five years for me."

"Yes, I know. If anything you look younger."

Suddenly she did smile, and that alone was the biggest transformation yet. But before I could tell her that, the navcom chimed softly through my phones. We were getting near Stuttgart, and I had to begin the long sweep down out of the clouds that would keep us clear of other flight corridors. I switched onto the local tower, and was about to start paging their controllers when the woman—no—Alison put a hand on my knee. The sudden intimacy was so unexpected I froze, though she only wanted to interrupt.

"Not at the heliport," she said over the link. "Can't you put us down as near as possible to wherever the Spear is? It'll be far safer."

I winced. The days when you could muck around like that were long gone; there'd been too many aircraft accidents over cities. On the other hand, we were headed for the edge of town; and it might be easier than trying to get a pack of hussars through airport security. I turned away to circle the city, and ducked down as if I were headed away again, lower and lower. If only the bloody landscape hadn't been so flat I could have got off radar more easily. I had to go a long way out and then come hedgehopping back by a zigzag route, praying I saw all the power lines, wind farms and similar obstructions in time. But at last the geometric patterns of the industrial development opened up before me, alongside a venous bunch of railway tracks, and I brought the little craft sideslipping in behind a conveniently large warehouse.

"We can't leave it here long," I hissed as we bumped down into the empty parking lot, the downdraft tipping a stack of empty cartons and whipping up a faint haze of spray. "Somebody's bound to report it and we'll have a police chopper overhead or on our tail. But we shouldn't need long!"

I slid back the door onto cool, rainwashed night air. Dragovic and the guards spilled out, groaning with relief and sticking fingers in their ringing ears. As the woman called Alison stepped down Dragovic moved swiftly to her side, and loomed there protectively when I ducked out. Was that the way the wind blew? It might explain his ruthless drive for success. "How far is it?" he growled.

"Two minutes," I said, and turned to the complex of lower buildings just across the lot.

"You know your way?" she demanded, as we padded swiftly across the slick tarmac, Dragovic and the guards casting dark glances around them. "Won't there be trouble with security men? Alarm systems? We know a few useful tricks for dealing with those."

"I'd rather you didn't. There won't be any trouble. I own this place—my company, anyhow." I fumbled for my keycase, hard to get out of these tight pockets, and fished out a strip of plastic with the spidery outline of a chip embedded into it. When we reached the gate I shoved it into a slot, spoke a few words into the shielded microphone and clapped my palm to the greenlit panel that uncovered below. There was an instant's delay, and the courtyard lighting went on. "Bugger! The local manager's been adding refinements, I didn't want that. Come on!"

I went through the same routine at an inner door, though this time I had to speak rather longer, and touch my index fingers to the panel as well. "ID, voice and print," nodded the woman. "Not bad. All the usual alarms, too?"

"The lot." We opened the building door and slipped inside, boots squeaking on the glossy black flooring with its broad colored stripes, eccentrically set. "But the main thing to watch out for is the automatic pallets—here's one now." Along the yellow line in front of us glided a low rectangle, edged with yellow stripes, topped with a pile of small crates and packages, plus its unloading arms and the gas supply for its ground-effect flotation pucks. Hissing faintly, it swung cumbersomely around to follow the inlaid line in the floor, and vanished among rows of stacks. Over to one side the arm mechanisms that had loaded it clacked back into their racks. The others watched it go, obviously impressed. I turned to the woman. "Lutz was even talking about getting those American guard-robots, too, for some buildings. Basically a mobile infrared scanner with programmable discrimination and patrol patterns, plus built-in high voltage stunguns. Or a Colt .35 auto mechanism, if you really want to be left alone; but I wouldn't have that, and nor would the local cops. We tried one stun model. The second night somebody left a nice warm computer running and the robot shocked the bejasus out of it. Shorted the whole network. Back it went."

The woman—no—Alison chuckled. "What on earth is this place?"

"The local C-Tran depot. I've never been here, but they're all to the same layout, more or less. What we need is a local terminal for the main freight computer—should be one right by the heavy-duty conveyor that brings in really massive pallets, machinery and so on, see there? And here it is. All the symbology's German, but that doesn't matter . . . "

It stood on a pedestal to the side of a long conveyor used for really heavy pallets, machinery and so on. I began tapping keys, and somewhere else in the warehouse we heard another pair of arms clack out, ready to shift a new load. Machinery hummed softly, and a pair of pallets swung into view, clearing the most direct path.

The others were visibly nervous, Dragovic tugging at his collar, Alison fidgeting with the panel's corner molding. "It's here, then?"

"Yes. Just a minute or two now. *Damn!*"

"What's wrong?" she spat.

I glared at the blinking characters.

URGENTIN IMMINENT EVENT SYSTEM WIPEOUT*INTERFACE PORT S WITH PORT G**URGENT**

"Nothing, nothing. Just some programmer playing silly buggers. It's here."

She sagged slightly. "Thank God. So you just parceled it up and sent it off down your freight system. You didn't know any better, but it was a terrible risk you took, even using a roundabout route. They could just have got into the computer and traced any packages sent from that office around that time. Lutz could do that, or somebody else;

they can get real experts. Or they could just have forced you to give away the route."

I grinned. "No, they couldn't. They couldn't force me, because I never knew; and the computer couldn't show any such package because there wasn't any."

"Then how—"

I chuckled. "You know how the system works? No? The idea's not so complex. I was getting fed up with all the delays in international shipping—consignments spending ages waiting for clearance or transshipment to road or rail or air, or just till somebody can fill a container or guarantee a return load, that kind of thing. Even when the EC brought down customs barriers they were replaced by a battery of checks that were ten times worse, security, health, you name it. Plus consignments would get lost, sidelined, mishandled; every delay increased the chances of that happening. I spent a lot of my time wishing the whole thing could be simplified, that the consignments could look after themselves. And I began to see how they could. A single freight network, in continuous motion, each road or rail or water or air link coordinated and continuously monitored by computer systems. And smart packaging—each consignment, even the smallest parcel, with its own on-board computer instead of a label. A pretty simple job, sturdy, fail-safe, but smart enough to know its own identity, contents, dispatch and delivery addresses and any other special conditions, and stay in touch with the main network. That way the network knows where each consignment is, each parcel knows where it is, and between them they choose the most efficient route, even from one end of a warehouse to the other—and if anything goes wrong on the way they can modify it. So our freight-carriers are always used to maximum capacity, nothing has to hang around, and we always know exactly where it is and when it'll get anywhere, when it leaves the system and so on. And it has total integrity, because the computer knows when it's being mucked about. And you can't get at the computer without destroying the packaging; and you can't do that without alerting the main computer. You can't even identify a consignment without alerting the main computer. That let us negotiate international agreements so that each consignment only needs to be checked at dispatch and delivery, when the label is programmed. Hey presto! No checks, no pilfering, no delays. Interfere with a consignment and it screams for help. Delay it, and it finds its own way around. Dead simple. All you need to do is make it work."

Alison grimaced. "Right. That's all. And how often've you reeled off *that* little spiel?"

I grimaced back. "You mean, apart from in my sleep? I've lost count."

"But if you say there wasn't any parcel or whatever . . ."

Between the two diverted pallets, their unloading arms raised as if in salute, glided another, empty except for a large plastic case, elegantly striped with the C-Tran logo and slogans in a host of languages, but already looking rather battered. "Pity I can't ever use this in an ad. You see, a system like ours depends one hundred percent on efficient circulation. One log-jam somewhere, one undetected breakdown and we lose a huge part of our advantage over more conventional methods. So it has to be monitored constantly, by including test loads in the system, always in motion, always circulating, never unloaded, reporting their progress and all the other conditions by onboard computers and telemetry gear, which is normally all they contain." I grinned. "Till now. Of course we have to divert them now and again to repair the gear and so on, but that's listed under maintenance, not freight. And they get checked to see they're not used for smuggling—but not within the EC, naturally. In the day or two since I put it in there your Spear's been on a free tour of Europe and back, untraceable and inaccessible except by someone who thought of the maintenance system and knew how to get into it—something my dear partner Lutz would never dream of dirtying his hands with. And who knew which of all the various test loads it might be, and had the skill to trace it. Force wouldn't leave me in any state to do that. Some kind of possession might, but not if I'm on my guard."

Alison the Graal Knight perched on the broad ledge alongside the conveyor and watched wide-eyed, swinging her legs, as the pallet sighed to a halt at her feet. "I read up on all this for your dossier," she said. "Never a word about test loads. And you know what? I should've realized you knew about the Spiral and the Core, too. You've gone and created a sort of microcosm here, a secret world, in constant flux."

I leaned over the case, slid another chip-key into its lock and popped open the lid. Alison gave an excited gasp. There, across a tangle of ribbon cables linking various sullen beige instrument boxes, lay the long metal casing Le Stryge had provided for the Spear. I was just stretching out a hand to lift it when I heard a metallic click that wasn't any of the usual warehouse noises—too close. My eyes flicked from one image to another, at the extreme edges of my vision.

Alison, mouth open to shout, grabbing for her sword hilt —which at that angle, even if she had Mall's bullet-splitting speed, she could never hope to draw.

Dragovic's hand half-way from his holster, thumb still resting on the safety catch he'd flicked, not realizing how loud it'd sound in that breathless instant. He'd alerted us both and he knew it. There'd be no stagey preliminaries; he was going to shoot, at once. He had to.

I froze, one hand hovering in mid-air, the other on the edge of the terminal. I thrust out those fingers and clamped down hard. I felt a function button in the top row give and click, but it seemed an eternity before anything happened, while the gun swung up to face us. Then an alarm shrieked, a red light flashed, and the conveyor lurched into life. In the same instant I threw myself forward, vaulting the case, cannoned into Alison and knocked her sprawling from her perch, right over the conveyor. I caught one topsy-turvy glimpse of Dragovic, mouth agape; then we were rolling entangled across the floor. He loosed off an echoing fusillade just as a high packing case chugged into his path; the bullets thudded hollowly, and kicked up a cloud of chips and splinters. The guards came running to his side, tugging out their heavy revolvers. Hardly a surprise: he'd chosen them.

We staggered to our feet, ducking from side to side, keeping behind the boxes as they bumped past, playing peek-a-boo with the guards. They snapped off a couple of shots which hit nothing but the merchandise and the frame of the conveyor. One, realizing he'd get nowhere, leaped up onto the side ledge to see over. I reached between packages and lunged at his foot, almost slashing the toe off his boot. He staggered, loosing a shot at the roof, and fell back with a heavy thud, triggering another wild shot. The other emptied his gun into the general area of the cases, and I scurried away with wood and shredded cardboard packaging flying around my ears.

The guards were yelling at Dragovic, demanding he finish us and fast; they sounded suitably rattled. He kept some semblance of brains and ordered them to jump across the belt further along, while he kept us pinned down. He glimpsed us and loosed another burst; we ducked down behind a tall heavy machinery case, while the guards scrambled noisily up onto the ledge and through a gap in the loads. One reached an arm around and fired twice, at random, to give them a clear moment to jump down. We weren't there. Without a word spoken—a look had been enough—we were both of us scrabbling up on top of the tall packing case, tipping it forward. The captain barely hopped away in time as it loomed over him, and we sprang free; it hit the floor with a booming thunderclap, he skidded back, collided with the first row of racking and dropped both the case with the Spear and his gun, which skidded away under the racks. He ducked after it. We went for him, only to jump back as a laden pallet slid innocently into our path, resuming its old preoccupations. A bullet bounced off it; the guard was firing from behind the conveyor. Then he threw down the empty pistol and they all jumped back across, drawing their sabres. We turned, and they were on us.

It was me they both went for, parrying Alison's swift lunge and ducking by, aiming a furious rain of cuts and slashes at me. They thought I was the weaker one, they meant to fell me fast by main force and leave themselves free to take her on. She didn't buy it; instead she was suddenly back to back with me, a supple, twisting presence, as they circled around us like snapping dogs. They were tough nuts, and fast, one of them almost as good as the captain. Evidently Alison thought I was the weak link too, because she wheeled us around after him, which wasn't getting us anywhere.

"Sod that!" I yelled—as good a battle cry as any, probably—and went for him, leaping forward into his attack with a swift stabbing lunge. He took my blade deftly and launched a hissing swipe at my face, I stopped it with a parry *quarte* and disengaged with what seemed to me deadly slowness; yet somehow my blade was on the other side of his, still across his body, and he was just bunching his arm for the riposte. I threw all my weight into a thrust that went right across his sword and drove down under his breastbone, pinning him to a neat pile of plastic sacks. I yanked loose and he folded with a groan as the heap collapsed on him. I whirled just in time to see why they'd been scared of Alison. She danced forward with a flickering attack that made her sabre look light as a foil, lanced past her opponent's guard and stabbed once and twice into his chest. He roared and lunged at her, she skipped away and abruptly parried with a circling, irresistible swing whose sheer strength flung his sword wide and wild, leaving him open to a leaping strike, a classic *flèche* that ran her blade deep under his armpit and killed him where he stood.

But even as she pulled free of the falling body a shot

plucked at her sleeve, and another smacked off the shelving. The captain had got his gun back. I meant to haul her back behind the racks, but she hauled me. "Pinning us down—" she panted. "Going for door! We jump him—wide apart! You take the left. Ready?" I nodded. "One—two— go!"

We dashed out together, but I jumped across the wide trackway, while she sprinted down the right flank. If the captain had delayed an instant longer he might never have got out; but he was already at the door, his hand on the handle, his gun leveled and the metal case under his arm. It was Alison's turn to launch herself at me; I fell, and the spray of fire splattered into stacked packages where I'd been that half heartbeat before. Then abruptly it stopped with a clicking snap. The Mauser had jammed; either that fall on the floor had done it no good, or he'd misloaded a clip in his haste. Complex machinery is hard to maintain on the Spiral, where industrial societies can't flourish. We were up and after him in the instant; but the door slammed behind him.

He might have been waiting outside to snipe at us as we emerged, but somehow I didn't think he'd risk lingering to clear the jam. We rushed out into the bleak white lighting of the yard, and saw the fence wire still vibrating where it had been scaled, the shreds of black material on the razor-wire along the top. Footsteps rattled away into the distance with frantic haste. Unlike the inner door, the gate needed a key from both sides, and that cost us a few more seconds. We rushed out; but whichever way we looked, there were only the bare brick and aluminum flanks of the buildings, smoothly sterile, and the empty rain-puddled streets between.

Chapter 8

Alison ground her teeth, audibly.

"Well, it's got to be one way or the other," I began, peering at the pavement where he'd jumped down. The rain-slicked tarmac was scuffed and slithered over, but one print stood out clearly in little streaks of muddy water. Suddenly Alison yelped and pointed to a smear of mud on the edge of the pavement further along. "So? Mud's not exactly in short supply in this weather."

"Maybe—but with grass and flowers in it?"

I glanced around at the arid industrial desert, new enough that nature hadn't started to reassert herself through cracks in the concrete façade. "It's better than nothing—come on!"

But she was running already. The road was a short one, doglegging left past a really impassable-looking fence and out into the main parking lot of the estate, empty now except for a few parked trucks. Beyond it was a main road into town, busy even at this time. Again we stared around wildly. "He can't have gone out there!"

"Why not?" she said, and ran on. But she sheathed her

sword, and I mine. The chances were that nobody would even notice them if we didn't draw attention to them; the Core is like that. But in the glare of headlights, say, a naked blade, highly reflective, might be another story. I'd had cop trouble before now. We reached the roadside and leaped the low fence onto the cycle track alongside, still peering ahead.

"He'll be out of sight by now," said Alison bitterly. "Out of town, probably, into the dark—"

I caught her shoulder. "No, by God! Look!"

Her eyes glittered under the street lights. "*Yes!* Tally-ho!"

She didn't strike me as the fox-hunting type, so I guessed she knew that old joke too. And there the bastard went, right enough. A hefty figure in black, with one sleeve showing white and a gleam of metal under his arm, was running hell for leather along the cycle track toward town. Even as we saw him he vanished down into an underpass. We ran again, our feet slapping on the harder surface. "He should've been long gone!" I panted. "I would have, and I think he's in better shape! Did we hurt him?"

"Never touched him!" gasped Alison. Then without stopping she twisted and looked back at the glowing callbox we'd just passed. "You don't think—"

"What—the Brocken's on the phone?"

"No, idiot!" she spat. "But the Baron is!"

"Oh. Right. A hundred miles away, mind. Better keep our eyes open, all the same."

We ran down through the underpass and up, and suddenly we were out of the industrial wilderness and into a world of neon signs and shop windows and streets still quite full. A ripple of turning heads, a flash of metal, a flicker of black led our eyes straight to the dark figure zigzagging through the crowds, and we went pounding after him, soft-drink cans and discarded pizza boxes whizzing across the pavement from under our feet, the usual debris of an urban evening. We attracted less attention than the captain; my black piratical gear and gaudy sweatband could be mistaken for expensively sleek athletics kit, Alison's uniform for a gray shellsuit. Most people probably just saw a pair of tall thirtysomethings out for their evening run, and anybody who noticed the swords had more sense than to say anything about it. We didn't speak, for we needed all our breath for running; but one flashing glance from Alison confirmed what I thought. We were gaining on the captain, strong though he was. We were close enough to see the occasional glint of the metal case, his tattered sleeve trailing free, the whites of his bulging eyes as he darted frantic looks back. Instant death ran at his heels, minutes behind, and he knew it. But then everything changed.

I felt it seconds before I saw it, and more seconds still before I could believe I saw it. I thought it was just exhaustion at first, the limits of my strength—much the way I'd felt on the last stretches of the Boston marathon. But I hadn't even run a half-marathon yet, and here was this leaden-limbed, suffocating sensation clamping down on me, pushing against my chest like the resistance on a cross-country ski simulator. I didn't say anything, I just pressed on, but I noticed Alison was looking tight-lipped and gray as well. But then, as the captain rounded a street corner, I did see something—something I remembered all too well. Hanging in the air like the ghost of a mist, tenuous, insubstantial, it filled the broad avenue from side to side; but it settled around me as I appeared, and the pressure grew worse. It clung as I ran, spreading out in streams from side to side like a wake. Now heads turned as we passed, and among some of those the mist seemed to settle, and the faces changed, struck by a sudden spasm, a flicker of sudden bestial anger. Not only a couple of skinheads, neo-Nazis probably, and a big hairy character in over-studded leathers, but also an ordinary young woman, *Hausfrau* type, a teenage girl with an ice-cream cone and a plump horn-rimmed *Burgerlicher*, an unlikely threat to anything except a second helping of *Kalbsfleisch*. Some of them only looked; but others moved out as if to follow. I tried to tell myself it was my imagination, but when I shot another look at

Alison I got a glance of horrified alertness in return, and a confirming nod. My lungs were laboring, but I was about to say something sensible back when I saw the faint hazy streamers drift out among the traffic, and worm their way into the path of a police car passing on the far side.

The reaction was instant: the driver stood on his brakes, the siren came on and the car pulled around in a screeching U-turn across the *Strassenbahn* tracks, straight toward us. Alison yelled in anger and clutched my arm, hauling me with her across the pavement to the shelter of a darker side-street. I didn't need any persuading; we ducked around the next corner, vaulted a barrier into an underground car park and clattered between the petrol-scented rows to the exit opposite.

"That—should—break our trail!" she wheezed as we staggered up into another shadowy side-street. She hung onto the gatepost and gasped for breath.

I doubled over to ease a developing stitch. "Right . . . got to get back . . . pick up captain's . . . " Then I hauled her back into the shadow of the wall and hissed, *"Look!"*

The exit was near the corner of a wider street, more poorly lit than the main streets and completely empty. But from an alley two blocks down a man tottered into it, a man in worse shape than we were, reeling like a drunk. That far ahead of us it wasn't easy to be sure; but somehow I was. He leaned against a lamppost for a moment, hugging something large to his chest; I didn't need to see what. Our involuntary short-cut had second-guessed his escape route; we only had to move in quietly, keep in the shadows and we'd have him.

But moving quietly is slow, especially when you're as blown as we were; even limping and gasping he was gaining on us. It was beginning to look like a geriatric speed trial, and there was a T-junction ahead, beyond it a building site with a towering crane as skeletal sentinel over its high wire fence—too many opportunities to ditch us. "Sod this!" I whispered, stalking out of a doorway. "Let's rush him! With any luck he'll trip and break his bloody—"

She grabbed my arm. "Wait! He's crossing the road! Get back in the shadow!"

Too late, because he wasn't crossing. He walked straight up to that forbidding fence, thrust the case into his jacket and began to climb. Only, as one does, he looked around first, and, of course, he saw us. Limping he might have been, but he was up that fence like a scared cat; still, he was only just at the top when we clattered up to the foot. I sprang up and slashed at him, but the blade passed a foot short as he swung himself off the top, over the razor-wire and onto one of the irregular heaps beyond, landing with a metallic clatter that seemed to go cascading away into the darkness. Alison was already clambering after him. I grabbed her heel and boosted her up to within reach of the top, she reached down an impatient hand and swung me up after her, then she sprang for the same heap, drawing her sword as she leaped. She landed with the same din and scrambled down the heap like a stair. I left my sword where it was, skidded as I landed and fell down onto metal that gave beneath me with a tinny thump. It was the bonnet of a rusty old car, and it slid me down onto another one beneath. I jumped, expecting solid ground; but I landed on a slope, a steep unstable slope that gave beneath my heels like shale or scree. I clung to the car and scrabbled for a foothold; below me darkness pooled like a lake in Hell. Something touched my leg, and I lashed out in alarm.

"Down here!" hissed Alison, and tugged again. I let go, leaned on her and together we went slipping and sliding down into the dark on little shifting slides of metal. I got my feet, she lost hers and almost fell head first under a cascade of clattering things as we struck the bottom. I helped her up, retrieved her sword, and together we peered into the cluttered dimness, listening for any sound of movement. A thousand empty eyes stared back, a macabre charnel-house of vacant sockets and gaping grins. They glimmered faintly in the city glow reflected off the clouds in place of moon or star, darkly mirrored in the iridescent puddle that slapped gently at our feet. This wasn't a building site, it was a graveyard, a communal plague-pit for the picked bones of planned obsolescence, the moldering corpses of cars. Their dismantled guts coated the slope we'd slid down.

"Dante would've loved this!" I muttered, and then suddenly I snapped my fingers. "Stuttgart! A big scrapyard, not far from the city center! *Metallwiederaufbereitungs Amerningen!* This belongs to one of Lutz's recycling companies. There could be a rendezvous here—"

The abrupt animal tension in Alison's stance silenced me quicker than any gesture. I looked where she looked, and instinctively clutched my arm around her shoulders. The cloud was back, drifting like wafts of cobweb silk outside the fence; and it was thicker. Suddenly it seemed to gather itself and roll, not through the mesh as you might expect, but over the top, as if it were a complete thing that couldn't stand separation. I noticed it avoided the razor-wire, too. We shivered, ready to run the moment it came after us. But it didn't. It plunged down, growing thicker and whiter all the time, like a waterfall out of emptiness, straight into the ground beyond the fence; a few seconds it fell, then vanished.

We weren't stupid. We turned to run, plashing exhaustedly through that bloody puddle. But Alison skidded, then me, as if the metal buried beneath was snagging feebly at our ankles; when the noise came we were barely across. Behind us the whole slope was heaving as if there was an earthquake, or something burrowing underneath. Long streaks of scattered small parts were flung up into the air, in loose sprays at first, then geysers, then in long stringy ribbons that wavered and convulsed before disintegrating again—all that, in the space of a second or two, while we gaped, appalled. Then there was a swift decisive clash, and out of the metallic rubble, waving long metallic pincers, lifted something like a head. Not a human head; it had two glinting lenses, but they were many-faceted domes bulging out of each apex of a triangular, featureless snout. Something clacked beneath it, like wide mandibles. Behind it a humped body arched and lifted on six dully gleaming legs, shedding showers of rusty metal and dribbling streams of ancient oil and dirty rainwater. It was made entirely of the stack debris, this thing, metallic, clanking, grinding, squeaking; yet it looked a lot more organic than mechanical. It could have been eight or ten yards across, something between a spider and a flattened mantis; and with a spider's gait it came scuttling forward through the churning pool.

The thing moved so fast that in our hypnotized horror we almost got caught. A claw swiped at us; Alison's sword barely parried it, and I hadn't even drawn mine. As it rattled back I ducked, scooped up a heavy driveshaft from the ground at my feet and swung it hammer-fashion. The clang was deafening, and a shower of debris rained down on our heads. The thing reeled back, forelimbs flailing in the air. I flung the steel rod like a javelin at one bulging eye, and we ran like hell.

The thing pattered after us, quieter now, the squeak and grind of rusty metal merging into a tooth-grinding hiss and chitter. Around the cars we ran, from one level of blind darkness to another, and always around a corner ahead or just at our heels that sinister chitter would sound. It would pounce suddenly from behind a stack, or clamber out into our path and stand there, waiting with nerve-fraying patience. No question, it was hunting us like a real animal, only with a more than animal cunning behind it. Twice I tried to strike at it, but it was ready now; once it caught the axle I was about to throw and very nearly dragged me in by it. Over and over we tried to dodge down narrow gaps between stacks, but the horrible thing simply squeezed itself up and pushed through with a grate and squeal of metal. We were tired already; now we were reeling, slipping, falling on our knees in the filth of automobile entrails. And far from reaching the fence, we'd been deftly driven deep into the heart of the huge yard, under the feet of the huge crane there.

"Climb it!" I yelled, but Alison shook her head slackly.

"No good—it'd climb too—or just pluck us off—"

It was then the darkness seemed to explode with light. I shook her, hard. "I'll climb!" I shouted. "You—circle! Keep dodging!"

Her eyes glinted as she looked up, wildly; and then of all things a grin flashed at me through the darkness. She'd actually sensed my idea, this amazing woman; and what was more, she'd accepted it without a word, even though it left her in terrible danger. She hefted something heavy, a cylinder-head I think, and hurled it right at the oncoming thing. It was a throw that wouldn't have disgraced an Olympic shot-put, and her aim was better than mine. One reflecting many-faceted eye went out in a scatter of broken headlamp lenses. You wouldn't have thought it would matter, but it did; the thing went wild, blundering from side to side for a moment, then it fixed on her and pounced. She was already away, and I was half-way up the ladder or further, praying I could manage this. She dodged around the base as the thing rushed again, never moving far away; and I reached the little metal gallery at the side of the crane's cab. It was old and battered, the doorlatch weak; but it might take seconds I didn't have to get it open. My sword went through the windscreen in a shower of safety glass, I went after it and began ripping out the dashboard leads to hot-wire a connection.

It felt like centuries before the engine spluttered and caught, and I slumped back into the greasy chair, working the levers as I went, kicking out for the pedals. For a moment my fuddled mind started flying a helicopter, but I'd been shown how to use a dockyard crane once, and this wasn't too different—except that there should be one extra control. I peered over the dashboard at the dirt-obscured German legends, and finally found one, the big red switch. I snapped it over.

Down below Alison shouted—or was it a scream? I leaned over, saw her scramble up on a car bonnet and crouch there, blade leveled before her. With terrible courage she stayed there as the thing advanced, slowly, as if suspicious of this sudden stand. And rightly so, for she'd given me just the position I needed. I didn't even have to swing the crane; I released the winch, the heavy cable screamed over its pulleys, the great grab at its tip with its electromagnet activated arrowed down like a harpoon onto that obscene bulk and clanged in deep. The thing convulsed with a screech like abrading steel, rearing back; and I seized the moment to rev the motor to its maximum and slam out the winch clutch. This isn't a good idea in normal circumstances; inertia being what it is, you might strip the gears or even pull the crane over. But I didn't give a damn; and to move so lightly that monster had to be hollow. Off the ground it lifted, twisting, kicking, a metal spider snared by a single webstrand of steel. Alison leaped down and away, around the base of the crane; and as she got clear I snapped the grab lever home, and twisted the red switch with the double lightnings to *aus*. The closing claw crushed and tore that kicking bulk; the magnet, turned off, let the mangled thing fall.

Only about twenty feet, but it was ample. It hit the ground and disintegrated in a great ringing explosion of bits, like a percussion group on self-destruct. Nuts, bolts, washers, valveheads, screws, springs, spark-plugs, shocks, half-shafts and millions of less identifiable components flew in all directions, some as high as the crane cab, and came raining and rattling down like hail on the grinning automobile corpses. By the time the last one fell nothing even remotely spider-like remained. I hardly gave the scattered heap a glance; I was swinging down the ladder, and shouting for Alison.

She was there, staggering up the lower rungs, clutching her forehead where some falling debris had caught it. But she let it go and grinned up at me, a wolfish grin, joying in mayhem, that made me want to hug her. *"Sic semper tyrannis!"* she carolled. I was just wondering whether to risk that hug when she grabbed me by the arms, and a deafening thudding roar shook the yard, as though all the ghostly engines were coming alive. It was another helicopter, a biggish, sleek machine coming in low between the buildings, dangerously low; and the searchlight at its shark-like nose nacelle snapped into searing life. For a minute I thought it must be the police; then the light struck the summit of a wide heap of cars at the far corner of the yard and hung there, circling slightly as the helicopter wavered. Up into the glare, keeping low, scrambled a human shape, and the light winked painfully off the case under one arm.

"Come on!" screamed Alison over the row, and together, staggering like drunks, we ran down the dark alleys of scrap. The figure looked around and cried out, gesturing urgently; a rope ladder came tumbling down, a short one, and he hooked his free arm onto it. As we stumbled closer hands reached down to grab him and haul him in, and suddenly the 'copter began to turn on its axis, the light tracked across the shattered stacks of bodies and pinned us down like rabbits at a burrow mouth. We broke for cover as the hammering burst of an automatic rifle drowned even the 'copter engines; a stream of bullets popped through car bodywork and richocheted screaming off chassis members and cylinder blocks, while the mud beyond flew up and danced. In that maelstrom we dived for what cover we could, cowering, while the 'copter made one swift circuit of the yard; then its light snapped off, and it climbed away into the mirk.

There was a long silence, until a rather tremulous voice inquired "Steve?"

My own came out as a sort of strangled croak. "Alison? You okay?"

"Suppose so. You?"

"Yes. Thank God they weren't trying too hard. That was one of Lutz's machines."

"Yes. And that—that sending, too, I expect."

"The cloud? And ... " Neither of us wanted to name it more closely. The very thought still made me shake. It was more than fear; it was the horrible wrongness of it, the gross mockery of life in that image—carefully chosen, no doubt. Spiders are one of the commonest phobias; I hadn't thought they were one of mine, but if I wasn't careful they could be. I didn't believe in Hell, either; but here in this horrible pit, with the taint of that evil still almost tangible in the air, a waft of corruption you could almost taste, it was getting harder. Whatever the source of such evil powers, it had to be wrong, it had to be something to meet, to stand up to, to obliterate before it could do more damage, because damage was all it could do. Hell was as good a name for it as any.

"It did what it was meant to, anyway," she said. "It got us off Dragovic's tail. Time for them to arrange a little air-taxi for him—straight to the Brocken, probably."

"By helicopter?"

"The same way you got to the Heilenthal." She sighed. "Come on, we'd better get back. There may still be something the Graal can do, even if we can't. I hope they haven't taken a moment to shoot up your machine; Dragovic knows where it is. Damn the man."

I looked at her as she got up, wincing at some unexpected bruise. I was gradually becoming aware that something had left a horrendous hacked bruise on my shin, but I was almost too numb to care. But she—what was she thinking? Here was a woman facing the ruin of everything she cared for, and in a cruelly ironic way she was partly responsible. I was prepared for storms, for tears; even a woman as self-possessed as my friend Jacquie would have cried. This one went on being calm, thinking logically, and I was almost offended. Idiotically, because I couldn't think why, unless, perhaps, it was at not being able to console and comfort her. I'd done that for women, often; I hadn't realized till now just how much I'd been comforting myself.

"Damn the man," she repeated, as we picked our way across the wasteland that spelled prosperity for Lutz. "And damn me, too. I would have to bring him along!"

I tried not to take the usual kind of line. It would have been insulting her, somehow. "I'm more to blame. This never would've happened if—"

"No," she said, quite flatly. "No, that was meant to happen, or at least not opposed. I'm to blame."

"You couldn't have known he was a traitor."

"I knew there were traitors. Everybody knew. But it's not that, in itself. It's that . . . " She looked at me. "I should have trusted you. Really trusted you, I mean, not just halfway. I was meant to, and I failed. I should have taken my cue from the Graal. But instead there must have been things hanging around, shreds of all that old resentment maybe. Or just the way I saw you; you still annoyed me the way you had—"

"Me? How?"

"Just . . . being what you are. Just *looking* the way you do . . . I don't know, I can't make sense of it. And that worries me. I shouldn't have given in to it, I should just have gone along with you the way my feelings told me to. And I didn't, I hesitated, I picked out that son of a bitch and let him pick his pet heavies and I . . . made all this possible."

"I don't see it that way," I said.

She gave something like a laugh. "Thanks! I need all the moral support I can get right now."

"Oh—even mine?"

"Oh, I didn't mean it like that! You—I value what you think, really. Seeing you in action tonight," she managed a laugh, "you earned that swagger of yours!"

"I don't bloody swagger!"

"Oh, yes, you do. A bit, even in your ordinary clothes; but put a sword at your side, and, well—your friend Jyp—"

"Okay, *he* swaggers. Do I do that?"

"Worse. But don't take it to heart. You—you've come a long way, I think, on the Spiral. And in a very short time.

You should try for esquire-probationer, really you should."

"Eh?"

"In the Graal's service. You'd make a Graal Knight, I'm sure of it. You fight like one already. As I've cause to know. And, of course, you've got the sword already."

"I'd sooner fight with you than *with* you, if you take my meaning. We make a good team."

"Yes. Yes, we do." She was silent a moment. "Dragovic was our best swordsman, outside the Knights. I was afraid he would kill you. I wish now I'd let him try. You'd have cut him into collops."

"I was tired. I'm glad you didn't. He just about had me." We came to the fence at the far end; it was tall, and we were weary, and the gate was way down the far end. We exchanged glances, and then I drew my sword. "I dub thee Lutz," I told the fence, and hit it, hard. There was a sound like somebody smashing a giant harp, and we jumped back as the wires parted and a great triangle of fence unrolled.

"I dub thee Dragovic!" said Alison, and swatted the swathe again. It twanged loose, tore away from the posts and sagged, leaving a nice wide gap. Somewhere alarms were probably going off, but that was the least of our problems.

"Dragovic," I repeated, as we stepped wearily out into the long street. "I wish it had been him. And what was that about everyone knows there are traitors? In that place? With the Graal there? How do they dare—and, come to that, why?"

"Oh, there always are traitors in times without a king. There's nothing to hold the loyalty of the ordinary townspeople, the ones who never normally go near the Graal. Not in the Graal's direct service, I'm certain." She smiled again suddenly, warmly. "Those it touches never renege. But among minor functionaries, postulants, maybe an occasional probationer—people hungry for success, but unsure of it—they might be tempted. Especially if they know they're unworthy. But him—no, I'd never have guessed. In fact I remember ruling him out. He seemed ... well, very dedicated, very good at organizing the City Guard, but ...a little absurd. Always straining after becoming a Knight when anyone could have told him he wasn't suitable—almost everyone did. But he was so ambitious, so determined to get into the Brotherhood, to bypass a spell as probationer—and that's just what a traitor wouldn't want, you see. Because it would mean facing the Graal."

"It would find him out? Kill him?"

"It would see right through him. But kill him, no! Try to cure him, maybe. The Graal's like that. The problem might be to stop him killing himself, when he saw his inner self laid bare like that. It's not a comfortable experience, however lightly the Graal tries to let you off."

"The Graal!" It was getting on my nerves, and other sensitive parts. Her voice went positively gooey every time she mentioned the thing. It seemed like a stupid weakness, a flaw in a bold, independent character like this. "You know you talk about that thing as if it was a person?"

She gave me a very wry look. "Not a person! Something much, much more ... But okay, I'm sure of this, it was somebody once. Part of it, anyway. When it speaks to you ... " For a moment her head lifted and she seemed to stare into infinity, like Jyp at his helm. "You can't help sensing the humanity there; everyone does. It isn't just some roaming intelligence from the Rim. It's experienced a human life; maybe many lives. It might have been many people once. But there's something else there, something ... " She made a vast expansive gesture, the flat of her hand tracing an arc above her head, as if a rainbow crowned it. It seemed to fill the darkness with eerie presence.

"You're saying ... a god?"

She laughed outright. "Oh, no! It's anything but infallible; it makes mistakes! And it can be defeated. It has been, often—but never entirely. Me, I'm a new face around there, but from what the older Knights tell me, it's been weak for a century or more, as the Core sees it. But it doesn't give up; it goes on. It goes on recruiting people, selecting them and refining them, sending them out to serve ... causes."

The word made me chuckle slightly, it sounded so Victorian and flannelly. "Good, worthy, virtuous ones, I hope."

And, of course, the woman took me seriously. "Oh, no! I'd have thought you knew. There aren't any purely good causes in the Core—it's not the place for absolutes, it's where everything mixes up and ferments. No, just causes that'll do mostly good—that's as much as you can ask for, here. That, and stop worse ones spreading—stop the old barbarism in its tracks. But that's mostly unnatural. That mostly comes from other forces outside, ones that feed on anarchy and pain. That's what the Brocken is—or rather, what dwells there. We've known that one for a long time, since the first waves of settlement came out of the East across Europe, thousands of years before Christ. A mountain-haunting power the Easterners knew simply as *Chernobog*."

"The Black God," I said, and involuntarily glanced around at the deep somber shadows of the back-streets as we passed. The cheerful buzz and chatter of the main drag seemed to come from an infinite, unbridgeable distance.

"Yes. In those days it lay very close to the Core, separated by the thinnest of veils, free to spread its insanity almost everywhere it chose. The Graal pushed it back, it and others. There are plenty of others."

"And you say most of the foul-ups in the Core and so on come from them? I don't buy it, sorry. I mean, sure these guys are bad, they've got to be fought and all that. But men—men seem determined to meet them half-way, given what they'll do to one another without any prompting. Or even to themselves. *Against stupidity*, remember? Nothing stands against that."

She whirled to face me. "*We* stand against that. We, the Knights, the Brotherhood—though there are plenty of women among us, in times and societies that permit it. In war we fight, in peace we work." She smiled one of those sweetly acid smiles. "Work like mine, often—the sort of thankless, gritty work that helps hold the fabric of a reasonable society together. A lot of people are recruited from jobs like that."

I caught something hanging in the air. "The way you were?"

"Yes, like me. Unhappy, embittered, out of tune with our time, like me. The Graal gives us strength to continue, and powers to help us. But it can't avoid a racking dilemma that seems to go with them. The further we advance, the more tension we feel about which world we really belong in, the more we feel torn apart—"

"Yes! Jesus, yes!" Suddenly my neck was aching, the tendons white-hot with the misuse they'd had tonight. A lot of old stress was back, and the dank chill of the night wasn't helping. Alison stared at me, astonished.

"Steve, what's—not you, too?" She caught my nod, and half laughed. "God, I'd never have believed it—I still don't, even! Steve Fisher, the sleek, the confident, the cat who's licked the cream, God's gift to suffering women—and all the time you were just as screwed up as me?" She leaned against a wall and rocked with silent laughter.

"Thanks for the thumbnail sketch!" I said sharply. "Maybe you should've looked a little closer, okay? I was just beginning to like you a bit."

She stopped laughing suddenly, but she didn't say anything else, not at first. Then she said, quietly, "Sorry. I could say the same. I did, didn't I? I thought we were on, well, less prickly terms, all right?"

She surprised me again, by putting a hand on my arm. I left it there; I suddenly felt very much in need of any human contact. I nodded. "We are. Forget it." I glanced around again. "You hit a sore spot, that was all. And I can't take much more of that right now. I'm spooked enough as it is. Keep thinking there's—" I stopped, and stared, back down the length of that straight dark street. So did Alison, and her fingers tightened on my arm. We could still see the scrapyard fence from here; and unquestionably now there were figures moving behind it, peering about, searching.

"So Lutz isn't going to leave things at that, after all!" My hand fell to my sword hilt. "Maybe we should just settle with them now—"

Her hand was still on my arm. "I wouldn't! Look!" The figures had spotted the slash in the fence, and converged on it, ducking through one at a time. We'd stepped through together, and we hadn't had to duck. "Night Children! Full-grown!"

We didn't need to say another word. We moved, quickly, quietly, keeping in shadow now and never quite running in case the flicker of movement caught some watcher's eye. "Back to the main street?" I whispered in Alison's ear. The prospect of lights and company seemed almost like sanctuary.

"No. Most likely there'll be half-grown cubs there, they can pass for human—well, you know, you've seen them. And we'd lose our lead. Best we keep moving, they're too heavy to catch up. That bastard!"

I glanced back again. "Lutz? Somehow I don't think this is him at all. He prefers human servants. I think we've got two of them on our trail, independently—no prizes for who. That'd account for a lot."

She cast me one alarmed glance and nodded. "You mean why Lutz tried to kill you the moment you'd rejected him? To deny you to Le Stryge? Could be. The old barbarism again, allies who can't trust each other. Might be why Lutz's boys didn't hang around."

"Hope so. The 'copter, as you said; we'll have to be careful. Look, at least that's a bend ahead. Once around that and we'll be out of sight—we can risk running."

We had maybe half a mile left in us, no more. After that we were near as dammit walking, despite the drizzle that was coming on again. Another half-mile and we had to stop, collapsing into a nice cosy stone doorway. A last chill drop from somewhere struck my cheek and trickled down. I looked up, and saw the moisture collecting on a brass plate commemorating some famous building that stood on this spot—until 1945. Alison followed my glance. "Barbarism. A souvenir."

I sighed. "Surely we're getting over that? I mean, okay, we're still bickering and bilking each other, but we're drifting into some kind of European union, aren't we? A lot nearer than we've ever been before?"

She rubbed her hands over her eyes. "That depends. In the Neolithic, when men traded metal and tools the length of Europe, and never fought a war? In the days of the Roman Empire? Or the Holy Roman Empire? Under Napoleon, even, though that one was distorted from the start; it was never meant to happen like that. The French Revolution got off to a good start, then something else took a hand. It gave us the Terror and then Napoleon running things, a megalomaniac military dictator instead of a constitutional monarchy under Necker."

"Who?"

"Exactly. And sometimes the Graal tried the cultural tack, pulling the politics after—the Carolingian era, the great monastic orders. In medieval times Europe was at peace, relatively speaking, for long periods; links between universities and scholars cut right across political boundaries, with Latin becoming a *lingua franca*. Then there was the Hundred Years War. There was the Enlightenment, then the Terror. There was the nineteenth century— Weimar and Bavaria, then Prussia and Bismarck. Victorian England, then World War I. And nationalism, Nazism, the Cold War, the Iron Curtain and its horrendous aftermath. But that ran its course soon enough, and it left the field wide open. Now, true, there are some signs of accord—oh, not so much the EC itself, with all its blundering and pomposities, more the underlying assumptions that let it exist. But we're not drifting toward that, as you said. The Graal

is the navigator—but there are contrary winds whipping
up, and storms ahead."

I didn't say anything. I was too busy thinking, trying to
reassess history as I'd been taught it, too busy feeling like
a small feather in a really big hurricane. She tucked a com-
panionable arm under mine, and huddled against me, welcome warmth.

"That's another apology we owe you. We were all on ten-
terhooks, you see, just wondering where the first assault
would come. That was why you got shot at on sight, that
first time you appeared. We were expecting some kind of
assault on the city, and the patrols were getting trigger-
happy. We'd already had troubles with Le Stryge daring to
wander around our mountain marches, him and those horrible creatures of his."

"You mean those Night Children things? What the hell
are they, anyhow?"

She glanced around quickly as something rattled in the
street behind us, but it was only a cool gust blowing at a
hanging sign. "We'd better be going. You know Wolves, of
course. Well, the Children appeared a lot more recently as
the Core counts time, but if the stories are true they're
making up for it fast."

I hauled myself to my feet. "Another sub-species from
the Spiral? Another cross, between humans and—"

"Others. Yes. The way I heard it is that last century, before the end of World War II, the Russians rounded up a
batch of *really* unpleasant Nazi POWs—concentration-
camp guards, psychopaths from the punitive battalions,
that sort, men and women both. There were some Croats
and Turkish SS too, I think. Their usual procedure with
these types was that they were kept in camps for KGB
screening and according to their potential put on show
trial, shot out of hand or recruited. This lot, men and
women both, were sent off under Russian guards—an
equally bad lot even by KGB standards, apparently—to a
specially remote part of Siberia; only there, it seems, they

were forgotten. Supplies dwindled and finally stopped. Life
in the camps degenerated; guards and prisoners mingled.
They began preying on the local population, such as it was.
The collectivization famines, the purges and the war had
left no responsible authority within hundreds of miles to
stop them. When they couldn't steal food they stole people.
That was common enough; it had happened all over Russia
during collectivization. But these creatures took to doing
it for pleasure, and to keeping their victims alive to hunt
down for sport. Soon enough they were alone in a vast area
of emptiness, and . . . something happened. Meanwhile Sta-
lin died, Beria was murdered; a lot of their officials were
liquidated, and secret files opened. Refugees from the area
didn't just vanish anymore—at least not without talking,
to the right people. When a KGB force was eventually detailed to deal with the camp, it could find no sign of it, and
the colonel in command concluded they'd all died in the
wilderness. They hadn't." I saw her grimace, and look behind, and walk that little bit faster. "Maybe they'd moved
out onto the Spiral of their own accord; but I think they
were taken there."

"By what? Who?"

"Something—some thing that sensed their presence and
reached out and drew them in. That area'd had a bad rep-
utation for centuries; and I've always wondered if somebody
put such a concentration of really evil people there deliberately, as an experiment—or a gift."

"God almighty!" was about the only response I could
make. The wind wailed behind me.

"Anyhow, one thing's certain. Out there in the Spiral,
out in timelessness they bred and evolved, even developed
a kind of culture, shaped according to their own psycho-
pathic rules—and they began to change. They became the
creatures you see now, with their own lovely habits. You
know what the Spiral's like, mingling past times with present and future out there in the shadows; well, I've always
wondered, those fairytale ogres in Grimm . . . "

"Fee-fi-fo-fum and all that?"

"And heads on posts, bodies on hooks, horrible cruelties—that's the way they live. But they've not been that common, the Children. People ran into them now and again, seldom for the better. It's always been assumed that they were a weaker strain, though, less numerous than Wolves or some of the others. Now, after they've started passing for human—the adolescents, at least—and popping up in all these riots, I'm not so sure. Maybe somebody's been saving them up, and this is his rainy day." She looked back again, away from me. "I thought it might be your friend the Baron—and you. That was one reason I was so hot on your trail and, of course, it was why I drew the wrong assumption that night I found you with them. Until I began to see that you didn't add up—no, that's wrong. Till I saw that the you I'd molded out of paper evidence and prejudice didn't fit the real you. Whatever that is."

"Don't you know yet?"

"I know I was wrong."

The rain came in earnest now, dashing down on the pavement like a shower of steel rods, shivering as they struck, stinging our heads and shoulders. We didn't dare stop any longer, so we trotted on, heads bowed, past talking, hardly able to see without shielding our eyes and shaking the drops from our eyelashes. I devoutly hoped the Children would be just as badly affected. At last, a very wet and miserable couple of miles on, it blew over, quite quickly, and left us chilling in the wind. We were out of town now, and in the industrial area; but all the developments looked alike. We cast about to get our bearings, chose a likely road and ran, exhausted as we were, to keep warm.

"What I said—" she burst out, "didn't sound like much of an apology, did it? But I am sorry, very. I should have realized. But then the Spear was stolen, and that tipped me right over the edge. A lot of us assumed the worst—and we were right to. Except that in the middle of it all was you, an innocent where there should have been a king pin;

you stood slap in the way of von Amerningen's aim of hijacking the transport service, you fouled up Le Stryge's plan to steal the Spear. It didn't figure, it didn't add up—and it still doesn't. How could they be so careless?"

"Unless . . . " All of a sudden I felt young and naive, the first time in a long while, confronted with a world view like this. "Unless—unless it didn't really matter whether these plans worked, as such. As if they were only incidentals, distractions, obscuring some larger plan."

Alison did laugh now, horrified and nervous. "Than stealing the Spear? Larger than that?"

I didn't answer; I clamped my fingers on hers, silently, and pointed. Ahead of us were the lights of the industrial estate, just as we'd left it; and there, cruising around slowly from the rail freight depot, was the flashing blue crest of a patrol car. But as we watched it glided by the gate of the C-Tran depot without even slowing, and out into the access road to the further half of the development. It was only estate security, too, not the real cops; and the rest was silent. So the row hadn't been heard, then—hardly surprising, at night in a deserted estate, with the alarms switched off. And the helicopter was out of sight of the road altogether.

We took our time reaching it. We stalked it, like some nervous steel bird that might flutter off at any instant. We searched the shadows around it till our eyes ached, though impatience ticked away on a time-fuse at the backs of our minds; and when we finally scuttled over to the machine we searched it high and low for the slightest sign of sabotage. There wasn't anything, though I still winced involuntarily when I started her up, and the shattering row re-echoed off the warehouse walls. Lutz's men hadn't thought of this, or didn't dare linger in case Le Stryge's creatures came after them. And we hadn't been spotted by the authorities, either. Shreds of luck, but sorely needed. I was glad it'd be a short flight; I wasn't fit for much more. I wheeled the little craft about as she lifted, much lighter now, and caught Alison's sardonic grin as she looked down on the C-Tran depot. Somebody down there was going to be calling the cops tomorrow morning; and the resulting memos would be serious enough to reach my desk. One hell of a mess, no sign of a break-in, and two unidentified stiffs in hussar rig—I could hardly wait to see them. Any manager who could explain away that lot would earn his next promotion and then some. But I'd have preferred that confrontation to the one that was brewing for me now.

All three of us looked up as the great door boomed softly open—or, more truthfully, we jumped. Alison stood there, and beside her a tall man in the same plain gray, his sword couched in the crook of one arm. Her face was expressionless, deliberately formal; but I thought I detected deep unease there. The man was equally unreadable, but at least there was no hostility or anger in his lined features, or in his easy stance, and his voice was deep and firm. "Which of you is Stephen Fisher? The Lady Alison has put your case to us, and we have agreed that in injuring us you are not substantially to blame for your actions. Furthermore, we appreciate your great efforts to remedy it."

I drew breath. "Thank you. That's extremely fair of you."

He inclined his head gravely. "Nevertheless, we feel that we must still see what the Graal itself makes of the matter, and learn if possible why you were permitted to remove the Spear. Your friends have permission to come with us."

Jyp's genial face froze slightly. "Oh—I do, huh? Well, thanks, mister, but if it's all the same to your good selves—"

"Jyp!" I murmured. "I asked, remember? And we agreed!"

"Listen, I've got back trouble!" he muttered. "Got this yellow streak running down it something terrible—"

"I know you! And you're not fooling anyone." I turned to Mall. "Mall, can't you tell him to—"

Mall turned an ashen face on me. Ashen, with little trickles of sweat at the temples; and her fingers were twining in her long blond curls. All she said was, "I stand ready," and it came out in a hoarse baritonal croak. Then she hastily added, "Almost!," and vanished back along the corridor behind us. A door banged shut, leaving me gaping after her. Mall was as transparently terrified as a little girl on her first day at kindergarten. And as Mall had been carving her own unhindered path along the haunted byways of the Spiral since the reign of James VI and I, a female paladin of startling strength and courage, that gave me pause for thought. And as she was the nearest thing among us to a power incarnate in her own right, that gave me still more. Why the hell wasn't I afraid? Because I was too ignorant, probably; it had happened before. Like some minor Aztec wondering why the Spaniards were aiming those strange tubes; or one of his Amazonian cousins wandering into an illicit toxic waste dump.

Mall reappeared, buckling her belt, and gave Alison an apologetic smile. She nodded, still formally, and led the way out of the Rittersaal's immense portico, where we'd been waiting, and across the square to the high bridge across the gorge. The river below had been full of small boats, but now they were moored or tied up at their quays; the water was empty except for a couple of low-lying vessels moored beyond the heavy grille of the water-gate, where the walls crossed the river lower down. Jyp jerked his head their way. "Gun-barges, big ones. And not mounting your ordinary cannon, either. Something like big naval guns, shell-firers, maybe breech-block loaders. You don't find many of those out along the Spiral—nor those," he added, indicating the airship that swung gently at its mooring mast on the far bank. "This place'd be a hard nut to crack, even with the weapons of your day. It's only having a real community here that makes it possible, so folk can settle and live out long lives without slipping back into the Core. Lets 'em build up complicated skills, industries even." He gazed up at the immense towers of the Graal Hall. "Holdin' all this whole city here, jehoshaphat! Takes a heap of power, that—

more'n I've ever come across before. And that's what we're going to pay a call on, Stevie boy! So you won't go gettin' too much on your high horse, huh? For all our sakes . . ."

"You're the pilot," I said, and he grinned.

"Not in these waters; I've set you the best course I can. Wind and shoals, that's your concern. Well, here we is. You okay, Mall girl?"

Mall's grip tightened on my arm, making the bones creak, and for an instant I saw real hesitation in her face; her legs seemed ready to give way. "Aye, needs must. I have sipped the drink, I must e'en down the draft. But I've *tremor cordis* on me, truly . . . " I supported her as best I could, and caught an odd look from Alison, still unreadable. She strode to the high door of the hall, and swung it wide before us. Darkness, a curtain swelling in an unseen draft, welled out above us. Mall's grip slipped from my arm; I caught her and practically had to lift her over the threshold.

Inside, though, she stiffened again, breathing hard, jumped only a little as the door shut out the light again. Jyp, at his foxiest, squinted around, sniffed the still air and then bobbed his head in a jaunty but respectful bow to the group who were waiting for us inside. Mall hastily swept an obeisance of such depth and panache her hair almost trailed on the flagstones. I managed the polite inclination from my course in Japanese business etiquette, and looked curiously at these formidable Knights. Most of them were old—an unusual thing in itself, as Alison had explained. They generally spent too much of their lives in the Core to benefit from the agelessness of the Spiral, though the Graal itself extended their youth and vigor far beyond normal. Only those who reached old age—not many, apparently— retired here, and ceased to age, until at last they grew weary and returned to the Core to die. It was mostly these older Knights who remained in the Heilenberg now, men and women who looked a strong sixty or so. I saw only a couple of younger men, both outwardly around my age, and two women besides Alison, one a little blond creature I'd have put at twenty-five and not a minute more. But her eyes had the same calm in them as the rest, and it was she who motioned us forward along the corridor. Alison and the Knights fell in on either side, suddenly in step, as if they were a guard, and we filed out into the main body of the hall.

It was brighter than I remembered it—or rather, it was as if the shadows had taken wing and were roosting head-down from the dome. Sunlight slanted across half the tessellated floor, warming the stone of the surrounding pillars; the dais and its charge still wore their mantle of gloom. I was about to step out onto the floor when the leading Knight politely but swiftly drew me back and steered us into the gallery behind the pillars. I remembered how the guards had circled after me, rather than rushed in, and watched as the Knights ranged themselves in a wide arc either side of the entrance. I calculated this gallery would hold around three hundred that way, if it was ever full. When everyone was in place I expected some ceremony, but all they did, those Knights, was stand and watch, fastening their eyes on the dais with an intensity you couldn't mistake. So did Mall, and though Jyp didn't seem to be making any particular effort I thought I'd better imitate them. I tried to concentrate, staring hard at the shadowy mass and fastening my thoughts on it. In five minutes all I got was spots before my eyes and a headache, and about the same response you would from a turned-off TV. The warm still air and the utter silence weighed on me like a blanket. I leaned against a sunwarmed pillar, my sore eyes slipped closed and I dozed where I stood—until the sound of Alison's voice, urgent and pleading, jolted me awake. She was standing out there, on the edge of the floor, and I thought she spoke; but though I heard her words echo in the dome above, her lips never moved.

"We need your advice—badly. You know what has happened. You know the story as I saw it. We are baffled, still, we do not know enough to act, we cannot agree on a plan. You must speak. You must advise us."

Nothing stirred; yet something happened. The angle of the light seemed to change, to expand and spread, till a patch of the bare wall was suddenly illuminated, highlighting a glowing fresco in that flat early medieval style, the figure of a bearded king enthroned, his hand upraised with authority. Shadow enfolded us still; yet beside me something gleamed and glinted. Mall's hair shone as if caught by a bright morning sun, and though the air was as warm and still as ever, it stirred and lifted. She tilted her head back, eyes closed, and raised her arms; and her ruddy cheeks blushed like fire. All around her was blackness; she bathed in light, and yet no ray reached her from the hall. The main beams shone squarely down on its center now, pouring gold on the low dais and on the circle-graven stone that stood there, half hidden by the mantle of rich dull red. Glowing dust motes danced above its cup, and the air tingled with a sense of presence. But there was no more; no voice spoke.

"Dare I ask again?" pleaded Alison, before her voice had left her lips. "The Spear—the Brocken might still be forestalled—there is so little time! We must act!"

I felt I ought to speak, to ask, as I should have here before. But I hadn't the faintest idea what; I was tongue-tied. And it didn't help that I was beginning to get angry with that impassive silence before us. The sincerity, the anguish in Alison's voice, the grave concern on the faces of the other Knights, all demanded some sort of response.

"We must have your word! Should we go after it? How many of us? How should we attack? Please!"

Silence.

I felt my face flush in the heat, in sheer fury. I spoke, all right, out loud and with a force that surprised me most of all. "*She's right!* Why don't you answer her? What d'you want, damn it? Me? All right, Sangraal or whatever you are, you've got me. I'll go. I'll go after this Spear of yours—

alone, if I have to! And you can at least say whether you're forbidding anyone to come along with me!"

I stopped dead there, because every eye in the hall was on me now. I was standing smack in the center of the floor; in that rush of anger I must have somehow gone barging straight out here. I stopped, shriveling; I'd committed some sort of sacrilege here. Or had I?

They seemed more astonished than angry, those Knights; and Alison's eyes glittered with a touch of gold. I turned on my heel and stamped back past them into the gloomy entrance. Suddenly I wanted the open air very badly, out of this stuffy mausoleum; I was burning inwardly. Behind me I heard footsteps, and a murmur of voices, very uneasy. The Knights were filing out after me, with no more ceremony than that. They'd had no answer either. Whatever its reasons, this great power was not responding, even to its own.

I caught Mall's firm arm. "You! You felt something. What was it? Did it tell you anything?"

She smiled, not her normal flash of teeth but an almost sleepy, lopsided beam. "I? No, no speech passed. It was there, that sufficed. How to lay't clear to you? If I hung my viol i' the trees, so that the strings resounded to the reverberant airs—like the windharp, the Aeolian device. The strings I, shivering i' the breath of that dread presence. The very fibers of my being sang its burden. What need of speech was there?"

High as a kite. I gave her up for a bad job and made for the way out. But as I laid my hand on the iron ring of the ancient door I thought I'd been electrocuted. Something juddered through me, a pulse that seemed to jolt my bones, every cell in my body, even. Not electricity; more like the tolling of a vast unseen bell, awaking reverberations all around. I stopped, breathless, caught in a play of great forces that seemed to stretch and flex my very bones. Tiredness, already fading in the tranquil air of the Heilenberg, shriveled and vanished in the electric thrill that invaded every part of me. It stung me, a sudden spray of icy water in my veins—not a pleasant sensation, and yet there was strength in it. The others bustled around me undisturbed, even Mall, rapt and remote. Nobody else had felt it.

Chapter 9

The atmosphere in the Rittersaal couldn't be called panic, but it was perilously close. The Knights weren't completely devastated. The Graal had been silent before, once or twice, generally when some great change or dramatic action had to be provided for and it couldn't spare the attention. As far as they could explain, it existed largely on some more rarefied level, and found it a strain to interact with ours except in certain ways its rite and ritual preserved. More rarely, it had refused to respond when it felt the Knights would gain in some way by coping on their own. Evidently that was what threw them. With only a handful left in the city, how could they be expected to cope?

I thought there'd be some sort of formal meeting, but among themselves the Knights seemed to be informal, gathering in small groups around the great hall of the Rittersaal to discuss the problem. In was an airy, open place, medieval in design but so tall and clear it reminded me of nineteenth-century Scandinavian architecture, Eliel Saarinen's romantic neo-castles, maybe. The warm carved wood and faded hangings covering its walls would have made it

a calm, pleasant place to sit, normally; and the banners in
the roof were an amazing pageant in themselves, crusader
crosses and gaudy pennants, Byzantine leather serpents and
war-torn medieval honors. There was even a legionary standard there, its shaft hung with gilded wreaths as battle honors, and older insignia too by the look of them, simple
plaited designs on poles and a huge bearskin and skull that
might have led the first charges out of the caves; they hung
next to the rich arms of eighteenth- and nineteenth-century
Europe, to a world of little principalities and dukedoms that
Napoleon and Bismarck between them swept away. It was
an intensely martial display; and yet the impression was
more of conflict stilled. For all that, though, an air of deep
unease and worry was building beneath it now. No shouting
or table-pounding here, but even the quietly emphatic gestures were charged with growing tension; and every so often a hand would caress a sabre hilt, or slide it quietly a
few inches from the sheath as if to check for rust.

Alison alone seemed close to losing her temper. She
paced the floor furiously between one little group and another, occasionally stopping at our corner of the massive
scarred table to report, or rummage around in the snow-
drift of maps and old reports, describing what little was
known of the Brocken. I'd read them all at least twice, and
I was struggling not to feel left out. It was good of the
Knights to have us in here at all, and several of them had
come to consult us at length about our experiences. But
nobody had actually asked our advice, or said whether
they'd accept my offer, and I couldn't help chafing at the
bit.

"Well, they're agreed on one thing!" was Alison's verdict.
"Whatever's to be done, we have to have more of the Order.
Most of those here can't leave. There must always be a
guard, in case of some direct assault on the City, or even
the Graal itself. And they're mostly old or young, with too
much experience or too little. So whatever we decide on,
we'll need others. But that's not easy. Most are committed

to the Graal's battles, scattered throughout the Spiral. The others are out on the search still, only to be contacted when they check back with us or pick up a message somewhere safe like the Tavern; we could put them in danger otherwise, break their cover. All that's too slow. And beyond that . . . " She kicked at the pale marble floor. "The Knights are divided. They like your plan, yes, but some want to wait till the Graal chooses to answer, build up our forces meanwhile, but wait. They say messing with the Brocken is so appallingly dangerous we daren't take chances, we should concentrate on defending the Heilenberg; and I can sympathize with that. But the others know it, too—and they're ready to act as we want, to go after the Spear."

"Then why don't we?" I said rebelliously. "The Graal can stop us if it wants to, can't it?"

She winced. "Yes, but what then? We're not puppets, you know, or slaves. The Graal doesn't choose us for that— would you? It knows it's not infallible, either. It selects us as well as it can, it helps us make the best of ourselves, it shares its power with us—and it trusts us. More than that, it makes us trust ourselves. Sometimes it makes us act for ourselves, stand or fall, because guiding us would interfere somehow."

"So it might not stop us even if we were doing the wrong thing?"

"Not if we were the only ones who'd suffer, and the responsibility was ours. If we all agreed on something that was wholly wrong, then it might intervene, I think."

I nodded. "I begin to follow its way of thinking. Get the right people to begin with, motivate them, give them the skills and the targets and then let them do the job. Sound management theory, as far as it goes. But there's another golden rule: *Be there when they need you*. Either it really has gone doolally, or it thinks you have the answer already." Even as I said it something filtered through the boredom and the bafflement and the dull besetting ache. "Wait a minute! Maybe you do. You can't get through to the searchers—but there must be some you can pull out of the fighting line. How about them?"

Alison looked very dubious. "Maybe a few—but it's no good, we can't contact them either. The Graal could, in an emergency, if it had the Spear. The Spear can carry its power far afield; it concentrates and directs it, it can guide our people through the deepest shadows of the Spiral, between the places and times that cast them. Without it the Graal's influence is confined to its own location, to this realm. Any messenger we sent would be as lost as you were that night of the riots—and in even more danger. Sorry, Steve—"

"No, hold your horses! I hadn't finished. All right, you can't recall them. Why not go out and pick them up?"

"Uh-*huh*!" exclaimed Jyp, with a snap of the fingers.

"What—"

"Sure. You got me. Name of Jyp the Pilot, remember?"

"He can speed you places not yet i' your dreams!" chimed in Mall. "Here, there and any the where! The swirlings of the Spiral are his playthings, its wastes his chessboard!"

"Yes, but we haven't any large ships in port, and we'd need to go to some places nowhere near the sea—"

Jyp's fingers drummed loudly on the table. "So? You got those damn great dirigible things there."

Alison blinked. "Those? Could you—"

"Anywhere. After a goddamn whirlybird those things'd come easy. Only it gets harder the longer we delay here."

Something like an echo of that strange shock ran through my bones. It left a kind of grim relief, like the loss of a broken tooth, the sick throb overtaken by a keener but more wholesome pain. "That's it!" I snapped, loudly enough to stop every voice in the hall. "That's what we'll do!" I rounded on the elderly Knight who'd come with Alison. "Torquil, isn't it? Is that bird down there ready for flight?"

"It is," he said. "But who would captain it? We are vowed to the city's defense. We are too old to be much use outside."

"You can spare me," said Alison. "I was only waiting to be assigned. And these three, Steve, Mall and Jyp, each one of them's as good as another Knight in their way. And as trustworthy."

I expected Torquil to balk at that. He only nodded, judiciously. "So I gather. Very well, then. I'll put it to the rest—"

"No time," I said sharply, feeling prickling fires spring up at the back of my neck, invading my mind. "Look, I don't mean to be rude, but we've wasted enough already. This is it, isn't it? This is the way we can both do something and leave the City guarded. So that answers both parties. What's the quickest way down to the far bank?"

The old man—how old?—looked at me for a long moment, then he shook his head. "No," he said. "No need."

The fires roared up. "Now you listen one damn minute—"

His gesture stopped me. "I meant, it would be quicker to bring it here. Raoul! The telegraph, if you please. My compliments to Ritter von Waldestein, and will he have the *Dove* brought over to the West Tower. Have them check the stores on the way over. And in the meantime," he added, "we will—inform—the others."

"You mean you agree? They'll agree?"

His smile was wry. "You leave us hardly a choice. The Lady Alison commands this expedition for us, she will find our brothers and sisters. But who is its real leader—of that I've little doubt. I have known men like you before; I am glad I have met another."

"But . . . I started this!" I blurted out. "I stole your bloody Spear, didn't I?"

"Who better to get it back?" He smiled. "You didn't realize what you did today, stepping on the floor of the Hall, speaking to the Graal. Not that it would have hurt you, willingly; but its very existence, so close, is a flame to those who lack fires of their own. The Lady Mall was warmed by it—but you, my friend, you were *kindled*."

He clicked his heels and bowed, then turned to the others clustered around him, speaking rapidly. He left me speechless. But maybe I did feel inspired, at that; or something more. Driven, fired—filled with fire. It was the memory of a shaft of flame that leaped and roared at the lightest touch, consuming, shriveling. The Spear would be at the Brocken; well then, so would I, and anything or anyone between me and it had better watch out. I needed it.

Through one of the tall windows I saw movement, and went to look. From the mast on the far bank the white dart shape of an airship swung up and out, cables trailing away and last of all the heavy mooring link. Its reflection glinted in the river as its propellers spun, gradually turning the weightless bulk in the air, swinging its nose around to face the island and the great hall of the Sangraal. Into my thoughts another bulk heaved up, as it had out of whatever hellish depths lay within that pentacle, the ridged spine of the Brocken; and it was greater by far. There was the Spear, and more; there was Katjka, if she had survived the transition. It was that thought that struck the real sparks within me. That was what the spear meant to me now. To get it back for these people, for this enigmatic Graal, for Alison—fine. But to have hold of that power, to have a chance, the only chance of rescuing Katjka—that was what mattered. That was what fed the flame. Just let me get it in my hand once more . . .

I jumped. Alison had touched my shoulder. "The *Dove's* mooring at the Graal Hall. We'd better go; there are a *lot* of stairs."

I looked at Mall and Jyp. "This isn't your fight, not anymore. It's so dangerous I don't even want to think about it. We'll drop you off once we've got the Knights we need."

Mall's face was wry. "Messire, did I not once tell you, upon a certain moonlit night, that I was sworn to set evil to rights, wheresoever I might set eyes upon it? And you laid the name of paladin upon me. A heavy burden, yet one I'd not willingly be discharg'd of." She caressed the worn hilt of her own great sword. "Then paladin let me be, and try not my pride with lesser esteem. That suffices."

"Yeah, and you can stick a hat on that an' a pipe in its kisser an' call it mine, too!" spluttered Jyp, though his face was grim. "Thought we got through all this crap before. 'Sides, how else're you ever gonna find the Brocken, 'less you happen to trip right over it?"

Racing to the rescue is all very well, but before we were more than half-way up that tower we were walking, sedately; by the top I was almost on all fours. We were already high up here, and the extra altitude of the tower-top made quite a difference. I hadn't felt like this since Cuzco. Fortunately the ladder above was quite short, and my straining lungs lasted the course; also, I had the sense not to look down. Crewmen in striped overalls hauled me into the gently swaying gondola, and then, at a sign from Alison, swung themselves down to the tower-top.

"Can't ask them to come along on this," she sighed. "We'll need all the capacity we have for combatants. Mall, would you haul up the ladder? Jyp, if you'd take the wheel—it's much like a ship's, but there are other controls, I'll show you. Steve? We're ready to go. If you wouldn't mind signaling them to cast off . . ."

I leaned through the doorway and waved down to the crewmen, who scurried to unlatch the moorings; it seemed almost sacrilegious having them hooked around that beautiful Gothic tracery. They swung free, I returned the crewmen's salutes—and looked down.

It was worse than my first look down from a swaying mast; it was worse than the first real rockface on the Eiger, with the glacier plunging away into nothingness and birds flying beneath my feet. The *Dove* swayed gently, her strange engines idling with little puffs of steam, just off the face of the tower. The lines of its sides struck down into the depths like arrows, carrying my mesmerized stare with them to the cobbles of the square and the tiny figures who clustered there. With the motion of the airship the red-tiled roof-tops surged beneath me like waves of blood, swelling and sinking in a peculiarly sickening slow motion. A strong hand caught my shoulder and pulled me back, just in time. "To spill one's jetsam from the maintop's poor enough, be the wind i' the wrong quarter," remarked Mall, sliding the door shut. "But from this height and onto innocent heads 'twould be counted ill-bred, I think. And no way to sail off to war."

I sat back on the gondola's polished wooden floor, closing my eyes for a moment. Behind us the engines altered suddenly from soft chugging to a pulsing thunder as Alison leaned on the throttle, though they were still far quieter than anything that powerful and steam-driven had a right to be. A flurry of startled pigeons fluttered past the window. The swaying stilled, and the *Dove* was no longer a helpless balloon-like bulk but a powerful nosing arrow, thrusting for the grayness above, the uncertainty of the Spiral, where the high peaks of stone and the ridges of shifting vapor became one, mountain-throne and mist-crest merged, each tracing the other's contours, each joined by common paths, the most and the least solid meeting at the far horizons of the Spiral. Where they joined, where wide roads opened between the ocean and the air and archipelagos stretched out into the clouds, the mighty shadows of all times, all places stretched; and men who spied their way could pass between. Jyp, grasping the controls with his usual uncanny ability, gunned the throttle to a deep drone, tilted the nose and brought us circling upward till all trace of the ground fell away like debris in our wake, and overhead the clouds drew back, outflung arms of a receding land, reaching out to the islands of the sunset sky. I stood at the gondola's forward window, and Alison joined me there. "Over the sunset," she whispered, and I wondered what had moved her to express it like that, so close to the helmsman's call I'd heard first on another such desperate chase.

"Over the airs of the Earth!" I answered. And something

of the old exultation did break out in me then, for all the gloomy cloud that overhung us and the danger of what was to come.

Jyp caught it, and his old grin broke through. Mall's smile flashed like the sun through an overcast, and she slapped the sheath at her thigh. "Over the airs of the Earth! We're under way! *We're coming!*"

"Whither away?" demanded Jyp, spinning the wheel experimentally. "Where first, Alison?"

"North-west ten degrees," she said, quite quietly. "Then north a degree, and I'll guide you in. The *Urwald*, the heartland forests of Europe. The late summer, fifteen years after Christ."

We came floating out of the clouds into darkness, a darkness more absolute than you could find almost anywhere in our light-polluted modern world. Alison had the wheel now, guiding us out of the shadows of the Spiral to the Core locations she knew. "In Rome Tiberius is still emperor," she said, steering us over hilly country whose skylines were a solid fringe of forest, broken only by a winding seam of dull silver. "Probably off in Capri just now. But down there somewhere his nephew Germanicus is leading a great campaign to drive the barbarians back from the Danube frontier . . ."

It didn't look as if anything could be stirring down below, let alone two sizeable armies, so dense were the trees under their faint carpet of chill mists. But Jyp, with his night eyes, suddenly pointed ahead, to where a tiny ember of red pulsed among the blackness. As we came closer we saw it was the wreck of a largish fort or township, walls reduced to stumps now but still crackling with fitful bursts of flame. We glided in under low power, almost brushing the pine tops, with our airscrews barely turning, and drifted like a cloud over the wreck below. Alison passed Jyp the helm, shot back the gondola door and swung down onto the unreeling ladder, waving. Under the forest shadow dull gleams of metal stirred, and a headcrest of high red plumes. A tall centurion in scarlet cloak moved out, peering suspiciously, with a dozen or so men behind him. Then he flashed a hand in quick salute. "What's this? Reinforcements?"

"Recall!" said Alison, thumping down onto the bushy slope. Within minutes, while she was still explaining, the centurion was chivvying the men up the ladder and through the gondola into the body of the machine. He sprang after them, loricated breastplate clanking and caligae squeaking, his hard face pale around the cheekbones, and tossed me a chest-thumping salute. *"Caio' Marco' Fevronio', centurio'!"* he announced, and then, with hardly an accent, "You're Fisher? The Lady Alison, she tells me we follow you. Okay, here we are. But we need more than my handful if we go lay siege to the Brocken, eh?" He blew out his cheeks. "More than one airship load!"

"Not siege," I told him. "Blitzkrieg. Alison, where next?"

"Westward," she said. "Western France, south-west of Paris on the Loire, summer of 732. Look for a battle and you're there."

Even in the dark we couldn't have missed it, even over our motors; the sounds drifted up to us, clanging, screaming, the snap of bows and the shrill neighing of horses. Here and there dark silhouettes capered against the light of burning buildings, widely separated; peasant farmsteads, I guessed. Alison was scanning the darkness, peering at the shoals of banners as they swept past the fires, following some kind of signals I couldn't even sense. "Our man's with the armies of Charles Martel, the Hammer, turning back the Moors," she said absently. "This was as far into Europe as they got."

I frowned. "Hang on a moment. Around that time the Moors weren't so bad, were they? They were the civilized ones, they built the Alhambra and all those other great buildings in Spain. More civilized than a load of Frankish headbangers, anyhow."

"It's not what they were," she said. "It's what they could become. And don't assume that cultured equals humane—

the Moorish nobles treated their own people like dirt. It helped bring them down during the reconquest—there!"

I couldn't make out one group from another, but we went drifting down like a stray cloud over a group of startled Moors, who let out one unison wail and bolted. The group of horsemen harrying them also bolted, except for a small knot who held their ground, calmed their plunging horses, and came trotting over, evidently well aware of what we were. Alison spoke to them hastily, and we held our breath every time an arrow sang past. Somebody blew a complicated horn signal, and within moments we had five or six chunky blond men with braids and moustaches clambering up into the gondola, their short mail shirts and studded belts clinking as they climbed. "That's all they could spare," Alison reported. "And they're leaving their horses, Charles is short of them for the pursuit."

I looked back at the long rear gondola, which had a ramp for loading horses up into the body of the airship. "We could use some horsemen. We may need to get somewhere fast, through rough country."

"It'll have to be later. They're too precious in these early periods, they'd be missed. We won't get them at the next stop either. That's eastward, Jyp. To the shadows of Byzantium, and beyond. Out into its northern territories, the steppes by the Dnieper, spring of the year 1091."

The centurion Marco nodded. "The Emperor Alexio' Comneno', where he defeats the Pecheneg horde. We go for Hastein, eh?"

Alison nodded. "If he's still all right."

oThere was no way we could approach that great circle of campfires and colorful tents across the rolling land. We came down swift but light, like a driven cloud, and Alison and Marco went to fetch their man while I stamped and fidgeted. The man who finally came clattering up the ladder was unexpected; I'd never seen anyone less Greek, a red-blond giant with a drooping handlebar moustache and embroidered fur-trimmed jacket over his scale-mail shirt, an

immense axe over his shoulder. He saluted me the same
way as the centurion, his English American-accented. "Hi.
Hastein Hallgrimsson, Icelander. Deputy *Spatharokandi-
dates* of the Varangian Guard. And, of course, Knight Commander of the Sangraal, at your orders. Even if it does
mean that hell-hole. We could only spare ten, but there's
one Knight and four squires, five probationers serving as
cataphracts."

"They'll do!" said Alison, herding a motley group up into
the body of the ship. Some were blonds like Hastein, the
five cataphracts short and dark and Greek-looking, with
lighter mail and bows; all of them were slathered with drying blood, apparently not their own. A couple of them
spared a curious glance for this non-Knight who was leading them, but they seemed as somberly calm as their
leaders.

"Hey, I don't suppose anyone's got a cigarette?" demanded Hastein.

"Got some cigars someplace," said Jyp.

"Not in an airship, as you very well know," snorted Alison. "You'll have to excuse him, Steve, he's from nineteen
forty-eight, apparently they smoked all day and night then."

"The Graal helped me break the compulsion," sighed Hastein. "But after ten years back here drinking watered Greek
wine you kind of revert. Besides, what harm'd just one do?
The hydrogen doesn't get down here into the gondola."

"No!" said Alison firmly. "Take us out of here, Jyp, before
he blows us all up."

Jyp gunned the throttle gently and spun the wheel; Alison worked the control surfaces. "You're heading north-
north-west now, Jyp. To France again, the north-west coast
in spring fourteen fifteen—the siege of Calais, under Henry
the Fifth."

Again the darkness, the smoke and flame and screams—
and this time the thud and crash of cannon, wafting bitter
powder smoke up to us as we glided over the glittering calm

of the Channel. "And what's this got to do with civilization?" I demanded.

"Unite England and France, that's what Henry tries to do," answered the centurion somberly. "And Bourgogne—that's Burgundy. A good enough man by the ways of his time; better than the French Dauphin. But he dies young, his lords squabble, and then there is this Giovanna d'Arco, who puts the worthless Dauphin on the throne of France. Pfft!"

I stared down at the mayhem below. Even as I watched, a sheet of flame leaped from the city walls at one point, leaving a smoking gap in the parapet. What good could come from all that, however long-term? But perhaps things like that would have happened anyway; better there was some point to them.

Through noise and fire and a sleeting, miserable drizzle a few bedraggled figures stumbled toward the sea coast where we'd landed, all the Knights here could spare; soon there'd be Agincourt to fight. We lifted away and slipped back into the shadows cast by this land and era, long and bloody shadows; and at their extremity they mingled with others, and Jyp's skilled hand slipped us between them, and out once more. Into the leaping flames of medieval Germany, to pluck bright-clad *landsknecht* mercenaries from lordly squabbles, Alison and I dashing into the midst of tramping ranks to find them, between wagons laden with pikes and loot. Into the blood-soaked mud of pastures by the Danube on a stifling August afternoon in 1526, as the vast Turkish armies rolled over the last diminished forces of Hungary, and thought them no more than an advance-guard. There, as thunder crashed and the skies opened, and the young king was swept to his death in the swollen river, we came on a little knot of riders, one of many making a last defiant stand. But when they heard our mission, they turned and came with us; and perhaps we did as much to delay the Turks, when they saw the *Dove* rising like a portent through the flickering lightnings. Into the sullen embers of Russia in 1609, shattered by years of famine and civil war after the death of Czar Boris, to pluck Polish cavalry from the invading army of King Sigismund—fierce, gallant men carrying curved sabres like those with which their descendants would launch one last charge against German tanks. From there to the same land a century later, as Peter the Great broke the Swedish Empire at Poltava, and King Charles fled to exile and death. In all these places smoke rose, blood fell; men lived, died, rose or were ruined, and the destinies of a continent were pulled and distorted, this way, that way, by forces no man caught up in them could ever have understood. Were we any better?

It grew harder now, as armies became more organized, to spirit away men who had often risen high in their commands and counsels; but we cruised unseen through the blizzards south of Moscow, to pull out some of the Russian irregulars who were harrying the retreating French, serf and nobleman fighting alongside one another to break the first great crack in Napoleon's dream of dominion. We settled among the smoke and flame at Leipzig, on a warm October afternoon in 1813, to hail a platoon of Scottish infantry as they drove some remnants of French *cuirassiers* off the field. We rescued Bavarian lancers as they broke before the Prussian guns in the last days of the Austro-Prussian war, and Bismarck forged the future in blood and iron. We came down amid eddying clouds of gas to bring in French cavalry at Ypres salient, five or six of them clattering on board, men and horses alike draped in stinking impregnated coats and hoods. I watched them somberly as they tore them off and hurled the hateful things away, and wondered at their calm demeanor. If they died with us, they would simply be thought to have vanished into the appalling rolls of death and disappearance in that shell-shattered morass. But if they survived, they might return.

Last of all—I thought—we glided among the north Italian hills, to pick up small groups of men and women in rough, torn clothes and battered hats, long knives in their belts and Stenguns and captured Schmeissers cradled in their arms, partisans fighting on when their armies had broken. I could imagine the same people coming off a mountainside in Greece or France, or out of the icy Russian marshland. They had the fierce haunted look of those who had seen too much, too many "security measures" and "due reprisals" in helpless villages, and had found themselves driven to do the same in turn, or worse.

And yet, like the doomed Hungarians, like the French cavalrymen, like all the rest whose lives might suddenly flare up and vanish like insects in a lamp-flame, they were ready to come back. Straight back from the nightmare of the Brocken to the man-made nightmares we had snatched them from, to tasks however hopeless and causes however lost—because in doing so they might make things that shade better, or at least less bad. Their chances were not good; that was why they'd been chosen, from causes already doomed, or firmly enough won to make their intervention only secondary—but still they were ready, because they might make that crucial difference, might perhaps save a hundred lives later, and from among those hundred one who might save a million. None of these people was under compulsion, none of them under orders; they were people who had been shown a truth, a pattern in which their life and if necessary their death had been given some greater meaning. Most of them had lived long lives already, far longer than the ordinary; but instead of clinging greedily to the rest they felt they were making some return in venturing it to help others. Neither the Graal nor its followers threw lives away; but they might, if they chose, invest them.

I wondered at that, wondered if ever I could come to think that way. I'd seen the near-immortality the Spiral made possible, and it made me uneasy. Age brought change; and those changes, however good, meant one was no longer entirely human. They extended you, concentrated you, heightened your abilities, brought out what was dominant in your inner self. That might be good, as it had been

for Jyp and Mall; but more often it might be ugly. It could
lead to near-divinity, or to things unimaginably hellish.
Something of that sort had happened to Katjka, and though
she'd pulled back, somehow, from the brink, it had remained there always a few steps in front of her, until at last
it had claimed her again. Living for ever at that sort of cost
wasn't something I wanted. Better to be content with an
ordinary life, and live it reasonably; it could be pretty good.
Mine was, by most people's standards, so why the hell was
I hankering after more? Why had I yearned for the Spiral
all these years, yet only dabbled in it, flirted with it, never
really taken the plunge? Was it because I really wanted
something else—like, for example, the strength and belief
and purpose these people had?

"... fifteen, sixteen!" counted Alison. "That's it, we've
enough! Set course northward, Jyp, we won't need to stop
at Stalingrad now."

"And Lord, am I thankful!" exclaimed Jyp, who'd sailed
in the North Sea convoys. "Freeze our asses off up there,
if the Jerries didn't shoot them off first—"

Alison shook her head. "We'd have been looking for the
German side. Obersturmbannführer Ewald Holzinger, for
one, and many others."

"Ober—" Jyp choked. "That's an SS rank! What kind of
goddamn game're you folks playing?"

"A very rough one," answered a leathery middle-aged
partisan woman. "I had hoped Ewald would be assigned to
our part of Italy, we could have prevented so much blood-
shed together. But Stalingrad is worse."

"You see," said Alison gently, "you need, sometimes, to
have good men serving an evil cause, to reform it, or at
worst restrain it. Even the SS was not beyond redemption,
once."

Jyp and I exchanged fairly eloquent glances.

I followed the partisans as they climbed up into the main
gallery that ran along the body of the airship, openwork
metal platforms that throbbed with the energy of the en-

gines as we pulled away northward, back into the shadows once more. There they all were, knight and squire, commoner and peasant crushed in together in a fuggy atmosphere of blood and sweat and horse dung, perched on every conceivable seat, joking quietly about the variety of smells each one had brought along, and which era had the biggest lice. (Byzantium won, by virtue of its bureaucrats.) They made a tremendous impression on me, a force of savage and dedicated fighters the SAS or Marines or samurai might have envied, yet radiating none of the aggression of a warrior caste. There was even a curious gentleness about them as they talked, swapped news of friends, soothed the restless horses in their wire-mesh stalls, snatched a hasty meal from the rations we handed out, or whatever sleep they could manage in those conditions. Some of them looked to me for more news about what had happened to the Spear; I suggested a briefing, thinking of Alison. They nodded sagely, and I called back down the ladder. "Alison, a word? And can somebody unpack that big chart? Thanks."

Rather to my surprise, Alison didn't come up; instead, she locked the control surfaces, took over the helm from Jyp and bent over the speaking tube. "Attention, all! In two minutes, a briefing on what's happened to the Spear, and what we're going to do about it!" She grinned at me, and added, "From the horse's mouth, right?"

I looked at all those hard, expectant faces, and I swallowed hard, wishing I was somewhere else, far, far away. These were the Knights of the Sangraal, its most dedicated followers, fanatical even; and I'd been playing fast and loose with the object of all that devotion. I was going to have to be pretty fast on my feet, verbally—or maybe literally.

But on the other hand, I'd been doing presentations all my life, and this wasn't too different, bar the bull. And there was Mall, sitting near me and watching me right through with those disconcerting green eyes. The Knights sat silent mostly, bar the odd question; I got some strange looks with my part in the theft, nothing more. But when I told them

about the captain, and the helicopter, a low growling mut-
ter ran through them, a horrible sound. Most of them knew
Dragovic, it seemed; and if he'd heard it, I think he might
have run to the ends of the earth, or simply cut his own
throat on the spot. So the hounds of heaven might give
tongue, and I was glad it wasn't after me. At last it broke
up, with nothing more than a few more questions, some
nodding and fingering of chins, and Hastein still trying to
cadge a cigarette.

"They accept you as their captain," Mall breathed in my
ear. "Never a doubt on't. That's well."

"I can't get over it!" Not sheeplike, not deferential even,
just accepting me with a confidence I didn't feel I even
remotely deserved. "I mean—people like these!"

"They're fierce, aye, and fell. But then . . . " her eyes sparkled in the gloom, "so am I! And I follow you, Master Stephen. So is the Pilot, and so are you also, after your fashion,
fierce and fast and proud as a goshawk when wrath o'er-
takes your quietness. Can you but enchain your doubts and
see but a little deeper into yourself, you'll have few masters.
Save one, I think." She bared her large teeth, and dug an
elbow into my side with her usual robust rib-cracking energy. By the time I had breath to speak she was down the
ladder again.

Somehow, despite the desperation of it all, I suddenly felt
good. If this pack of fighters could accept their fate, stand
or fall, could I do any less? If they accepted me as leader I
owed them the best I could do. I had Mall by my side, and
Jyp—and Alison too, of course. I owed them even more. I
might be adequate or I might not; but whatever there was
in me, they were going to get it.

Clouds rolled by us, cloud battlements, cloud towers,
cloud castles, vast insubstantial fortresses of nebulous history and misty ideals. They loomed like all the challenges
I'd ever faced, all the heights I'd ever hoped to storm, as
gray and forbidding as my imagination could make them.
All the demands of life, exams, college courses, graduation

with a good degree, getting the right job, landing the right contracts, handling the new promotion, launching my brainchild C-Tran—mist, all mist. A clammy veil that blotted out things that really mattered, that shaped itself into seductive phantoms I could chase and catch, only to have them melt away in my fingers and leave me no satisfaction, no real achievement, no solid ground beneath. And then one day, drawn by urges I hadn't understood, I'd wandered out onto the Spiral. Here, among this shifting morass of space and time and history and legend, I'd begun to face real challenges, real adventures with life as the prize and the forfeit both. Real, amid unreality; real friendships, real relationships. Other people I knew had stepped briefly over the bounds as I had—my colleague Dave, my ex-girlfriend Jacquie—only to step back, hurriedly. See and step back, to wrap the cold fixed Core around them like a security blanket. Dave had long forgotten; I hoped Jacquie hadn't, not entirely, if only for the odd fond memory of me. I couldn't do that, I knew it now. Like Alison, I'd been torn, this way and that, afraid of rejecting what my reason insisted must be the hard, the firm, the only true reality. Now, about to walk straight into what stood to be the most hellish thing I'd ever encountered—and by now that covered quite a pack—the mere vapors had been stripped away. This was real, for me at least; this moment now was life, existence. My past life, that had seemed so involving, so important, that was the fog. The cloud castles around us, they were real.

Jyp spun the wheel, took us down a little. The clouds thinned to flying streamers, and we headed west now, straight into the dying sun's last angry glance before an endless night. I stood beside him, swaying on my feet as small gusts swung and shook us. "This is it?"

"Surely is. Near as I can get it. Any nearer, we might be too early and scare 'em off."

"Okay. Stay in among the lower clouds," I warned him, "the driven stuff. Hide, as long and as completely as you can. Circle if you have to. It's our best hope."

He grinned; his teeth were on edge. "Nope. It isn't, you are. Don't go losing a holt of that."

I hung onto the brass handrail instead, and watched grimly. Not alone; I heard the little buzz and whisper that ran through the ship, audible even over the soft engine drone. The dull horizon swallowed up the sun and sucked the color from the sky, changing the world to lead. The cockpit lights were out, and we were sunk in shadow. This was glacial country, ground out by the great ice sheets, a broad, broken land seamed with river valleys. Against a swathe of pallid clouds the worn teeth of the ancient Harzgebirge stood out dark gray, and above them, twice their height, a vast mountainside shouldered upward. Out of its shroud of forest a central peak protruded, bare and stark, its nooks and crannies gleaming with grayish snow. The sharp little winds that buffeted us herded the clouds in a swirl around it, and it tore at them and shredded them and sent them reeling away in tatters, over the face of the rising moon.

I'd seen the Brocken, in the Core—the real Brocken, I might once have called it. Even there it was a presence, brooding, dominant, looming over the little town in the valley with its quaint station. Only the lure of the Harz mountain railway, with its beautifully preserved steam locomotives, had happened to take me up there, a footloose, footsore student wandering around Europe on a pre-college rail pass. It had impressed me, yes. The dense green forest of its lower slopes, still visibly divided by criss-crossed scars like an old *Junker*'s sabre cuts where the late unlamented East German border fortifications had been taken up, and their defoliated no man's land where the greenery was only just returning; high crags, with big birds wheeling around them; the bare and bony flanks of the peak, capped by the concrete blockhouse and spiny antennae set up to improve the border guards' view and ruin everyone else's. I'd paused a moment, whistled, made a mental note to pick up some postcards (I never did) then shambled off down into town with nothing more on my mind than the youth hostel, the girls I might meet there, the local *Bierstube*. That was all; no mysterious chills, no portents, nothing. Nothing to suggest it might somehow become the thing that had risen at me out of the pentacle, that swelled in bulk and menace ahead of me. I'd have laughed myself sick; but I never felt less like laughing now.

The moon was full, and its pallid light shone down upon a nightmarish transfiguration. The enshrouding *Urwald* was tangled and choked, a mass of struggling, distorted trees like one long frozen death-struggle spread out across the whole mountain flank. Swirling bands of mist shrouded the twisted branches, clinging to them wraithlike, while billows of darker smoke rose up and rolled between them. The tree shadows were alive with lights—pale lights, unhealthy phosphoric glows of green and yellow, sudden flaring actinic blues that hurt the eyes but illuminated nothing, pulsing specks of scarlet the shade of rubies and of fresh blood, sparking among the smoke. Fierce white glares shot out their rays into the blackness, lit up only the infinite tangle, and were swallowed up into the dark once more. There was noise, too, audible even from this far away, an indistinct, incessant row punctuated by impossibly deep, slow sounds that seemed to originate from within the mountain itself, carried to us on the wailing wind; and every so often fragments of sound would break through, a sudden keening in many voices, a brutal rattle and thud like drumming on metal. Always, in front of the lights, shapes flickered, brief blinks of movement rising and falling almost in patterns, like a great sweeping net of ribbons that arched from depths to heights and back again. The big brass telescope mounted over the binnacle showed me they were insubstantial, as if the mountain was surrounded by a constant flock of flying creatures, great moths or monstrous bats, maybe. And above it all lifted that bare jagged peak, escalating crags of granite whose peculiar shapes cast monstrous moon shadows across the mist.

One thing above all else it radiated: terror. Even I could feel it, as strong at this range as when it contorted space and time to drag us down into its ant-lion's pit, and all the time growing stronger, a cavernous cold feeling that seemed to suck the marrow from my bones. It was partly the sheer size of the thing; it was a mountain, a whole huge peak filled with the influence of whatever dreadful force it was that dwelt there. But there was more to it than that; something inside me shrank away—and something, bolder but nastier, licked its chops and was curious. And that was what I feared most. I reached out, unthinking, and felt a hand slip into mine and clutch it tight. Alison stood beside me. "The lion's den," I whispered. "This is too much like walking straight into it. Wish we could land some way off—"

"A *long* way," she agreed. "And move in under cover. But it wouldn't work."

"I know." We'd discussed it all, and it came down to speed. One of the great forces from the Rim had moved in to touch the earth here, and there was no telling what it might do if it was alerted. Our only hope was to move in fast. If we recovered the Spear, then it might be a different story; then we ought at least to be able to defend ourselves even against . . .

"Even against that," said Alison quietly, and I realized suddenly, horribly, that I desperately didn't want her going anywhere near that place. I never learned; often enough before I'd only come to realize how much I valued something when I was closest to losing it. Or some person. I let her hand fall suddenly and wrapped my arm around her shoulders, tightly, drawing her close. She looked up at me, startled.

"Stay with the ship!" I said tightly. "Somebody's got to—"

She gave a breathless half-grin. "Oh, Steve, you know I

can't do that. I'm a Knight of the Sangraal! That's meant
more to me than anything—than almost anything. I took
the privilege, I pay the price, and this is it."

"Sod the privilege!" I muttered, and she half laughed,
wrapped an arm around my waist and gave a companion-
able squeeze in return. I rounded on her suddenly, and
pulled her hard against me, and kissed her, also hard. She
was almost the first woman apart from Mall I hadn't had
to bend down to. Her body pressed against mine, serpen-
tine, slender, softer somehow than I'd expected even as she
stiffened with surprise. I felt her arms shift as if to push
me away; instead they clapped around my shoulder blades
and pressed, hard, pulling me closer. Her dry lips parted,
and they weren't dry anymore. She shifted slightly against
me, and I felt all of her, the texture of her skin almost, as
if there were no clothes at all between us, as if we were
welded close by the swelling heat. I slid my hand up to the
back of her neck and twined my fingers in the close-cut
curls, slid them over the soft neck beneath the soft uniform
collar. My other hand slowly traced down her spine—

You need to breathe at the damnedest times. I wanted to
come up for air, my lips were bruising against my teeth,
and she wouldn't let me. Those arms were whipcord and
steel cable. I hauled myself free and stared into her wide
startled dark eyes. How, in God's name, had I ever thought
this woman was plain? It was just that habitual look she'd
had, all anger and resentment, that and the ghost of it
lingering on in my memory which had blinded me to her.
With that wiped away and filled out a little, the dark eyes
wide instead of permanently narrowed, the softer outline
and the fine bones beneath made the best of that firm chin
and full lips and put her face back into balance. Wide-eyed,
open-mouthed, startled and unguarded, the look suited her.
At least as pretty as half the faces I'd seen that close, prettier
than I ever deserved and then some, because there was
something more than just the prettiness there. She didn't
fight, she said nothing, she just stared back. I couldn't

think what to say; I had a hundred handy responses for situations like this, and every one of them turned sour on me, cheap and stale and stinking of lies. I was scared to say anything; it seemed too important somehow. It was a mercy when Jyp's hail broke the spell.

"Ahoy all! West away! A light! Navigation lights!"

We sprang apart, still staring at each other, then wildly around at a cockpit and company we'd completely forgotten. Maybe they hadn't seen us in the dark, maybe—

The dark; the sky; lights. I pulled myself together, and saw where Jyp was pointing, a faint flashing gleam barely above the western horizon. "Are you sure?" whispered Alison, grabbing the telescope. But before she'd finished asking it was obvious, a constellation of faint glows surrounding one brighter flashing light; and over the clamor of the mountain and the soft purr of our engines a distant, deeper sound was growing, a distinctive, thudding roar we'd last heard in a Munich scrapyard.

"Jyp," I whispered, "you're amazing. I think you could chart a course back to the Big Bang."

"Maybe so; wouldn't bank on the round trip, mind. But I'll steer you a course between a girl's first and second thoughts of her lover, and that's tighter yet. And with more shoals." Alison made a small sound. I concentrated fervently on the incoming machine. It was bigger than I'd realized, a fast, long-range 'copter of the kind favored by oil exploration teams and narc agents.

"He's coming in very low," I told Jyp. "Why? It's slower. He must have a reason."

"Yah. Where's he going to land?" We scanned the immense expanse of *Urwald* surrounding the mountain's base, but there were no major breaks in it at all along that flank.

Alison frowned. "It has to be the summit, then . . . unless—yes, look there!"

Just at the treeline, beneath one of the granite outcrops, a wide shelf stretched out over the slope, half hidden by the tangle of distorted, half-uprooted pines around it. As we watched from cloud height, hardly daring to breathe, the big 'copter rumbled its way around, banking till we looked down on its rotors, obviously preparing to come in.

"Quickly, Jyp!" I hissed, but he and Alison were already at the controls. In the shadow of a cloud the airship sank swiftly but smoothly, so any chance watcher would be hard put to it to make it out. I snapped out my orders, and there was a general scramble as the Knights in the gondola moved to their stations, unshipping the small breechloader at the rear of the platform. It swung on its mount, brass shellcases were charged, one slammed home and the breech dogged down. Very quietly the rear door was unlatched, and the gun swung back. Still we sank, slow as a leaf now, till it seemed that the wood would reach up and swallow us like a sea anemone after a fish.

"Wish we could shoot the bastard out of the air!" murmured one of the World War I esquires. "Wouldn't hurt the Spear!"

Alison frowned. She still looked beautiful. "No—but would you want to have to go hunting for it? Through all *that* down there?"

The squire shuddered. "I surely wouldn't! And I'd have competition fast enough, I bet!"

"No takers," I whispered. "Quiet now!" The airship rocked slightly, and I heard a soft scratching as the pine tops brushed the base of the gondola. The helicopter's engine thundered as it came to a hover, and then rumbled slowly down as it sank to the earth of the bare mountain. Even as its skids touched the bare stony soil, blasting up clouds of dusty gravel, figures appeared at the margins of the wood and came streaming toward it. Horrible figures, for all their human-like outlines, mostly like Le Stryge's ogreish henchmen but some even weirder, bloated, rolling monsters of horrendous height and bulk; their swollen arms flailed as they crashed forward on legs grown conical and stubby to support their bulk. This was the ultimate development of this mingled race of demons, human and otherwise, the fully adult stage of the Children of the Night—giants, vast, coarse, primevally strong. It looked as if the helicopter had strayed into one of those nightmarish illustrations from an old Grimm's. But its door slid back, and a familiar figure jumped down and strode confidently forward; metal gleamed underneath his arm. He must have had more nerve than I'd given him credit for, even if they were on his side.

"Now!"

I'd meant it to be an inspiring shout. It came out as a sort of falsetto eunuch shriek.

"Go, Jyp, go-go-go!"

Alison's hand tilted the control surfaces; Jyp's slammed down the throttles, and he spun the helm. We'd sunk down, right down below the shelf, unnoticed as I'd hoped we'd be while the 'copter was landing. And now, even as the captain stepped out from beneath the circle of the blades, we rose like an avenging angel to the edge of the shelf, and over. The gondola lurched violently as its base scraped and screeched along the stones, but we stayed upright. I snatched up the speaking tube that linked us to the rear gondola, shouted an order, then threw open our forward door and sprang down, stumbling on the stark earth of the Brocken. Behind me sprang Alison, and Mall after her. The monsters swung toward us, glaring; their faces were impossibly bestial, lumpy, misshapen, fanged and filthy, with slitted eyes glittering under pouchy lids, like a living satire written on human flesh. From the rear gondola the wide ramp boomed down, scraping against the stone. They started at the noise; and then they fell back as a loud metallic jingle sounded. The first horses came slipping and sliding down the ramp, their riders crouching low in the saddle to pass through. It didn't slow them in the least; they came out with lances already lowered, sabres in hand, to the charge. Utterly taken aback, the monsters howled and scattered, some in aimless panic, others for the trees; but I had no eyes for them. Dragovic, as stunned as the rest, was frantically dodging the monstrous stampede, running for the helicopter. Understandably it was already gunning its rotors, and he screamed at them to wait. He needn't have bothered; I'd given my orders. As the last horse sprang out the airship swung around, and from the after door the breechloader spat fire. A cracking explosion, and the 'copter jerked forward and crashed back on its skids, its rotor smashed and its cabin roof chewed open. A figure slumped out of the co-pilot's door, held back by the cords of his helmet. The captain gaped for an instant; then he saw us coming, and he turned to run.

A fearful mêlée filled the shelf now, as many of the giant Children, overtaken, turned with horrible savagery on the soldiers who milled around them. Some of them were fifteen feet tall or more, much bigger than Kodiak grizzlies or polar bears, and stronger, by the look of it; those puffy, bowed arms picked up warhorses and broke their necks, or threw their riders spinning headlong. But they feared the lances and heavy sabres that left great slashing wounds, and the arrows of the cataphracts; and when they tried to mass another shell burst in among them, the survivors scattered and the axemen and foot soldiers closed in and hewed down the monsters like trees. Through the middle of the slaughter the captain ran for his life, and at his tail, keeping together as we'd arranged and leaving the fight to the Knights, came Alison, Mall, and myself. Dragovic leaped violently as a pistol shot whizzed past his ear; Jyp, who'd been seeing the airship made fast, sprang down and joined the pursuit. Dragovic swerved to avoid him, and so into our path. We lunged frantically, thought we had him, collided—and he ducked in among the trees and away, shouting loudly for help.

Slashing branches, leaping stones, we kept after him, turning at every turn he made, cutting off his attempts to double back. He kept on screaming and screaming for help, but nothing happened, and I came so close my sword slashed a wide half-moon flap out of his ragged shirt. But then, as swiftly as the telling of it, a great curtain of gray flew up in my face, a puff of dense fog that filled the air and blotted out my sight, so that abruptly, unnervingly, I was alone.

I took a cautious step. My foot skidded on some puffy fungus; I caught myself on an overhanging limb then jerked my hand away, thick with slime and decay. *"Alison!"* I yelled. *"Mall! Jyp! This way! Keep together!"*

But it was as if the vapor drank my voice. Out of the fog a dark figure appeared—and then a sword flashed, lance-straight in a lightning lunge, almost too fast to see. I parried, barely, staggered back, saw Dragovic's eyes glitter, and again only just parried a cut to take my throat out. I tried to launch my own attack and was countered with a force that jarred my wrist, and nearly skewered on another lunge. I knew in a moment of cold panic that Dragovic really was a better swordsman, and nearly as strong; I'd no advantages of muscle or stamina here. How about nerves? I launched a fearful wild swing at his head and a horrible cracked wolf-howl. His sword jerked even as it caught mine, and he jumped back and vanished into the mist. From somewhere another voice called out, muffled as if by great distance; I couldn't tell whose. Silence fell again.

I hated fog, ever since the Gates. I stepped forward—and something loomed up in front of me, tall, misshapen, fantastical. I yelled and struck at it. My sword slashed the fog, and I almost fell over. Again it appeared, to the side this time. Again I struck at it, again there was nothing there. I bounded forward a few steps, found a stout tree and put my back to it. Nothing—and then abruptly it was there again right in front of me. I sprang forward, slashing wildly, and this time I did fall over, hard. A rock caught me sickeningly in the kidneys. I rolled over—and there the thing came again, more shapeless than ever, rippling across the face of the mist. My sword lay feet away. I snatched up that rock and threw it, a poor throw. It passed straight through the thing and went rattling away into sudden silence. A crash

echoed up from somewhere below. I snatched up my sword
and scrabbled forward on all fours. Where the thing had
appeared the ground dropped away abruptly, that was all I
could see. I tossed another rock, there was a delay, then
another crash. I sank back, sweating. Whatever that image
was, it had almost led me right over quite a respectable
cliff—

"No more than a simple natural illusion."

I sprang up, swearing, and stared wildly around me. That
voice had sounded right in my ear.

It was there again, papery and cold. "Have you not heard
of the Specter of the Brocken? An effect of light and shadows, no more."

"Stryge?"

"A votre service comme toujours, mon seigneur. But
kindly enlighten me, boy. If you cannot cope with so slight
a thing, what chance have you against the power that dwells
upon this mountain?"

His voice almost concealed the slight scraping sound at
my back. Almost. I half turned, barely in time. The captain's
stabbing lunge, meant for my kidneys, slid along my left
arm, leaving a shallow cut, and stuck me awkwardly in the
side. The impact was bruising, but the blow was indirect;
the tough, taut merhorse skin of my top turned the point
and sent it skidding over my ribs. I yelped with pain and
lashed out a cut, as he should have done; he'd tried to kill
me painfully instead of cleanly. He ducked hastily away
again.

"There will be others to help me!" hissed the captain,
from somewhere nearby. "Any minute! Then you and your
friends will be slaughtered piecemeal in your misty traps!
Cut to pieces! Eh?"

Rubbing my ribs, I didn't answer. I wouldn't have given
him the satisfaction. There were other voices in the fog,
but I ignored them.

"Was sagt er denn daran? Do you hear me?" I had the
direction. Not something I'd ever made a habit of, this, but

it gave me a certain satisfaction now; I pursed my mouth and spat forcefully out into the mist.

The captain should have waited. I was afraid he would, despite my provocation; but I suspect he wasn't very sane by then. He sprang in suddenly, from a different direction, aiming the killing thrust he should have started with—too predictable, for such a good swordsman. It passed through the mist above me. I'd ducked down easily; and my own cut rose almost from the ground, with two hands behind it and all the force of my anger and my fear. It struck right into Dragovic's exposed side, and across him from stomach to shoulder, trailing a spraying scarlet banner into the air. He flew up and over backwards, legs akimbo, hit the ground like a sack of potatoes and lay twisting. I leveled my sword and sprang forward, but one look was more than enough.

All the same, I jumped violently when one scrabbling arm slid down suddenly, with a metallic clatter. But it was only the thing he'd been carrying. I sprang on it as it rattled free among the stones, fumbled desperately with the blood-slicked catches and flung back the lid.

It should have been a dramatic moment, a little thrill of satisfaction at least. It wasn't; things were too urgent for that. The Spear gleamed against the soft lining, its obsidian head deeply lustrous even in this dim mirk. I took a deep breath, banished all hesitation, and closed my left hand about the shaft. It felt glassy smooth itself, polished by untold ages of being grasped perhaps—and by who knows what hands? The thought gave me a sudden thrill, as if I teetered on the brink of some startling understanding. I plucked up my courage and easily, carefully, I lifted it from the case.

In the faint wind of its passage the mist fell back and began to grow thinner and disperse. I let my arm fall, and found myself standing on the narrow bare margin of the hillside above a very respectable cliff indeed, part of the same formation as the larger shelf. Below me, among the trees behind it, the bloody battle was still raging; the shelf was a mass of bodies. Around me, startlingly close, were Alison and the others, thankfully all right, staring down at the dying captain.

"Said you were better!" she muttered softly. But she wouldn't have sounded that relieved if she'd been sure.

I shook my head. "Nearly had me!" I panted. "Would have, if he hadn't tried a low one!"

"Not the better sword," she said quietly. "The better man." Then her eyes lifted and widened, as she saw what I held.

Careful of the tangle around, I brandished it high above my head. The tattered streamers of mist boiled up suddenly into the crest of a great wave, collapsed, sank back on themselves and faded. The mountain loomed above now, vaster and more terrible than it had seemed from the air; and as I saw it for the first time clearly, saw something of what those lights were, and those flying swirls, my brief moment of triumph and relief sank down like lead.

And worse; for a dry cough drew my attention back to the ground I stood on. In front of us, perched comfortably on a granite outcropping, was the old necromancer himself, Le Stryge.

Chapter 10

Those lights were fires, fires in clearings dotted all over the hillside, and the nearest ones were easy to see. The fires were made before great stones set up like altars, and before and around those altars figures shuffled and danced, silhouettes passing in front of the flames, some grotesque, some monstrous, some nakedly, fallibly human, whirling in the grip of frenzy, screaming and mouthing and gibbering. It was impossible to make out all the things that were going on, but there were worse things there than Children of Night—worse even than anything I'd seen in the dark *tonnelle* when the malformed *loa* of Don Petro descended, worse than the dead legions of Rangda. I thought I made out shadows with spidery spindled limbs and sunken ribcages, monstrous heads sunk between their shoulders, black hunched figures that trailed their hands or waddled along on all fours, and worse, crawling, flapping worse; I could never be sure. What must this Brocken creature, this residing power, look like, if those were only its servants? Some of them seemed to change shape instant by instant, or maybe that was only the flickering of the flames.

Things were done, rites carried out; that was clear, though what they were or why I couldn't guess and didn't want to. No wonder the medievals interpreted them as parodies of church rites, deliberate blasphemies; so they were, but against every concept of reason or sense I could imagine, even warped ones. I'd heard somewhere that fetishes and obsessions carried to extremes usually lose any resemblance at all to sex, at least to outsiders who don't share the secret; what I saw here felt like that, only far worse. As if at the center of the bizarre ritual was emptiness, its meaning that it had no meaning; but even emptiness hid a tiny twisted core, malice and evil too arcane to expose fully to itself. And even on the surface the rites were cruel.

Some of the human shapes didn't dance or caper; they were dragged along, half slumping, loose-limbed. Figures jigged around them, postured, gestured; suddenly at the nearest fire something was cast into the flame so it blazed reddish-green, and by that sickly light I saw some of their faces, lank and sick and miserable, jaws sagging like their exhausted bodies so that dark slaver trickled down onto their sunken chests. Their limbs bled, they were spilling their guts and I guessed they wailed, though I couldn't make it out among the clamor. They looked exhausted, but more than that—they seemed spent or used-up, like a coal half turned to ash and clinging together in a shadow of its outward solidity, only to collapse suddenly and disintegrate. The other dancers, human or monstrous, had no mercy on these drained things, but pawed and mauled them and flung them around in their filth like sacks with manic shrieks and laughter. It was ghastly, like plague burial pits come to life; but what was above them was worse. For all the shock of the old villain's appearance, it held our horrified eyes entirely.

Those swirling haloes, those swooping flocks that circled the mountain crest like the bands of an airy crown—those were figures too. All of them human, as far as I could make out; they moved almost too fast to see, except when a flow-

ing band stooped low above our heads, trailing a terrible
clamor of wailing and screams and a waft of choking vom-
itous stench. What held them so high I couldn't imagine;
there was nothing of flight about them, a writhing tangled
mass like eels in a torrent. It was more as if they were
pinioned within rushing currents of wind that flung and
tumbled and battered them against one another, but never
let them drop. Even as the wind collided them they scrabbled and they clawed at one another, fighting like drowning
people in a current, so that they were a mass of blood and
bruises and horrible injuries, faces screaming with eyeless
sockets, an ear torn away or a cheek as they spun and
spilled over one another, dangling shreds of clothes and
flesh. Not only panic drove them as they clutched at each
other, scrabbling indiscriminately for any shred of sensation, pawing and coupling—there wasn't a better word for
it—at frenzied random in the cascading, boiling tumult of
flesh. Some of their appetite, horribly, was hunger; for
many tore the living flesh around them and stuffed it in
their mouths, and I glimpsed some who licked and sucked
the blood and snarled at neighbors like hyenas on a kill.
All this at once, a living hymn of hatred to human flesh
and human senses, twisted about the mountain like a living
crown. I'd only glanced at Dante, but I remembered something like this; and I wondered what infernos that man
really had passed through. It was only afterwards I thought
of Hieronymus Bosch, and Breughel.

Now I understood what those halo-things were that had
plucked at Katjka as she dangled, that had torn her from
me. So did the others. Jyp was suddenly and violently sick.
Mall closed her eyes in agony, that awful sudden empathy
of hers stiffening her rigid. Alison, her clenched fist
jammed against her lips, was the gray shade of her uniform.

Le Stryge gave his thin cold laugh, and clicked his
knobbed knuckles. "What is amiss, ladies and gentlemen?
The brave pilot, is he airsick? The harridan who'd right the
wrongs of womankind, does she blanch at the play they

make with men—or recall her own beginnings? A Knight
of the Graal, surely she doesn't falter at the sight of blood,
hein?" He turned toward me. "But you, boy, you surprise
me, truly. This I would have thought is your everyday life
in its essence, eh. The world of finances and affairs, the
struggle for survival, dog-eat-dog, the mindless, incessant
mating and eating. So much your true *milieu* I feared you
might have to be restrained from plunging into it. Headlong."

"No, Stryge," I said tightly. "No, I wouldn't."

He flapped a hand. "Bah! There's no pleasing some people. In any event, you may as well relax and take what pleasure you can, because no more is left you. Your mission
has failed. Those rabble Knights of yours now blunder
wildly throughout this hospitable forest, led ever more
apart and astray by visions and delusions, torn by thorn
and briar, falling into snares or simply the consequences of
their own carelessness. Those that are not picked off one
by one will soon become irrelevant, as have you."

"And this?" I lowered the Spear, and held it out before
me, carefully, testing the ground ahead before I put my
weight on it. "You ran from this before. What do you think
it's about to do to all your bloody pretensions?"

He shrugged, and waggled his fingers in a contemptuous
gesture. "Why, nothing, boy. Nothing at all. Here, upon the
very flanks of the Brocken, I could shield myself for some
time against such an enfeebled force—far longer than I will
in fact need. I never did care so very much about the thing,
you know, except as its loss furthered my real plan. Do by
all means retain it if you wish—no, please, I beg you!"

Those stark mad eyes of his fastened on me with a weird
intensity, part menacing, part politely pleading. Behind us
the wind shook and rattled those skeletal trees. I lowered
the Spear again slightly; I'd been about to lunge, and the
old bastard had spotted it somehow.

"I would have to stop you, and you would not like it,"
he said sharply. "A word of Arraignment, at the least, if you

try any such foolishness. I do strive to warn you; you may
remember, I am not without a sense of obligation. And you,
truly, are the one responsible for all this."

Alison touched my arm. "Is he hell! He's never willingly
done anything to help you and you know it! We know it!"

"That's so!" snapped Mall. "Sneck up thy tongue, old
blindworm, it stings us not!"

"Goes for me too!" said Jyp. "I know you and your goddamn obligations, Stryge! Know him, too, and he's none of
yours!"

Stryge smiled. "Now there, I may inform you, you are
both right and wrong. He has become mine, this empty-
headed boy, because he was not himself. Right from our
first encounter, when he began to dabble in things beyond
his measure, I sensed something about this Stephen Fisher.
Something I did not like, something that made me itch."

I wheezed with laughter. "No shortage of those around
you!"

His eyes flamed an instant. "You! What would *you* know
of necessary austerities, of ritual abasement? That, I, *I*,
should have to humble myself thus in the quest of power—
and be insulted for it by you, you base-born scraper after
filthy commerce." He shrugged again, dismissive. "But you
are chiefly appearance, why should I expect more? It was
that very emptiness that intrigued me, for beneath it lay a
hint of something else, something disturbing. That was one
reason I agreed to help, even at great risk to myself; and
when even my powers were spent I saw you—*you*—
summon down an Invisible, a near-divine, and contain it,
and share its powers so fluently . . . " He breathed deep, and
steepled his long bony fingers. "The watch I set on you
found nothing at first. As well I was patient; for then came
that business in the East, and you somehow contained and
challenged a still greater power. Then I set out to trace you
in both directions, to find your ancestry, and from that to
divine your destiny." He nodded sourly. "I traced your family back to the Rhineland of medieval days, and beyond. It

began at the heart of modern Europe, with the bastard child of a Merovingian princess at the Frankish court of Rheims."

I shrugged. "I could have told you that, the Rhineland, anyway. Glad I didn't save you the trouble. So what difference does it make?"

The twist of his bloodless lips was nothing like a smile. "You are correct, of course. It makes little, now. But it was unusual enough to set me on the quest of your destiny also. And do you know? It proved both hard and costly, to my surprise, for I had sharper tools at my disposal than a witchling's cards." He gave a sudden cackle. "Oh, you start? A little friend forgotten, is that it? But who can tell where she may be by now? Or whether you would know her if you saw her. Warlocks and witches as she was, they are swept up for a brief spell of frenzied indulgence and excess, the ultimate communion of the Sabbat; most survive. But those the Brocken punishes touch the earth no more. The winds are scarcely merciful, and they are never still." He sniggered softly. "She should have read her cards more closely. What did she read for you? Very little, I guess. That in itself was the most intriguing thing of all. I sought events which would shape your fate, and found almost nothing." He rubbed his hands with a businesslike gleefulness, while the rest of us, I suppose, simply gaped at him. "You do not comprehend? Of course you do not. It is rare, boy, very rare. As if the course of destiny depends upon you, not you upon it; as if you yourself are some great fulcrum, a point of balance upon which historic forces hang. Naturally no divination involving such a person would ever yield any clear results."

I might have laughed myself sick at that; but nothing in that harsh corvine croak made laughter possible. I believed him, and that belief sank down around me with the stifling weight of a leaden cover, of unimaginable responsibilities. He seemed to see that, and smirked.

"All this suggested, shall we say, an avenue, through which you might be of service to me. The forces involved were so great I could not be sure of handling them myself. That was what brought me here, to find an ally sufficiently powerful and knowledgeable, in its way. The price was high, perhaps, but the benefits were great, and the potential triumph . . . " He closed his eyes and shivered, and crooned softly. I remembered him making the same noise over a seagull he was about to use in a cruel spell. *"Vast!"*

"And Lutz?" I demanded, watching for an instant when his vigilance might slip, feeling as if I really did stand astride that unsteady balance. "Where did he come in?"

Le Stryge twitched his lips contemptuously. "The Herr Baron von Amerningen? Through my new ally, as you suspect. He was already a rising adept and as viciously ambitious as such creatures tend to be. Some of his companies dealt with your business already. It was easy to improve the acquaintance, and when you launched this absurd money-grubbing scheme of yours I instructed him to become one of its backers and draw you into his circles. He seemed quite surprised when it began to make him money."

I nodded. "He would. Maybe I do owe you one thing, Stryge. I've always wondered how an aging playboy with an inherited business and about as much vision as a blind slug ever had enough faith in my idea. It worried me, at times. Now I know it was pure accident."

Le Stryge chuckled. "An apt description. Yes, he found you hard work, I believe. When he failed to corrupt you indirectly I grew impatient, seeking to gain a more direct hold over you and try the power I suspected. Luring you, with your straggling romantic notions, to the margins of the Heilenthal was easy enough, only those idiot Knights interfered, and you broke free somehow. Completely, I feared; I frightened von Amerningen into making a more direct approach, to lure you here. And then, *potz sapermentz*, some mischance or other alerts you against him and the idiot panics and tries to kill you!" He struck his brow. "You, upon whom my whole scheme hung! I was quite hard put to it to forestall him."

A great light dawned. "So it was you who intervened on the *Autobahn*? That truck?"

"A sending, to save your life. Still more obligation, if I chose to claim it."

"When you endangered me in the first place? Bugger that!"

"I? You would have been in danger anyway, believe me. Nothing you do, no idea you have, is truly called coincidental; it is all part of your self, your personality, and its potential. That was why I needed you for the task, knowing that you were the only ordinary human who could touch the weapon without dire peril. And you still don't know why, do you?" He chuckled, and his fingers wove a distracting pattern in the air. "If I tell you now, you . . ."

He paused, and looked up expectantly, as if he somehow heard something over that horrendous babel. The moment his eyes were off me, I lunged.

Not fast enough. Warped branches that hadn't been there a moment before were suddenly whipping forward as if a gale bent them; they lashed painfully at my arms, my ankles, around my bruised side. Straight thorns sank deep into my flesh. They tangled around me and tightened, till my feet left the ground and my breathing was constricted. Only my hand with the Spear was left free; they wouldn't go anywhere near that. But I couldn't move it enough to do anything, even to touch the wood; it might if I let it fall, but I wasn't about to risk that. I struggled uselessly, gasping; I could barely twist around enough to see the others just as entangled. I seethed bitterly at my own stupidity. With Le Stryge nothing had only one purpose. Those extravagant gestures, perhaps some of his very words, had been the subtle medium for some kind of spell. "So it was all a ploy!" I choked. "The goading, the threats—just to hold us while you worked up all this! All those carefully measured revelations—"

The old man made a modest *moue*. "But naturally. Even honesty has its uses, and truth can be turned to account.

Nothing less than frankness would have held you. Why else should I bother to reveal anything? Now be quiet, or you will suffer more greatly." As a swirling streak of lost souls reeled away toward the heights again I heard what he'd heard—a deep buzzing drone in the air somewhere very close, too quiet to be a helicopter.

Stryge unfolded himself and hopped nimbly down from his perch. "That will be the other airship."

"What?" yelled Alison.

"The *Raven*, I believe you call it. Please do not trouble yourselves with hope; it bears only my followers. For this," he drew a deep breath, "this is the real fulfillment of my plan."

Alison sagged in that cruel grasp, and closed her eyes. Le Stryge evidently saw no need to explain any further, but she seemed to guess just what the old beast meant; and I had the awful feeling I was beginning to see it, too. I struggled against the entangling, trying to ignore the pain and the little patches of stickiness starting as the thorns punctured clothes and skin. An instant's hope burgeoned as the branches beside me heaved and seemed about to loosen; but it was Mall, with all her great strength, barely tearing free an arm. She shouted with raw triumph, and for an instant it looked as if she would explode out of the entwining mass; but Le Stryge's cold gaze lit upon her, and suddenly her struggles seemed diminished, her achievement useless. I saw her hand sag. He gave that straight-lipped little smirk. "Ah, madam! However hot the flames within you, in this place they are all but quenched. I know you, I have seen you; and I am greater than you."

"You sawn-off little ratfink!" yelled Jyp, flailing against his own bonds. "You're no greater'n all shit, y' hear?"

"You are scarcely equipped to judge, Pilot," said the little man imperturbably. "But even you can perceive the scale of the force that dwells here—and the power of the Brocken, remember, is mine. It will become more so, as only through me it achieves its ancient ends, which began when the first men spread across this land in the wake of the retreating Ice. Then . . . ah, yes, then!" His chilly eyes became gloating suddenly. "A new Master is about to emerge."

Jyp stared, and I understood what had struck him. That wasn't at all like the old Stryge, austere and cruel but never betraying such bare ambition. He was a monster, in his way; but this was Le Stryge plus something else, and far, far worse. This was a devouring devil. And yet obscurely, impossibly, I found myself pitying him.

The airship was circling now, easing in toward the landing shelf with a hesitant care that made me realize just how good Jyp and Alison had been at piloting it. Le Stryge nodded, amused; he seemed to be thinking the same. "You have talents, abilities beyond the common, all of you. That is my only reason for keeping you alive. It would be criminal to let such gifts perish needlessly. Therefore, if you do not all wish to be thrown away and wasted utterly, if you wish some tiny shred of your individuality and identity to remain, then you would do well to hold yourself in readiness and accept what comes. Remember, I am not a sadistic little idiot like that fool Don Petro. I will rule, not despoil."

I looked at him; and I remembered his dark brand of magic, the awful familiars in human form he kept and the black suspicions of how he'd come by them, the murderous cold wrath he'd more than once displayed. And now, I guessed, he was hardly more himself than Don Petro had been; he'd plunged too deeply into dark waters, and been overwhelmed. Like so many others I'd encountered, he'd made what he thought was an alliance and turned out to be servitude. It was the mysterious creature of this mountain, wherever it dwelt, that looked out from behind those eyes now, as much as the man himself. The fate he was predicting he had already met himself. He'd swallowed fire in order to breathe it, and become the first to burn.

There was no need to ask what that force would do; the example was all around us. A degradation and depravity beyond ordinary comprehension, almost infantile in its viciousness; that was what the alliance of these two dark minds would create. No doubt they meant to spread it, too. Now I could guess the point of Lutz's neo-Nazi links, and the Children of Night fomenting riot and murder in a peaceful demonstration. Their corrupting purpose would spread like gangrene from country to country by that kind of means, by old suspicions and hatreds inflamed, by war even. I could just imagine that cold face gloating over the aftermath of a battle or a brisk bout of ethnic cleansing, then stirring up the losers to return the favor, until in the end the whole human race was swept up. A fate like Katjka's, with no chance to fly from it—

Like Katjka's. Voices rode the air, tearing at my ears.

The winds are scarcely merciful. And they are never still.

The image was bitter in my mind, bitter and terrible; I hardly dared confront it. Katjka dangling over that impossible gulf, with the creatures of the winds plucking at her like sharks at a struggling swimmer, and that fearful blend of terror and longing distorting her face.

But me—leave me where I belong!

Her hand, slipping away from mine. Her shape whirling away, barely visible against the smoke and the glare. The creatures hadn't pulled her down. It was Katjka herself. Even after centuries of remorse the things she had done, the unhallowed pleasures she'd taken in them, those had weighed her down. The remembered lure, the scarred self-image; they had made her want to fall. As a dog returns to his vomit, the addict to his drug, pleasure and punishment together; and if only I'd understood I might have reached out more than a hand to her, more than merely physical support. But there hadn't been time. It was too late.

Was it—entirely?

I reached out with my free hand, my Spear hand, straining hard against the binding withies; but my arm was still held down. Le Stryge glared at me; but after a second he laughed contemptuously, and turned away to watch the other airship wobble in to land. In my heart I knew he was right; alone, unaided, I couldn't shift anything. I needed something extra, something that came from within, I needed to burst into flame like Mall—

I twisted violently about to catch her eye, but her head sagged, and I didn't dare make a noise in case Le Stryge noticed. Desperately I willed her to just glance my way, even for an instant; but deep gouges on her neck and arm leaked blood over the thorns, and her hair overhung her face. Softly I pursed my lips and blew; the curls stirred, and I caught a flash of green. But beneath it, on her cheek, I saw something that shocked me more deeply, a single smudged streak. On her? *Mall*? I mouthed at her, furiously, praying she wouldn't make a sound. Her eye was dull and dazed, as if the weight of this place had settled on her more heavily. But she seemed to understand what I was saying, because slowly, hesitantly, she burrowed her free arm back into the branches again, wincing as the thorns pawed at her. But she kept it coming, until there was a stirring in the branches that caged me, and her strong bony fingers entwined with mine and held fast. I clenched my grip, pulled myself as close as I could, feeling my own neck savaged, and risked the faintest of whispers. *"Fire, Mall! That can save us . . ."*

The answer came softer still, barely a breath. *"Stephen, heart, I have none—darker and older than mine, these flames here—alone I cannot assail them—I am embers . . ."*

"But you're not alone! With Katjka the flame changed—and with the Graal! He said I was kindled! Mall, woman—*kindle me!*"

Her jaw dropped; but her eye glittered with green mischief, and her fingers clamped so hard on mine I almost yelled. "I' love o' God's will!" she murmured. "Will the man never stop trying!" And, wonder of wonders, she chuckled; and yet in that chuckle I sensed something else, and at last I began to understand what fired her spirit.

It was nothing I hadn't felt in myself often, only enlarged

and broadened by century upon century of bruising life.
Anger seethed and bubbled till at last it boiled dry; and the
residue was laughter. Laughter at cruelty, laughter at crime
unpunished, laughter at the torment of the weak, laughter
at injustice, laughter at fear and agony and the final dev-
astating kicks of destiny. Laughter, because tears were helpless; tears were defeat. A laughter that scraped against anger
like a match against a wall, that left a trail of stinging
sparks and finally, when it seemed there could be no more,
struck a flame within the mind, pure and sharp and cleansing. In a lifetime you might see no more than a glitter in
the eye, a piercing brightness to a sudden glance; but Mall
had known many lifetimes, and her laughter could make
the corners of the wide world ring.

She laughed silently now, but the tremor of it passed
through her grip to me. My own swelled up in answer, till
holding it back strained my ribs and brought me near to
choking. Jyp was laughing too, with the cold manic glitter
his eyes wore in a fight; and he was staring at me. So was
Alison, where it should have been Mall they watched; because there was a light in her eye again, a flash in her
sudden grin, a swift transparency under her face as if the
bones had turned to frozen milk. Her hair stirred and
heaved, and I felt my own scalp crawl as I watched it lift
and billow in some private wind of its own, some interplay
of vast forces from the margins of human experience. Yet
they were still staring at me—her too. I struggled to point;
then I understood. In front of my eyes, over the back of
that hand sparks were passing, little crackling arcs, not blue
like Mall's, but yellow, golden even. And they ran along the
Spear, right to its tip.

Then I laughed aloud. The golden fire blazed up in blinding corona, and hurled a long black shadow of Le Stryge
upon the ground. He turned quickly, only to hide his eyes
and howl. "Idiot! That will avail you nothing! You will only
summon worse!"

And that decided me; because it was exactly what I had

in mind. I reached out with the Spear, as high as I could, and when I could reach no higher I pulled it back and threw. High into the seething smoky air that glittering spearhead rose, and out of its black glass the golden fire blazed like a beacon. I gathered my breath and yelled out, with all the strength I could summon, one word, one name.

Katjka's.

The Spear tumbled in the air. The light faded. The hollow bestial howlings devoured my voice. The branches heaved and clutched about my throat, my chest, squeezing the breath from me more surely than any constrictor. Beside me Mall jerked, gargled; her fingers slipped from mine. The Spear fell, and I strained my fingers desperately to reach it again. Le Stryge opened his mouth to cackle.

Instead he gaped. Beyond us, up at that endless ribbon of humanity that rolled above, stooping down now, low, lower, roaring close above our heads. With the last gasp in me I whistled, shrilly, on the same high note as that keening wind. To my astonishment Le Stryge slapped his hands to his ears in sudden anguish—and the living cord lashed apart, recoiling like a snapped sinew. Out of it, tumbling, gliding along that note in the air as if it was a bridge, came a human shape, naked, torn, terrible, one eye still visible in a mask of rawness and filth; and the branches sprang and split with the force of her answering, avenging shriek. Out of the air, inches from my hand, she plucked the Spear—and with the force of her fall, unstoppably, she cannoned right into Le Stryge. His arms flew wide as the primeval weapon lanced through his breastbone and stood out a foot behind his back; and his scream was lost in the roar of the flame that enveloped them both.

Katjka recoiled and fell among smoke. The ensnaring branches vanished, spilling us to the ground in a gasping heap; they had never been there at all. What had held us half strangled in the air was the force of Le Stryge's spell. I hurled myself into the smoke, hand outstretched, and for an instant I touched warm living fingertips; but as my hand

closed over Katjka's it sank inward with a feathery insubstantial touch, and a faint rustling sigh, to ash as fine and
soft as talcum, and as clean, that blew away almost before
it touched the ground. But Le Stryge, shrieking, struggled
with the flames, beating them down only to have them billow out anew, prolonging his agony. He stumbled past us,
ignoring us, arms outstretched as if he reached out for
something. Looking around, we saw why.

There at the clearing's edge stood Lutz, tall and white-
haired and fleshily handsome as ever even in a bloodstained
black uniform, his ridiculous monocle popping from his eye
as he goggled thunderstruck at the scene. But we can't have
been much better; because beside him, at the head of a little
knot of human thugs, all armed and dressed in bloodied
City guard uniforms, stood Leutnant von Albersweg. And
in their hands between them, encased in a shielding cage
of metal, they held the rough stone mass that was the Graal
itself.

Nobody said anything; nobody needed to. The same sinking instant of cold understanding hit us all. That had been
Le Stryge's scheme from the start—to strip the Graal of its
warlike, outgoing aspect, the Spear, and of most of its human defenders in searching. Normally the Graal was too
strong even for him to assault; but that way, and aided by
otreachery from within, a small force might seize it. He
would have struck at once, if I hadn't run off with the thing;
then he could never be sure the weapon wouldn't suddenly
show up somehow and devastate his attack. But the moment the captain was on his way with it, he'd ordered Lutz
to launch the attack, and bring the Graal here—to where,
however great its power, it would be imprisoned apart from
its other half, and so weakened, altered, even destroyed. Its
realm and all its aims would collapse, and into that void
would step Le Stryge. And within his iron, austere will the
almost infantile drives of the force that had created this
revolting place, destruction and degradation. That would be
the new heart of Europe.

It was a vision worthy of Hell; and he'd come within an ace of it. He hadn't even wholly failed, perhaps; not yet. Towards the vision of the Graal the old man staggered even as the flames tore at him within and without, reaching for it, clawing for it, whether for power or for redemption no one could ever say. But Lutz and the lieutenant recoiled in terror from the flaming, gibbering thing, and Le Stryge staggered, screamed despairingly and stiffened in a last agonized rictus. His will must have slackened then, because the fire roared out again in untrammeled triumph, and he fell backwards like a log, stiff and unresponding. The flames were out before he hit the ground; and among the smoke, untouched, the Spear struck the hillside and stood upright, quivering.

For a moment the air seemed to sing with vast energies, then—

The ground erupted. Crackling black char scattered across the slope, smoking, as the earth where the old necromancer had fallen heaved and shook, spitting stone. The slope juddered, sending everyone sprawling, and a great raw crack went racing across it between the trees, widening with every convulsive heave. Tree roots waved and writhed as the soil split like a broken shell. Another crack went popping and screeching off at right angles, flinging clouds of stinking soil into the air. A tall tree tore free from the entangled mass and collapsed near us with a jarring thud.

Alison was on her feet before me, but off them as quickly. Sailors fared better on this swaying ground; Mall was afoot and retrieving her sword, and Jyp, though lurching wildly, already held his. I staggered over to the patch of blackened debris that had once been the old enchanter, and with an effort I tore free the Spear, rejoicing in the crackle of power in my fingers. Then, without the least hesitation, I went straight for Lutz von Amerningen's throat.

He and the lieutenant were already running. Turmoil was breaking out around us, more cracks zigzagging out in every direction, toppling tall rocks or splitting them where they stood. Out of the widest crack, higher up the mountainside, something bubbled and burst like boiling mud, and beneath it things glistened and stirred. Another fountain spewed up behind us, shrilling like a broken steampipe, and the ground around it caved in on a pool of the stinking slime. Avalanches of scree came rattling and roaring down between the pines, fires went out or blazed up wildly and their dark frequenters screeched and scattered or were smashed down in their tracks. Suddenly we were enveloped in a fleeing mass of creatures, humans, Children of Night in all their stages, even some of those monster shapes hobbling through the trees like blighted blendings of man and beast, lower than either.

The trees were bunching and swaying now, bending independent of the wind as if some huge unseen hand twisted and tormented them. Or as if more than tanglings and twinings linked them, as if this whole dense forest had itself been changed and united by forces beneath the soil, into one organism. I believe it was; it writhed like tendrils or tentacles in a slow-motion spasm of anguish and wrath. But, miracle of miracles, among the revolting crush of creatures it disgorged came some of our own men and women, generally by ones and twos, swept by in the flood and fighting it hard still; but those who saw us and the Spear still had the strength to cheer. We struggled to break through the black tide, but it was like fighting a moving wall now, that hurled us off at every contact.

The humans and the smaller Children seemed hardly to see us in their panic, and the main threat was in being kicked or trampled or sent slithering away down into blackness; but one or two, maddened or bloodthirsty, hewed and hacked at us at sight. The first one fell to Jyp, and another two, an instant later, to Alison, who sent them rolling among the stones before either of us could intervene. The giant Children were easier to dodge, more concerned with keeping their feet because if once they fell their less massive counterparts would swarm over them like a parade of ants;

I saw it happen a couple of times. One toppled down the slope, and his own gross weight skewered him kicking upon a slanted tree. We only had to slash at them or shout, and they cleared the paths. It was the unhuman creatures, minor powers or half-incarnate spirits maybe, who were the worst danger. Even as they fled they stopped and turned to fight, as if in their malformed shells self-preservation counted for less than the eternal nagging malice in their minds. A great bowed brute with a longhorned bovine skull came slithering down the rockface and in among us, swiping about with its huge blunt claws so that we had to duck and scatter. I slashed off one blacktipped horn; Mall's blow cut the sinews of its neck and it crashed roaring among the heaving roots. Its feet were human, calloused and scorched but strangely ordinary; perhaps it had been as human as us once. Its fall broke a path through the stampede, and Alison and I sprang through, toward the downhill flank. Mall and Jyp were following, when the sounds above sent warning.

That wind-blown web of bodies still whipped and flailed like a broken belt, sloughing off bodies and filth, and suddenly its severed end came lashing down against the hillside, hard, twice, where we'd been. Screaming voices were suddenly cut off, and an awful rain spattered down onto the trees. "*Avaunt!*" yelled Mall, and positively threw Alison out of the way as the other end came smashing down, much closer. The trees upslope flew into matchwood, spraying blood and bodies in all directions.

Alison and I, clinging together, struggled out from under that lashing mass as it thrashed the wood again where we'd been that minute earlier, skidding downhill in a mass of tumbling rocks and rotten tree-limbs. I lifted the Spear in the hope it might somehow shield us, and looked back desperately to see if there was any sign of the others, or of our quarry; but in that flickering, sparking confusion it was impossible to tell. In the wan moonlight the flanks of the mountain ran with great rippling shudders like the skin of a branded horse, the cracks oozed and bubbled. As those lashing ends slashed and struck, almost at random now, more and more soil fell away. Where there should have been rock, it exposed a glistening dark stuff beneath, not solid but churning and writhing, forms that scrabbled and heaved across one another in a sink of dark slime. It looked organic—but only when I saw the oddly misshapen limb that stuck out of it did I begin to understand.

Nothing dwelt on the mountain, or even within it. The Brocken *was* the mountain, a kind of single living creature, composed of cells like any other, like ourselves. But here the cells were not its own; they were the human bodies it had gathered to itself, and gradually degenerated and subsumed until they were no more than mindless things sliding in a morass. Somewhere beneath, at the heart of the mountain, there must lurk the center, the queen, the directing mind that ensnared and degraded—Chernobog.

That dark intellect, that black near-Absolute from the misty margins of the Rim, had built itself a physical body from its followers, deluded and entrapped. It was a cult become a colony organism, like a giant coelenterate, and as venomous. Those swirling skeins of humanity served it like tentacles, the individuals in them of no more concern than any few cells in my fingertips were to me—except for that extra touch of malice, reveling in the things it wasted. And naturally, like any body, it had strong defenses. Now it was wounded, maybe in a vital organ, and flailing in anguish; and those defenses were turning on their tormentors. This flood wasn't as random as it looked. It was a way of getting its defense resources, as quick and thoroughly wasteful as white cells, to one place fast.

"You're right!" gasped Alison. "They're its immune system, and we're the infection. Let's spread! Any sign of the others?"

Anxiously we scanned uphill, and spotted some of our people toiling across the slopes, ducking into cover to avoid random shots and flying stones and sludge. A darting ra-

diance still defied the shadows, Mall bounding from one
little group to another, helping them against the howling
flocks which fought to reject or absorb their infecting presence. I saw Jyp not far behind, daring wrath from above to
slither across the hillside, evidently spying out anxiously
for us. We waved, and it was Mall who saw us first; but she
didn't wave back, she pointed, again and again, with furious
emphasis to the hillside below us. "The shelf!" shouted Alison suddenly. "The landing ground! She can see it from
up there!"

And she wouldn't just tell us to get out for nothing—
"*Lutz*! He must be headed for it!"

Jyp was gesticulating, just as urgently.

"They're cut off!" snapped Alison. "And we aren't—
but . . ."

She looked at the slope below, impassable with monstrous flows. "It's too far!" she gasped. "Got to go around!"

"Get him!" came a yell from above. *"Seize the wight!
Carve the codpiece off him if a' can—but save the Graal!"*
As an angelic summons it left something to be desired, but
it was far louder and clearer than it should have been over
that row, even with Mall's lungs, and it seemed to set new
spring in my bruised heels. Alison went bounding down the
unstable rocks with gazelle energy, after her beloved Graal;
while I leaped and stumbled over them with my heart in
my mouth, ready to feel the avalanche pull my aching ankles from under me any second, or be stamped flat by a
horde of stinking diabolical abortions. Only one thing kept
me going, the desire to get my hands on that bastard Lutz;
and I grated my teeth as I heard the sound of airship engines being warmed up below.

"We can't do it!" I yelled to Alison as I caught her up.
"There's got to be a faster way—"

She shook me off. "Know where you can hire a bloody
horse?" That gave me a jolt. I looked down vaguely at the
Spear in my hand; and then I leaped about six feet as something warm and wet snuffled in my ear. The white horse

looked at me as if I was a total idiot, the way horses do. Giddily I beckoned him, and he came, snuffling at my pockets. "Later, chum," I told him, and swung myself into the stirrups, the same perfect fit. I seized the reins, and prodded him gently with my heels. "Watch your footing—and follow the lady!"

A hundred yards downslope a new rush of horrors was bursting out of the tormented wood, and we overtook Alison as she crossed its path. She half turned at the sound of hooves, and screamed aloud as I reached down to haul her up behind. The big horse hardly checked at the extra load. "Where did you *get* this?"

"Courtesy of Le Stryge—and my straggling romantic notions. But I think he likes me better—" I broke off as the horse sprang suddenly, clearing a low boulder and carrying us beyond the main stream of the oncoming horrors. We landed with hardly a jolt, though Alison hung onto every bit of me she could reach. One of the things sprang in our path, a big-headed biped with gaping jaws, bloated genitals and no eyes I could see before I cut it down. "And he came when I called, the way my sword does. Maybe the Spear helped, too."

Another pack of creatures boiled up around us, flowing out of a narrow gully above the shelf. The first one went down under those heavy hooves, the second to Alison as it tried to rake the horse's haunch; the ones on my side scattered before the sword could reach them, and the horse clattered into the gap. He wafted us along those last few vital strides like the breath of a gale, bounding and unstoppable. At last we burst out of that nightmare undergrowth into the clearing where the wreck of the helicopter still smoked, and the *Dove* rolled and swayed at her moorings. But in the space between, the *Raven*, less securely tethered and with its engines still warm from flight, was already feet off the ground and rising steadily. We galloped forward over the open ground, but even the dangling mooring lines were already out of our reach. Lutz was a poor

pilot, though, trying to bank the craft about like one of his
private planes. The control surfaces flapped, the rudder
went hard over and the great airship rolled like an elephant
in a mud wallow; its stern dipped sharply. Suddenly the
stern lines were trailing—and I urged the horse on, stood
in my stirrups and grabbed. Ponderously the tail lifted, and
I was abruptly twirling around forty feet off the ground,
kicking my legs about to get my feet on the rope, thrusting
the precious Spear into my belt. Then I was face to face
with Alison, grinning wildly and shinning up her rope as if
there was no tomorrow—which, come to think of it, there
wasn't. Unless we got the Graal back in one piece.

    And Alison.

Chapter 11

I went shinning after her, monkey on a stick fashion. It mightn't look very graceful, but it kept me too busy to look down. I was afraid I'd impale myself on the Spear, but somehow I never quite did. We were more than half-way up when the engines' drone became uneven. The airship's roll increased suddenly, swinging Alison out and me back in, then the other way around, never close enough to the gondolas. I thought for a moment they were trying to dislodge us, but if they'd seen us they could just have cut the cables; it was plain idiot piloting.

It almost did the job, all the same. We swung back and forth, slowly but with an utterly sickening motion. I nearly yelled as I saw Alison lose her foothold on the line and begin to slide down, but she got it back almost at once. Then the same thing happened to me, and I wasn't so lucky; I slid, gathering momentum with the rope burning my fingers, and barely managed to stop by more or less wrapping it around my legs. That fetched me up with a jolt and left me swinging head down over the abyss. I was a lot higher now than I'd realized; we were almost level with the barren summit of the Brocken, and a more terrible sight I didn't want to imagine.

Among the tentacles of the beast, still lashing in agony, the whole crest of the mountain was unfolding, earth and stones rattling away in slides to reveal a churning organic mass, seething like a mass of maggots, white in liquid brown putrescence. Once, maybe, those had been individuals, bodies with minds. Now they were lumps of cells whose writhings reflected only the wounded will they housed. And even with that thought the mass changed, split. Across its lower edge near the treeline a great gash opened and ran, vomiting a rush of pale liquid down among the trees. I was sure they'd become part of it, somehow, some kind of sense organ—maybe even, through photosensitivity, a gigantic eye. I was afraid for Mall and Jyp, and that wonderful horse; nowhere looked safe beneath that thing. Then the new trench opened and lifted, the crest changed shape, seemed almost to tilt back. In ice-black silhouette the monster opened its mouth and bellowed its pain and wrath beneath the sickle moon.

Parts of that undulating crest lifted, others sank. The boiling surface heaved itself into the semblance of a face, eyes tight shut, blunt nostrils flared, thin lipless mouth gaping in that deafening shriek of self-pitying agony. Whose face, I couldn't say; but it was recognizable, individual, human in every line, though the stuff that made it was in constant motion. It was as distinctive as a molded death mask, and it lived. A memory, maybe, a haunting semblance of somebody the creature had once known; or of what, or who, some part of that awesome malevolent intelligence had been. But whatever it had been, now it was a mask of primal torment, a face from the rack or the flaying or the wires and clamps. It held its form, that monstrous thing, and it wailed, a rending, sobbing howl of infinite pain and implacable anger. The tentacles it had shaped for itself, like a wounded sea-anemone, flailed and beat at the forest as you might at the unbearable pain of an eye injury. And then they lashed up into the skies around, barely below us, and the wind of their passage shook the airship still further. The nose dipped suddenly, the swing changed, and I arrowed in toward the gondola, close enough to risk a hand to grab its mounting struts.

I caught it, let go the rope and clung on with everything but my teeth. I reached out a foot and kicked down the door handle, hooked back the door and swung in, landing with a crash on the metal floor as the door slammed again behind me. The Spear went skidding down to the end of the car, under the spiral ladder leading up into the ship. The next thing I knew I was being jumped on by two bloody figures in guard uniforms, evidently a couple of Lutz's thugs who'd been left to nurse their wounds. They weren't in prime condition, but then neither was I, and I couldn't shift them. We swayed and bounced from side to side of the car, skidding on the flooring, hauling and punching at one another to little effect, while I kept catching glimpses of Alison, white-faced, struggling to swing back in. Finally I managed to sway us back against the door, and at the cost of being half throttled I freed a hand for the handle. The door rumbled back and hung there, there was a sudden rush of air and the game plan changed. Now it was throw or be thrown, with me clinging onto the frame and hammering at the others as they tried to dislodge me without being tipped out themselves. Suddenly the curly-haired thug on my left let go with a squawk as a pair of legs wrapped themselves around his neck, and flailed at them with his unwounded arm. Next moment he was gone, and my heart froze as a faint cry died away in the dark. The other man tried to take advantage, but I threw him back against the far side of the frame; he rebounded with a knife in his fist. But even as he raised it, Alison swung through the door and her boots caught him right in the stomach and threw him against the far wall with a very decisive crash. He slumped down and lost interest.

I grabbed her, hauled her in and held her, hard. "That's *twice*! Ye gods, girl—"

"Let go!" she hissed. "They saw something, or heard it maybe. One of them climbed up from the forward car!"

I let her go and ran for the Spear. But as I scooped it up, somebody swung down through the hatch, and his boots almost landed on my back. He'd probably have broken my neck; but I threw myself aside, slipped and fell, and then so did he as he landed, and I ran him through. Another one clanked down and went for Alison, who met him running, sword to sword. I scrambled up, and the next pair of boots retreated hastily up the ladder. I swarmed after them into the dim belly of the airship, but as I stuck my head through the hatch there was a burst of fire around me, and I ducked and dropped back hastily. A furious shout came aft.

"Du Sau-Idiot! Kein Schuss mehr! Willst du die ganze Schiff im Brand setzen?"

Do you want to set the whole ship on fire? God, yes, these things were full of hydrogen! I caught the sides of the hatch and catapulted myself up. This was the spacious area for the horses, with rows of mesh-sided stalls and tethers, but it was a strange stuffy place with a dead feel to the air, a skeleton of spindly structural members surrounded by the great gas balloons, stinking of impregnated canvas like an old-fashioned tent, only worse. They killed the drone of the engines, muffled the clash of the metal catwalks and the singing vibration of the lines of bare control cables flexing overhead, bulged out over them in deep concealing shadows like heavy clouds.

My adversary was backing away, trying to holster a long parabellum revolver, but he dropped it and snatched out his sabre. It was the lieutenant, and he had a nasty gleam in his eye as he weighed me up, battered, tired and bleeding. I put the Spear down carefully; I didn't fancy any sudden spouts of flame in here. I had the idea it wouldn't necessarily act as a casual weapon, anyhow. From below there came a hoarse cry and a sliding thud; I couldn't help looking back, and the lieutenant was on me with one of those vicious slashing cuts to the face. I turned it, hacked at him and drove him back a few steps. Boots clanged on the ladder behind me, and Alison, as I was sure it would be, flew up through the hatch. But she hardly spared us a glance, and ran along the catwalk aft. There was a sudden twang and rattle, and one of the cables overhead vibrated violently. The lieutenant swore hoarsely and tried to drive me back with a furious attack. I stood my ground and parried, then dodged behind the hatch as his sword clanged on the upright cover. With the moment that gained me I risked a look around and saw Alison leaping up to slash at one particular cable among the mass; it had a deep notch in it already.

"Leave him!" yelled Alison. "Come and help!"

Easier said than done; he closed with me, locking hilt to hilt, and tried to knee me in the groin. *"Typisch!"* I sneered in his face. "No swordsman, just a street goon in a fancy uniform! A knife in a parking lot, that's your weapon—in the back, most likely!"

He snarled and tried to free his blade, and what developed was more like a back-street rumble than a duel. It spilled us back and forth across the floor in a furious twisting clinch, banging each other's heads against the structural members, trying to tip each other off the catwalk and in among the webs of netting, while Alison hacked away at the cables. I managed to get my knee up into his stomach, trying to wind him, but he punched his sword hilt into my face and sprang to his feet. He missed his balance and staggered backwards, arms windmilling. But not far enough; he caught himself, sword above head, and aimed a chopping downstroke I wasn't sure I could stop.

Then his eyes widened, Alison yelled a warning, there was a tremendous singing twang and something whipped through the air—a length of thin wire cable. It hissed right over my head; but it caught him square across the chest, coiled itself around him with constrictor force and cracked taut. I heard bones break. The airship gave a violent lurch, and the engines droned violently. Something whined loudly, then stopped with a thud. The wire slackened, then went taut again, releasing its mangled captive. The body slid down the tilting floor and fell limply through the forward hatchway; there was a muffled cry.

Alison ducked down beside me. "You're not hurt? That was the starboard rudder cable I cut, it's locked hard to port now. This ship's not going anywhere anymore—"

She stopped. There was a growing smell of burning. From behind us came the rising hum of a stalled electric motor, and little bursts of crackling. "It's snagged the winch!" cried Alison, and sprang up, just as something fizzled and a spray of sparks erupted up under the catwalk. In the sudden glare I saw Lutz rising from the forward hatchway, a perfect entrance for the Demon King—monocle gone, white hair flying, florid face suffused with blood. I didn't need to read the desperation on it; he had a very modern little automatic in his hand. If he wasn't going anywhere, neither were we.

Desperately I twisted around to shout a warning, but even as I drew the breath I heard the shot. I saw it strike, actually saw the spatter of blood and fragments punched from the base of Alison's ribs, saw her whirled around by the impact and fall on her side with a soundless gasp of anguish. By some miracle the shot didn't go into the gasholders, but another might; and he was swinging around to aim at me. The lieutenant's pistol lay on the deck, but I didn't dare fire it. I might still have something to lose. So instead I threw it, and it took Lutz nicely on the chin. He staggered, fell backwards across the hatch and away down the suddenly tilting catwalk, dropping his own gun. They skittered off together into the dark.

I was up and after him. But as I passed the hatch I peered quickly down into the gondola, saw the lieutenant's mangled body at the foot of the ladder—and something a lot more chilling. The side door was flapping open, as the airship slowly wavered and rocked; and each motion sent the Graal, in its metal cage, sliding that little bit further down the floor toward it. I was about to leap down after it, when a dry cough stopped me. Lutz, fingering a bleeding chin, stood barely a sword's length away, his handsome features twisted in a positively impish smile; the tic at the corner of his eye spoiled it.

"Wenn man nur wusste . . . " he began, half laughing. "If you only knew just what *things* I have been through, all the nasty, tiresome, dirty, filthy, degrading, plain damn *stupid* things I've had to do to get this far . . . "

"I can guess. Sucking up to that thing down there. And leading other people into the net." We were circling it now, that lashing monster; but we wouldn't circle forever. We were losing height already, and soon we'd be within reach of those tentacles.

Lutz laughed out loud now. There were slithering sounds from behind me. "And then you come along, you little small-time pedlar from your nation of shopkeepers, and you louse it up. *You!* And you know something, little pedlar? I never felt so degraded ever as I did associating with you!"

My turn to laugh. "You should have spoken to Le Stryge. He says I have royal blood in me, German royal blood, descended from a princess at Charlemagne's court, he said! Oh, a long time back, but better than a mere baron's, don't you think?"

I didn't expect that to have the effect it did. His blue eyes bulged, and he almost cowered away. *"You?* Fisher? *Lieber Gott in Himmel!"*

I felt a flare of renewed fury. Katjka. Alison. Mall and Jyp, maybe. Myself, probably. "I wouldn't bandy His name about, if I were you. If He exists, you're going to have some pretty slick excuses to—*naughty!"*

He'd made a sudden dive for the hatch, and the Graal and the door, no doubt. My sabre slashed the air between, and he skidded back, drawing his own heavy *Schlager.*

"I've been promising myself this," he said tautly. "That fool Dragovic reported you were a good swordsman. Maybe you were, beside him; Dragovic was a passable competition *sabreur*. But I tell you this, little pedlar, whatever prophecies were made for you, whatever is predestined, a sharp sword always can cut it. You come into my hands too early, too inexperienced."

I laughed. "You're going to tell me you're the finest swordsman in all France?"

He smirked. "France, no. On the other hand, I have been sabre champion of Thuringia!"

And so he evidently was, from the moment he saluted and came on guard, left arm tucked comfortably in the small of his back, right arm high with the blade facing forward. I fell into the more modern stance, arm straight, blade angled up. Lutz chuckled. "I'm sorry, I have no little foils for us, pedlar. You will just have to learn the gentleman's way of handling a weapon. *Nun—fahren Sie fort!*"

Our blades kissed, scraped, clashed lightly at the tips— and suddenly his wasn't there, whizzing by my head in a fierce lunge-cut. Barely in time I took it and launched a stabbing counter at his exposed forearm. But he disengaged as lightly as if we were using foils, and riposted fiercely. As rarely happens in real bloodletting swordplay, we fell into the fast shifting rhythms of a competition *piste*, moving little, hailing swift short moves in complex sequence at every close-range opening the other left. It was frenetic, dazzling play; and I was exhausted. Even if I hadn't been, Lutz was far better at it than I was, conserving his energy, fighting mostly from the wrist, never launching a really vicious stroke but never, never letting the smallest opening go unchallenged. Playboy that he was, he'd had the time for this sort of thing, not just a few hours snatched from lunchtimes or evenings. I guessed I was the stronger, despite his tennis wrists, but that wouldn't count much longer, the way he was wearing me down. And I kept hearing those noises—

Something clattered beside me, as Lutz's latest sequence of attacks backed me up a pace. For a minute I was afraid the lieutenant had revived somehow. Then, with all the peripheral vision I could spare, I saw Alison, upright, hanging onto the ladder with her face turned away from me, and the slather of blood on the rung she held. Lutz's eyes widened in surprise, his attack slackened slightly and I lunged right into it, disengaging to deflect his blade past me. My point ripped into his right sleeve. He sprang back, swearing, but there wasn't any blood.

I bared my teeth. "Shouldn't mix it with shopkeepers, Herr Baron! Too good at minding the store!"

He snorted. "Your store, pedlar, is all but bankrupt!"

Alison slid the last few steps, sagged down onto the gondola floor and didn't move—and Lutz's blade whirled so fast I never even saw it, only felt the jar against my own blade as it was driven down and his lunge speared at my guts. I turned it, just, but the effort left me staggering, and Lutz launched a savage slash at my throat. But that I did stop, and thoroughly, so that its momentum recoiled on him; he staggered back and our blades met and hissed in a quick side-to-side action, each trying to trap the other's against the catwalk railing. His clanged free; but mine sheared through the light metal tubing with a tooth-grating screech and straight at his leg. Lutz jumped back, skidded in some blood, Alison's or the lieutenant's, crashed onto the broken railing and almost went over into the gas-holders. Only the airship's sudden list saved him, and he fell flat.

I couldn't take advantage of it; I was too spent, hauling in air in great hoarse breaths. I peered down the hatchway, looking for Alison, but she wasn't at the bottom of the ladder anymore. She was crawling, slowly but steadily with her long limbs starfished, toward the cage that held the Graal. Lutz, on his knees, also saw, and sprang for the ladder. I kicked him on the shin. He rolled back with a curse then thrust, hard between the rungs of the ladder. It connected, and scraped against a rib. The pain was excruciating, but it didn't do any major damage; it did wake up the little souvenir the captain left me, though, and threw me back, doubled up. Lutz cackled. "So much for your back-alley tactics!"

"Thought streetfighting was a Nazi speciality!"

"Nazi?" he panted, as we tried to struggle up. "You don't understand the meaning of the word! The Nazis were a blind, a gaudy banner to please the peasants, nothing more! The *SchutzStaffel* was the home of my spirit, yet even of that, only a tiny core—honor, purity, courage—I have never ceased to fight."

The ship tilted again, and it was my turn to be slid away, down toward the stern and the shorting winch motor. But instead of getting up and coming after me, Lutz grabbed up the lieutenant's sword and hurled it down the hatchway. Clumsily; it clattered. But I heard Alison scream with pain; and I went just a trace crazy. Not wild, very calm, very cold, seeing that I'd been fighting on Lutz's terms, not mine. I had to force the advantage, what little I had. There were things I was used to, and he wasn't; but how to get him into them?

That was where the madness came in. He was about to jump down that hatch; he had to be stopped. I drew one deep painful breath, levered myself to my feet, and, struggling to ignore my shakiness, I ran at him. For one minute, two, I forced myself to do what Lutz had done, to delay the killing stroke and go for the advantage; only in my case that wasn't skill. But it could be—it would be—ground. Though I wasn't reaching through his guard, he was getting nowhere with me either; and that seemed to disturb him. I forced him in, then out again; I retreated, drawing him back with clumsy defenses, then circled him, herded him with swift reckless attacks. It couldn't last; I was tiring fast, and any minute now I'd leave the fatal opening. But Lutz was nonplussed, slackening his own barrage to figure out what I was doing. He found out when his heels teetered over the rim of the hatchway, and I suddenly pressed the attack home. In danger of losing his balance, free arm windmilling for support, he found the ladder at his back, parried to gain an instant and swung himself onto it.

I could almost see his mind working, and I willed it on. It was swordplay that gave us the upper hand as an expression. Height lends weight and freedom to your attack— technically. If he tried to climb down the ladder, I'd have it. Even if he let go and dropped—risky enough in itself, with a body at the foot—I might well skewer him on the way down. So he climbed up a couple of steps, and I cringed a little under his cuts, which wasn't at all hard. He laughed, tried a couple more and I swung around the hatch and slashed his leg wide open from thigh to calf. Or rather, the leg of his riding breeches, because there was hardly any blood; I'd only pinked him. But it took a fair-sized slice out of his boottop, and it unnerved him. Instinctively he hopped up another step or two—and I'd won my ground. I ducked under his blow, and through the hatch I caught a glimpse of Alison as she slumped down over the cage, her hands clasped tight around its bars. I suppose I half expected her to spring up healed, but she didn't. I gave her an encouraging shout, knocked the hatch-cover free and slammed it beneath Lutz; and I slashed a sliver off his bootsole into the bargain.

He should have risked jumping down and facing me on the level again; but his nerve was going. There was another hatch overhead; he launched a couple of wild slashes that nearly parted my hair, then turned away and began to climb frantically, faster than I could manage with my aching ribs. We were up among the balloons, now, the stuffy darkness aft lit by a flickering glow I didn't want to think about. But it showed me Lutz frantically spinning the wheel of the next hatch, desperate for some level surface to fight on. He'd get one, all right; but I didn't think he was going to like it.

The hatch slammed right back, and the inrush of chill clear air was startling. I found it refreshing, but Lutz quailed and hesitated. I hauled myself up with an effort, and stabbed him in the calf, hard. He cried out and almost fell off the ladder, then hauled himself hastily up through the opening. I could see him kneeling, hanging on with one hand and scrabbling at the hatch, hoping to slam it on me, but I didn't give him the time. I was at the top before he'd got the catch loose, and swinging up and out as he had, onto the open upper surface of the airship. But I stood up straight.

"Never did go in for mountaineering, did you, Herr Baron? Not one of your sports, was it?"

I padded around the hatch, and he shuffled away from me on all fours, fingers clawing at the hull fabric, drum-taut and unyielding. The wind ruffled our hair, and wafted up the unbelievable stench of the mountain below. I laughed a little at the way the moonlight sparkled on my sword. I jabbed it at him, and he yelped and almost lost his balance, seeing the flank of the airship curve away below him.

"And you've never gone in for climbing mastheads, have you? You'd crewmen to do that, on your racing yachts, with tackle and harness, while you stuck to the helm, right? *Nicht wahr?*" I jabbed at him again, he hunched back, slid a little and caught himself with frantic quickness.

"This is not fair fighting!" he blustered, but I hadn't even the energy to laugh.

"Don't be a bloody fool! Who'd risk being fair with you? I'll kill you any way I can." I hoped I could.

Then the question was academic. I'd hesitated just too long. He had a better grip than he pretended; he clung tight, shot out a boot and hacked me on the shin again. Then, as I skidded back and grabbed the hatchway for support, he did something unexpectedly clever; he dug his sword hard into the fabric and hauled himself upright on it, testing the bounce like a drumskin. Careful not to look to starboard or port now, where the mountain-beast's tentacles were sweeping alarmingly close, he advanced with

short determined steps. I stood up too, feeling the anger
and the futility of it all. There was red light flickering
through the tail fabric, beneath the rudder; any moment it
might reach one of the gas-holders, and that would be that.
We were dead men already, squabbling over the right to
snuff out each other's last few seconds; better, perhaps, to
go by a sword thrust than by what was brewing below us.
But I couldn't help it, and neither could he; neither could
countenance the least, unlikeliest chance that the other
might live. We were in too deep.

Again we squared up. Again the blades slithered against
one another, like mating snakes, tapping, edging—and
again Lutz was faster. A fiery torch dug into me above the
heart, burning through pectoral meat and grating horribly
against my left collarbone. My knees gave, and I sank down.
It was his kind of stroke, a swift conclusive competition
point, a touch, not a killer—at first. The moon showed me
the glint of his teeth as he leaned his weight on the blade
to drive it home, preparing the swift wrist twist that would
tear ligaments and open veins beyond hope of staunching.

But in that agonized instant I remembered the great Wolf
captain, Rooke, and how I'd finished him. With a start like
that, just scoring points was something I'd never really
learned. I gave before the stroke, sagged back, so that Lutz's
own force brought him staggering forward—

Right onto my own last lunge.

His arms flew out, his sword fell away from my wound
and down into the dark. I forgot the pain, snarling like a
Wolf myself, slamming my own blow home till the hilt
clanked against the breast-buttons of his tunic, and the
blade stood out scarlet behind his neck. Then I tore it loose,
and he doubled up and fell to all fours again, gasping,
coughing. His feet scrabbled for purchase, found none, and
he began to slide. His hands found the tear in the fabric
and clung hard; but it tore wider now under his weight, he
slid faster and it tore still faster, the coarse doped silk rip-

ping away in a great triangular patch that sent him sliding
helplessly down the side.

"Zu Hilfe!" he screamed, between coughs of blood. *"Rette
mir doch! Um Gottes Name! Steve!"*

But I was already turning away, hardly listening, shoving
the sword back in my belt. I scarcely cared about him now,
or about anything else. There was red light shimmering up
through the hatch, and only one place I wanted to be. One-
handed, head singing with the pain, I scrambled back down
the ladder into the smoky cauldron below, and saw, to my
utter astonishment, the hatch thrown back, and Alison,
swaying and chalk-faced, a swathe of her jacket wrapped
around her side, staring up at me.

"I thought you were dead!"

We both wheezed it at once, and Alison managed a dry
croak of a laugh.

"Not . . . completely."

"Ditto. Why . . . "

She swallowed, with nothing to swallow. "Get to . . .
Spear. Mustn't lose . . . keep together, even in crash . . . so
can be found . . . "

"Ri' . . . I'll go." We sounded like a couple of drunks. I
almost fell, but managed to slither the rest of the way down
to the catwalk, and retrieve the Spear. Fighting for breath,
I looked up and saw that the tear in the fabric had widened,
and the flames were roaring out through it; that was what
had saved us this long, keeping them from the gas-holders.
But it was fanning them higher, too. If Lutz was still hanging on, he must be roasting alive; and we'd be joining him
any minute. I thrust the smooth cool shaft into my belt,
but no sooner had I swung painfully back onto the ladder
than there was a brilliant flash and a thudding, jarring con-
cussion. I ducked down hastily, just in time. A wall of flame
roared down the catwalk and across the hatch, so close it
scorched the hair on my hands. The fire-proofing treatment
was starting to go. I slid down in a heap beside Alison,
seized her hand, knowing this was the end.

There was another explosion, even louder. Flame spewed down through the hatchway, knocked the cover off the catch and slammed it down. The airship rocked sickeningly, the motors labored and stuttered; but the gondola was untouched.

"Why're we still here?" she demanded, almost angrily.

"The *Hindenburg*!" I yelled. "Haven't you seen the film? People got out of that—hydrogen burns *upwards!*"

I slid along the floor, and hauled myself up by the control panel. We were still circling, but losing altitude fast. I hated to think of the inferno developing overhead. Another minute, another couple of bags going off, and we'd come down somewhere in the rocky lower slopes. The rudder was broken, but the control surfaces might still do something. I slammed up the port surface, hard, and gunned the faltering motors on that side. The ship lurched, swung around and went sliding on in.

Suddenly something brushed at the window, and it smashed. For an instant I thought it was one of the tentacles. It wasn't; it was a tree-top. And with it an awful burden weighed down on my heart; because when you've already abandoned hope, it can be the most agonizing thing of all.

We had seconds, no more, to reach that door. And that cage was too much for us now. Angrily I tore it open, hesitated an instant before touching the thing it held. Alison balked at the Spear. We giggled idiotically. What had we to lose?

We grabbed them both. Nothing happened, except that the rough granite scraped my fingers. The ship lurched violently as another gasbag went, and we crawled for the door. I moaned a bit; even sliding it along, the weight of that lump of stone tore at my lacerated shoulder. But Alison wrapped her free arm around my waist, and suddenly, for all the pain that creased her face, she was grinning.

"Out of the frying-pan—"

The gondola bumped and squeaked across another tree-top, another blast of orange flame blossomed above us, and because jumping was beyond us, clutching our swords and our burdens to us, we rolled out.

The next instants were a blur; lashing branches, stinging pains, rushing air and sudden sickening impact. I must have lingered a moment awake, because I have one last memory of the blazing airship lurching by overhead, a grasping tentacle blasting apart as another gas-holder exploded, and another, leaving the ship an arrow of leaping flames falling right as I'd aimed it.

Onto that barren mountain crest, and right into that awful face.

The sound was fearsome, louder far than the airship exploding. It had too many components, as I heard them; volcanic rumbles, liquid sizzlings and spittings, mindless yelling and in amidst it all, yet somehow audible, one anguished but articulated, all too human cry. The whole ground juddered, those demonic tentacles flew up, fell inward, fragmented in mid-air into a cascading rain—

Then blackness, abrupt and stifling.

But the blackness wasn't empty. I was condemned to death, and I was asking why why, why. I was tapping it out on a computer keyboard because that was all they'd given me. If I could just get through to somebody important with my plea it might help—Alison, if not me. But all I kept getting was that bloody error message:

```
**URGENT**IN IMMINENT EVENT SYSTEM
WIPEOUT*INTERFACE PORT S WITH PORT
G**URGENT**
**URGENT**IN IMMINENT EVENT SYSTEM
WIPEOUT*INTERFACE PORT S WITH PORT
G**URGENT**
**URGENT**IN IMMINENT EVENT SYSTEM
WIPEOUT*INTERFACE PORT S WITH PORT
G**URGENT**
```

—over and over and over until I wanted to scream.

It couldn't have lasted long, though—seconds, according to Jyp, because they were already running toward us as we fell. "If it was the Baron," he explained, "we kind of wanted to get our hands on him. Where is he, anyhow?"

I struggled to focus my swimming thoughts; and then Jyp noticed my shoulder, and stopped shaking me. "Jehoshaphat! A mite lower and he'd have skewered your heart!"

"Not . . . quite. Alison?"

"She's here. But she's bad. The bullet wound, a broken leg, maybe something internal. Lucky, at that; if the forest hadn't been so tangled and all this goddamn underbrush that thick, you'd've been succotash. Mall's getting some branches for a stretcher. Don't know if we can get you folks away from here, but we're damn well going to try."

I pushed him aside, because I hadn't the words, and levered myself up on my elbow. Alison was beside me, face gray, lips dark, the Spear lying limp in her fingers; the slab of stone had fallen from my arms, only a few feet away. I looked at the mountain crest, a howling, heaving mass of flame in which something thrashed and spouted, setting the whole mountainside quaking, and the milling, baying shadows running in renewed panic—chaos rampant. The fire was spilling down among the trees now; that meant it would soon be spreading wholesale. Who was Jyp kidding? And the little knot of people gathering around him, the survivors. Here a Byzantine archer without his horse or his bow, helping along a wounded doughboy still clutching the shattered stock of his rifle, bayonet attached. There, two of the partisans, quietly slipping cartridges from their pockets into the magazines of their Schmeissers while an English archer covered us with his last shaft. There were others, but not many; fourteen, fifteen, maybe, from all our force. The centurion was gone; Hastein was there, one arm in a bloody sling. They watched over us, these battered warriors, their eyes wide in wonder; and they waited. "This . . . is all?"

"All," echoed Mall somberly. "No man or woman more, no horses. Nor any food or water, or aught to ease your pain—no clean herb grows in this place."

"Save . . . yourselves," said Alison faintly. "Take the Graal and the Spear. Steve might still make it. Leave me . . . "

I reached out to her; but my hand touched something else.

"No," I said.

Mall chuckled faintly. "The very word I fumbled after! Well, now that's reasoned out, let's to our road—"

"No," I said again, feeling the hair on the back of my neck prickle. "Mall, help me up—"

"And have you bleed your life out on me? I'll do no such thing—"

"*Help me up, damn you!* You don't know what's going on." I'd been going to swear at her again, but I softened my tone. "There's another way—and it'll work! You see—you see—they told me all along—all along—"

Without another word Mall took my good arm and hauled me to my feet. It did start the wound bleeding again, but that didn't matter. I took two steps, to that slab of stone, and I knelt again, before it. The pain was jarring, and as I struggled to raise my arms above my head it made my head sing and my guts heave; but none of that mattered now, not in the slightest. In my hands I held a power that was greater than the Brocken, greater by far; for its schemes reached farther and longer, and even when those schemes failed, they carried within them the germs of new success. When they succeeded, however high the cost, the success was absolute. They'd told me; they'd prepared me for this, all along, knowing there was no way I could possibly understand until now—until I held both Graal and Spear together in my hands.

I guessed it now, I saw the relationship between them; and once seen, I saw what the Graal had once been, in what guise it had appeared to the first shamans of the first men, stumbling after knowledge and succor in their desperate struggle to survive. I might have laughed, if I hadn't been so filled with awe. I knew what that ancient ceremony must have been, and in imitation of it, with reverence and even with fear, I swung the Spear high above my head. Alison saw, and summoned energy enough to scream, *"No, Steve! You haven't the right! Only one man—"*

Too late.

The spearhead struck; but not into the base of the rough stone chalice. Into the shimmering pool of light it contained.

Interface—

And the light overflowed, and spilled, and came racing up the shaft to envelop my hands and draw me down, down to the death I expected, and out of my pain embraced. My momentum carried me on and down, down like a swimmer into deep waters.

There were clouds, clouds everywhere, and they closed over me like waves, and I thought I was going to drown. Involuntarily, stupidly I kicked out, and rose to the surface again. Looking up, I saw the shadowy coastlines of the cloud archipelago high overhead, and above them the great arching tunnel of cloud that framed a glittering arc of starry sky, moonless and clear. And coursing through it, sails billowing with moonlight, spray leaping from beneath her bows, rose the high stern of a mighty merchantman, ablaze with lanterns, laden with strange cargoes for stranger destinations. It was the same surreal seascape I'd commissioned so carefully for my office wall. But this was its great original, those eerie seas of cloud and night, those shadows the waters of the Core cast deep into the Spiral, infinite where they were only endless, the oceans over the airs of the Earth, the seas I'd sailed so often. Never without peril; yet never, also, without friends.

Now, in all their vastness, I drifted alone. No bark to bear me, no ship to succor me; and my strength was failing. The cool clouds closed over me, and I sank back—

There was a soft discreet hiss, and the chair's pneumatic damper stopped me. I crossed my legs and settled back comfortably, enjoying the luxurious give of the white kid upholstery, contemplating the seascape with detached pleasure. Then my intercom chimed discreetly, and I sighed and touched the hidden control.

"Your visitor is here," said Claire's voice.

"Oh," I said, trying not to sound nonplussed or admit I'd completely forgotten I was expecting anyone—you never knew if they could hear. "Thanks, yes. Please ask him to come in!"

I sat up hastily, glanced around the office, wished I'd remembered to clear away those reports. No matter; just time to straighten my tie, and the door was opening. I was glad I'd closed the blinds; the sunlight through the outer office was blinding. That thought brought on a moment of confusion. Claire wasn't my PA anymore, hadn't been for—what? Twelve years or more. So why—perhaps she'd brought whoever this was up, that must be it. Something from Personnel, then: oh, God. And who the hell was this, opening the door with the sun behind him?

Part of me shriveled with potential embarrassment. Had I met him before, this character? I must have; but the face eluded me. It was a strong, distinctive face, and yet it was somehow hard to pin down; he looked very much like a number of well-groomed middle-aged businessmen, right down to the quietly immaculate suit and the silvery streaks at his temples—a touch handsomer, perhaps, and fitter, but nothing exceptional. And yet I kept seeing flashes I recognized, his tall build—only a little heavier than mine—a lithe energy in his walk, the general outline of his head, the wry lop-sided lift to his smile as he held out his hand to me, his deep resonant voice as he spoke my name. Resonant, but not just deep; it echoed all kinds of accents, but with relentless clarity. All told, an impressive-looking character, not the sort you forget meeting; yet damned if I could put a name to him, or remember where.

That made me a touch too effusive as I seated him in my best guest chair, and he waved an apologetic hand as he settled back. "Very comfortable," he remarked, looking around. "Like the rest of this office, in fact. Well-designed, elegant even, yet, if you don't mind my saying so, not at all pretentious. None of this investment art rubbish." He nodded at my skyscape. "A nice mixture of the romantic and the practical. A strong expression of personality, both the company's, and your own. I remember liking the old atlases. I'm glad you kept those."

An old client, from my early days in the office; that would be it. "Yes, I inherited those from Barry," I said as I poured him coffee, wondering vaguely who had brought the tray in, and where all these compliments were leading. "He had an even bigger collection once, but it was destroyed in a burglary."

"Ah yes," said my visitor, "I believe I heard. Well, Mr. Fisher, I expect you're wondering why I'm here and what I'm leading up to. I know you've a lot on your mind just at the moment, going through a busy period, people depending on you ... "

"Well, since you put it that way ... "

"Exactly. But I assure you, this will take little or no time, and it may be well worth your while. Mr. Fisher," he said seriously, as I settled back into my chair, "you're very comfortable here, that's evident. And I don't doubt you look equally at home over at C-Tran, though I don't like those high-tech offices as much. But comfort isn't always satisfaction. Are you satisfied? Mr. Fisher, you have shown considerable skill at creating companies that run themselves."

"No company does that," I objected, a little nettled. "If they seem to, that's just slow stagnation. You need active minds at the top, always—questioning, reshaping, continually seeking new business or new ways of operating. Like the old joke about the swan, you know? Floating serenely above the water, paddling like hell underneath."

He grinned. I liked that grin; I just wished I knew where

I'd seen it before. "Of course that's so. And you've built in mechanisms to keep that happening. You yourself are part of them, but your scope is limited. You leave most of the running of this company to David Oshukwe."

"Of course. He's better at it than I am. And there are people at C-Tran who I hope will be able to take over in the same way from me and Baron von Amerningen—" Something jarred in my head, and I stopped, uncertainly.

"And that's precisely my point!" said my visitor. "Mr. Fisher, you are or will soon be as rich as most men ever feel the need for. You have no real motive to struggle, to compete. Are you not a little lacking in . . . challenges? Are you not ready to try something new?"

I steepled my fingers. I didn't like having my thoughts read. "Now *that*," I said severely, "is a loaded question, the kind that affects share prices and brings speculators circling around in droves."

My visitor sipped his coffee and smiled. "Mr. Fisher, you don't need to answer it, not outright. The fact is that I've come here to offer you just such a venture. Our prospectus. . . " He reached into his briefcase, pulled out a neat-looking morocco binder and laid it gently on my desk. "You're very welcome to read it now, if you can spare the time, and while I'm here to answer any immediate questions you may have. But be warned, you may be surprised at our longer-term planning; and the fact that some of it already involves yourself."

"What?"

"We have assumed that because we didn't dare assume anything else. Before you judge us, please read to the end."

I treated him to my most suspicious frown as I picked up the folder and opened it. My hair prickled, my heart gave that leaping extra breathless beat. There at the head of the first page, embossed on the heavy cream paper, the emblem of a dove flew above two graceful—and suddenly very familiar—towers.

I read that page, and the next, and the next, with eyes

widening and astonishment building. I glared at my visitor over the top of it. "So this—all of this—is something you *planned*?" Astonishment vanished under growing fury. "Are you trying to tell me you—you sacrificed all these people in some half-baked bloody—"

"No, no, no," he said, a little irritated. "I did ask you to read on. We knew something was stirring, yes—call it a hostile takeover bid. In a sense, it was remembered—though over a gulf you really couldn't imagine—but only in the most general terms, so we had to evolve a general plan, a broad strategy to cover as many instances as possible. But Le Stryge's secrets were never quite as secret as he liked to think. He was following a trail; we followed it in both directions, the way he'd come, the way he was going. Either way, at either end, there was you. It was clear that you were going to be involved, though at that time we had no idea why; so we kept on searching, and we were both surprised and appalled when we found out, and realized the significance of your name. It required us, at so many stages, to have faith in you, in what you could do. We had no idea who Le Stryge's master was, or Baron von Amerningen's when he became involved—or even that it was the same power." He grinned briefly. "Or that Alison would take such a fancy to you when we prompted her to keep an eye on you, a fancy, of course, that she resented like hell because she thought you were the same sort as the late Baron. We're not gods or tyrants—we don't confine the human heart, or compel it. It's a fearful handicap when dealing with adversaries who do—but, then, it's one of the chiefest things that set us apart from them. Some of them started with the best intentions, but—"

I nodded. "I can guess. Means determine ends. Absolute power corrupts—"

"Absolutely. So we couldn't map everything out neatly; we had to narrow it down to definitions, and provide for them. It was inevitable some attempt would be made to steal the Spear, using you, and that an assault to steal the

Graal would follow; we couldn't stop that. We had several possible definitions of success in varying degrees: you never took the Spear; we got it back without you; you got it back without trouble; you got it back *with* trouble, before it got into enemy territory. Any of those, and the assault on the Heilenberg never coming. We had one ultimate failure standard—the Spear and the Graal both taken and reaching our enemy."

"God!" I slumped back, feeling the blood leave my cheeks. "Was it that close, after all?"

The tall man's face grew somber. "It was. But it was also our ultimate standard of success—getting the source of our power into the enemy camp. Provided, that is, you were there to do the necessary, namely retrieve one or the other and let fly. If you hadn't come through we'd have been sunk. And if we'd tried to direct you somehow we might have cramped your style, fatally. That's why we didn't dare say anything, one way or another, when you asked for guidance. So in the end all we could do was try to see that if Spear or Graal did reach the enemy, so would you, with the knowledge you needed to use them. Knowledge that wouldn't make sense till the time came, yet would stick in your mind." He grinned again. "So it kept popping up on your computers. Irritating as hell, wasn't it?"

I bridled. "Too damn right! But me—why all this on *me*?"

"Because you were there. Because of your name. Because only you could do it."

"That's a load of—that's rubbish. A lot of people did it. Alison, Jyp, Mall—Katjka. Her especially. What about her? Did your plan involve compelling her?"

He looked somber. "No. She chose. She knew what was coming, and she chose it, to wipe out a past that wouldn't leave her. Remember those extra cards that seemed to deal themselves? She was warned, and she chose. True, she did a lot to aid you. But even without her you'd have managed. Differently, but you would have. The same with your friend

Jyp. He played an important part, but there were other ways to get through—the pentacle at Baron von Amerningen's, for example. And other ways of launching an assault than by recalling the Graal Knights. There was no way to know which would work. We had to trust you."

I was rapidly getting furious with this urbane creature. "I wish I'd had your bloody confidence! You used me, you son of a bitch! You used my friends, you threw them away the way you throw away those Knights of yours! Okay for them, maybe, they've chosen to serve. But I never got the chance to choose, did I? So let's just run that one by again. *Why me?*"

"Because you're special." He sipped at his coffee, and reached for a biscuit I'd forgotten to offer him. "Excellent. Because Le Stryge did do something clever, in ferreting you out. His mind was blinkered by its own narrowness, of course. He only saw how you could be of use to him; but we saw in you the germ of a greater success than just restoring the *status quo ante bellum*. He told you about your ancestry, didn't he?"

"You mean that I'm descended from a Frankish princess's little mistake? Yes. What's that got to do with the price of tomatoes?"

"Is that all he thought of it? She was one of Charlemagne's daughters, man, the first Holy Roman Emperor, the first king to unify any part of Europe, however sketchily, since the Romans. And incidentally, the last reigning monarch who was also the Graal King."

"What?"

"Oh, yes. A rather rough and rumbustious character, but a genius in his way. You have to make allowances. Late in life he even tried to learn to read. That was fearfully progressive for those days. And you're a direct descendant, via a line of sturdy peasantry in Germany, France and England, mostly the richer sort. There's a good gene for making money somewhere in that line."

I sat back. "I see. And—what? I'm sort of a favorite

nephew, am I? That was why I could touch that bloody Spear without being incinerated?"

"That's right. That's why Le Stryge thought he could use you. Actually we wouldn't seriously hurt anyone who didn't deserve it, but we don't advertise that. It's better to seem untouchable. People are people; there's always some treason, especially when we don't have a king to interpret for us. It's hard to love just a cup and a spear."

I shook my head. "Then why take that shape? Why not appear as you're appearing now, a sort of smug father-figure wolfing bloody chocolate biscuits? Always good for a friendly chat, the chocolate biscuits . . . "

He contemplated one of them a little sadly, and bit into it again. "Would that we could. I told you you were exceptional. It's a long time since we were in any shape to appear to anyone. Out by the Rim things get a little . . . refined, would you say?"

"How the hell would I know? I've never been there."

"You will, one day. If you're the right sort you gain . . . rather a lot. But you lose a lot of other things, too. We had bodies once, very good ones. They lasted rather longer than you might expect, and even then we kept them around for occasional use, poor old threadbare things. But they wouldn't fit us very well anymore. They'd cramp our style; and we're not as . . . individual as we once were. We can only maintain the barest toehold in the material; and even that has to reflect different forces at work within us. The Cup and the Spear were convenient symbols for the first men, easy to understand; and we've never really improved on them. A syringe and a phial? A Kalashnikov rifle and a TV set? Hardly as compelling. And they don't express so succinctly just what we're capable of—in our opposing states. Think of them as poles together and poles apart, if you want. Apart, thrusting strength and deep knowledge, war and peace, defense and consolidation, wounding and healing. Together . . . " he chuckled, "well, let's call it creative friction. It's a potent symbol everyone responds to, the primitive mind and the modern, even if they don't wholly understand. Opposites working together instead of apart; and conceiving something new."

"Yes, but what's the point?"

"The point is that it provides a simplified way of directing some of our power—power even you could never normally handle, because you can't imagine it. Your mind literally can't conceive of its origins or its action. But equally we who possess it don't have a clear enough view of the more material world, so—"

I snapped my fingers. "So—you delegate?"

He grinned again. "Yes. Sound management practice, isn't it? We choose someone we know can be trusted, and let him—or her!—direct it through the symbolic intermediary of the Graal and the Spear, and through rites which have many layers of psychological meaning. That speak directly to the inner self, as clearly to a CroMagnon shaman as they do to you, today."

I looked at him, astonished. "To—"

"Oh, yes. That's why having a king makes such a difference. When the Graal has one it's strong, and when there isn't one it's weakened; so much of its power it just doesn't dare to wield. And the trouble is that these types don't grow on trees—individuals with the leadership, the responsibility, the sense of adventure and the ability to carry it through ... In short, Mr. Fisher—call it corporate recruitment if you'd rather, but the fact is, I've come here to headhunt you."

I almost laughed aloud at the sudden return of business jargon. "Away from companies that are my first loyalty and my creation?"

"From companies that need your loyalty and creativity no longer, to one that does. Desperately, if I may say so, Mr. Fisher. We believe that somebody like you is our only chance, not only of success but of survival itself. And in this present generation we can find few in any way like you, and no one person at all."

That made me blink again. "I'm sure you're overstating things." He steepled his fingers, which annoyed me because I was just about to. "I am not. Even among those who live long lifetimes on the Spiral, they're rare; because most people do not grow as they live, but become only more intensely what they are."

"Like Jyp, yes—from a good navigator to something like the ultimate."

"Not quite that; but yes, the principle holds. Or Mall, even, who has progressed so far and will go further, yet is a leader only when she has to be, and doesn't enjoy it. Our chosen few must be leaders from the beginning, but other things as well. We haven't any easy way of finding such people, even of shortlisting candidates. We can't choose by heredity—though when we do find one there's almost always a clear blood link of some kind. The right mix seems to be a little heredity, a dash of environment and a lot of shuffling the pack—of genes, of destiny, of whatever. But fortunately such people very often gravitate to us. And when we see them, we know them. We knew you."

I drew a deep breath. "And . . . it seems to me that I know you."

That grin again, only it wasn't quite the same. For an instant he looked like somebody else altogether. "Ah, you do. A bit already, but you'll get to know us better yet."

"If I say yes?"

"You don't need to."

I exploded. "You arrogant SOB! What right have you got to take me for granted? To think that you know what I'm going to say?"

My visitor stood up. "None, and we don't. It's just that circumstances are rather unusual. You'll understand." His eyes narrowed for a moment in an enigmatic smile I'd seen before somewhere; but not on anyone who looked like him. "I'm afraid we know that, too. Remember it, I should say; but the pain is, our memories are very faint, by now. Inevitable, when we have so many others; and that's not the only complication. But I'd better be going now, before I annoy you any further." He glanced around. "I enjoyed our little talk, and just being here. It brings so much back to me. I remember you used to be—well, let's say a bit of a cold fish. It's good to see you've outgrown it already."

"Now wait a minute," I said, leaping to my feet. "I? What's happened to '*we*'? I'm going to need to know a damn sight more—"

"It's all in the prospectus," he said reassuringly. "Set out fair and square with the minimum of jargon and even less sales talk. Just the way you like these things done. Just sit and read it, take all the time you like."

"Like hell!" I barked, looking around wildly. "My friends—I've got to get back to them!"

He shook his head. "No problem . . . really. You could take all day, and still go back to them as you left them, not a half second later."

"But . . . who are you?" I breathed. "What are you? And . . . why?"

"Ah," he said, a little glumly. "Hardest ones last, eh? Well, as to the last, we're not a hundred percent sure ourselves. And maybe not about the one before, either. Offhand I'd say it all depends on whether you see us as a stone or as a chalice. As a power from within man, or from outside."

"How do you see yourselves? Which are you, really?"

He whistled softly. "Wow! We've been chewing over that one, researching it and arguing about it for time that— well, has no meaning. We've never found out, not for sure. All the answers we've ever found turned out to be just more questions, when we looked a mite closer. This I'll say for sure, that all the powers we've ever met, and they're legion, they've had their roots in humankind. Whatever they were, however far they'd traveled, however remote they and their concerns might seem, once they'd all of them lived and walked as you do. And they knew no more of the answer than we do. What we have found, though, is that it makes no difference."

He looked at something beyond me, beyond the confines of this little space. "Where we've been, out toward the infinity of the Rim, in realms you can't guess, Right and Wrong, to give them the nearest names you have, they're flames that burn, trees that grow, minds that plan, colors, tastes, smells—everything. They exist in themselves; they're absolutes. But even they don't know the whys and wherefores of everything. It's beyond them, beyond the Rim, and what lies there is hidden. Only by getting beyond the margins of the Spiral, beyond the Rim, will we ever find any answers. But they also know that the way beyond isn't to be found out there; it's back here, right here, in the Core. And that's why the Brocken, the Graal, the Invisibles, the Ape—all the powers that have taken wing from here—that's why they all come back."

He moved toward the door, and I was powerless to stop him. But with his hand on the handle he paused, scratching his head in a slightly puzzled fashion. "You know, all those times you've been out East, did you ever hear that old saying? Buddhist, or Taoist or something like that. I can't quite remember the exact phrasing, but it went something like this: 'You can fly like a dragon to the Truth, through the airs, or you can burrow your head to it through the mud, like a worm; but in the end—both ways are the same.'"

He looked thoughtful. "By the time you even get near the Rim, you've existed so long, been through so much that you forget the early stuff, however important. By the time you come back it's hardly the shadow of a lost dream. And even then you can't rely on the little that remains, not just because it's faint, but because simply by coming back you change it, hopefully for the better. It doesn't all happen the same, the second time around, or what would be the point? That's why you came as such a shock. You, and Alison, and the others, when we recognized them. And why we simply had to trust you."

I stared at him, speechless, and he smiled again. "With that sort of stimulus we can remember our human roots, after a fashion, the selves we once were. The way you might remember a childhood friend, something like that; well enough, but you've changed a lot yourself. It's pleasant to see them again—and feel that they were people to be, well, proud of." His voice changed slightly. "And every bit the way you remembered them. Bye, Steve, we'll be seeing you again. Soon."

He opened the door quietly, and stepped through it; but the burst of radiance beyond it came through no ordinary window, ever.

I stared after my visitor awhile. And then, because I had all the time he said, I sat down to read. From time to time I poured myself another coffee, ate another biscuit; he was right, they were good. But in the end, in the fullness of something that was not time, I stood up, and stepped out from behind the desk; but I remembered to tab the intercom. "Just to say I'll be going back now."

"Very good, Steve," said a voice, and it chuckled. That wasn't Claire; it sounded more like Alison. I strode to the door, drew a deep breath, and put my hand to the handle.

There was no light. It wasn't a doorhandle in my hand, it was the smooth shaft of the Spear, and I was lifting it high against the wall of smoke that welled up beyond, shot with flames and stench. My other hand lay upon the Graal. The pain had gone, the weariness and the terror I'd been too busy to recognize had sloughed away like the grime of a long day's labor under a cleansing shower. A clear mountain river leaped and bubbled through my veins, my limbs had the strength of ancient oaks and lindens, my body was the rock they rooted in; and over me shone the sun of the Heilenthal. For that moment I was the Graal's kingdom, from earth to sky; I was the channel and the repository of

its power. Awe gripped me at the ageless weight of it, and
the turbulent strength that seemed to shake and buffet the
weapon in my hand; but it was mine to channel, mine to
direct, mine, as now, to unleash. I swung it, in a great
sweeping gesture, around and about me; and light leaped
from it, golden light that sprayed and crackled with lightning intensity.

Light that leaped, that blazed, that mocked dull surfaces
and turned bright ones into liquid flame. Light that showered down upon the upturned faces around me and shone
warmth into them as if they were glass. Light that fell
around them like a barrier, that dimmed the world of ug-
liness beyond, and yet within its own brilliant circle didn't
dazzle or blind. Light that showed you your friends; light
that shone through their very flesh, and set their eyes glittering, their hair bristling with its sheer energy. Through
my own hand it blazed, and made it a film of clear glass
over molten gold. Over the wounded it settled like a glowing web. Blood staunched itself, pain rebelled and became
immediate flooding relief, torn flesh sank back into unity
as its cells doubled and redoubled in healing fervor, joining
without a scar. I saw Alison, upon a crude brush stretcher,
stiffen suddenly in that acute cramping agony which follows
sudden surcease; yet even that was wiped out as it seized
her. Mall, beside her, half rose in shock; but as she did so
her hair streamed out in an unseen wind, her eyes shimmered and like a brand held close to the heat she herself
blazed up with silvery radiance. She became a molten outline against the darkness, a human fountain of fire; the
sword in her hand trailed a great sweep of it in the air. But
in the midst of that incandescent gold even her inward
furnace flames seemed pale.

Through it I reached out to them, reached through the
fascinated eyes to tap what lay behind, the sources of their
selves. As the fire enveloped them, they too took light from
me, glowing in many colors and intensities from Jyp's light
flickering red, darkening to scarlet as he stared unbelieving

at his hands, to Alison in shimmering blue-green, like dark glass or the twilit ocean, running her hands through her sparkling hair and laughing. Then without warning there was a sense of yielding, of falling into sudden openness, and a roar of thoughts, a shifting blur of images, burst into my mind. Eighteen images, slightly blurred by each viewpoint, each personal perception, images of a superhuman shape like a statue fallen white-hot from the casting, brandishing aloft a shaft of solid light. It dominated their thoughts, that fearful vision, it possessed their minds; and in mental communion they mirrored the light of it back at me. Reflected, the fires grew till I felt as if I could contain them no longer, as if I was rising from the earth on columns of sparking, coruscating flame.

That was what I needed! I—we—reached down and snatched up the Graal, and it lifted as if it was no more substantial than a soap bubble. I turned to face the forest, and all the rest turned with me, easily, acquiescent, sharing each other's bodies in a constant ebb and flow. But when I lifted the Spear that flow grew fierce, a torrent, and the power of the Graal burst out in thunderous array.

The advancing forest fires roared and flattened as if a great wind blew over them, and the creatures of the Brocken, fleeing them, fell also, and scrabbled in the dust. The enshrouding trees convulsed as the golden light flew across their crests, and in the straight path of the beam the rising earth heaved them aside. Rocks splintered, cracks and chasms closed with a snap, or were filled by a rushing wave of soil and stone. A wide swathe of ground lay clear and leveled, leading along the mountainside directly to the landing ledge, where, miracle of miracles, the *Dove* still rolled, its stern mooring snapped, but bow and midships still holding. And beneath it, pawing the dusty earth, a white horse tossed its head impatiently. Slowly, unhurriedly, I passed through the rest, and in solemn procession, amid a pulsating curtain of light, we made our way down the slopes of the dying mountain. The others joined hands, gasping as light leaped between them; but mine were full. It didn't matter. I was bound to them by ties far closer than mere touch.

That was what the Graal sought—a state not unlike the Brocken's, but in a far less horrible and parasitic way. Incomers both from the remoteness of the Rim, they had the same strengths, the same limitations. The Graal also sought embodiment in the flesh; but by the free will of free minds, and for a while only. It would take nothing, only give.

The forest parted before us, and fell away. But as we passed the open ground I glanced uphill, to where Le Stryge's rock had stood; it lay fallen and shattered now, and among the churned-up soil only a few scraps of black remained. I stared in vain for any sign of paler ash; but my thought touched Jyp's, and he shook his head slowly.

No orders were given; none were needed, not even to the horse. The *Dove* was hauled in—it felt impossibly weird, my hands on every rope, but not unpleasant—and we scrambled aboard, into the forward gondola, up the horseramp, any way; no danger of leaving anyone behind. The stallion went easily to a stall. Starting the motors and slashing the moorings was swift and silent, and we lifted on a swelling upsurge of gladness and relief, so strong we felt it could have carried us without the aid of hydrogen. Standing at the open door, I watched the boiling mountain crest in its ring of flame, and the things that struggled there; surely there was nothing more to do there. Yet I thought of that twisted face, and it was with a sudden impulse of revulsion and even of mercy that I lifted the Spear one last time.

Even the SS . . .

"By the sign you coveted," I said softly, "I defy your power. As other wounds must be healed, I heal yours, and shatter the walls of torment you raised to relieve your own. Fall, and find peace!"

The light was silent and swift, a dancing, coursing network of flame. The Brocken was in no state to resist, or even shield itself, not so close. The mountain shook visibly, and part of its flank slumped away in a single drumming avalanche. Already I saw the reports in tomorrow's bulletins, of the small earth tremors that had shaken the Harz mountains, causing only minor damage to the landscape of that popular holiday area. Apart, that is, from the collapse of that bunker. Commentators would be making little jokes about it being symbolic; and they'd be right. They wouldn't see, as I did, the flicker of dark radiance around that summit, like the uncoiling of vast ragged wings. Something was departing, maybe, something diminished almost to transparency, so it could no longer hold back the dawn.

And with that last effort our light also faded, and our unity. We were ourselves again, and weary; and with the last traces of it a common shadow enveloped us, for those who were not coming back. "You were thinking about Katjka," said Jyp quietly, as he joined me at the door, where I'd slumped down, the Graal at my feet, the Spear across my knees.

"Yes."

"You shouldn't. I've known her a hell of a lot longer than you, remember? She's got what she needed now, needed and courted, surely; and got it well, very well. That's fine. It was a transformation for her, held up too long."

"Transformation?" I asked quietly.

"Or just an end?" added Alison, from the wheel. "A dead end?"

"That was no creed of hers," sniffed Mall, unsticking her long hair from her sweat-plastered face. She leaned over Alison's shoulder, a trace too closely. "Whatever she became, once she was a true Christian soul and none of your miserable unbelieving heathens such as you twain. And that's what's the matter, surely? What ending one may choose for oneself?"

Alison nodded; and so did I, remembering the single smoky little icon in Katjka's room. Jyp and Mall were Christians, as you'd expect from their times and places; Alison was like me, agnostic at best. But we could share a viewpoint out here on the Spiral, where life could be endless and death transient; who was I to argue about something the Graal itself couldn't be sure of?

Itself. Or themselves?

I looked down at the stone beneath my knees, wondering vaguely why it hadn't broken my wrist. Only it wasn't a stone; it was a broad chalice of slightly tarnished white metal, with a scrolling ornament of flowers, the kind of bowl in which Romans mixed their wine. And across my knees lay a long metal shaft with a short stabbing head. I swallowed; and getting to my feet I laid them, carefully and reverentially, across the ledge of the gondola window ahead of the wheel, secure and out of reach.

Clouds rolled down before them as we rose once again, and the blasted remnant of the Brocken was hidden by the clean cool grayness. Jyp came to take the controls, and Alison moved away to stand by me. Nobody spoke much; nobody needed to. We had all been too recently in the flow of one another's thoughts, and there was a responsiveness, quiet but strong, I'd only ever seen among people who'd known each other a lifetime. The only one who still felt strange to me among them all was Alison, stranger and more exciting the closer I drew to her, unknown territory, uncharted seas; and I guessed from the resonances I still felt that that was a reflection of her feelings toward me. But because people are the way they are, it only drew me closer. We stood together, and we watched as the *Dove* climbed high over the ramparts and battlements of the clouds, high into the first delicate beams of a glorious sunrise.

Caught in it, their traceries silhouetted against the reddening sky, the towers of the Graal Hall showed us our way home. Under Jyp's easy direction we came around the curve of what was now a solid mountainside, cruising low over a mountain meadow where my helicopter seemed to be grazing among a herd of complacent cows. Maybe I should put it out to grass, at that, and look into airship shares, if there were any; I was acquiring a taste for a quieter kind of flight.

But the sight of the city put it out of my mind, and the sound, audible even over the engines; the sound of guns, sudden and chilling. But then we heard the bells behind them, great clashing cascades of bells and Belgian carillons and English change-ringing and hammering Russian counter-rhythms; it was a salute, a greeting, a homecoming in grand style.

"It's almost as if they know already—" I exclaimed, and Alison smiled.

"Do you think they wouldn't know, the moment the Graal returned here?"

The celebration impressed me all the more as we came gliding in, and I saw how many of the figures waving along the walls were bandaged and bloodied, how many still shapes were laid out under white coverings in the guard-house square. Those would be Lutz's men, no doubt; but how many had they killed in their turn, of those older Knights, those esquires and plain city folk? Even those pristine buildings had suffered in the fighting, scarred by fire and explosion, windows shattered, columns cracked, here and there a house burned down to bare blackened walls. It was shocking, like raw scars marring a young girl's face.

I looked at Alison. "I remember thinking this place ought to reflect a more up-to-date Europe. I should have kept my trap shut. It does now, all right—bloodied, wounded, shell-shocked . . . "

She took my hand and squeezed it, not quite hard enough to bring on gangrene. "Europe recovered; so will they. I think right now they'll be more uncertain than anything else. They need to know that the cost was worth it, that a victory's been won."

"Well, we're bringing them back the Graal and the Spear."

She gave an exasperated chuckle. "No, idiot! You know that's not what I mean. They need more. Not just things as they were, or the cost would be too high! They need a new ideal to look to, some kind of assurance that the old weakness and stagnation are gone, that all the awful things won't just come rushing back again. More than just another day dawning, even a bright one. This place needs . . . healing, Steve."

"But what makes me the one to do it? I hardly know it, I—"

"You felt at home, though, didn't you? Right from the start. Because you were meant for it, destined for it. Don't you see? That was what Le Stryge must have meant about your bloodline, why he knew you'd be able to touch the Spear safely. All those centuries it's been working down to you. I'm amazed I didn't see it earlier. From your name, even!"

"Not you too! Look, just what is this about my name? Stephen, what's with Stephen?"

She laughed, softly. "Quite a lot. I could get to like it. No, Steve! Your surname! You still don't see, do you? I suppose you never even read the legends you're inheriting, of the Wounded Land, that must find healing. And its ruler, the Fisher King."

"Aye, so it was foretold us," said Mall, her strong voice riding the tide of the bells below. "The Fisher King, himself maimed, no more than half a man, should himself find healing, and so make whole the Wounded Land once more. So it is fulfilled today." She shook her head. "And I stand amazed I live to see't made manifest."

"Goes double for me!" chipped in Jyp cheerfully. "Say, think you can swing us a couple of front-row duckets for the coronation? Anyone know where I can borrow a stovepipe hat?"

"The *what*?"

Alison grinned. "Not a coronation, exactly; the Graal King wears no crown. Only the mantle."

I groaned. I knew what those bells heralded; I could almost feel the weight of that heavy gold weave bearing me down, of ages of dusty responsibility settling on my back. "I hope they shake the moths out, at least."

"There won't be any! That thing's ancient. They say it was made for Charlemagne."

Him again! "For shoulders broader than mine, I'll bet—in every sense."

"Yeah, give the poor guy a break!" grinned Jyp. "After all, what's he been all his life but a businessman? It'll be hard having to give that up."

"I'm not going to," I said, and was startled to see just how alarmed every face in that cockpit became. "I mean, not all at once! I've got a life in the Core as well; I don't want to just vanish. I'll keep on with it, keep up the expansion of C-Tran, develop some other projects; maybe even go into politics as I always planned to. In the EC, maybe; after all, the Graal looks to the whole of Europe. And now people are finally getting fed up with trying to unite it by war and conquest and religion and ideology, maybe it's time to let trade have a go. So fine, I'll be your king here as well, the way destiny and just about everyone else and his dog seems determined to make me. But I'm damn well going to do it the way this destiny seems to have shaped for me. I'll be a merchant king, like Christian the Fourth of Denmark; and see what I can do to feed the body of the state as well as heal its soul. Okay, it may not be as glorious an empire as Charlemagne's, or the Romans, or whoever. But with any luck it'll cost a lot fewer lives, and last a damn sight longer. Until maybe this time people can get it right for themselves!"

There was amazement on their faces; but there was also a growing excitement, like a light growing stronger and clearer. What I saw in Alison's face confirmed it. "Is that anything like—"

"Yes. Oh, yes. If you knew how, how bloody *proud* of you I feel. But there's more, isn't there? Much more."

I took both her hands in mine, and kissed them. "There's that, for a start."

"Steve! Everybody's *looking*—oh, you don't distract me that easily. You know what I meant."

"Yes," I admitted. "Much more. But I can't tell you, not now."

She shook her head. "It doesn't matter. I know you'll tell me one day."

"Mean to be around, do you?"

She gave an elaborate shrug. "I'm sworn to the Graal, remember?"

"Feel like dividing your loyalties a bit?"

"No," she said. And then, in a surprisingly small voice, "There is no division between the Graal and the King. And the rites are very much the—"

"Ah!" I said, and grabbed her. It was around about then, or a little while later, that the ground staff cottoned onto our mooring ropes, and the whole ship lurched lightly. Alison being as tall as I am, I was forced to shift my handhold well below the usual center of gravity; at least that was my story. I hadn't realized how close we were to the ground. Close enough for Mall and Jyp, with malice aforethought, to fling open the door.

"But that's how a new king should be shown to his people," protested Jyp. "Gettin' a grip on his responsibilities."

"Remind me to find out whether there's a vacancy for a court fool," I said acidly, but I was too happy to be annoyed. Too happy, even, to be weighed down any longer by what I couldn't tell Alison.

More? Much, much more. Only a short time back I'd felt torn between Core and Spiral, reluctant to quit the one for the other. Had it been some foreboding of just how thoroughly the Spiral was going to claim me, of the vast stretch of existence laid out before me, like a pilgrim's road?

Of one day, if the promise was true, going beyond even this place, this existence, of voyaging outward and ever outward toward those eerie outer reaches of the Spiral, toward those realms where the illusions and the follies of things material fall away, and absolutes are approached—and then to return, transfigured, to that first unimaginable beginning.

A voyage so long, and so bitterly hard, that it didn't matter that I knew it would succeed; for nothing less, no promise or guidance, could sustain me on the way. The prospect terrified and exalted me; but I knew now that at least I wouldn't be treading it alone. From last to first I'd have friends, comrades, companions, close to me, always close and growing closer, until at last we would, in some way unimaginable, merge and become part of one another, components of a greater whole. Such a being, that if it somehow managed to regain human form, would talk with a voice familiar and yet unfamiliar, echoing with the vagrant identities it never wholly lost. One of them, at least, I was sure of now.

I stepped down to the cobbled square, blinking slightly in the fullness of early day. I balanced the Spear carefully across the chalice, and, hoping it wouldn't revert to stone just yet, I raised it high above my head. The whole island seemed to shake under the thunder of a cheering people. Alison sprang down, and together, with the rest of our party falling in behind, we strode slowly toward the great doors of the Graal Hall—slowly, because ritual and reverent respect came naturally, with such an awesome power in my grasp. The doors swung open as we approached—and if I had anything to say about it they'd stay that way more often.

As always in the realm of the Sangraal the sky had a deeper blue of its own, the white clouds seemed brighter, billowing up in ramparts and turrets behind the towers of the Hall. Alison's cheeks were glowing, her eyes afire; and looking at her, borne along on the tide of that rejoicing, I felt I could overtop the towers at a leap, go soaring over those haughty castles of cloud at will. My isolation was over, my loneliness and my lack of purpose at an end. I had been the Wounded Land, also. For, in closing its wounds, I'd healed my own, and my last emptiness was filled.

I'd heal others yet.

Like *Chase the Morning* and *The Gates of Noon*, this book is set some years in the future, and no reference to present-day individuals or organizations is intended. In the interests of classical scholarship I should point out that on page 144, despite his linguistic abilities, Stephen Fisher evidently just can't understand the heavy Ithacan accent.

MSR